Les Misérables

Volume III: Marius

Les Misérables

Volume III: Marius

Victor Hugo

MINT EDITIONS

Les Misérables was first published in 1862.

This edition published by Mint Editions 2020.

ISBN 9781513279787 | E-ISBN 9781513284804

Published by Mint Editions®

**MINT
EDITIONS**

minteditionbooks.com

Publishing Director: Jennifer Newens
Design & Production: Rachel Lopez Metzger
Project Manager: Micaela Clark
Translated by: Isabel F. Hapgood
Typesetting: Westchester Publishing Services

Contents

BOOK FIRST
PARIS STUDIED IN ITS ATOM

I

Parvulus

Paris has a child, and the forest has a bird; the bird is called the sparrow; the child is called the gamin.

Couple these two ideas which contain, the one all the furnace, the other all the dawn; strike these two sparks together, Paris, childhood; there leaps out from them a little being. *Homuncio*, Plautus would say.

This little being is joyous. He has not food every day, and he goes to the play every evening, if he sees good. He has no shirt on his body, no shoes on his feet, no roof over his head; he is like the flies of heaven, who have none of these things. He is from seven to thirteen years of age, he lives in bands, roams the streets, lodges in the open air, wears an old pair of trousers of his father's, which descend below his heels, an old hat of some other father, which descends below his ears, a single suspender of yellow listing; he runs, lies in wait, rummages about, wastes time, blackens pipes, swears like a convict, haunts the wine-shop, knows thieves, calls gay women *thou*, talks slang, sings obscene songs, and has no evil in his heart. This is because he has in his heart a pearl, innocence; and pearls are not to be dissolved in mud. So long as man is in his childhood, God wills that he shall be innocent.

If one were to ask that enormous city: "What is this?" she would reply: "It is my little one."

II

Some of his Particular Characteristics

The gamin—the street Arab—of Paris is the dwarf of the giant.

Let us not exaggerate, this cherub of the gutter sometimes has a shirt, but, in that case, he owns but one; he sometimes has shoes, but then they have no soles; he sometimes has a lodging, and he loves it, for he finds his mother there; but he prefers the street, because there he finds liberty. He has his own games, his own bits of mischief, whose foundation consists of hatred for the bourgeois; his peculiar metaphors: to be dead is *to eat dandelions by the root*; his own occupations, calling hackney-coaches, letting down carriage-steps, establishing means of transit between the two sides of a street in heavy rains, which he calls *making the bridge of arts*, crying discourses pronounced by the authorities in favor of the French people, cleaning out the cracks in the pavement; he has his own coinage, which is composed of all the little morsels of worked copper which are found on the public streets. This curious money, which receives the name of *loques*—rags—has an invariable and well-regulated currency in this little Bohemia of children.

Lastly, he has his own fauna, which he observes attentively in the corners; the lady-bird, the death's-head plant-louse, the daddy-long-legs, "the devil," a black insect, which menaces by twisting about its tail armed with two horns. He has his fabulous monster, which has scales under its belly, but is not a lizard, which has pustules on its back, but is not a toad, which inhabits the nooks of old lime-kilns and wells that have run dry, which is black, hairy, sticky, which crawls sometimes slowly, sometimes rapidly, which has no cry, but which has a look, and is so terrible that no one has ever beheld it; he calls this monster "the deaf thing." The search for these "deaf things" among the stones is a joy of formidable nature. Another pleasure consists in suddenly prying up a paving-stone, and taking a look at the wood-lice. Each region of Paris is celebrated for the interesting treasures which are to be found there. There are ear-wigs in the timber-yards of the Ursulines, there are millepeds in the Pantheon, there are tadpoles in the ditches of the Champs-de-Mars.

As far as sayings are concerned, this child has as many of them as Talleyrand. He is no less cynical, but he is more honest. He is endowed with a certain indescribable, unexpected joviality; he upsets the composure of the shopkeeper with his wild laughter. He ranges boldly from high comedy to farce.

A funeral passes by. Among those who accompany the dead there is a doctor. "Hey there!" shouts some street Arab, "how long has it been customary for doctors to carry home their own work?"

Another is in a crowd. A grave man, adorned with spectacles and trinkets, turns round indignantly: "You good-for-nothing, you have seized my wife's waist!"—"I, sir? Search me!"

III

He is Agreeable

In the evening, thanks to a few sous, which he always finds means to procure, the *homuncio* enters a theatre. On crossing that magic threshold, he becomes transfigured; he was the street Arab, he becomes the titi. Theatres are a sort of ship turned upside down with the keel in the air. It is in that keel that the titi huddle together. The titi is to the gamin what the moth is to the larva; the same being endowed with wings and soaring. It suffices for him to be there, with his radiance of happiness, with his power of enthusiasm and joy, with his hand-clapping, which resembles a clapping of wings, to confer on that narrow, dark, fetid, sordid, unhealthy, hideous, abominable keel, the name of Paradise.

Bestow on an individual the useless and deprive him of the necessary, and you have the gamin.

The gamin is not devoid of literary intuition. His tendency, and we say it with the proper amount of regret, would not constitute classic taste. He is not very academic by nature. Thus, to give an example, the popularity of Mademoiselle Mars among that little audience of stormy children was seasoned with a touch of irony. The gamin called her *Mademoiselle Muche*— "hide yourself."

This being bawls and scoffs and ridicules and fights, has rags like a baby and tatters like a philosopher, fishes in the sewer, hunts in the cesspool, extracts mirth from foulness, whips up the squares with his wit, grins and bites, whistles and sings, shouts, and shrieks, tempers Alleluia with Matanturlurette, chants every rhythm from the De Profundis to the Jack-pudding, finds without seeking, knows what he is ignorant of, is a Spartan to the point of thieving, is mad to wisdom, is lyrical to filth, would crouch down on Olympus, wallows in the dunghill and emerges from it covered with stars. The gamin of Paris is Rabelais in this youth.

He is not content with his trousers unless they have a watch-pocket.

He is not easily astonished, he is still less easily terrified, he makes songs on superstitions, he takes the wind out of exaggerations, he twits mysteries, he thrusts out his tongue at ghosts, he takes the poetry out of stilted things, he introduces caricature into epic extravaganzas. It is not that he is prosaic; far from that; but he replaces the solemn vision by the farcical phantasmagoria. If Adamastor were to appear to him, the street Arab would say: "Hi there! The bugaboo!"

IV

He May Be of Use

Paris begins with the lounger and ends with the street Arab, two beings of which no other city is capable; the passive acceptance, which contents itself with gazing, and the inexhaustible initiative; Prudhomme and Fouillou. Paris alone has this in its natural history. The whole of the monarchy is contained in the lounger; the whole of anarchy in the gamin.

This pale child of the Parisian faubourgs lives and develops, makes connections, "grows supple" in suffering, in the presence of social realities and of human things, a thoughtful witness. He thinks himself heedless; and he is not. He looks and is on the verge of laughter; he is on the verge of something else also. Whoever you may be, if your name is Prejudice, Abuse, Ignorance, Oppression, Iniquity, Despotism, Injustice, Fanaticism, Tyranny, beware of the gaping gamin.

The little fellow will grow up.

Of what clay is he made? Of the first mud that comes to hand. A handful of dirt, a breath, and behold Adam. It suffices for a God to pass by. A God has always passed over the street Arab. Fortune labors at this tiny being. By the word "fortune" we mean chance, to some extent. That pigmy kneaded out of common earth, ignorant, unlettered, giddy, vulgar, low. Will that become an Ionian or a Bœotian? Wait, *currit rota*, the Spirit of Paris, that demon which creates the children of chance and the men of destiny, reversing the process of the Latin potter, makes of a jug an amphora.

V

His Frontiers

The gamin loves the city, he also loves solitude, since he has something of the sage in him. *Urbis amator*, like Fuscus; *ruris amator*, like Flaccus.

To roam thoughtfully about, that is to say, to lounge, is a fine employment of time in the eyes of the philosopher; particularly in that rather illegitimate species of campaign, which is tolerably ugly but odd and composed of two natures, which surrounds certain great cities, notably Paris. To study the suburbs is to study the amphibious animal. End of the trees, beginning of the roofs; end of the grass, beginning of the pavements; end of the furrows, beginning of the shops, end of the wheel-ruts, beginning of the passions; end of the divine murmur, beginning of the human uproar; hence an extraordinary interest.

Hence, in these not very attractive places, indelibly stamped by the passing stroller with the epithet: *melancholy*, the apparently objectless promenades of the dreamer.

He who writes these lines has long been a prowler about the barriers of Paris, and it is for him a source of profound souvenirs. That close-shaven turf, those pebbly paths, that chalk, those pools, those harsh monotonies of waste and fallow lands, the plants of early market-garden suddenly springing into sight in a bottom, that mixture of the savage and the citizen, those vast desert nooks where the garrison drums practise noisily, and produce a sort of lisping of battle, those hermits by day and cut-throats by night, that clumsy mill which turns in the wind, the hoisting-wheels of the quarries, the tea-gardens at the corners of the cemeteries; the mysterious charm of great, sombre walls squarely intersecting immense, vague stretches of land inundated with sunshine and full of butterflies,—all this attracted him.

There is hardly any one on earth who is not acquainted with those singular spots, the Glacière, the Cunette, the hideous wall of Grenelle all speckled with balls, Mont-Parnasse, the Fosse-aux-Loups, Aubiers on the bank of the Marne, Mont-Souris, the Tombe-Issoire, the Pierre-Plate de Châtillon, where there is an old, exhausted quarry which no longer serves any purpose except to raise mushrooms, and which is closed, on a level with the ground, by a trap-door of rotten planks. The campagna of Rome is one idea, the banlieue of Paris is another; to behold nothing but fields, houses, or trees in what a stretch of country offers us, is to remain on the surface; all aspects of things are thoughts of God. The spot where a plain effects its junction with a city is always stamped with a certain piercing melancholy. Nature and humanity both appeal to you at the same time there. Local originalities there make their appearance.

Any one who, like ourselves, has wandered about in these solitudes contiguous to our faubourgs, which may be designated as the limbos of Paris, has seen here and there, in the most desert spot, at the most unexpected moment, behind a meagre hedge, or in the corner of a lugubrious wall, children grouped tumultuously, fetid, muddy, dusty, ragged, dishevelled, playing hide-and-seek, and crowned with corn-flowers. All of them are little ones who have made their escape from poor families. The outer boulevard is their breathing space; the suburbs belong to them. There they are eternally playing truant. There they innocently sing their repertory of dirty songs. There they are, or rather, there they exist, far from every eye, in the sweet light of May or June, kneeling round a hole in the ground, snapping marbles with their thumbs, quarrelling over half-farthings, irresponsible, volatile, free and happy; and, no sooner do they catch sight of you than they recollect that they have an industry, and that they must earn their living, and they offer to sell you an old woollen stocking filled with cockchafers, or a bunch of lilacs. These encounters with strange children are one of the charming and at the same time poignant graces of the environs of Paris.

Sometimes there are little girls among the throng of boys,—are they their sisters?—who are almost young maidens, thin, feverish, with sunburnt hands, covered with freckles, crowned with poppies and ears of rye, gay, haggard, barefooted. They can be seen devouring cherries among the wheat. In the evening they can be heard laughing. These groups, warmly illuminated by the full glow of midday, or indistinctly seen in the twilight, occupy the thoughtful man for a very long time, and these visions mingle with his dreams.

Paris, centre, banlieue, circumference; this constitutes all the earth to those children. They never venture beyond this. They can no more escape from the Parisian atmosphere than fish can escape from the water. For them, nothing exists two leagues beyond the barriers: Ivry,

Gentilly, Arcueil, Belleville, Aubervilliers, Ménilmontant, Choisy-le-Roi, Billancourt, Meudon, Issy, Vanvre, Sèvres, Puteaux, Neuilly, Gennevilliers, Colombes, Romainville, Chatou, Asnières, Bougival, Nanterre, Enghien, Noisy-le-Sec, Nogent, Gournay, Drancy, Gonesse; the universe ends there.

VI

A Bit of History

At the epoch, nearly contemporary by the way, when the action of this book takes place, there was not, as there is to-day, a policeman at the corner of every street (a benefit which there is no time to discuss here); stray children abounded in Paris. The statistics give an average of two hundred and sixty homeless children picked up annually at that period, by the police patrols, in unenclosed lands, in houses in process of construction, and under the arches of the bridges. One of these nests, which has become famous, produced "the swallows of the bridge of Arcola." This is, moreover, the most disastrous of social symptoms. All crimes of the man begin in the vagabondage of the child.

Let us make an exception in favor of Paris, nevertheless. In a relative measure, and in spite of the souvenir which we have just recalled, the exception is just. While in any other great city the vagabond child is a lost man, while nearly everywhere the child left to itself is, in some sort, sacrificed and abandoned to a kind of fatal immersion in the public vices which devour in him honesty and conscience, the street boy of Paris, we insist on this point, however defaced and injured on the surface, is almost intact on the interior. It is a magnificent thing to put on record, and one which shines forth in the splendid probity of our popular revolutions, that a certain incorruptibility results from the idea which exists in the air of Paris, as salt exists in the water of the ocean. To breathe Paris preserves the soul.

What we have just said takes away nothing of the anguish of heart which one experiences every time that one meets one of these children around whom one fancies that he beholds floating the threads of a broken family. In the civilization of the present day, incomplete as it still is, it is not a very abnormal thing to behold these fractured families pouring themselves out into the darkness, not knowing clearly what has become of their children, and allowing their own entrails to fall on the public highway. Hence these obscure destinies. This is called, for this sad thing has given rise to an expression, "to be cast on the pavements of Paris."

Let it be said by the way, that this abandonment of children was not discouraged by the ancient monarchy. A little of Egypt and Bohemia in the lower regions suited the upper spheres, and compassed the aims of the powerful. The hatred of instruction for the children of the people was a dogma. What is the use of "half-lights"? Such was the countersign. Now, the erring child is the corollary of the ignorant child.

Besides this, the monarchy sometimes was in need of children, and in that case it skimmed the streets.

Under Louis XIV, not to go any further back, the king rightly desired to create a fleet. The idea was a good one. But let us consider the means. There can be no fleet, if, beside the sailing ship, that plaything of the winds, and for the purpose of towing it, in case of necessity, there is not the vessel which goes where it pleases, either by means of oars or of steam; the galleys were then to the marine what steamers are to-day. Therefore, galleys were necessary; but the galley is moved only by the galley-slave; hence, galley-slaves were required. Colbert had the commissioners of provinces and the parliaments make as many convicts as possible. The magistracy showed a great deal of complaisance in the matter. A man kept his hat on in the presence of a procession—it was a Huguenot attitude; he was sent to the galleys. A child was encountered in the streets; provided that he was fifteen years of age and did not know where he was to sleep, he was sent to the galleys. Grand reign; grand century.

Under Louis XV children disappeared in Paris; the police carried them off, for what mysterious purpose no one knew. People whispered with terror monstrous conjectures as to the king's baths of purple. Barbier speaks ingenuously of these things. It sometimes happened that the exempts of the guard, when they ran short of children, took those who had fathers. The fathers, in despair, attacked the exempts. In that case, the parliament intervened and had some one hung. Who? The exempts? No, the fathers.

VII

The Gamin Should Have his Place in the Classifications of India

The body of street Arabs in Paris almost constitutes a caste. One might almost say: Not every one who wishes to belong to it can do so.

This word *gamin* was printed for the first time, and reached popular speech through the literary tongue, in 1834. It is in a little work entitled *Claude Gueux* that this word made its appearance. The horror was lively. The word passed into circulation.

The elements which constitute the consideration of the gamins for each other are very various. We have known and associated with one who was greatly respected and vastly admired because he had seen a man fall from the top of the tower of Notre-Dame; another, because he had succeeded in making his way into the rear courtyard where the statues of the dome of the Invalides had been temporarily deposited, and had "prigged" some lead from them; a third, because he had seen a diligence tip over; still another, because he "knew" a soldier who came near putting out the eye of a citizen.

This explains that famous exclamation of a Parisian gamin, a profound epiphonema, which the vulgar herd laughs at without comprehending,—*Dieu de Dieu! What ill-luck I do have! to think that I have never yet seen anybody tumble from a fifth-story window!* (*I have* pronounced *I'ave* and *fifth* pronounced *fift'*.)

Surely, this saying of a peasant is a fine one: "Father So-and-So, your wife has died of her malady; why did you not send for the doctor?" "What would you have, sir, we poor folks *die of ourselves*." But if the peasant's whole passivity lies in this saying, the whole of the free-thinking anarchy of the brat of the faubourgs is, assuredly, contained in this other saying. A man condemned to death is listening to his confessor in the tumbrel. The child of Paris exclaims: "He is talking to his black cap! Oh, the sneak!"

A certain audacity on matters of religion sets off the gamin. To be strong-minded is an important item.

To be present at executions constitutes a duty. He shows himself at the guillotine, and he laughs. He calls it by all sorts of pet names: The End of the Soup, The Growler, The Mother in the Blue (the sky), The Last Mouthful, etc., etc. In order not to lose anything of the affair, he scales the walls, he hoists himself to balconies, he ascends trees, he suspends himself to gratings, he clings fast to chimneys. The gamin is born a tiler as he is born a mariner. A roof inspires him with no more fear than a mast. There is no festival which comes up to an execution on the Place de Grève. Samson and the Abbé Montès are the truly popular names. They hoot at the victim in order to encourage him. They sometimes admire him. Lacenaire, when a gamin, on seeing the hideous Dautin die bravely, uttered these words which contain a future: "I was jealous of him." In the brotherhood of gamins Voltaire is not known, but Papavoine is. "Politicians" are confused with assassins in the same legend. They have a tradition as to everybody's last garment. It is known that Tolleron had a fireman's cap, Avril an otter cap, Losvel a round hat, that old Delaporte was bald and bareheaded, that Castaing was all ruddy and very handsome, that Bories had a romantic small beard, that Jean Martin kept on his suspenders, that Lecouffé and his mother quarrelled. "Don't reproach each other for your basket," shouted a gamin to them. Another, in order to get a look at Debacker as he passed, and being too small in the crowd, caught sight of the lantern on the quay and climbed it. A gendarme stationed opposite frowned. "Let me climb up, m'sieu le gendarme," said the gamin. And, to soften the heart of the authorities he added: "I will not fall." "I don't care if you do," retorted the gendarme.

In the brotherhood of gamins, a memorable accident counts for a great deal. One reaches the height of consideration if one chances to cut one's self very deeply, "to the very bone."

The fist is no mediocre element of respect. One of the things that the gamin is fondest of saying is: "I am fine and strong, come now!" To be left-handed renders you very enviable. A squint is highly esteemed.

VIII

In Which the Reader Will Find a Charming Saying of the Last King

In summer, he metamorphoses himself into a frog; and in the evening, when night is falling, in front of the bridges of Austerlitz and Jena, from the tops of coal wagons, and the washerwomen's boats, he hurls himself headlong into the Seine, and into all possible infractions of the laws of modesty and of the police. Nevertheless the police keep an eye on him, and the result is a highly dramatic situation which once gave rise to a fraternal and memorable cry; that cry which was celebrated about 1830, is a strategic warning from gamin to gamin; it scans like a verse from Homer, with a notation as inexpressible as the eleusiac chant of the Panathenæa, and in it one encounters again the ancient Evohe. Here it is: "Ohé, Titi, ohééé! Here comes the bobby, here comes the p'lice, pick up your duds and be off, through the sewer with you!"

Sometimes this gnat—that is what he calls himself—knows how to read; sometimes he knows how to write; he always knows how to daub. He does not hesitate to acquire, by no one knows what mysterious mutual instruction, all the talents which can be of use to the public; from 1815 to 1830, he imitated the cry of the turkey; from 1830 to 1848, he scrawled pears on the walls. One summer evening, when Louis Philippe was returning home on foot, he saw a little fellow, no higher than his knee, perspiring and climbing up to draw a gigantic pear in charcoal on one of the pillars of the gate of Neuilly; the King, with that good-nature which came to him from Henry IV, helped the gamin, finished the pear, and gave the child a louis, saying: "The pear is on that also." The gamin loves uproar. A certain state of violence pleases him. He execrates "the curés." One day, in the Rue de l'Université, one of these scamps was putting his thumb to his nose at the carriage gate of No. 69. "Why are you doing that at the gate?" a passer-by asked. The boy replied: "There is a curé there." It was there, in fact, that the Papal Nuncio lived.

Nevertheless, whatever may be the Voltairianism of the small gamin, if the occasion to become a chorister presents itself, it is quite possible that he will accept, and in that case he serves the mass civilly. There are two things to which he plays Tantalus, and which he always desires without ever attaining them: to overthrow the government, and to get his trousers sewed up again.

The gamin in his perfect state possesses all the policemen of Paris, and can always put the name to the face of any one which he chances to meet. He can tell them off on the tips of his fingers. He studies their habits, and he has special notes on each one of them. He reads the souls of the police like an open book. He will tell you fluently and without flinching: "Such an one is a *traitor*; such another is very *malicious*; such another is *great*; such another is *ridiculous*." (All these words: traitor, malicious, great, ridiculous, have a particular meaning in his mouth.) That one imagines that he owns the Pont-Neuf, and he prevents *people* from walking on the cornice outside the parapet; that other has a mania for pulling *person's* ears; etc., etc.

IX

The Old Soul of Gaul

There was something of that boy in Poquelin, the son of the fish-market; Beaumarchais had something of it. Gaminerie is a shade of the Gallic spirit. Mingled with good sense, it sometimes adds force to the latter, as alcohol does to wine. Sometimes it is a defect. Homer repeats himself eternally, granted; one may say that Voltaire plays the gamin. Camille Desmoulins was a native of the faubourgs. Championnet, who treated miracles brutally, rose from the pavements of Paris; he had, when a small lad, inundated the porticos of Saint-Jean de Beauvais, and of Saint-Étienne du Mont; he had addressed the shrine of Sainte-Geneviève familiarly to give orders to the phial of Saint Januarius.

The gamin of Paris is respectful, ironical, and insolent. He has villainous teeth, because he is badly fed and his stomach suffers, and handsome eyes because he has wit. If Jehovah himself were present, he would go hopping up the steps of paradise on one foot. He is strong on boxing. All beliefs are possible to him. He plays in the gutter, and straightens himself up with a revolt; his effrontery persists even in the presence of grape-shot; he was a scapegrace, he is a hero; like the little Theban, he shakes the skin from the lion; Barra the drummer-boy was a gamin of Paris; he Shouts: "Forward!" as the horse of Scripture says "Vah!" and in a moment he has passed from the small brat to the giant.

This child of the puddle is also the child of the ideal. Measure that spread of wings which reaches from Molière to Barra.

To sum up the whole, and in one word, the gamin is a being who amuses himself, because he is unhappy.

X

Ecce Paris, Ecce Homo

To sum it all up once more, the Paris gamin of to-day, like the *græculus* of Rome in days gone by, is the infant populace with the wrinkle of the old world on his brow.

The gamin is a grace to the nation, and at the same time a disease; a disease which must be cured, how? By light.

Light renders healthy.

Light kindles.

All generous social irradiations spring from science, letters, arts, education. Make men, make men. Give them light that they may warm you. Sooner or later the splendid question of universal education will present itself with the irresistible authority of the absolute truth; and then, those who govern under the superintendence of the French idea will have to make this choice; the children of France or the gamins of Paris; flames in the light or will-o'-the-wisps in the gloom.

The gamin expresses Paris, and Paris expresses the world.

For Paris is a total. Paris is the ceiling of the human race. The whole of this prodigious city is a foreshortening of dead manners and living manners. He who sees Paris thinks he sees the bottom of all history with heaven and constellations in the intervals. Paris has a capital, the Town-Hall, a Parthenon, Notre-Dame, a Mount Aventine, the Faubourg Saint-Antoine, an Asinarium, the Sorbonne, a Pantheon, the Pantheon, a Via Sacra, the Boulevard des Italiens, a temple of the winds, opinion; and it replaces the Gemoniæ by ridicule. Its *majo* is called "faraud," its Transteverin is the man of the faubourgs, its *hammal* is the market-porter, its lazzarone is the pègre, its cockney is the native of Ghent. Everything that exists elsewhere exists at Paris. The fishwoman of Dumarsais can retort on the herb-seller of Euripides, the discobols Vejanus lives again in the Forioso, the tight-rope dancer. Therapontigonus Miles could walk arm in arm with Vadeboncœur the grenadier, Damasippus the second-hand dealer would be happy among bric-à-brac merchants, Vincennes could grasp Socrates in its fist as just as Agora could imprison Diderot, Grimod de la Reynière discovered larded roast beef, as Curtillus invented roast hedgehog, we see the trapeze which figures in Plautus reappear under the vault of the Arc of l'Etoile, the sword-eater of Pœcilus encountered by Apuleius is a sword-swallower on the Pont-Neuf, the nephew of Rameau and Curculio the parasite make a pair, Ergasilus could get himself presented to Cambacères by d'Aigrefeuille; the four dandies of Rome: Alcesimarchus, Phœdromus, Diabolus, and Argyrippus, descend from Courtille in Labatut's posting-chaise; Aulus Gellius would halt no longer in front of Congrio than would Charles Nodier in front of Punchinello; Marto is not a tigress, but Pardalisca was not a dragon; Pantolabus the wag jeers in the Café Anglais at Nomentanus the fast liver, Hermogenus is a tenor in the Champs-Élysées, and round him, Thracius the beggar, clad like Bobèche, takes up a collection; the bore who stops you by the button of your coat in the Tuileries makes you repeat after a lapse of two thousand years Thesprion's apostrophe: *Quis properantem me prehendit pallio?* The wine on Surêne is a parody of the wine of Alba, the red border of Desaugiers forms a balance to the great cutting of Balatro, Père-Lachaise exhales beneath nocturnal rains the same gleams as the Esquiliæ, and the grave of the poor bought for five years, is certainly the equivalent of the slave's hived coffin.

Seek something that Paris has not. The vat of Trophonius contains nothing that is not in Mesmer's tub; Ergaphilas lives again in Cagliostro; the Brahmin Vâsaphantâ become incarnate in the Comte de Saint-Germain; the cemetery of Saint-Médard works quite as good miracles as the Mosque of Oumoumié at Damascus.

Paris has an Æsop-Mayeux, and a Canidia, Mademoiselle Lenormand. It is terrified, like Delphos at the fulgurating realities of the vision; it makes tables turn as Dodona did tripods. It places the grisette on the throne, as Rome placed the courtesan there; and, taking it altogether, if Louis XV is worse than Claudian, Madame Dubarry is better than Messalina. Paris combines in an unprecedented type, which has existed and which we have elbowed, Grecian nudity, the Hebraic ulcer, and the Gascon pun. It mingles Diogenes, Job, and Jack-pudding, dresses up a spectre in old numbers of the *Constitutional*, and makes Chodruc Duclos.

Although Plutarch says: *the tyrant never grows old*, Rome, under Sylla as under Domitian, resigned itself and willingly put water in its wine. The Tiber was a Lethe, if the rather doctrinary eulogium made of it by Varus Vibiscus is to be credited: *Contra Gracchos Tiberim habemus, Bibere Tiberim, id est seditionem oblivisci.* Paris drinks a million litres of water a day, but that does not prevent it from occasionally beating the general alarm and ringing the tocsin.

With that exception, Paris is amiable. It accepts everything royally; it is not too particular about its Venus; its Callipyge is Hottentot; provided that it is made to laugh, it condones; ugliness cheers it, deformity provokes it to laughter, vice diverts it; be eccentric and you may be an eccentric; even hypocrisy, that supreme cynicism, does not disgust it; it is so literary that it does not hold its nose before Basile, and is no more scandalized by the prayer of Tartuffe than Horace was repelled by the "hiccup" of Priapus. No trait of the universal face is lacking in the profile of Paris. The bal Mabile is not the polymnia dance of the Janiculum, but the dealer in ladies' wearing apparel there devours the lorette with her eyes, exactly as the procuress Staphyla lay in wait for the virgin Planesium. The Barrière du Combat is not the Coliseum, but people are as ferocious there as though Cæsar were looking on. The Syrian hostess has more grace than Mother Saguet, but, if Virgil haunted the Roman wine-shop, David d'Angers, Balzac and Charlet have sat at the tables of Parisian taverns. Paris reigns. Geniuses flash forth there, the red tails prosper there. Adonaï passes on his chariot with its twelve wheels of thunder and lightning; Silenus makes his entry there on his ass. For Silenus read Ramponneau.

Paris is the synonym of Cosmos, Paris is Athens, Sybaris, Jerusalem, Pantin. All civilizations are there in an abridged form, all barbarisms also. Paris would greatly regret it if it had not a guillotine.

A little of the Place de Grève is a good thing. What would all that eternal festival be without this seasoning? Our laws are wisely provided, and thanks to them, this blade drips on this Shrove Tuesday.

XI

To Scoff, To Reign

There is no limit to Paris. No city has had that domination which sometimes derides those whom it subjugates. To please you, O Athenians! exclaimed Alexander. Paris makes more than the law, it makes the fashion; Paris sets more than the fashion, it sets the routine. Paris may be stupid, if it sees fit; it sometimes allows itself this luxury; then the universe is stupid in company with it; then Paris awakes, rubs its eyes, says: "How stupid I am!" and bursts out laughing in the face of the human race. What a marvel is such a city! it is a strange thing that this grandioseness and this burlesque should be amicable neighbors, that all this majesty should not be thrown into disorder by all this parody, and that the same mouth can to-day blow into the trump of the Judgment Day, and to-morrow into the reed-flute! Paris has a sovereign joviality. Its gayety is of the thunder and its farce holds a sceptre.

Its tempest sometimes proceeds from a grimace. Its explosions, its days, its masterpieces, its prodigies, its epics, go forth to the bounds of the universe, and so also do its cock-and-bull stories. Its laugh is the mouth of a volcano which spatters the whole earth. Its jests are sparks. It imposes its caricatures as well as its ideal on people; the highest monuments of human civilization accept its ironies and lend their eternity to its mischievous pranks. It is superb; it has a prodigious 14th of July, which delivers the globe; it forces all nations to take the oath of tennis; its night of the 4th of August dissolves in three hours a thousand years of feudalism; it makes of its logic the muscle of unanimous will; it multiplies itself under all sorts of forms of the sublime; it fills with its light Washington, Kosciusko, Bolivar, Bozzaris, Riego, Bem, Manin, Lopez, John Brown, Garibaldi; it is everywhere where the future is being lighted up, at Boston in 1779, at the Isle de Léon in 1820, at Pesth in 1848, at Palermo in 1860, it whispers the mighty countersign: Liberty, in the ear of the American abolitionists grouped about the boat at Harper's Ferry, and in the ear of the patriots of Ancona assembled in the shadow, to the Archi before the Gozzi inn on the seashore; it creates Canaris; it creates Quiroga; it creates Pisacane; it irradiates the great on earth; it was while proceeding whither its breath urge them, that Byron perished at Missolonghi, and that Mazet died at Barcelona; it is the tribune under the feet of Mirabeau, and a crater under the feet of Robespierre; its books, its theatre, its art, its science, its literature, its philosophy, are the manuals of the human race; it has Pascal, Régnier, Corneille, Descartes, Jean-Jacques: Voltaire for all moments, Molière for all centuries; it makes its language to be talked by the universal mouth, and that language becomes the word; it constructs in all minds the idea of progress, the liberating dogmas which it forges are for the generations trusty friends, and it is with the soul of its thinkers and its poets that all heroes of all nations have been made since 1789; this does not prevent vagabondism, and that enormous genius which is called Paris, while transfiguring the world by its light, sketches in charcoal Bouginier's nose on the wall of the temple of Theseus and writes *Credeville the thief* on the Pyramids.

Paris is always showing its teeth; when it is not scolding it is laughing.

Such is Paris. The smoke of its roofs forms the ideas of the universe. A heap of mud and stone, if you will, but, above all, a moral being. It is more than great, it is immense. Why? Because it is daring.

To dare; that is the price of progress.

All sublime conquests are, more or less, the prizes of daring. In order that the Revolution should take place, it does not suffice that Montesquieu should foresee it, that Diderot should preach it, that Beaumarchais should announce it, that Condorcet should calculate it, that Arouet should prepare it, that Rousseau should premeditate it; it is necessary that Danton should dare it.

The cry: *Audacity!* is a *Fiat lux*. It is necessary, for the sake of the forward march of the human race, that there should be proud lessons of courage permanently on the heights. Daring deeds dazzle history and are one of man's great sources of light. The dawn dares when it rises. To attempt, to brave, to persist, to persevere, to be faithful to one's self, to grasp fate bodily, to astound catastrophe by the small amount of fear that it occasions us, now to affront unjust power, again to insult drunken victory, to hold one's position, to stand one's ground; that is the example which nations need, that is the light which electrifies them. The same formidable lightning proceeds from the torch of Prometheus to Cambronne's short pipe.

XII

The Future Latent in the People

As for the Parisian populace, even when a man grown, it is always the street Arab; to paint the child is to paint the city; and it is for that reason that we have studied this eagle in this arrant sparrow. It is in the faubourgs, above all, we maintain, that the Parisian race appears; there is the pure blood; there is the true physiognomy; there this people toils and suffers, and suffering and toil are the two faces of man. There exist there immense numbers of unknown beings, among whom swarm types of the strangest, from the porter of la Râpée to the knacker of Montfaucon. *Fex urbis*, exclaims Cicero; *mob*, adds Burke, indignantly; rabble, multitude, populace. These are words and quickly uttered. But so be it. What does it matter? What is it to me if they do go barefoot! They do not know how to read; so much the worse. Would you abandon them for that? Would you turn their distress into a malediction? Cannot the light penetrate these masses? Let us return to that cry: Light! and let us obstinately persist therein! Light! Light! Who knows whether these opacities will not become transparent? Are not revolutions transfigurations? Come, philosophers, teach, enlighten, light up, think aloud, speak aloud, hasten joyously to the great sun, fraternize with the public place, announce the good news, spend your alphabets lavishly, proclaim rights, sing the Marseillaises, sow enthusiasms, tear green boughs from the oaks. Make a whirlwind of the idea. This crowd may be rendered sublime. Let us learn how to make use of that vast conflagration of principles and virtues, which sparkles, bursts forth and quivers at certain hours. These bare feet, these bare arms, these rags, these ignorances, these abjectnesses, these darknesses, may be employed in the conquest of the ideal. Gaze past the people, and you will perceive truth. Let that vile sand which you trample under foot be cast into the furnace, let it melt and seethe there, it will become a splendid crystal, and it is thanks to it that Galileo and Newton will discover stars.

XIII

LITTLE GAVROCHE

Eight or nine years after the events narrated in the second part of this story, people noticed on the Boulevard du Temple, and in the regions of the Château-d'Eau, a little boy eleven or twelve years of age, who would have realized with tolerable accuracy that ideal of the gamin sketched out above, if, with the laugh of his age on his lips, he had not had a heart absolutely sombre and empty. This child was well muffled up in a pair of man's trousers, but he did not get them from his father, and a woman's chemise, but he did not get it from his mother. Some people or other had clothed him in rags out of charity. Still, he had a father and a mother. But his father did not think of him, and his mother did not love him.

He was one of those children most deserving of pity, among all, one of those who have father and mother, and who are orphans nevertheless.

This child never felt so well as when he was in the street. The pavements were less hard to him than his mother's heart.

His parents had despatched him into life with a kick.

He simply took flight.

He was a boisterous, pallid, nimble, wide-awake, jeering, lad, with a vivacious but sickly air. He went and came, sang, played at hopscotch, scraped the gutters, stole a little, but, like cats and sparrows, gayly laughed when he was called a rogue, and got angry when called a thief. He had no shelter, no bread, no fire, no love; but he was merry because he was free.

When these poor creatures grow to be men, the millstones of the social order meet them and crush them, but so long as they are children, they escape because of their smallness. The tiniest hole saves them.

Nevertheless, abandoned as this child was, it sometimes happened, every two or three months, that he said, "Come, I'll go and see mamma!" Then he quitted the boulevard, the Cirque, the Porte Saint-Martin, descended to the quays, crossed the bridges, reached the suburbs, arrived at the Salpêtrière, and came to a halt, where? Precisely at that double number 50–52 with which the reader is acquainted—at the Gorbeau hovel.

At that epoch, the hovel 50–52 generally deserted and eternally decorated with the placard: "Chambers to let," chanced to be, a rare thing, inhabited by numerous individuals who, however, as is always the case in Paris, had no connection with each other. All belonged to that indigent class which begins to separate from the lowest of petty bourgeoisie in straitened circumstances, and which extends from misery to misery into the lowest depths of society down to those two beings in whom all the material things of civilization end, the sewer-man who sweeps up the mud, and the rag-picker who collects scraps.

The "principal lodger" of Jean Valjean's day was dead and had been replaced by another exactly like her. I know not what philosopher has said: "Old women are never lacking."

This new old woman was named Madame Bourgon, and had nothing remarkable about her life except a dynasty of three paroquets, who had reigned in succession over her soul.

The most miserable of those who inhabited the hovel were a family of four persons, consisting of father, mother, and two daughters, already well grown, all four of whom were lodged in the same attic, one of the cells which we have already mentioned.

At first sight, this family presented no very special feature except its extreme destitution; the father, when he hired the chamber, had stated that his name was Jondrette. Some time after his moving in, which had borne a singular resemblance to *the entrance of nothing at all*, to borrow the memorable expression of the principal tenant, this Jondrette had said to the woman, who, like her predecessor, was at the same time portress and stair-sweeper: "Mother So-and-So, if any one should chance to come and inquire for a Pole or an Italian, or even a Spaniard, perchance, it is I."

This family was that of the merry barefoot boy. He arrived there and found distress, and, what is still sadder, no smile; a cold hearth and cold hearts. When he entered, he was asked: "Whence come you?" He replied: "From the street." When he went away, they asked him: "Whither are you going?" He replied: "Into the streets." His mother said to him: "What did you come here for?"

This child lived, in this absence of affection, like the pale plants which spring up in cellars. It did not cause him suffering, and he blamed no one. He did not know exactly how a father and mother should be.

Nevertheless, his mother loved his sisters.

We have forgotten to mention, that on the Boulevard du Temple this child was called Little Gavroche. Why was he called Little Gavroche?

Probably because his father's name was Jondrette.

It seems to be the instinct of certain wretched families to break the thread.

The chamber which the Jondrettes inhabited in the Gorbeau hovel was the last at the end of the corridor. The cell next to it was occupied by a very poor young man who was called M. Marius.

Let us explain who this M. Marius was.

BOOK SECOND
THE GREAT BOURGEOIS

I

NINETY YEARS AND THIRTY-TWO TEETH

In the Rue Boucherat, Rue de Normandie and the Rue de Saintonge there still exist a few ancient inhabitants who have preserved the memory of a worthy man named M. Gillenormand, and who mention him with complaisance. This good man was old when they were young. This silhouette has not yet entirely disappeared—for those who regard with melancholy that vague swarm of shadows which is called the past—from the labyrinth of streets in the vicinity of the Temple to which, under Louis XIV, the names of all the provinces of France were appended exactly as in our day, the streets of the new Tivoli quarter have received the names of all the capitals of Europe; a progression, by the way, in which progress is visible.

M. Gillenormand, who was as much alive as possible in 1831, was one of those men who had become curiosities to be viewed, simply because they have lived a long time, and who are strange because they formerly resembled everybody, and now resemble nobody. He was a peculiar old man, and in very truth, a man of another age, the real, complete and rather haughty bourgeois of the eighteenth century, who wore his good, old bourgeoisie with the air with which marquises wear their marquisates. He was over ninety years of age, his walk was erect, he talked loudly, saw clearly, drank neat, ate, slept, and snored. He had all thirty-two of his teeth. He only wore spectacles when he read. He was of an amorous disposition, but declared that, for the last ten years, he had wholly and decidedly renounced women. He could no longer please, he said; he did not add: "I am too old," but: "I am too poor." He said: "If I were not ruined—Héée!" All he had left, in fact, was an income of about fifteen thousand francs. His dream was to come into an inheritance and to have a hundred thousand livres income for mistresses. He did not belong, as the reader will perceive, to that puny variety of octogenaries who, like M. de Voltaire, have been dying all their life; his was no longevity of a cracked pot; this jovial old man had always had good health. He was superficial, rapid, easily angered. He flew into a passion at everything, generally quite contrary to all reason. When contradicted, he raised his cane; he beat people as he had done in the great century. He had a daughter over fifty years of age, and unmarried, whom he chastised severely with his tongue, when in a rage, and whom he would have liked to whip. She seemed to him to be eight years old. He boxed his servants' ears soundly, and said: "Ah! carogne!" One of his oaths was: "By the pantoufloche of the pantouflochade!" He had singular freaks of tranquillity; he had himself shaved every day by a barber who had been mad and who detested him, being jealous of M. Gillenormand on account of his wife, a pretty and coquettish barberess. M. Gillenormand admired his own discernment in all things, and declared that he was extremely sagacious; here is one of his sayings: "I have, in truth, some penetration; I am able to say when a flea bites me, from what woman it came."

The words which he uttered the most frequently were: *the sensible man*, and *nature*. He did not give to this last word the grand acceptation which our epoch has accorded to it, but he made it enter, after his own fashion, into his little chimney-corner satires: "Nature," he said, "in order that civilization may have a little of everything, gives it even specimens of its amusing barbarism. Europe possesses specimens of Asia and Africa on a small scale. The cat is a drawing-room tiger, the lizard is a pocket crocodile. The dancers at the opera are pink female savages. They do not eat men, they crunch them; or, magicians that they are, they transform them into oysters and swallow them. The Caribbeans leave only the bones, they leave only the shell. Such are our morals. We do not devour, we gnaw; we do not exterminate, we claw."

II

LIKE MASTER, LIKE HOUSE

He lived in the Marais, Rue des Filles-du-Calvaire, No. 6. He owned the house. This house has since been demolished and rebuilt, and the number has probably been changed in those revolutions of numeration which the streets of Paris undergo. He occupied an ancient and vast apartment on the first floor, between street and gardens, furnished to the very ceilings with great Gobelins and Beauvais tapestries representing pastoral scenes; the subjects of the ceilings and the panels were repeated in miniature on the armchairs. He enveloped his bed in a vast, nine-leaved screen of Coromandel lacquer. Long, full curtains hung from the windows, and formed great, broken folds that were very magnificent. The garden situated immediately under his windows was attached to that one of them which formed the angle, by means of a staircase twelve or fifteen steps long, which the old gentleman ascended and descended with great agility. In addition to a library adjoining his chamber, he had a boudoir of which he thought a great deal, a gallant and elegant retreat, with magnificent hangings of straw, with a pattern of flowers and fleurs-de-lys made on the galleys of Louis XIV and ordered of his convicts by M. de Vivonne for his mistress. M. Gillenormand had inherited it from a grim maternal great-aunt, who had died a centenarian. He had had two wives. His manners were something between those of the courtier, which he had never been, and the lawyer, which he might have been. He was gay, and caressing when he had a mind. In his youth he had been one of those men who are always deceived by their wives and never by their mistresses, because they are, at the same time, the most sullen of husbands and the most charming of lovers in existence. He was a connoisseur of painting. He had in his chamber a marvellous portrait of no one knows whom, painted by Jordaens, executed with great dashes of the brush, with millions of details, in a confused and hap-hazard manner. M. Gillenormand's attire was not the habit of Louis XIV nor yet that of Louis XVI; it was that of the Incroyables of the Directory. He had thought himself young up to that period and had followed the fashions. His coat was of light-weight cloth with voluminous revers, a long swallow-tail and large steel buttons. With this he wore knee-breeches and buckle shoes. He always thrust his hands into his fobs. He said authoritatively: "The French Revolution is a heap of blackguards."

III

LUC-ESPRIT

At the age of sixteen, one evening at the opera, he had had the honor to be stared at through opera-glasses by two beauties at the same time—ripe and celebrated beauties then, and sung by Voltaire, the Camargo and the Sallé. Caught between two fires, he had beaten a heroic retreat towards a little dancer, a young girl named Nahenry, who was sixteen like himself, obscure as a cat, and with whom he was in love. He abounded in memories. He was accustomed to exclaim: "How pretty she was—that Guimard-Guimardini-Guimardinette, the last time I saw her at Longchamps, her hair curled in sustained sentiments, with her come-and-see of turquoises, her gown of the color of persons newly arrived, and her little agitation muff!" He had worn in his young manhood a waistcoat of Nain-Londrin, which he was fond of talking about effusively. "I was dressed like a Turk of the Levant Levantin," said he. Madame de Boufflers, having seen him by chance when he was twenty, had described him as "a charming fool." He was horrified by all the names which he saw in politics and in power, regarding them as vulgar and bourgeois. He read the journals, the *newspapers, the gazettes* as he said, stifling outbursts of laughter the while. "Oh!" he said, "what people these are! Corbière! Humann! Casimir Périer! There's a minister for you! I can imagine this in a journal: 'M. Gillenorman, minister!' that would be a farce. Well! They are so stupid that it would pass"; he merrily called everything by its name, whether decent or indecent, and did not restrain himself in the least before ladies. He uttered coarse speeches, obscenities, and filth with a certain tranquillity and lack of astonishment which was elegant. It was in keeping with the unceremoniousness of his century. It is to be noted that the age of periphrase in verse was the age of crudities in prose. His god-father had predicted that he would turn out a man of genius, and had bestowed on him these two significant names: Luc-Esprit.

IV

A Centenarian Aspirant

He had taken prizes in his boyhood at the College of Moulins, where he was born, and he had been crowned by the hand of the Duc de Nivernais, whom he called the Duc de Nevers. Neither the Convention, nor the death of Louis XVI, nor the Napoleon, nor the return of the Bourbons, nor anything else had been able to efface the memory of this crowning. *The Duc de Nevers* was, in his eyes, the great figure of the century. "What a charming grand seigneur," he said, "and what a fine air he had with his blue ribbon!"

In the eyes of M. Gillenormand, Catherine the Second had made reparation for the crime of the partition of Poland by purchasing, for three thousand roubles, the secret of the elixir of gold, from Bestucheff. He grew animated on this subject: "The elixir of gold," he exclaimed, "the yellow dye of Bestucheff, General Lamotte's drops, in the eighteenth century,—this was the great remedy for the catastrophes of love, the panacea against Venus, at one louis the half-ounce phial. Louis XV sent two hundred phials of it to the Pope." He would have been greatly irritated and thrown off his balance, had any one told him that the elixir of gold is nothing but the perchloride of iron. M. Gillenormand adored the Bourbons, and had a horror of 1789; he was forever narrating in what manner he had saved himself during the Terror, and how he had been obliged to display a vast deal of gayety and cleverness in order to escape having his head cut off. If any young man ventured to pronounce an eulogium on the Republic in his presence, he turned purple and grew so angry that he was on the point of swooning. He sometimes alluded to his ninety years, and said, "I hope that I shall not see ninety-three twice." On these occasions, he hinted to people that he meant to live to be a hundred.

V

BASQUE AND NICOLETTE

He had theories. Here is one of them: "When a man is passionately fond of women, and when he has himself a wife for whom he cares but little, who is homely, cross, legitimate, with plenty of rights, perched on the code, and jealous at need, there is but one way of extricating himself from the quandry and of procuring peace, and that is to let his wife control the purse-strings. This abdication sets him free. Then his wife busies herself, grows passionately fond of handling coin, gets her fingers covered with verdigris in the process, undertakes the education of half-share tenants and the training of farmers, convokes lawyers, presides over notaries, harangues scriveners, visits limbs of the law, follows lawsuits, draws up leases, dictates contracts, feels herself the sovereign, sells, buys, regulates, promises and compromises, binds fast and annuls, yields, concedes and retrocedes, arranges, disarranges, hoards, lavishes; she commits follies, a supreme and personal delight, and that consoles her. While her husband disdains her, she has the satisfaction of ruining her husband." This theory M. Gillenormand had himself applied, and it had become his history. His wife—the second one—had administered his fortune in such a manner that, one fine day, when M. Gillenormand found himself a widower, there remained to him just sufficient to live on, by sinking nearly the whole of it in an annuity of fifteen thousand francs, three-quarters of which would expire with him. He had not hesitated on this point, not being anxious to leave a property behind him. Besides, he had noticed that patrimonies are subject to adventures, and, for instance, become *national property*; he had been present at the avatars of consolidated three per cents, and he had no great faith in the Great Book of the Public Debt. "All that's the Rue Quincampois!" he said. His house in the Rue des Filles-du-Calvaire belonged to him, as we have already stated. He had two servants, "a male and a female." When a servant entered his establishment, M. Gillenormand re-baptized him. He bestowed on the men the name of their province: Nîmois, Comtois, Poitevin, Picard. His last valet was a big, foundered, short-winded fellow of fifty-five, who was incapable of running twenty paces; but, as he had been born at

Bayonne, M. Gillenormand called him *Basque*. All the female servants in his house were called Nicolette (even the Magnon, of whom we shall hear more farther on). One day, a haughty cook, a cordon bleu, of the lofty race of porters, presented herself. "How much wages do you want a month?" asked M. Gillenormand. "Thirty francs." "What is your name?" "Olympie." "You shall have fifty francs, and you shall be called Nicolette."

VI

In Which Magnon and Her
Two Children are Seen

With M. Gillenormand, sorrow was converted into wrath; he was furious at being in despair. He had all sorts of prejudices and took all sorts of liberties. One of the facts of which his exterior relief and his internal satisfaction was composed, was, as we have just hinted, that he had remained a brisk spark, and that he passed energetically for such. This he called having "royal renown." This royal renown sometimes drew down upon him singular windfalls. One day, there was brought to him in a basket, as though it had been a basket of oysters, a stout, newly born boy, who was yelling like the deuce, and duly wrapped in swaddling-clothes, which a servant-maid, dismissed six months previously, attributed to him. M. Gillenormand had, at that time, fully completed his eighty-fourth year. Indignation and uproar in the establishment. And whom did that bold hussy think she could persuade to believe that? What audacity! What an abominable calumny! M. Gillenormand himself was not at all enraged. He gazed at the brat with the amiable smile of a good man who is flattered by the calumny, and said in an aside: "Well, what now? What's the matter? You are finely taken aback, and really, you are excessively ignorant. M. le Duc d'Angoulême, the bastard of his Majesty Charles IX, married a silly jade of fifteen when he was eighty-five; M. Virginal, Marquis d'Alluye, brother to the Cardinal de Sourdis, Archbishop of Bordeaux, had, at the age of eighty-three, by the maid of Madame la Présidente Jacquin, a son, a real child of love, who became a Chevalier of Malta and a counsellor of state; one of the great men of this century, the Abbé Tabaraud, is the son of a man of eighty-seven. There is nothing out of the ordinary in these things. And then, the Bible! Upon that I declare that this little gentleman is none of mine. Let him be taken care of. It is not his fault." This manner of procedure was good-tempered. The woman, whose name was Magnon, sent him another parcel in the following year. It was a boy again. Thereupon, M. Gillenormand capitulated. He sent the two brats back to their mother, promising to pay eighty francs a month for their maintenance, on the condition that the said mother would not do so any more. He added: "I insist upon it that the mother shall treat them well. I shall go to see them from time to time." And this he did. He had had a brother who was a priest, and who had been rector of the Academy of Poitiers for three and thirty years, and had died at seventy-nine. "I lost him young," said he. This brother, of whom but little memory remains, was a peaceable miser, who, being a priest, thought himself bound to bestow alms on the poor whom he met, but he never gave them anything except bad or demonetized sous, thereby discovering a means of going to hell by way of paradise. As for M. Gillenormand the elder, he never haggled over his alms-giving, but gave gladly and nobly. He was kindly, abrupt, charitable, and if he had been rich, his turn of mind would have been magnificent. He desired that all which concerned him should be done in a grand manner, even his rogueries. One day, having been cheated by a business man in a matter of inheritance, in a gross and apparent manner, he uttered this solemn exclamation: "That was indecently done! I am really ashamed of this pilfering. Everything has degenerated in this century, even the rascals. Morbleu! this is not the way to rob a man of my standing. I am robbed as though in a forest, but badly robbed. *Silvæ sint consule dignæ!*" He had had two wives, as we have already mentioned; by the first he had had a daughter, who had remained unmarried, and by the second another daughter, who had died at about the age of thirty, who had wedded, through love, or chance, or otherwise, a soldier of fortune who had served in the armies of the Republic and of the Empire, who had won the cross at Austerlitz and had been made colonel at Waterloo. *"He is the disgrace of my family,"* said the old bourgeois. He took an immense amount of snuff, and had a particularly graceful manner of plucking at his lace ruffle with the back of one hand. He believed very little in God.

VII

Rule: Receive No One Except in the Evening

S uch was M. Luc-Esprit Gillenormand, who had not lost his hair,— which was gray rather than white,—and which was always dressed in "dog's ears." To sum up, he was venerable in spite of all this.

He had something of the eighteenth century about him; frivolous and great.

In 1814 and during the early years of the Restoration, M. Gillenormand, who was still young,—he was only seventy-four,— lived in the Faubourg Saint Germain, Rue Servandoni, near Saint-Sulpice. He had only retired to the Marais when he quitted society, long after attaining the age of eighty.

And, on abandoning society, he had immured himself in his habits. The principal one, and that which was invariable, was to keep his door absolutely closed during the day, and never to receive any one whatever except in the evening. He dined at five o'clock, and after that his door was open. That had been the fashion of his century, and he would not swerve from it. "The day is vulgar," said he, "and deserves only a closed shutter. Fashionable people only light up their minds when the zenith lights up its stars." And he barricaded himself against every one, even had it been the king himself. This was the antiquated elegance of his day.

VIII

Two Do Not Make a Pair

We have just spoken of M. Gillenormand's two daughters. They had come into the world ten years apart. In their youth they had borne very little resemblance to each other, either in character or countenance, and had also been as little like sisters to each other as possible. The youngest had a charming soul, which turned towards all that belongs to the light, was occupied with flowers, with verses, with music, which fluttered away into glorious space, enthusiastic, ethereal, and was wedded from her very youth, in ideal, to a vague and heroic figure. The elder had also her chimera; she espied in the azure some very wealthy purveyor, a contractor, a splendidly stupid husband, a million made man, or even a prefect; the receptions of the Prefecture, an usher in the antechamber with a chain on his neck, official balls, the harangues of the town-hall, to be "Madame la Préfète,"—all this had created a whirlwind in her imagination. Thus the two sisters strayed, each in her own dream, at the epoch when they were young girls. Both had wings, the one like an angel, the other like a goose.

No ambition is ever fully realized, here below at least. No paradise becomes terrestrial in our day. The younger wedded the man of her dreams, but she died. The elder did not marry at all.

At the moment when she makes her entrance into this history which we are relating, she was an antique virtue, an incombustible prude, with one of the sharpest noses, and one of the most obtuse minds that it is possible to see. A characteristic detail; outside of her immediate family, no one had ever known her first name. She was called *Mademoiselle Gillenormand, the elder*.

In the matter of *cant*, Mademoiselle Gillenormand could have given points to a miss. Her modesty was carried to the other extreme of blackness. She cherished a frightful memory of her life; one day, a man had beheld her garter.

Age had only served to accentuate this pitiless modesty. Her guimpe was never sufficiently opaque, and never ascended sufficiently high. She multiplied clasps and pins where no one would have dreamed of looking. The peculiarity of prudery is to place all the more sentinels in proportion as the fortress is the less menaced.

Nevertheless, let him who can explain these antique mysteries of innocence, she allowed an officer of the Lancers, her grand nephew, named Théodule, to embrace her without displeasure.

In spite of this favored Lancer, the label: *Prude*, under which we have classed her, suited her to absolute perfection. Mademoiselle Gillenormand was a sort of twilight soul. Prudery is a demi-virtue and a demi-vice.

To prudery she added bigotry, a well-assorted lining. She belonged to the society of the Virgin, wore a white veil on certain festivals, mumbled special orisons, revered "the holy blood," venerated "the sacred heart," remained for hours in contemplation before a rococo-jesuit altar in a chapel which was inaccessible to the rank and file of the faithful, and there allowed her soul to soar among little clouds of marble, and through great rays of gilded wood.

She had a chapel friend, an ancient virgin like herself, named Mademoiselle Vaubois, who was a positive blockhead, and beside whom Mademoiselle Gillenormand had the pleasure of being an eagle. Beyond the Agnus Dei and Ave Maria, Mademoiselle Vaubois had no knowledge of anything except of the different ways of making preserves. Mademoiselle Vaubois, perfect in her style, was the ermine of stupidity without a single spot of intelligence.

Let us say it plainly, Mademoiselle Gillenormand had gained rather than lost as she grew older. This is the case with passive natures. She had never been malicious, which is relative kindness; and then, years wear away the angles, and the softening which comes with time had come to her. She was melancholy with an obscure sadness of which she did not herself know the secret. There breathed from her whole person the stupor of a life that was finished, and which had never had a beginning.

She kept house for her father. M. Gillenormand had his daughter near him, as we have seen that Monseigneur Bienvenu had his sister with him. These households comprised of an old man and an old spinster are not rare, and always have the touching aspect of two weaknesses leaning on each other for support.

There was also in this house, between this elderly spinster and this old man, a child, a little boy, who was always trembling and mute in the presence of M. Gillenormand. M. Gillenormand never addressed this child except in a severe voice, and sometimes, with uplifted cane: "Here, sir! rascal, scoundrel, come here!—Answer me, you scamp! Just let me see you, you good-for-nothing!" etc., etc. He idolized him.

This was his grandson. We shall meet with this child again later on.

I

AN ANCIENT SALON

When M. Gillenormand lived in the Rue Servandoni, he had frequented many very good and very aristocratic salons. Although a bourgeois, M. Gillenormand was received in society. As he had a double measure of wit, in the first place, that which was born with him, and secondly, that which was attributed to him, he was even sought out and made much of. He never went anywhere except on condition of being the chief person there. There are people who will have influence at any price, and who will have other people busy themselves over them; when they cannot be oracles, they turn wags. M. Gillenormand was not of this nature; his domination in the Royalist salons which he frequented cost his self-respect nothing. He was an oracle everywhere. It had happened to him to hold his own against M. de Bonald, and even against M. Bengy-Puy-Vallée.

About 1817, he invariably passed two afternoons a week in a house in his own neighborhood, in the Rue Férou, with Madame la Baronne de T., a worthy and respectable person, whose husband had been Ambassador of France to Berlin under Louis XVI. Baron de T., who, during his lifetime, had gone very passionately into ecstasies and magnetic visions, had died bankrupt, during the emigration, leaving, as his entire fortune, some very curious Memoirs about Mesmer and his tub, in ten manuscript volumes, bound in red morocco and gilded on the edges. Madame de T. had not published the memoirs, out of pride, and maintained herself on a meagre income which had survived no one knew how.

Madame de T. lived far from the Court; "a very mixed society," as she said, in a noble isolation, proud and poor. A few friends assembled twice a week about her widowed hearth, and these constituted a purely Royalist salon. They sipped tea there, and uttered groans or cries of horror at the century, the charter, the Bonapartists, the prostitution of the blue ribbon, or the Jacobinism of Louis XVIII, according as the wind veered towards elegy or dithyrambs; and they spoke in low tones of the hopes which were presented by Monsieur, afterwards Charles X.

The songs of the fishwomen, in which Napoleon was called *Nicolas*, were received there with transports of joy. Duchesses, the most delicate and charming women in the world, went into ecstasies over couplets like the following, addressed to "the federates":—

> *Refoncez dans vos culottes*
> *Le bout d' chemis' qui vous pend.*
> *Qu'on n' dis' pas qu' les patriotes*
> *Ont arboré l' drapeau blanc?*

There they amused themselves with puns which were considered terrible, with innocent plays upon words which they supposed to be venomous, with quatrains, with distiches even; thus, upon the Dessolles ministry, a moderate cabinet, of which MM. Decazes and Deserre were members:—

> *Pour raffermir le trône ébranlé sur sa base,*
> *Il faut changer de sol, et de serre et de case.*

Or they drew up a list of the chamber of peers, "an abominably Jacobin chamber," and from this list they combined alliances of names, in such a manner as to form, for example, phrases like the following: *Damas. Sabran. Gouvion-Saint-Cyr.*—All this was done merrily. In that society, they parodied the Revolution. They used I know not what desires to give point to the same wrath in inverse sense. They sang their little *Ça ira:* —

> *Ah! ça ira ça ira ça ira!*
> *Les Bonapartistes à la lanterne!*

Songs are like the guillotine; they chop away indifferently, to-day this head, to-morrow that. It is only a variation.

In the Fualdès affair, which belongs to this epoch, 1816, they took part for Bastide and Jausion, because Fualdès was "a Buonapartist." They designated the liberals as *friends and brothers*; this constituted the most deadly insult.

Like certain church towers, Madame de T.'s salon had two cocks. One of them was M. Gillenormand, the other was Comte de Lamothe-Valois, of whom it was whispered about, with a sort of respect: "Do you know? That is the Lamothe of the affair of the necklace." These singular amnesties do occur in parties.

Let us add the following: in the bourgeoisie, honored situations decay through too easy relations; one must beware whom one admits; in the same way that there is a loss of caloric in the vicinity of those who are cold, there is a diminution of consideration in the approach of despised persons. The ancient society of the upper classes held themselves above this law, as above every other. Marigny, the brother of the Pompadour, had his entry with M. le Prince de Soubise. In spite of? No, because. Du Barry, the god-father of the Vaubernier, was very welcome at the house of M. le Maréchal de Richelieu. This society is Olympus. Mercury and the Prince de Guémenée are at home there. A thief is admitted there, provided he be a god.

The Comte de Lamothe, who, in 1815, was an old man seventy-five years of age, had nothing remarkable about him except his silent and sententious air, his cold and angular face, his perfectly polished manners, his coat buttoned up to his cravat, and his long legs always crossed in long, flabby trousers of the hue of burnt sienna. His face was the same color as his trousers.

This M. de Lamothe was "held in consideration" in this salon on account of his "celebrity" and, strange to say, though true, because of his name of Valois.

As for M. Gillenormand, his consideration was of absolutely first-rate quality. He had, in spite of his levity, and without its interfering in any way with his dignity, a certain manner about him which was imposing, dignified, honest, and lofty, in a bourgeois fashion; and his great age added to it. One is not a century with impunity. The years finally produce around a head a venerable dishevelment.

In addition to this, he said things which had the genuine sparkle of the old rock. Thus, when the King of Prussia, after having restored Louis XVIII, came to pay the latter a visit under the name of the Count de Ruppin, he was received by the descendant of Louis XIV somewhat as though he had been the Marquis de Brandebourg, and with the most delicate impertinence. M. Gillenormand approved: "All kings who are not the King of France," said he, "are provincial kings." One day, the following question was put and the following answer returned in his presence: "To what was the editor of the *Courrier Français* condemned?" "To be suspended." "*Sus* is superfluous," observed M. Gillenormand. Remarks of this nature found a situation.

At the Te Deum on the anniversary of the return of the Bourbons, he said, on seeing M. de Talleyrand pass by: "There goes his Excellency the Evil One."

M. Gillenormand was always accompanied by his daughter, that tall mademoiselle, who was over forty and looked fifty, and by a handsome little boy of seven years, white, rosy, fresh, with happy and trusting eyes, who never appeared in that salon without hearing voices murmur around him: "How handsome he is! What a pity! Poor child!" This child was the one of whom we dropped a word a while ago. He was called "poor child," because he had for a father "a brigand of the Loire."

This brigand of the Loire was M. Gillenormand's son-in-law, who has already been mentioned, and whom M. Gillenormand called "the disgrace of his family."

II

One of the Red Spectres of That Epoch

Any one who had chanced to pass through the little town of Vernon at this epoch, and who had happened to walk across that fine monumental bridge, which will soon be succeeded, let us hope, by some hideous iron cable bridge, might have observed, had he dropped his eyes over the parapet, a man about fifty years of age wearing a leather cap, and trousers and a waistcoat of coarse gray cloth, to which something yellow which had been a red ribbon, was sewn, shod with wooden sabots, tanned by the sun, his face nearly black and his hair nearly white, a large scar on his forehead which ran down upon his cheek, bowed, bent, prematurely aged, who walked nearly every day, hoe and sickle in hand, in one of those compartments surrounded by walls which abut on the bridge, and border the left bank of the Seine like a chain of terraces, charming enclosures full of flowers of which one could say, were they much larger: "these are gardens," and were they a little smaller: "these are bouquets." All these enclosures abut upon the river at one end, and on a house at the other. The man in the waistcoat and the wooden shoes of whom we have just spoken, inhabited the smallest of these enclosures and the most humble of these houses about 1817. He lived there alone and solitary, silently and poorly, with a woman who was neither young nor old, neither homely nor pretty, neither a peasant nor a bourgeoise, who served him. The plot of earth which he called his garden was celebrated in the town for the beauty of the flowers which he cultivated there. These flowers were his occupation.

By dint of labor, of perseverance, of attention, and of buckets of water, he had succeeded in creating after the Creator, and he had invented certain tulips and certain dahlias which seemed to have been forgotten by nature. He was ingenious; he had forestalled Soulange Bodin in the formation of little clumps of earth of heath mould, for the cultivation of rare and precious shrubs from America and China. He was in his alleys from the break of day, in summer, planting, cutting, hoeing, watering, walking amid his flowers with an air of kindness, sadness, and sweetness, sometimes standing motionless and thoughtful for hours, listening to the song of a bird in the trees, the babble of a child in a house, or with his eyes fixed on a drop of dew at the tip of a spear of grass, of which the sun made a carbuncle. His table was very plain, and he drank more milk than wine. A child could make him give way, and his servant scolded him. He was so timid that he seemed shy, he rarely went out, and he saw no one but the poor people who tapped at his pane and his curé, the Abbé Mabeuf, a good old man. Nevertheless, if the inhabitants of the town, or strangers, or any chance comers, curious to see his tulips, rang at his little cottage, he opened his door with a smile. He was the "brigand of the Loire."

Any one who had, at the same time, read military memoirs, biographies, the *Moniteur*, and the bulletins of the grand army, would have been struck by a name which occurs there with tolerable frequency, the name of Georges Pontmercy. When very young, this Georges Pontmercy had been a soldier in Saintonge's regiment. The revolution broke out. Saintonge's regiment formed a part of the army of the Rhine; for the old regiments of the monarchy preserved their names of provinces even after the fall of the monarchy, and were only divided into brigades in 1794. Pontmercy fought at Spire, at Worms, at Neustadt, at Turkheim, at Alzey, at Mayence, where he was one of the two hundred who formed Houchard's rearguard. It was the twelfth to hold its ground against the corps of the Prince of Hesse, behind the old rampart of Andernach, and only rejoined the main body of the army when the enemy's cannon had opened a breach from the cord of the parapet to the foot of the glacis. He was under Kléber at Marchiennes and at the battle of Mont-Palissel, where a ball from a biscaïen broke his arm. Then he passed to the frontier of Italy, and was one of the thirty grenadiers who defended the Col de Tende with Joubert. Joubert was appointed its adjutant-general, and Pontmercy sub-lieutenant. Pontmercy was by Berthier's side in the midst of the grape-shot of that day at Lodi which caused Bonaparte to say: "Berthier has been cannoneer, cavalier, and grenadier." He beheld his old general, Joubert, fall at Novi, at the moment when, with uplifted sabre, he was shouting: "Forward!" Having been embarked with his company in the exigencies of the campaign, on board a pinnace which was proceeding from Genoa to some obscure port on the coast, he fell into a wasps'-nest of seven or eight English vessels. The Genoese commander wanted to throw his cannon into the sea, to hide the soldiers between decks, and to slip along in the dark as a merchant vessel. Pontmercy had the colors hoisted to the peak, and sailed proudly past under the guns of the British frigates.

Twenty leagues further on, his audacity having increased, he attacked with his pinnace, and captured a large English transport which was carrying troops to Sicily, and which was so loaded down with men and horses that the vessel was sunk to the level of the sea. In 1805 he was in that Malher division which took Günzberg from the Archduke Ferdinand. At Weltingen he received into his arms, beneath a storm of bullets, Colonel Maupetit, mortally wounded at the head of the 9th Dragoons. He distinguished himself at Austerlitz in that admirable march in echelons effected under the enemy's fire. When the cavalry of the Imperial Russian Guard crushed a battalion of the 4th of the line, Pontmercy was one of those who took their revenge and overthrew the Guard. The Emperor gave him the cross. Pontmercy saw Wurmser at Mantua, Mélas, and Alexandria, Mack at Ulm, made prisoners in succession. He formed a part of the eighth corps of the grand army which Mortier commanded, and which captured Hamburg. Then he was transferred to the 55th of the line, which was the old regiment of Flanders. At Eylau he was in the cemetery where, for the space of two hours, the heroic Captain Louis Hugo, the uncle of the author of this book, sustained alone with his company of eighty-three men every effort of the hostile army. Pontmercy was one of the three who emerged alive from that cemetery. He was at Friedland. Then he saw Moscow. Then La Bérésina, then Lutzen, Bautzen, Dresden, Wachau, Leipzig, and the defiles of Gelenhausen; then Montmirail, Château-Thierry, Craon, the banks of the Marne, the banks of the Aisne, and the redoubtable position of Laon. At Arnay-Le-Duc, being then a captain, he put ten Cossacks to the sword, and saved, not his general, but his corporal. He was well slashed up on this occasion, and twenty-seven splinters were extracted from his left arm alone. Eight days before the capitulation of Paris he had just exchanged with a comrade and entered the cavalry. He had what was called under the old regime, *the double hand*, that is to say, an equal aptitude for handling the sabre or the musket as a soldier, or a squadron or a battalion as an officer. It is from this aptitude, perfected by a military education, which certain special branches of the service arise, the dragoons, for example, who are both cavalry-men and infantry at one and the same time. He accompanied Napoleon to the Island of Elba. At Waterloo, he was chief of a squadron of cuirassiers, in Dubois' brigade. It was he who captured the standard of the Lunenburg battalion. He came and cast the flag at the Emperor's feet. He was covered with blood. While tearing down the banner he had received a sword-cut across his face. The Emperor, greatly pleased, shouted to him: "You are a colonel, you are a baron, you are an officer of the Legion of Honor!" Pontmercy replied: "Sire, I thank you for my widow." An hour later, he fell in the ravine of Ohain. Now, who was this Georges Pontmercy? He was this same "brigand of the Loire."

We have already seen something of his history. After Waterloo, Pontmercy, who had been pulled out of the hollow road of Ohain, as it will be remembered, had succeeded in joining the army, and had dragged himself from ambulance to ambulance as far as the cantonments of the Loire.

The Restoration had placed him on half-pay, then had sent him into residence, that is to say, under surveillance, at Vernon. King Louis XVIII, regarding all that which had taken place during the Hundred Days as not having occurred at all, did not recognize his quality as an officer of the Legion of Honor, nor his grade of colonel, nor his title of baron. He, on his side, neglected no occasion of signing himself "Colonel Baron Pontmercy." He had only an old blue coat, and he never went out without fastening to it his rosette as an officer of the Legion of Honor. The Attorney for the Crown had him warned that the authorities would prosecute him for "illegal" wearing of this decoration. When this notice was conveyed to him through an officious intermediary, Pontmercy retorted with a bitter smile: "I do not know whether I no longer understand French, or whether you no longer speak it; but the fact is that I do not understand." Then he went out for eight successive days with his rosette. They dared not interfere with him. Two or three times the Minister of War and the general in command of the department wrote to him with the following address: *"A Monsieur le Commandant Pontmercy."* He sent back the letters with the seals unbroken. At the same moment, Napoleon at Saint Helena was treating in the same fashion the missives of Sir Hudson Lowe addressed to *General Bonaparte.* Pontmercy had ended, may we be pardoned the expression, by having in his mouth the same saliva as his Emperor.

In the same way, there were at Rome Carthaginian prisoners who refused to salute Flaminius, and who had a little of Hannibal's spirit.

One day he encountered the district-attorney in one of the streets of Vernon, stepped up to him, and said: "Mr. Crown Attorney, am I permitted to wear my scar?"

He had nothing save his meagre half-pay as chief of squadron. He had hired the smallest house which he could find at Vernon. He lived there alone, we have just seen how. Under the Empire, between two wars, he had found time to marry Mademoiselle Gillenormand. The old bourgeois, thoroughly indignant at bottom, had given his consent with a sigh, saying: "The greatest families are forced into it." In 1815, Madame Pontmercy, an admirable woman in every sense, by the way, lofty in sentiment and rare, and worthy of her husband, died, leaving a child. This child had been the colonel's joy in his solitude; but the grandfather had imperatively claimed his grandson, declaring that if the child were not given to him he would disinherit him. The father had yielded in the little one's interest, and had transferred his love to flowers.

Moreover, he had renounced everything, and neither stirred up mischief nor conspired. He shared his thoughts between the innocent things which he was then doing and the great things which he had done. He passed his time in expecting a pink or in recalling Austerlitz.

M. Gillenormand kept up no relations with his son-in-law. The colonel was "a bandit" to him. M. Gillenormand never mentioned the colonel, except when he occasionally made mocking allusions to "his Baronship." It had been expressly agreed that Pontmercy should never attempt to see his son nor to speak to him, under penalty of having the latter handed over to him disowned and disinherited. For the Gillenormands, Pontmercy was a man afflicted with the plague. They intended to bring up the child in their own way. Perhaps the colonel was wrong to accept these conditions, but he submitted to them, thinking that he was doing right and sacrificing no one but himself.

The inheritance of Father Gillenormand did not amount to much; but the inheritance of Mademoiselle Gillenormand the elder was considerable. This aunt, who had remained unmarried, was very rich on the maternal side, and her sister's son was her natural heir. The boy, whose name was Marius, knew that he had a father, but nothing more. No one opened his mouth to him about it. Nevertheless, in the society into which his grandfather took him, whispers, innuendoes, and winks, had eventually enlightened the little boy's mind; he had finally understood something of the case, and as he naturally took in the ideas and opinions which were, so to speak, the air he breathed, by a sort of infiltration and slow penetration, he gradually came to think of his father only with shame and with a pain at his heart.

While he was growing up in this fashion, the colonel slipped away every two or three months, came to Paris on the sly, like a criminal breaking his ban, and went and posted himself at Saint-Sulpice, at the hour when Aunt Gillenormand led Marius to the mass. There, trembling lest the aunt should turn round, concealed behind a pillar, motionless, not daring to breathe, he gazed at his child. The scarred veteran was afraid of that old spinster.

From this had arisen his connection with the curé of Vernon, M. l'Abbé Mabeuf.

That worthy priest was the brother of a warden of Saint-Sulpice, who had often observed this man gazing at his child, and the scar on his cheek, and the large tears in his eyes. That man, who had so manly an air, yet who was weeping like a woman, had struck the warden. That face had clung to his mind. One day, having gone to Vernon to see his brother, he had encountered Colonel Pontmercy on the bridge, and had recognized the man of Saint-Sulpice. The warden had mentioned the circumstance to the curé, and both had paid the colonel a visit, on some pretext or other. This visit led to others. The colonel, who had been extremely reserved at first, ended by opening his heart, and the curé and the warden finally came to know the whole history, and how Pontmercy was sacrificing his happiness to his child's future. This caused the curé to regard him with veneration and tenderness, and the colonel, on his side, became fond of the curé. And moreover, when both are sincere and good, no men so penetrate each other, and so amalgamate with each other, as an old priest and an old soldier. At bottom, the man is the same. The one has devoted his life to his country here below, the other to his country on high; that is the only difference.

Twice a year, on the first of January and on St. George's day, Marius wrote duty letters to his father, which were dictated by his aunt, and which one would have pronounced to be copied from some formula; this was all that M. Gillenormand tolerated; and the father answered them with very tender letters which the grandfather thrust into his pocket unread.

III

REQUIESCANT

M adame de T.'s salon was all that Marius Pontmercy knew of the world. It was the only opening through which he could get a glimpse of life. This opening was sombre, and more cold than warmth, more night than day, came to him through this skylight. This child, who had been all joy and light on entering this strange world, soon became melancholy, and, what is still more contrary to his age, grave. Surrounded by all those singular and imposing personages, he gazed about him with serious amazement. Everything conspired to increase this astonishment in him. There were in Madame de T.'s salon some very noble ladies named Mathan, Noé, Lévis,—which was pronounced Lévi,—Cambis, pronounced Cambyse. These antique visages and these Biblical names mingled in the child's mind with the Old Testament which he was learning by heart, and when they were all there, seated in a circle around a dying fire, sparely lighted by a lamp shaded with green, with their severe profiles, their gray or white hair, their long gowns of another age, whose lugubrious colors could not be distinguished, dropping, at rare intervals, words which were both majestic and severe, little Marius stared at them with frightened eyes, in the conviction that he beheld not women, but patriarchs and magi, not real beings, but phantoms.

With these phantoms, priests were sometimes mingled, frequenters of this ancient salon, and some gentlemen; the Marquis de Sass****, private secretary to Madame de Berry, the Vicomte de Val***, who published, under the pseudonym of *Charles-Antoine*, monorhymed odes, the Prince de Beauff*******, who, though very young, had a gray head and a pretty and witty wife, whose very low-necked toilettes of scarlet velvet with gold torsades alarmed these shadows, the Marquis de C***** d'E******, the man in all France who best understood "proportioned politeness," the Comte d'Am*****, the kindly man with the amiable chin, and the Chévalier de Port-de-Guy, a pillar of the library of the Louvre, called the King's cabinet, M. de Port-de-Guy, bald, and rather aged than old, was wont to relate that in 1793, at the age of sixteen, he had been put in the galleys as refractory and chained with an octogenarian, the Bishop of Mirepoix, also refractory, but as a priest, while he was so in the capacity of a soldier. This was at Toulon. Their business was to go at night and gather up on the scaffold the heads and bodies of the persons who had been guillotined during the day; they bore away on their backs these dripping corpses, and their red galley-slave blouses had a clot of blood at the back of the neck, which was dry in the morning and wet at night. These tragic tales abounded in Madame de T.'s salon, and by dint of cursing Marat, they applauded Trestaillon. Some deputies of the undiscoverable variety played their whist there; M. Thibord du Chalard, M. Lemarchant de Gomicourt, and the celebrated scoffer of the right, M. Cornet-Dincourt. The bailiff de Ferrette, with his short breeches and his thin legs, sometimes traversed this salon on his way to M. de Talleyrand. He had been M. le Comte d'Artois' companion in pleasures and unlike Aristotle crouching under Campaspe, he had made the Guimard crawl on all fours, and in that way he had exhibited to the ages a philosopher avenged by a bailiff. As for the priests, there was the Abbé Halma, the same to whom M. Larose, his collaborator on *la Foudre*, said: "Bah! Who is there who is not fifty years old? a few greenhorns perhaps?" The Abbé Letourneur, preacher to the King, the Abbé Frayssinous, who was not, as yet, either count, or bishop, or minister, or peer, and who wore an old cassock whose buttons were missing, and the Abbé Keravenant, Curé of Saint-Germain-des-Prés; also the Pope's Nuncio, then Monsignor Macchi, Archbishop of Nisibi, later on Cardinal, remarkable for his long, pensive nose, and another Monsignor, entitled thus: Abbate Palmieri, domestic prelate, one of the seven participant prothonotaries of the Holy See, Canon of the illustrious Liberian basilica, Advocate of the saints, *Postulatore dei Santi*, which refers to matters of canonization, and signifies very nearly: Master of Requests of the section of Paradise. Lastly, two cardinals, M. de la Luzerne, and M. de Cl****** T*******. The Cardinal of Luzerne was a writer and was destined to have, a few years later, the honor of signing in the *Conservateur* articles side by side with Chateaubriand; M. de Cl****** T******* was Archbishop of Toul****, and often made trips to Paris, to his nephew, the Marquis de T*******, who was Minister of Marine and War. The Cardinal of Cl****** T******* was a merry little man, who displayed his red stockings beneath his tucked-up cassock; his specialty was a hatred of the Encyclopædia, and his desperate play at billiards, and persons who, at that epoch, passed through the Rue M***** on summer evenings, where the hotel de Cl****** T******* then stood, halted to listen to the shock of the balls and the piercing voice of the Cardinal shouting to his conclavist, Monseigneur Cotiret, Bishop *in partibus* of Caryste: "Mark, Abbé, I make a cannon." The Cardinal de Cl****** T******* had been brought to Madame de T.'s by his most intimate friend, M. de Roquelaure, former Bishop of Senlis, and one of the Forty. M. de Roquelaure was notable for his lofty figure and his assiduity at the Academy; through the glass door of the neighboring hall of the library where the French Academy then held its meetings, the curious could, on every Tuesday, contemplate the Ex-Bishop of Senlis, usually standing erect, freshly powdered, in violet hose, with his back turned to the door, apparently for the purpose of allowing a better view of his little collar. All these ecclesiastics, though for the most part as much courtiers as churchmen, added to the gravity of the T. salon, whose seigniorial aspect was accentuated by five peers of France, the Marquis de Vib****, the Marquis de Tal***, the Marquis de Herb*******, the Vicomte Damb***, and the Duc de Val********. This Duc de Val********, although Prince de Mon***, that is to say a reigning prince abroad, had so high an idea of France and its peerage, that he viewed everything through their medium. It was he who said: "The Cardinals are the peers of France of Rome; the lords are the peers of France of England." Moreover, as it is indispensable that the Revolution should be everywhere in this century, this feudal salon was, as we have said, dominated by a bourgeois. M. Gillenormand reigned there.

There lay the essence and quintessence of the Parisian white society. There reputations, even Royalist reputations, were held in quarantine. There is always a trace of anarchy in renown. Chateaubriand, had he entered there, would have produced the effect of Père Duchêne. Some of the scoffed-at did, nevertheless, penetrate thither on sufferance. Comte Beug*** was received there, subject to correction.

The "noble" salons of the present day no longer resemble those salons. The Faubourg Saint-Germain reeks of the fagot even now. The Royalists of to-day are demagogues, let us record it to their credit.

At Madame de T.'s the society was superior, taste was exquisite and haughty, under the cover of a great show of politeness. Manners there admitted of all sorts of involuntary refinements which were the old régime itself, buried but still alive. Some of these habits, especially in the matter of language, seem eccentric. Persons but superficially acquainted with them would have taken for provincial that which was only antique. A woman was called *Madame la Générale. Madame la Colonelle* was not entirely disused. The charming Madame de Léon, in memory, no doubt, of the Duchesses de Longueville and de Chevreuse, preferred this appellation to her title of Princesse. The Marquise de Créquy was also called *Madame la Colonelle*.

It was this little high society which invented at the Tuileries the refinement of speaking to the King in private as *the King*, in the third person, and never as *Your Majesty*, the designation of *Your Majesty* having been "soiled by the usurper."

Men and deeds were brought to judgment there. They jeered at the age, which released them from the necessity of understanding it. They abetted each other in amazement. They communicated to each other that modicum of light which they possessed. Methuselah bestowed information on Epimenides. The deaf man made the blind man acquainted with the course of things. They declared that the time which had elapsed since Coblentz had not existed. In the same manner that Louis XVIII was by the grace of God, in the five and twentieth year of his reign, the emigrants were, by rights, in the five and twentieth year of their adolescence.

All was harmonious; nothing was too much alive; speech hardly amounted to a breath; the newspapers, agreeing with the salons, seemed a papyrus. There were some young people, but they were rather dead. The liveries in the antechamber were antiquated. These utterly obsolete personages were served by domestics of the same stamp.

They all had the air of having lived a long time ago, and of obstinately resisting the sepulchre. Nearly the whole dictionary consisted of *Conserver, Conservation, Conservateur; to be in good odor*,—that was the point. There are, in fact, aromatics in the opinions of these venerable groups, and their ideas smelled of it. It was a mummified society. The masters were embalmed, the servants were stuffed with straw.

A worthy old marquise, an *emigrée* and ruined, who had but a solitary maid, continued to say: "My people."

What did they do in Madame de T.'s salon? They were ultra.

To be ultra; this word, although what it represents may not have disappeared, has no longer any meaning at the present day. Let us explain it.

To be ultra is to go beyond. It is to attack the sceptre in the name of the throne, and the mitre in the name of the altar; it is to ill-treat the thing which one is dragging, it is to kick over the traces; it is to cavil at the fagot on the score of the amount of cooking received by heretics; it is to reproach the idol with its small amount of idolatry; it is to insult through excess of respect; it is to discover that the Pope is not sufficiently papish, that the King is not sufficiently royal, and that the night has too much light; it is to be discontented with alabaster, with snow, with the swan and the lily in the name of whiteness; it is to be a partisan of things to the point of becoming their enemy; it is to be so strongly for, as to be against.

The ultra spirit especially characterizes the first phase of the Restoration.

Nothing in history resembles that quarter of an hour which begins in 1814 and terminates about 1820, with the advent of M. de Villèle, the practical man of the Right. These six years were an extraordinary moment; at one and the same time brilliant and gloomy, smiling and sombre, illuminated as by the radiance of dawn and entirely covered, at the same time, with the shadows of the great catastrophes which still filled the horizon and were slowly sinking into the past. There existed in that light and that shadow, a complete little new and old world, comic and sad, juvenile and senile, which was rubbing its eyes; nothing resembles an awakening like a return; a group which regarded France with ill-temper, and which France regarded with irony; good old owls of marquises by the streetful, who had returned, and of ghosts, the "former" subjects of amazement at everything, brave and noble gentlemen who smiled at being in France but wept also, delighted to behold their country once more, in despair at not finding their monarchy; the nobility of the Crusades treating the nobility of the Empire, that is to say, the nobility of the sword, with scorn; historic races who had lost the sense of history; the sons of the companions of Charlemagne disdaining the companions of Napoleon. The swords, as we have just remarked, returned the insult; the sword of Fontenoy was laughable and nothing but a scrap of rusty iron; the sword of Marengo was odious and was only a sabre. Former days did not recognize Yesterday. People no longer had the feeling for what was grand. There was some one who called Bonaparte Scapin. This Society no longer exists. Nothing of it, we repeat, exists to-day. When we select from it some one figure at random, and attempt to make it live again in thought, it seems as strange to us as the world before the Deluge. It is because it, too, as a matter of fact, has been engulfed in a deluge. It has disappeared beneath two Revolutions. What billows are ideas! How quickly they cover all that it is their mission to destroy and to bury, and how promptly they create frightful gulfs!

Such was the physiognomy of the salons of those distant and candid times when M. Martainville had more wit than Voltaire.

These salons had a literature and politics of their own. They believed in Fiévée. M. Agier laid down the law in them. They commentated M. Colnet, the old bookseller and publicist of the Quay Malaquais. Napoleon was to them thoroughly the Corsican Ogre. Later on the introduction into history of M. le Marquis de Bonaparte, Lieutenant-General of the King's armies, was a concession to the spirit of the age.

These salons did not long preserve their purity. Beginning with 1818, doctrinarians began to spring up in them, a disturbing shade. Their way was to be Royalists and to excuse themselves for being so. Where the ultras were very proud, the doctrinarians were rather ashamed. They had wit; they had silence; their political dogma was suitably impregnated with arrogance; they should have succeeded. They indulged, and usefully too, in excesses in the matter of white neckties and tightly buttoned coats. The mistake or the misfortune of the doctrinarian party was to create aged youth. They assumed the poses of wise men. They dreamed of engrafting a temperate power on the absolute and excessive principle. They opposed, and sometimes with rare intelligence, conservative liberalism to the liberalism which demolishes. They were heard to say: "Thanks for Royalism! It has rendered more than one service. It has brought back tradition, worship, religion, respect. It is faithful, brave, chivalric, loving, devoted. It has mingled, though with regret, the secular grandeurs of the monarchy with the new grandeurs of the nation. Its mistake is not to understand the Revolution, the Empire, glory, liberty, young ideas, young generations, the age. But this mistake which it makes with regard to us,—have we not sometimes been guilty of it towards them? The Revolution, whose heirs we are, ought to be intelligent on all points. To attack Royalism is a misconstruction of liberalism. What an error! And what blindness! Revolutionary France is wanting in respect towards historic France, that is to say, towards its mother, that is to say, towards itself. After the 5th of September, the nobility of the monarchy is treated as the nobility of the Empire was treated after the 5th of July. They were unjust to the eagle, we are unjust to the fleur-de-lys. It seems that we must always have something to proscribe! Does it serve any purpose to ungild the crown of Louis XIV, to scrape the coat of arms of Henry IV? We scoff at M. de Vaublanc for erasing the N's from the bridge of Jena! What was it that he did? What are we doing? Bouvines belongs to us as well as Marengo. The fleurs-de-lys are ours as well as the N's. That is our patrimony. To what purpose shall we diminish it? We must not deny our country in the past any more than in the present. Why not accept the whole of history? Why not love the whole of France?"

It is thus that doctrinarians criticised and protected Royalism, which was displeased at criticism and furious at protection.

The ultras marked the first epoch of Royalism, congregation characterized the second. Skill follows ardor. Let us confine ourselves here to this sketch.

In the course of this narrative, the author of this book has encountered in his path this curious moment of contemporary history; he has been forced to cast a passing glance upon it, and to trace once more some of the singular features of this society which is unknown to-day. But he does it rapidly and without any bitter or derisive idea. Souvenirs both respectful and affectionate, for they touch his mother, attach him to this past. Moreover, let us remark, this same petty world had a grandeur of its own. One may smile at it, but one can neither despise nor hate it. It was the France of former days.

Marius Pontmercy pursued some studies, as all children do. When he emerged from the hands of Aunt Gillenormand, his grandfather confided him to a worthy professor of the most purely classic innocence. This young soul which was expanding passed from a prude to a vulgar pedant.

Marius went through his years of college, then he entered the law school. He was a Royalist, fanatical and severe. He did not love his grandfather much, as the latter's gayety and cynicism repelled him, and his feelings towards his father were gloomy.

He was, on the whole, a cold and ardent, noble, generous, proud, religious, enthusiastic lad; dignified to harshness, pure to shyness.

IV

End of the Brigand

The conclusion of Marius' classical studies coincided with M. Gillenormand's departure from society. The old man bade farewell to the Faubourg Saint-Germain and to Madame de T.'s salon, and established himself in the Marais, in his house of the Rue des Filles-du-Calvaire. There he had for servants, in addition to the porter, that chambermaid, Nicolette, who had succeeded to Magnon, and that short-breathed and pursy Basque, who have been mentioned above.

In 1827, Marius had just attained his seventeenth year. One evening, on his return home, he saw his grandfather holding a letter in his hand.

"Marius," said M. Gillenormand, "you will set out for Vernon to-morrow."

"Why?" said Marius.

"To see your father."

Marius was seized with a trembling fit. He had thought of everything except this—that he should one day be called upon to see his father. Nothing could be more unexpected, more surprising, and, let us admit it, more disagreeable to him. It was forcing estrangement into reconciliation. It was not an affliction, but it was an unpleasant duty.

Marius, in addition to his motives of political antipathy, was convinced that his father, *the slasher*, as M. Gillenormand called him on his amiable days, did not love him; this was evident, since he had abandoned him to others. Feeling that he was not beloved, he did not love. "Nothing is more simple," he said to himself.

He was so astounded that he did not question M. Gillenormand. The grandfather resumed:—

"It appears that he is ill. He demands your presence."

And after a pause, he added:—

"Set out to-morrow morning. I think there is a coach which leaves the Cour des Fontaines at six o'clock, and which arrives in the evening. Take it. He says that here is haste."

Then he crushed the letter in his hand and thrust it into his pocket. Marius might have set out that very evening and have been with his father on the following morning. A diligence from the Rue du Bouloi took the trip to Rouen by night at that date, and passed through Vernon. Neither Marius nor M. Gillenormand thought of making inquiries about it.

The next day, at twilight, Marius reached Vernon. People were just beginning to light their candles. He asked the first person whom he met for "M. Pontmercy's house." For in his own mind, he agreed with the Restoration, and like it, did not recognize his father's claim to the title of either colonel or baron.

The house was pointed out to him. He rang; a woman with a little lamp in her hand opened the door.

"M. Pontmercy?" said Marius.

The woman remained motionless.

"Is this his house?" demanded Marius.

The woman nodded affirmatively.

"Can I speak with him?"

The woman shook her head.

"But I am his son!" persisted Marius. "He is expecting me."

"He no longer expects you," said the woman.

Then he perceived that she was weeping.

She pointed to the door of a room on the ground floor; he entered.

In that room, which was lighted by a tallow candle standing on the chimney-piece, there were three men, one standing erect, another kneeling, and one lying at full length, on the floor in his shirt. The one on the floor was the colonel.

The other two were the doctor, and the priest, who was engaged in prayer.

The colonel had been attacked by brain fever three days previously. As he had a foreboding of evil at the very beginning of his illness, he had written to M. Gillenormand to demand his son. The malady had grown worse. On the very evening of Marius' arrival at Vernon, the colonel had had an attack of delirium; he had risen from his bed, in spite of the servant's efforts to prevent him, crying: "My son is not coming! I shall go to meet him!" Then he ran out of his room and fell prostrate on the floor of the antechamber. He had just expired.

The doctor had been summoned, and the curé. The doctor had arrived too late. The son had also arrived too late.

By the dim light of the candle, a large tear could be distinguished on the pale and prostrate colonel's cheek, where it had trickled from his dead eye. The eye was extinguished, but the tear was not yet dry. That tear was his son's delay.

Marius gazed upon that man whom he beheld for the first time, on that venerable and manly face, on those open eyes which saw not, on those white locks, those robust limbs, on which, here and there, brown lines, marking sword-thrusts, and a sort of red stars, which indicated bullet-holes, were visible. He contemplated that gigantic sear which stamped heroism on that countenance upon which God had imprinted goodness. He reflected that this man was his father, and that this man was dead, and a chill ran over him.

The sorrow which he felt was the sorrow which he would have felt in the presence of any other man whom he had chanced to behold stretched out in death.

Anguish, poignant anguish, was in that chamber. The servant-woman was lamenting in a corner, the curé was praying, and his sobs were audible, the doctor was wiping his eyes; the corpse itself was weeping.

The doctor, the priest, and the woman gazed at Marius in the midst of their affliction without uttering a word; he was the stranger there. Marius, who was far too little affected, felt ashamed and embarrassed at his own attitude; he held his hat in his hand; and he dropped it on the floor, in order to produce the impression that grief had deprived him of the strength to hold it.

At the same time, he experienced remorse, and he despised himself for behaving in this manner. But was it his fault? He did not love his father? Why should he!

The colonel had left nothing. The sale of big furniture barely paid the expenses of his burial.

The servant found a scrap of paper, which she handed to Marius. It contained the following, in the colonel's handwriting:—

"*For my son*.—The Emperor made me a Baron on the battle-field of Waterloo. Since the Restoration disputes my right to this title which I purchased with my blood, my son shall take it and bear it. That he will be worthy of it is a matter of course." Below, the colonel had added: "At that same battle of Waterloo, a sergeant saved my life. The man's name was Thénardier. I think that he has recently been keeping a little inn, in a village in the neighborhood of Paris, at Chelles or Montfermeil. If my son meets him, he will do all the good he can to Thénardier."

Marius took this paper and preserved it, not out of duty to his father, but because of that vague respect for death which is always imperious in the heart of man.

Nothing remained of the colonel. M. Gillenormand had his sword and uniform sold to an old-clothes dealer. The neighbors devastated the garden and pillaged the rare flowers. The other plants turned to nettles and weeds, and died.

Marius remained only forty-eight hours at Vernon. After the interment he returned to Paris, and applied himself again to his law studies, with no more thought of his father than if the latter had never lived. In two days the colonel was buried, and in three forgotten.

Marius wore crape on his hat. That was all.

V

The Utility of Going to Mass, In Order to Become a Revolutionist

Marius had preserved the religious habits of his childhood. One Sunday, when he went to hear mass at Saint-Sulpice, at that same chapel of the Virgin whither his aunt had led him when a small lad, he placed himself behind a pillar, being more absent-minded and thoughtful than usual on that occasion, and knelt down, without paying any special heed, upon a chair of Utrecht velvet, on the back of which was inscribed this name: *Monsieur Mabeuf, warden*. Mass had hardly begun when an old man presented himself and said to Marius:—

"This is my place, sir."

Marius stepped aside promptly, and the old man took possession of his chair.

The mass concluded, Marius still stood thoughtfully a few paces distant; the old man approached him again and said:—

"I beg your pardon, sir, for having disturbed you a while ago, and for again disturbing you at this moment; you must have thought me intrusive, and I will explain myself."

"There is no need of that, Sir," said Marius.

"Yes!" went on the old man, "I do not wish you to have a bad opinion of me. You see, I am attached to this place. It seems to me that the mass is better from here. Why? I will tell you. It is from this place, that I have watched a poor, brave father come regularly, every two or three months, for the last ten years, since he had no other opportunity and no other way of seeing his child, because he was prevented by family arrangements. He came at the hour when he knew that his son would be brought to mass. The little one never suspected that his father was there. Perhaps he did not even know that he had a father, poor innocent! The father kept behind a pillar, so that he might not be seen. He gazed at his child and he wept. He adored that little fellow, poor man! I could see that. This spot has become sanctified in my sight, and I have contracted a habit of coming hither to listen to the mass. I prefer it to the stall to which I have a right, in my capacity of warden. I knew that unhappy gentleman a little, too. He had a father-in-law, a wealthy aunt, relatives,

I don't know exactly what all, who threatened to disinherit the child if he, the father, saw him. He sacrificed himself in order that his son might be rich and happy some day. He was separated from him because of political opinions. Certainly, I approve of political opinions, but there are people who do not know where to stop. Mon Dieu! a man is not a monster because he was at Waterloo; a father is not separated from his child for such a reason as that. He was one of Bonaparte's colonels. He is dead, I believe. He lived at Vernon, where I have a brother who is a curé, and his name was something like Pontmarie or Montpercy. He had a fine sword-cut, on my honor."

"Pontmercy," suggested Marius, turning pale.

"Precisely, Pontmercy. Did you know him?"

"Sir," said Marius, "he was my father."

The old warden clasped his hands and exclaimed:—

"Ah! you are the child! Yes, that's true, he must be a man by this time. Well! poor child, you may say that you had a father who loved you dearly!"

Marius offered his arm to the old man and conducted him to his lodgings.

On the following day, he said to M. Gillenormand:—

"I have arranged a hunting-party with some friends. Will you permit me to be absent for three days?"

"Four!" replied his grandfather. "Go and amuse yourself."

And he said to his daughter in a low tone, and with a wink, "Some love affair!"

VI

The Consequences of Having
Met a Warden

Where it was that Marius went will be disclosed a little further on. Marius was absent for three days, then he returned to Paris, went straight to the library of the law-school and asked for the files of the *Moniteur*.

He read the *Moniteur*, he read all the histories of the Republic and the Empire, the *Memorial de Sainte-Hélène*, all the memoirs, all the newspapers, the bulletins, the proclamations; he devoured everything. The first time that he came across his father's name in the bulletins of the grand army, he had a fever for a week. He went to see the generals under whom Georges Pontmercy had served, among others, Comte H. Church-warden Mabeuf, whom he went to see again, told him about the life at Vernon, the colonel's retreat, his flowers, his solitude. Marius came to a full knowledge of that rare, sweet, and sublime man, that species of lion-lamb who had been his father.

In the meanwhile, occupied as he was with this study which absorbed all his moments as well as his thoughts, he hardly saw the Gillenormands at all. He made his appearance at meals; then they searched for him, and he was not to be found. Father Gillenormand smiled. "Bah! bah! He is just of the age for the girls!" Sometimes the old man added: "The deuce! I thought it was only an affair of gallantry. It seems that it is an affair of passion!"

It was a passion, in fact. Marius was on the high road to adoring his father.

At the same time, his ideas underwent an extraordinary change. The phases of this change were numerous and successive. As this is the history of many minds of our day, we think it will prove useful to follow these phases step by step and to indicate them all.

That history upon which he had just cast his eyes appalled him.

The first effect was to dazzle him.

Up to that time, the Republic, the Empire, had been to him only monstrous words. The Republic, a guillotine in the twilight; the Empire, a sword in the night. He had just taken a look at it, and where he had expected to find only a chaos of shadows, he had beheld, with a sort of unprecedented surprise, mingled with fear and joy, stars sparkling, Mirabeau, Vergniaud, Saint-Just, Robespierre, Camille, Desmoulins, Danton, and a sun arise, Napoleon. He did not know where he stood. He recoiled, blinded by the brilliant lights. Little by little, when his astonishment had passed off, he grew accustomed to this radiance, he contemplated these deeds without dizziness, he examined these personages without terror; the Revolution and the Empire presented themselves luminously, in perspective, before his mind's eye; he beheld each of these groups of events and of men summed up in two tremendous facts: the Republic in the sovereignty of civil right restored to the masses, the Empire in the sovereignty of the French idea imposed on Europe; he beheld the grand figure of the people emerge from the Revolution, and the grand figure of France spring forth from the Empire. He asserted in his conscience, that all this had been good. What his dazzled state neglected in this, his first far too synthetic estimation, we do not think it necessary to point out here. It is the state of a mind on the march that we are recording. Progress is not accomplished in one stage. That stated, once for all, in connection with what precedes as well as with what is to follow, we continue.

He then perceived that, up to that moment, he had comprehended his country no more than he had comprehended his father. He had not known either the one or the other, and a sort of voluntary night had obscured his eyes. Now he saw, and on the one hand he admired, while on the other he adored.

He was filled with regret and remorse, and he reflected in despair that all he had in his soul could now be said only to the tomb. Oh! if his father had still been in existence, if he had still had him, if God, in his compassion and his goodness, had permitted his father to be still among the living, how he would have run, how he would have precipitated himself, how he would have cried to his father: "Father! Here I am! It is I! I have the same heart as thou! I am thy son!" How he would have embraced that white head, bathed his hair in tears, gazed upon his scar, pressed his hands, adored his garment, kissed his feet! Oh! Why had his father died so early, before his time, before the justice, the love of his son had come to him? Marius had a continual sob in his heart, which said to him every moment: "Alas!" At the same time, he became more truly serious, more truly grave, more sure of his thought and his faith. At each instant, gleams of the true came to complete his reason. An inward growth seemed to be in progress within him. He was conscious of a sort of natural enlargement, which gave him two things that were new to him—his father and his country.

As everything opens when one has a key, so he explained to himself that which he had hated, he penetrated that which he had abhorred; henceforth he plainly perceived the providential, divine and human sense of the great things which he had been taught to detest, and of the great men whom he had been instructed to curse. When he reflected on his former opinions, which were but those of yesterday, and which, nevertheless, seemed to him already so very ancient, he grew indignant, yet he smiled.

From the rehabilitation of his father, he naturally passed to the rehabilitation of Napoleon.

But the latter, we will confess, was not effected without labor.

From his infancy, he had been imbued with the judgments of the party of 1814, on Bonaparte. Now, all the prejudices of the Restoration, all its interests, all its instincts tended to disfigure Napoleon. It execrated him even more than it did Robespierre. It had very cleverly turned to sufficiently good account the fatigue of the nation, and the hatred of mothers. Bonaparte had become an almost fabulous monster, and in order to paint him to the imagination of the people, which, as we lately pointed out, resembles the imagination of children, the party of 1814 made him appear under all sorts of terrifying masks in succession, from that which is terrible though it remains grandiose to that which is terrible and becomes grotesque, from Tiberius to the bugaboo. Thus, in speaking of Bonaparte, one was free to sob or to puff up with laughter, provided that hatred lay at the bottom. Marius had never entertained— about *that man*, as he was called—any other ideas in his mind. They had combined with the tenacity which existed in his nature. There was in him a headstrong little man who hated Napoleon.

On reading history, on studying him, especially in the documents and materials for history, the veil which concealed Napoleon from the eyes of Marius was gradually rent. He caught a glimpse of something immense, and he suspected that he had been deceived up to that moment, on the score of Bonaparte as about all the rest; each day he saw more distinctly; and he set about mounting, slowly, step by step, almost regretfully in the beginning, then with intoxication and as though attracted by an irresistible fascination, first the sombre steps, then the vaguely illuminated steps, at last the luminous and splendid steps of enthusiasm.

One night, he was alone in his little chamber near the roof. His candle was burning; he was reading, with his elbows resting on his table close to the open window. All sorts of reveries reached him from space, and mingled with his thoughts. What a spectacle is the night! One hears dull sounds, without knowing whence they proceed; one beholds Jupiter, which is twelve hundred times larger than the earth, glowing like a firebrand, the azure is black, the stars shine; it is formidable.

He was perusing the bulletins of the grand army, those heroic strophes penned on the field of battle; there, at intervals, he beheld his father's name, always the name of the Emperor; the whole of that great Empire presented itself to him; he felt a flood swelling and rising within him; it seemed to him at moments that his father passed close to him like a breath, and whispered in his ear; he gradually got into a singular state; he thought that he heard drums, cannon, trumpets, the measured tread of battalions, the dull and distant gallop of the cavalry; from time to time, his eyes were raised heavenward, and gazed upon the colossal constellations as they gleamed in the measureless depths of space, then they fell upon his book once more, and there they beheld other colossal things moving confusedly. His heart contracted within him. He was in a transport, trembling, panting. All at once, without himself knowing what was in him, and what impulse he was obeying, he sprang to his feet, stretched both arms out of the window, gazed intently into the gloom, the silence, the infinite darkness, the eternal immensity, and exclaimed: "Long live the Emperor!"

From that moment forth, all was over; the Ogre of Corsica,—the usurper,—the tyrant,—the monster who was the lover of his own sisters,—the actor who took lessons of Talma,—the poisoner of Jaffa,— the tiger,—Buonaparte,—all this vanished, and gave place in his mind to a vague and brilliant radiance in which shone, at an inaccessible height, the pale marble phantom of Cæsar. The Emperor had been for his father only the well-beloved captain whom one admires, for whom one sacrifices one's self; he was something more to Marius. He was the predestined constructor of the French group, succeeding the Roman group in the domination of the universe. He was a prodigious architect, of a destruction, the continuer of Charlemagne, of Louis XI, of Henry IV, of Richelieu, of Louis XIV, and of the Committee of Public Safety, having his spots, no doubt, his faults, his crimes even, being a man, that is to say; but august in his faults, brilliant in his spots, powerful in his crime.

He was the predestined man, who had forced all nations to say: "The great nation!" He was better than that, he was the very incarnation of France, conquering Europe by the sword which he grasped, and the world by the light which he shed. Marius saw in Bonaparte the dazzling spectre which will always rise upon the frontier, and which will guard the future. Despot but dictator; a despot resulting from a republic and summing up a revolution. Napoleon became for him the man-people as Jesus Christ is the man-God.

It will be perceived, that like all new converts to a religion, his conversion intoxicated him, he hurled himself headlong into adhesion and he went too far. His nature was so constructed; once on the downward slope, it was almost impossible for him to put on the drag. Fanaticism for the sword took possession of him, and complicated in his mind his enthusiasm for the idea. He did not perceive that, along with genius, and pell-mell, he was admitting force, that is to say, that he was installing in two compartments of his idolatry, on the one hand that which is divine, on the other that which is brutal. In many respects, he had set about deceiving himself otherwise. He admitted everything. There is a way of encountering error while on one's way to the truth. He had a violent sort of good faith which took everything in the lump. In the new path which he had entered on, in judging the mistakes of the old regime, as in measuring the glory of Napoleon, he neglected the attenuating circumstances.

At all events, a tremendous step had been taken. Where he had formerly beheld the fall of the monarchy, he now saw the advent of France. His orientation had changed. What had been his East became the West. He had turned squarely round.

All these revolutions were accomplished within him, without his family obtaining an inkling of the case.

When, during this mysterious labor, he had entirely shed his old Bourbon and ultra skin, when he had cast off the aristocrat, the Jacobite and the Royalist, when he had become thoroughly a revolutionist, profoundly democratic and republican, he went to an engraver on the Quai des Orfévres and ordered a hundred cards bearing this name: *Le Baron Marius Pontmercy*.

This was only the strictly logical consequence of the change which had taken place in him, a change in which everything gravitated round his father.

Only, as he did not know any one and could not sow his cards with any porter, he put them in his pocket.

By another natural consequence, in proportion as he drew nearer to his father, to the latter's memory, and to the things for which the colonel had fought five and twenty years before, he receded from his grandfather. We have long ago said, that M. Gillenormand's temper did not please him. There already existed between them all the dissonances of the grave young man and the frivolous old man. The gayety of Géronte shocks and exasperates the melancholy of Werther. So long as the same political opinions and the same ideas had been common to them both, Marius had met M. Gillenormand there as on a bridge. When the bridge fell, an abyss was formed. And then, over and above all, Marius experienced unutterable impulses to revolt, when he reflected that it was M. Gillenormand who had, from stupid motives, torn him ruthlessly from the colonel, thus depriving the father of the child, and the child of the father.

By dint of pity for his father, Marius had nearly arrived at aversion for his grandfather.

Nothing of this sort, however, was betrayed on the exterior, as we have already said. Only he grew colder and colder; laconic at meals, and rare in the house. When his aunt scolded him for it, he was very gentle and alleged his studies, his lectures, the examinations, etc., as a pretext. His grandfather never departed from his infallible diagnosis: "In love! I know all about it."

From time to time Marius absented himself.

"Where is it that he goes off like this?" said his aunt.

On one of these trips, which were always very brief, he went to Montfermeil, in order to obey the injunction which his father had left him, and he sought the old sergeant to Waterloo, the inn-keeper Thénardier. Thénardier had failed, the inn was closed, and no one knew what had become of him. Marius was away from the house for four days on this quest.

"He is getting decidedly wild," said his grandfather.

They thought they had noticed that he wore something on his breast, under his shirt, which was attached to his neck by a black ribbon.

VII

SOME PETTICOAT

We have mentioned a lancer.

He was a great-grand-nephew of M. Gillenormand, on the paternal side, who led a garrison life, outside the family and far from the domestic hearth. Lieutenant Théodule Gillenormand fulfilled all the conditions required to make what is called a fine officer. He had "a lady's waist," a victorious manner of trailing his sword and of twirling his moustache in a hook. He visited Paris very rarely, and so rarely that Marius had never seen him. The cousins knew each other only by name. We think we have said that Théodule was the favorite of Aunt Gillenormand, who preferred him because she did not see him. Not seeing people permits one to attribute to them all possible perfections.

One morning, Mademoiselle Gillenormand the elder returned to her apartment as much disturbed as her placidity was capable of allowing. Marius had just asked his grandfather's permission to take a little trip, adding that he meant to set out that very evening. "Go!" had been his grandfather's reply, and M. Gillenormand had added in an aside, as he raised his eyebrows to the top of his forehead: "Here he is passing the night out again." Mademoiselle Gillenormand had ascended to her chamber greatly puzzled, and on the staircase had dropped this exclamation: "This is too much!"—and this interrogation: "But where is it that he goes?" She espied some adventure of the heart, more or less illicit, a woman in the shadow, a rendezvous, a mystery, and she would not have been sorry to thrust her spectacles into the affair. Tasting a mystery resembles getting the first flavor of a scandal; sainted souls do not detest this. There is some curiosity about scandal in the secret compartments of bigotry.

So she was the prey of a vague appetite for learning a history.

In order to get rid of this curiosity which agitated her a little beyond her wont, she took refuge in her talents, and set about scalloping, with one layer of cotton after another, one of those embroideries of the Empire and the Restoration, in which there are numerous cart-wheels. The work was clumsy, the worker cross. She had been seated at this for several hours when the door opened. Mademoiselle Gillenormand raised her nose. Lieutenant Théodule stood before her, making the regulation salute. She uttered a cry of delight. One may be old, one may be a prude, one may be pious, one may be an aunt, but it is always agreeable to see a lancer enter one's chamber.

"You here, Théodule!" she exclaimed.

"On my way through town, aunt."

"Embrace me."

"Here goes!" said Théodule.

And he kissed her. Aunt Gillenormand went to her writing-desk and opened it.

"You will remain with us a week at least?"

"I leave this very evening, aunt."

"It is not possible!"

"Mathematically!"

"Remain, my little Théodule, I beseech you."

"My heart says 'yes,' but my orders say 'no.' The matter is simple. They are changing our garrison; we have been at Melun, we are being transferred to Gaillon. It is necessary to pass through Paris in order to get from the old post to the new one. I said: 'I am going to see my aunt.'"

"Here is something for your trouble."

And she put ten louis into his hand.

"For my pleasure, you mean to say, my dear aunt."

Théodule kissed her again, and she experienced the joy of having some of the skin scratched from her neck by the braidings on his uniform.

"Are you making the journey on horseback, with your regiment?" she asked him.

"No, aunt. I wanted to see you. I have special permission. My servant is taking my horse; I am travelling by diligence. And, by the way, I want to ask you something."

"What is it?"

"Is my cousin Marius Pontmercy travelling so, too?"

"How do you know that?" said his aunt, suddenly pricked to the quick with a lively curiosity.

"On my arrival, I went to the diligence to engage my seat in the coupé."

"Well?"

"A traveller had already come to engage a seat in the imperial. I saw his name on the card."

"What name?"

"Marius Pontmercy."

"The wicked fellow!" exclaimed his aunt. "Ah! your cousin is not a steady lad like yourself. To think that he is to pass the night in a diligence!"

"Just as I am going to do."

"But you—it is your duty; in his case, it is wildness."

"Bosh!" said Théodule.

Here an event occurred to Mademoiselle Gillenormand the elder,— an idea struck her. If she had been a man, she would have slapped her brow. She apostrophized Théodule:—

"Are you aware whether your cousin knows you?"

"No. I have seen him; but he has never deigned to notice me."

"So you are going to travel together?"

"He in the imperial, I in the coupé."

"Where does this diligence run?"

"To Andelys."

"Then that is where Marius is going?"

"Unless, like myself, he should stop on the way. I get down at Vernon, in order to take the branch coach for Gaillon. I know nothing of Marius' plan of travel."

"Marius! what an ugly name! what possessed them to name him Marius? While you, at least, are called Théodule."

"I would rather be called Alfred," said the officer.

"Listen, Théodule."

"I am listening, aunt."

"Pay attention."

"I am paying attention."

"You understand?"

"Yes."

"Well, Marius absents himself!"

"Eh! eh!"

"He travels."

"Ah! ah!"

"He spends the night out."

"Oh! oh!"

"We should like to know what there is behind all this."

Théodule replied with the composure of a man of bronze:—

"Some petticoat or other."

And with that inward laugh which denotes certainty, he added:—
"A lass."

"That is evident," exclaimed his aunt, who thought she heard M. Gillenormand speaking, and who felt her conviction become irresistible at that word *fillette*, accentuated in almost the very same fashion by the granduncle and the grandnephew. She resumed:—

"Do us a favor. Follow Marius a little. He does not know you, it will be easy. Since a lass there is, try to get a sight of her. You must write us the tale. It will amuse his grandfather."

Théodule had no excessive taste for this sort of spying; but he was much touched by the ten louis, and he thought he saw a chance for a possible sequel. He accepted the commission and said: "As you please, aunt."

And he added in an aside, to himself: "Here I am a duenna."

Mademoiselle Gillenormand embraced him.

"You are not the man to play such pranks, Théodule. You obey discipline, you are the slave of orders, you are a man of scruples and duty, and you would not quit your family to go and see a creature."

The lancer made the pleased grimace of Cartouche when praised for his probity.

Marius, on the evening following this dialogue, mounted the diligence without suspecting that he was watched. As for the watcher, the first thing he did was to fall asleep. His slumber was complete and conscientious. Argus snored all night long.

At daybreak, the conductor of the diligence shouted: "Vernon! relay of Vernon! Travellers for Vernon!" And Lieutenant Théodule woke.

"Good," he growled, still half asleep, "this is where I get out."

Then, as his memory cleared by degrees, the effect of waking, he recalled his aunt, the ten louis, and the account which he had undertaken to render of the deeds and proceedings of Marius. This set him to laughing.

"Perhaps he is no longer in the coach," he thought, as he rebuttoned the waistcoat of his undress uniform. "He may have stopped at Poissy; he may have stopped at Triel; if he did not get out at Meulan, he may have got out at Mantes, unless he got out at Rolleboise, or if he did not go on as far as Pacy, with the choice of turning to the left at Évreus, or to the right at Laroche-Guyon. Run after him, aunty. What the devil am I to write to that good old soul?"

At that moment a pair of black trousers descending from the imperial, made its appearance at the window of the coupé.

"Can that be Marius?" said the lieutenant.

It was Marius.

A little peasant girl, all entangled with the horses and the postilions at the end of the vehicle, was offering flowers to the travellers. "Give your ladies flowers!" she cried.

Marius approached her and purchased the finest flowers in her flat basket.

"Come now," said Théodule, leaping down from the coupé, "this piques my curiosity. Who the deuce is he going to carry those flowers to? She must be a splendidly handsome woman for so fine a bouquet. I want to see her."

And no longer in pursuance of orders, but from personal curiosity, like dogs who hunt on their own account, he set out to follow Marius.

Marius paid no attention to Théodule. Elegant women descended from the diligence; he did not glance at them. He seemed to see nothing around him.

"He is pretty deeply in love!" thought Théodule.

Marius directed his steps towards the church.

"Capital," said Théodule to himself. "Rendezvous seasoned with a bit of mass are the best sort. Nothing is so exquisite as an ogle which passes over the good God's head."

On arriving at the church, Marius did not enter it, but skirted the apse. He disappeared behind one of the angles of the apse.

"The rendezvous is appointed outside," said Théodule. "Let's have a look at the lass."

And he advanced on the tips of his boots towards the corner which Marius had turned.

On arriving there, he halted in amazement.

Marius, with his forehead clasped in his hands, was kneeling upon the grass on a grave. He had strewn his bouquet there. At the extremity of the grave, on a little swelling which marked the head, there stood a cross of black wood with this name in white letters: COLONEL BARON PONTMERCY. Marius' sobs were audible.

The "lass" was a grave.

VIII

Marble Against Granite

It was hither that Marius had come on the first occasion of his absenting himself from Paris. It was hither that he had come every time that M. Gillenormand had said: "He is sleeping out."

Lieutenant Théodule was absolutely put out of countenance by this unexpected encounter with a sepulchre; he experienced a singular and disagreeable sensation which he was incapable of analyzing, and which was composed of respect for the tomb, mingled with respect for the colonel. He retreated, leaving Marius alone in the cemetery, and there was discipline in this retreat. Death appeared to him with large epaulets, and he almost made the military salute to him. Not knowing what to write to his aunt, he decided not to write at all; and it is probable that nothing would have resulted from the discovery made by Théodule as to the love affairs of Marius, if, by one of those mysterious arrangements which are so frequent in chance, the scene at Vernon had not had an almost immediate counter-shock at Paris.

Marius returned from Vernon on the third day, in the middle of the morning, descended at his grandfather's door, and, wearied by the two nights spent in the diligence, and feeling the need of repairing his loss of sleep by an hour at the swimming-school, he mounted rapidly to his chamber, took merely time enough to throw off his travelling-coat, and the black ribbon which he wore round his neck, and went off to the bath.

M. Gillenormand, who had risen betimes like all old men in good health, had heard his entrance, and had made haste to climb, as quickly as his old legs permitted, the stairs to the upper story where Marius lived, in order to embrace him, and to question him while so doing, and to find out where he had been.

But the youth had taken less time to descend than the old man had to ascend, and when Father Gillenormand entered the attic, Marius was no longer there.

The bed had not been disturbed, and on the bed lay, outspread, but not defiantly the great-coat and the black ribbon.

"I like this better," said M. Gillenormand.

And a moment later, he made his entrance into the salon, where Mademoiselle Gillenormand was already seated, busily embroidering her cart-wheels.

The entrance was a triumphant one.

M. Gillenormand held in one hand the great-coat, and in the other the neck-ribbon, and exclaimed:—

"Victory! We are about to penetrate the mystery! We are going to learn the most minute details; we are going to lay our finger on the debaucheries of our sly friend! Here we have the romance itself. I have the portrait!"

In fact, a case of black shagreen, resembling a medallion portrait, was suspended from the ribbon.

The old man took this case and gazed at it for some time without opening it, with that air of enjoyment, rapture, and wrath, with which a poor hungry fellow beholds an admirable dinner which is not for him, pass under his very nose.

"For this evidently is a portrait. I know all about such things. That is worn tenderly on the heart. How stupid they are! Some abominable fright that will make us shudder, probably! Young men have such bad taste nowadays!"

"Let us see, father," said the old spinster.

The case opened by the pressure of a spring. They found in it nothing but a carefully folded paper.

"From the same to the same," said M. Gillenormand, bursting with laughter. "I know what it is. A billet-doux."

"Ah! let us read it!" said the aunt.

And she put on her spectacles. They unfolded the paper and read as follows:—

"For my son.—The Emperor made me a Baron on the battlefield of Waterloo. Since the Restoration disputes my right to this title which I purchased with my blood, my son shall take it and bear it. That he will be worthy of it is a matter of course."

The feelings of father and daughter cannot be described. They felt chilled as by the breath of a death's-head. They did not exchange a word.

Only, M. Gillenormand said in a low voice and as though speaking to himself:—

"It is the slasher's handwriting."

The aunt examined the paper, turned it about in all directions, then put it back in its case.

At the same moment a little oblong packet, enveloped in blue paper, fell from one of the pockets of the great-coat. Mademoiselle Gillenormand picked it up and unfolded the blue paper.

It contained Marius' hundred cards. She handed one of them to M. Gillenormand, who read: *Le Baron Marius Pontmercy*.

The old man rang the bell. Nicolette came. M. Gillenormand took the ribbon, the case, and the coat, flung them all on the floor in the middle of the room, and said:—

"Carry those duds away."

A full hour passed in the most profound silence. The old man and the old spinster had seated themselves with their backs to each other, and were thinking, each on his own account, the same things, in all probability.

At the expiration of this hour, Aunt Gillenormand said:—"A pretty state of things!"

A few moments later, Marius made his appearance. He entered. Even before he had crossed the threshold, he saw his grandfather holding one of his own cards in his hand, and on catching sight of him, the latter exclaimed with his air of bourgeois and grinning superiority which was something crushing:—

"Well! well! well! well! well! so you are a baron now. I present you my compliments. What is the meaning of this?"

Marius reddened slightly and replied:—

"It means that I am the son of my father."

M. Gillenormand ceased to laugh, and said harshly:—

"I am your father."

"My father," retorted Marius, with downcast eyes and a severe air, "was a humble and heroic man, who served the Republic and France gloriously, who was great in the greatest history that men have ever made, who lived in the bivouac for a quarter of a century, beneath grape-shot and bullets, in snow and mud by day, beneath rain at night, who captured two flags, who received twenty wounds, who died forgotten and abandoned, and who never committed but one mistake, which was to love too fondly two ingrates, his country and myself."

This was more than M. Gillenormand could bear to hear. At the word *republic*, he rose, or, to speak more correctly, he sprang to his feet. Every word that Marius had just uttered produced on the visage of the old Royalist the effect of the puffs of air from a forge upon a blazing brand. From a dull hue he had turned red, from red, purple, and from purple, flame-colored.

"Marius!" he cried. "Abominable child! I do not know what your father was! I do not wish to know! I know nothing about that, and I do not know him! But what I do know is, that there never was anything but scoundrels among those men! They were all rascals, assassins, red-caps, thieves! I say all! I say all! I know not one! I say all! Do you hear me, Marius! See here, you are no more a baron than my slipper is! They were all bandits in the service of Robespierre! All who served B-u-o-naparté were brigands! They were all traitors who betrayed, betrayed, betrayed their legitimate king! All cowards who fled before the Prussians and the English at Waterloo! That is what I do know! Whether Monsieur your father comes in that category, I do not know! I am sorry for it, so much the worse, your humble servant!"

In his turn, it was Marius who was the firebrand and M. Gillenormand who was the bellows. Marius quivered in every limb, he did not know what would happen next, his brain was on fire. He was the priest who beholds all his sacred wafers cast to the winds, the fakir who beholds a passer-by spit upon his idol. It could not be that such things had been uttered in his presence. What was he to do? His father had just been trampled under foot and stamped upon in his presence, but by whom? By his grandfather. How was he to avenge the one without outraging the other? It was impossible for him to insult his grandfather and it was equally impossible for him to leave his father unavenged. On the one hand was a sacred grave, on the other hoary locks.

He stood there for several moments, staggering as though intoxicated, with all this whirlwind dashing through his head; then he raised his eyes, gazed fixedly at his grandfather, and cried in a voice of thunder:—

"Down with the Bourbons, and that great hog of a Louis XVIII!"

Louis XVIII had been dead for four years; but it was all the same to him.

The old man, who had been crimson, turned whiter than his hair. He wheeled round towards a bust of M. le Duc de Berry, which stood on the chimney-piece, and made a profound bow, with a sort of peculiar majesty. Then he paced twice, slowly and in silence, from the fireplace to the window and from the window to the fireplace, traversing the whole length of the room, and making the polished floor creak as though he had been a stone statue walking.

On his second turn, he bent over his daughter, who was watching

VICTOR HUGO

this encounter with the stupefied air of an antiquated lamb, and said to her with a smile that was almost calm: "A baron like this gentleman, and a bourgeois like myself cannot remain under the same roof."

And drawing himself up, all at once, pallid, trembling, terrible, with his brow rendered more lofty by the terrible radiance of wrath, he extended his arm towards Marius and shouted to him:—

"Be off!"

Marius left the house.

On the following day, M. Gillenormand said to his daughter:

"You will send sixty pistoles every six months to that blood-drinker, and you will never mention his name to me."

Having an immense reserve fund of wrath to get rid of, and not knowing what to do with it, he continued to address his daughter as *you* instead of *thou* for the next three months.

Marius, on his side, had gone forth in indignation. There was one circumstance which, it must be admitted, aggravated his exasperation. There are always petty fatalities of the sort which complicate domestic dramas. They augment the grievances in such cases, although, in reality, the wrongs are not increased by them. While carrying Marius' "duds" precipitately to his chamber, at his grandfather's command, Nicolette had, inadvertently, let fall, probably, on the attic staircase, which was dark, that medallion of black shagreen which contained the paper penned by the colonel. Neither paper nor case could afterwards be found. Marius was convinced that "Monsieur Gillenormand"—from that day forth he never alluded to him otherwise—had flung "his father's testament" in the fire. He knew by heart the few lines which the colonel had written, and, consequently, nothing was lost. But the paper, the writing, that sacred relic,—all that was his very heart. What had been done with it?

Marius had taken his departure without saying whither he was going, and without knowing where, with thirty francs, his watch, and a few clothes in a hand-bag. He had entered a hackney-coach, had engaged it by the hour, and had directed his course at hap-hazard towards the Latin quarter.

What was to become of Marius?

BOOK FOURTH
THE FRIENDS OF THE A B C

I

A Group Which Barely Missed
Becoming Historic

At that epoch, which was, to all appearances indifferent, a certain revolutionary quiver was vaguely current. Breaths which had started forth from the depths of '89 and '93 were in the air. Youth was on the point, may the reader pardon us the word, of moulting. People were undergoing a transformation, almost without being conscious of it, through the movement of the age. The needle which moves round the compass also moves in souls. Each person was taking that step in advance which he was bound to take. The Royalists were becoming liberals, liberals were turning democrats. It was a flood tide complicated with a thousand ebb movements; the peculiarity of ebbs is to create intermixtures; hence the combination of very singular ideas; people adored both Napoleon and liberty. We are making history here. These were the mirages of that period. Opinions traverse phases. Voltairian royalism, a quaint variety, had a no less singular sequel, Bonapartist liberalism.

Other groups of minds were more serious. In that direction, they sounded principles, they attached themselves to the right. They grew enthusiastic for the absolute, they caught glimpses of infinite realizations; the absolute, by its very rigidity, urges spirits towards the sky and causes them to float in illimitable space. There is nothing like dogma for bringing forth dreams. And there is nothing like dreams for engendering the future. Utopia to-day, flesh and blood to-morrow.

These advanced opinions had a double foundation. A beginning of mystery menaced "the established order of things," which was suspicious and underhand. A sign which was revolutionary to the highest degree. The second thoughts of power meet the second thoughts of the populace in the mine. The incubation of insurrections gives the retort to the premeditation of *coups d'état*.

There did not, as yet, exist in France any of those vast underlying organizations, like the German *tugendbund* and Italian Carbonarism; but here and there there were dark underminings, which were in process of throwing off shoots. The Cougourde was being outlined at Aix; there existed at Paris, among other affiliations of that nature, the society of the Friends of the A B C.

What were these Friends of the A B C? A society which had for its object apparently the education of children, in reality the elevation of man.

They declared themselves the Friends of the A B C,—the *Abaissé*,— the debased,—that is to say, the people. They wished to elevate the people. It was a pun which we should do wrong to smile at. Puns are sometimes serious factors in politics; witness the *Castratus ad castra*, which made a general of the army of Narses; witness: *Barbari et Barberini*; witness: *Tu es Petrus et super hanc petram*, etc., etc.

The Friends of the A B C were not numerous, it was a secret society in the state of embryo, we might almost say a coterie, if coteries ended in heroes. They assembled in Paris in two localities, near the fish-market, in a wine-shop called *Corinthe*, of which more will be heard later on, and near the Pantheon in a little café in the Rue Saint-Michel called the *Café Musain*, now torn down; the first of these meeting-places was close to the workingman, the second to the students.

The assemblies of the Friends of the A B C were usually held in a back room of the Café Musain.

This hall, which was tolerably remote from the café, with which it was connected by an extremely long corridor, had two windows and an exit with a private stairway on the little Rue des Grès. There they smoked and drank, and gambled and laughed. There they conversed in very loud tones about everything, and in whispers of other things. An old map of France under the Republic was nailed to the wall,—a sign quite sufficient to excite the suspicion of a police agent.

The greater part of the Friends of the A B C were students, who were on cordial terms with the working classes. Here are the names of the principal ones. They belong, in a certain measure, to history: Enjolras, Combeferre, Jean Prouvaire, Feuilly, Courfeyrac, Bahorel, Lesgle or Laigle, Joly, Grantaire.

These young men formed a sort of family, through the bond of friendship. All, with the exception of Laigle, were from the South.

THIS WAS A REMARKABLE GROUP. It vanished in the invisible depths which lie behind us. At the point of this drama which we have now reached, it will not perhaps be superfluous to throw a ray of light upon these youthful heads, before the reader beholds them plunging into the shadow of a tragic adventure.

Enjolras, whose name we have mentioned first of all,—the reader shall see why later on,—was an only son and wealthy.

Enjolras was a charming young man, who was capable of being terrible. He was angelically handsome. He was a savage Antinous. One would have said, to see the pensive thoughtfulness of his glance, that he had already, in some previous state of existence, traversed the revolutionary apocalypse. He possessed the tradition of it as though he had been a witness. He was acquainted with all the minute details of the great affair. A pontifical and warlike nature, a singular thing in a youth. He was an officiating priest and a man of war; from the immediate point of view, a soldier of the democracy; above the contemporary movement, the priest of the ideal. His eyes were deep, his lids a little red, his lower lip was thick and easily became disdainful, his brow was lofty. A great deal of brow in a face is like a great deal of horizon in a view. Like certain young men at the beginning of this century and the end of the last, who became illustrious at an early age, he was endowed with excessive youth, and was as rosy as a young girl, although subject to hours of pallor. Already a man, he still seemed a child. His two and twenty years appeared to be but seventeen; he was serious, it did not seem as though he were aware there was on earth a thing called woman. He had but one passion—the right; but one thought—to overthrow the obstacle. On Mount Aventine, he would have been Gracchus; in the Convention, he would have been Saint-Just. He hardly saw the roses, he ignored spring, he did not hear the carolling of the birds; the bare throat of Evadne would have moved him no more than it would have moved Aristogeiton; he, like Harmodius, thought flowers good for nothing except to conceal the sword. He was severe in his enjoyments. He chastely dropped his eyes before everything which was not the Republic. He was the marble lover of liberty. His speech was harshly inspired, and had the thrill of a hymn. He was subject to unexpected outbursts of soul. Woe to the love-affair which should have risked itself beside him! If any grisette of the Place Cambrai or the Rue Saint-Jean-de-Beauvais, seeing that face of a youth escaped from college, that page's mien, those long, golden lashes, those blue eyes, that hair billowing in the wind, those rosy cheeks, those fresh lips, those exquisite teeth, had conceived an appetite for that complete aurora, and had tried her beauty on Enjolras, an astounding and terrible glance would have promptly shown her the abyss, and would have taught her not to confound the mighty cherub of Ezekiel with the gallant Cherubino of Beaumarchais.

By the side of Enjolras, who represented the logic of the Revolution, Combeferre represented its philosophy. Between the logic of the Revolution and its philosophy there exists this difference—that its logic may end in war, whereas its philosophy can end only in peace. Combeferre complemented and rectified Enjolras. He was less lofty, but broader. He desired to pour into all minds the extensive principles of general ideas: he said: "Revolution, but civilization"; and around the mountain peak he opened out a vast view of the blue sky. The Revolution was more adapted for breathing with Combeferre than with Enjolras. Enjolras expressed its divine right, and Combeferre its natural right. The first attached himself to Robespierre; the second confined himself to Condorcet. Combeferre lived the life of all the rest of the world more than did Enjolras. If it had been granted to these two young men to attain to history, the one would have been the just, the other the wise man. Enjolras was the more virile, Combeferre the more humane. *Homo* and *vir*, that was the exact effect of their different shades. Combeferre was as gentle as Enjolras was severe, through natural whiteness. He loved the word *citizen*, but he preferred the word *man*. He would gladly have said: *Hombre*, like the Spanish. He read everything, went to the theatres, attended the courses of public lecturers, learned the polarization of light from Arago, grew enthusiastic over a lesson in which Geoffroy Sainte-Hilaire explained the double function of the external carotid artery, and the internal, the one which makes the face, and the one which makes the brain; he kept up with what was going on, followed science step by step, compared Saint-Simon with Fourier, deciphered hieroglyphics, broke the pebble which he found and reasoned on geology, drew from memory a silkworm moth, pointed out the faulty French in the Dictionary of the Academy, studied Puységur and Deleuze, affirmed nothing, not even miracles; denied nothing, not even ghosts; turned over the files of the *Moniteur*, reflected. He declared that the future lies in the hand of the schoolmaster, and busied himself with educational questions. He desired that society should labor without relaxation at the elevation of the moral and intellectual level, at coining science, at putting ideas into circulation, at increasing the mind in youthful persons, and he feared lest the present poverty of method, the paltriness from a literary point of view confined to two or three centuries called classic, the tyrannical dogmatism of official pedants, scholastic prejudices and routines should end by converting our colleges into artificial oyster beds. He was learned, a purist, exact, a graduate of the Polytechnic, a close student, and at the same time, thoughtful "even to chimæras," so his friends said. He believed in all dreams, railroads, the suppression of suffering in chirurgical operations, the fixing of images in the dark chamber, the electric telegraph, the steering of balloons. Moreover, he was not much alarmed by the citadels erected against the human mind in every direction, by superstition, despotism, and prejudice. He was one of those who think that science will eventually turn the position. Enjolras was a chief, Combeferre was a guide. One would have liked to fight under the one and to march behind the other. It is not that Combeferre was not capable of fighting, he did not refuse a hand-to-hand combat with the obstacle, and to attack it by main force and explosively; but it suited him better to bring the human race into accord with its destiny gradually, by means of education, the inculcation of axioms, the promulgation of positive laws; and, between two lights, his preference was rather for illumination than for conflagration. A conflagration can create an aurora, no doubt, but why not await the dawn? A volcano illuminates, but daybreak furnishes a still better illumination. Possibly, Combeferre preferred the whiteness of the beautiful to the blaze of the sublime. A light troubled by smoke, progress purchased at the expense of violence, only half satisfied this tender and serious spirit. The headlong precipitation of a people into the truth, a '93, terrified him; nevertheless, stagnation was still more repulsive to him, in it he detected putrefaction and death; on the whole, he preferred scum to miasma, and he preferred the torrent to the cesspool, and the falls of Niagara to the lake of Montfaucon. In short, he desired neither halt nor haste. While his tumultuous friends, captivated by the absolute, adored and invoked splendid revolutionary adventures, Combeferre was inclined to let progress, good progress, take its own course; he may have been cold, but he was pure; methodical, but irreproachable; phlegmatic, but imperturbable. Combeferre would have knelt and clasped his hands to enable the future to arrive in all its candor, and that nothing might disturb the immense and virtuous evolution of the races. *The good must be innocent*, he repeated incessantly. And in fact, if the grandeur of the Revolution consists in keeping the dazzling ideal fixedly in view, and of soaring thither athwart the lightnings, with fire and blood in its talons, the beauty of progress lies in being spotless; and there exists between Washington, who represents the one, and Danton, who incarnates the other, that difference which separates the swan from the angel with the wings of an eagle.

Jean Prouvaire was a still softer shade than Combeferre. His name was Jehan, owing to that petty momentary freak which mingled with the powerful and profound movement whence sprang the very essential study of the Middle Ages. Jean Prouvaire was in love; he cultivated a pot of flowers, played on the flute, made verses, loved the people, pitied woman, wept over the child, confounded God and the future in the same confidence, and blamed the Revolution for having caused the fall of a royal head, that of André Chénier. His voice was ordinarily delicate, but suddenly grew manly. He was learned even to erudition, and almost an Orientalist. Above all, he was good; and, a very simple thing to those who know how nearly goodness borders on grandeur, in the matter of poetry, he preferred the immense. He knew Italian, Latin, Greek, and Hebrew; and these served him only for the perusal of four poets: Dante, Juvenal, Æschylus, and Isaiah. In French, he preferred Corneille to Racine, and Agrippa d'Aubigné to Corneille. He loved to saunter through fields of wild oats and corn-flowers, and busied himself with clouds nearly as much as with events. His mind had two attitudes, one on the side towards man, the other on that towards God; he studied or he contemplated. All day long, he buried himself in social questions, salary, capital, credit, marriage, religion, liberty of thought, education, penal servitude, poverty, association, property, production and sharing, the enigma of this lower world which covers the human ant-hill with darkness; and at night, he gazed upon the planets, those enormous beings. Like Enjolras, he was wealthy and an only son. He spoke softly, bowed his head, lowered his eyes, smiled with embarrassment, dressed badly, had an awkward air, blushed at a mere nothing, and was very timid. Yet he was intrepid.

Feuilly was a workingman, a fan-maker, orphaned both of father and mother, who earned with difficulty three francs a day, and had but one thought, to deliver the world. He had one other preoccupation, to educate himself; he called this also, delivering himself. He had taught himself to read and write; everything that he knew, he had learned by himself. Feuilly had a generous heart. The range of his embrace was immense. This orphan had adopted the peoples. As his mother had failed him, he meditated on his country. He brooded with the profound divination of the man of the people, over what we now call the *idea of the nationality*, had learned history with the express object of raging with full knowledge of the case. In this club of young Utopians, occupied chiefly with France, he represented the outside world. He had for his specialty Greece, Poland, Hungary, Roumania, Italy. He uttered these names incessantly, appropriately and inappropriately, with the tenacity of right. The violations of Turkey on Greece and Thessaly, of Russia on Warsaw, of Austria on Venice, enraged him. Above all things, the great violence of 1772 aroused him. There is no more sovereign eloquence than the true in indignation; he was eloquent with that eloquence. He was inexhaustible on that infamous date of 1772, on the subject of that noble and valiant race suppressed by treason, and that three-sided crime, on that monstrous ambush, the prototype and pattern of all those horrible suppressions of states, which, since that time, have struck many a noble nation, and have annulled their certificate of birth, so to speak. All contemporary social crimes have their origin in the partition of Poland. The partition of Poland is a theorem of which all present political outrages are the corollaries. There has not been a despot, nor a traitor for nearly a century back, who has not signed, approved, counter-signed, and copied, *ne variatur*, the partition of Poland. When the record of modern treasons was examined, that was the first thing which made its appearance. The congress of Vienna consulted that crime before consummating its own. 1772 sounded the onset; 1815 was the death of the game. Such was Feuilly's habitual text. This poor workingman had constituted himself the tutor of Justice, and she recompensed him by rendering him great. The fact is, that there is eternity in right. Warsaw can no more be Tartar than Venice can be Teuton. Kings lose their pains and their honor in the attempt to make them so. Sooner or later, the submerged part floats to the surface and reappears. Greece becomes Greece again, Italy is once more Italy. The protest of right against the deed persists forever. The theft of a nation cannot be allowed by prescription. These lofty deeds of rascality have no future. A nation cannot have its mark extracted like a pocket handkerchief.

Courfeyrac had a father who was called M. de Courfeyrac. One of the false ideas of the bourgeoisie under the Restoration as regards aristocracy and the nobility was to believe in the particle. The particle, as every one knows, possesses no significance. But the bourgeois of the epoch of *la Minerve* estimated so highly that poor *de*, that they thought themselves bound to abdicate it. M. de Chauvelin had himself called M. Chauvelin; M. de Caumartin, M. Caumartin; M. de Constant de Robecque, Benjamin Constant; M. de Lafayette, M. Lafayette.

Courfeyrac had not wished to remain behind the rest, and called himself plain Courfeyrac.

We might almost, so far as Courfeyrac is concerned, stop here, and confine ourselves to saying with regard to what remains: "For Courfeyrac, see Tholomyès."

Courfeyrac had, in fact, that animation of youth which may be called the *beauté du diable* of the mind. Later on, this disappears like the playfulness of the kitten, and all this grace ends, with the bourgeois, on two legs, and with the tomcat, on four paws.

This sort of wit is transmitted from generation to generation of the successive levies of youth who traverse the schools, who pass it from hand to hand, *quasi cursores*, and is almost always exactly the same; so that, as we have just pointed out, any one who had listened to Courfeyrac in 1828 would have thought he heard Tholomyès in 1817. Only, Courfeyrac was an honorable fellow. Beneath the apparent similarities of the exterior mind, the difference between him and Tholomyès was very great. The latent man which existed in the two was totally different in the first from what it was in the second. There was in Tholomyès a district attorney, and in Courfeyrac a paladin.

Enjolras was the chief, Combeferre was the guide, Courfeyrac was the centre. The others gave more light, he shed more warmth; the truth is, that he possessed all the qualities of a centre, roundness and radiance.

Bahorel had figured in the bloody tumult of June, 1822, on the occasion of the burial of young Lallemand.

Bahorel was a good-natured mortal, who kept bad company, brave, a spendthrift, prodigal, and to the verge of generosity, talkative, and at times eloquent, bold to the verge of effrontery; the best fellow possible; he had daring waistcoats, and scarlet opinions; a wholesale blusterer, that is to say, loving nothing so much as a quarrel, unless it were an uprising; and nothing so much as an uprising, unless it were a revolution; always ready to smash a window-pane, then to tear up the pavement, then to demolish a government, just to see the effect of it; a student in his eleventh year. He had nosed about the law, but did not practise it. He had taken for his device: "Never a lawyer," and for his armorial bearings a nightstand in which was visible a square cap. Every time that he passed the law-school, which rarely happened, he buttoned up his frock-coat,—the paletot had not yet been invented,—and took hygienic precautions. Of the school porter he said: "What a fine old man!" and of the dean, M. Delvincourt: "What a monument!" In his lectures he espied subjects for ballads, and in his professors occasions for caricature. He wasted a tolerably large allowance, something like three thousand francs a year, in doing nothing.

He had peasant parents whom he had contrived to imbue with respect for their son.

He said of them: "They are peasants and not bourgeois; that is the reason they are intelligent."

Bahorel, a man of caprice, was scattered over numerous cafés; the others had habits, he had none. He sauntered. To stray is human. To saunter is Parisian. In reality, he had a penetrating mind and was more of a thinker than appeared to view.

He served as a connecting link between the Friends of the A B C and other still unorganized groups, which were destined to take form later on.

In this conclave of young heads, there was one bald member.

The Marquis d'Avaray, whom Louis XVIII made a duke for having assisted him to enter a hackney-coach on the day when he emigrated, was wont to relate, that in 1814, on his return to France, as the King was disembarking at Calais, a man handed him a petition.

"What is your request?" said the King.

"Sire, a post-office."

"What is your name?"

"L'Aigle."

The King frowned, glanced at the signature of the petition and beheld the name written thus: LESGLE. This non-Bonaparte orthography touched the King and he began to smile. "Sire," resumed the man with the petition, "I had for ancestor a keeper of the hounds surnamed Lesgueules. This surname furnished my name. I am called Lesgueules, by contraction Lesgle, and by corruption l'Aigle." This caused the King to smile broadly. Later on he gave the man the posting office of Meaux, either intentionally or accidentally.

The bald member of the group was the son of this Lesgle, or Légle, and he signed himself, Légle (de Meaux). As an abbreviation, his companions called him Bossuet.

Bossuet was a gay but unlucky fellow. His specialty was not to succeed in anything. As an offset, he laughed at everything. At five and twenty he was bald. His father had ended by owning a house and a field; but he, the son, had made haste to lose that house and field in a bad speculation. He had nothing left. He possessed knowledge and wit, but all he did miscarried. Everything failed him and everybody deceived him; what he was building tumbled down on top of him. If he were splitting wood, he cut off a finger. If he had a mistress, he speedily discovered that he had a friend also. Some misfortune happened to him every moment, hence his joviality. He said: "I live under falling tiles." He was not easily astonished, because, for him, an accident was what he had foreseen, he took his bad luck serenely, and smiled at the teasing of fate, like a person who is listening to pleasantries. He was poor, but his fund of good humor was inexhaustible. He soon reached his last sou, never his last burst of laughter. When adversity entered his doors, he saluted this old acquaintance cordially, he tapped all catastrophes on the stomach; he was familiar with fatality to the point of calling it by its nickname: "Good day, Guignon," he said to it.

These persecutions of fate had rendered him inventive. He was full of resources. He had no money, but he found means, when it seemed good to him, to indulge in "unbridled extravagance." One night, he went so far as to eat a "hundred francs" in a supper with a wench, which inspired him to make this memorable remark in the midst of the orgy: "Pull off my boots, you five-louis jade."

Bossuet was slowly directing his steps towards the profession of a lawyer; he was pursuing his law studies after the manner of Bahorel. Bossuet had not much domicile, sometimes none at all. He lodged now with one, now with another, most often with Joly. Joly was studying medicine. He was two years younger than Bossuet.

Joly was the "malade imaginaire" junior. What he had won in medicine was to be more of an invalid than a doctor. At three and twenty he thought himself a valetudinarian, and passed his life in inspecting his tongue in the mirror. He affirmed that man becomes magnetic like a needle, and in his chamber he placed his bed with its head to the south, and the foot to the north, so that, at night, the circulation of his blood might not be interfered with by the great electric current of the globe. During thunder storms, he felt his pulse. Otherwise, he was the gayest of them all. All these young, maniacal, puny, merry incoherences lived in harmony together, and the result was an eccentric and agreeable being whom his comrades, who were prodigal of winged consonants, called Jolllly. "You may fly away on the four *L's*," Jean Prouvaire said to him.

Joly had a trick of touching his nose with the tip of his cane, which is an indication of a sagacious mind.

All these young men who differed so greatly, and who, on the whole, can only be discussed seriously, held the same religion: Progress.

All were the direct sons of the French Revolution. The most giddy of them became solemn when they pronounced that date: '89. Their fathers in the flesh had been, either royalists, doctrinaires, it matters not what; this confusion anterior to themselves, who were young, did not concern them at all; the pure blood of principle ran in their veins. They attached themselves, without intermediate shades, to incorruptible right and absolute duty.

Affiliated and initiated, they sketched out the ideal underground.

Among all these glowing hearts and thoroughly convinced minds, there was one sceptic. How came he there? By juxtaposition. This sceptic's name was Grantaire, and he was in the habit of signing himself with this rebus: R. Grantaire was a man who took good care not to believe in anything. Moreover, he was one of the students who had learned the most during their course at Paris; he knew that the best coffee was to be had at the Café Lemblin, and the best billiards at the Café Voltaire, that good cakes and lasses were to be found at the Ermitage, on the Boulevard du Maine, spatchcocked chickens at Mother Sauget's, excellent matelotes at the Barrière de la Cunette, and a certain thin white wine at the Barrière du Compat. He knew the best place for everything; in addition, boxing and foot-fencing and some dances; and he was a thorough single-stick player. He was a tremendous drinker to boot. He was inordinately homely: the prettiest boot-stitcher of that day, Irma Boissy, enraged with his homeliness, pronounced sentence on him as follows: "Grantaire is impossible"; but Grantaire's fatuity was not to be disconcerted. He stared tenderly and fixedly at all women, with the air of saying to them all: "If I only chose!" and of trying to make his comrades believe that he was in general demand.

All those words: rights of the people, rights of man, the social contract, the French Revolution, the Republic, democracy, humanity, civilization, religion, progress, came very near to signifying nothing whatever to Grantaire. He smiled at them. Scepticism, that caries of the intelligence, had not left him a single whole idea. He lived with irony. This was his axiom: "There is but one certainty, my full glass." He sneered at all devotion in all parties, the father as well as the brother, Robespierre junior as well as Loizerolles. "They are greatly in advance to be dead," he exclaimed. He said of the crucifix: "There is a gibbet which has been a success." A rover, a gambler, a libertine, often drunk, he displeased these young dreamers by humming incessantly: "J'aimons les filles, et j'aimons le bon vin." Air: Vive Henri IV.

However, this sceptic had one fanaticism. This fanaticism was neither a dogma, nor an idea, nor an art, nor a science; it was a man: Enjolras. Grantaire admired, loved, and venerated Enjolras. To whom did this anarchical scoffer unite himself in this phalanx of absolute minds? To the most absolute. In what manner had Enjolras subjugated him? By his ideas? No. By his character. A phenomenon which is often observable. A sceptic who adheres to a believer is as simple as the law of complementary colors. That which we lack attracts us. No one loves the light like the blind man. The dwarf adores the drum-major. The toad always has his eyes fixed on heaven. Why? In order to watch the bird in its flight. Grantaire, in whom writhed doubt, loved to watch faith soar in Enjolras. He had need of Enjolras. That chaste, healthy, firm, upright, hard, candid nature charmed him, without his being clearly aware of it, and without the idea of explaining it to himself having occurred to him. He admired his opposite by instinct. His soft, yielding, dislocated, sickly, shapeless ideas attached themselves to Enjolras as to a spinal column. His moral backbone leaned on that firmness. Grantaire in the presence of Enjolras became some one once more. He was, himself, moreover, composed of two elements, which were, to all appearance, incompatible. He was ironical and cordial. His indifference loved. His mind could get along without belief, but his heart could not get along without friendship. A profound contradiction; for an affection is a conviction. His nature was thus constituted. There are men who seem to be born to be the reverse, the obverse, the wrong side. They are Pollux, Patrocles, Nisus, Eudamidas, Ephestion, Pechmeja. They only exist on condition that they are backed up with another man; their name is a sequel, and is only written preceded by the conjunction *and*; and their existence is not their own; it is the other side of an existence which is not theirs. Grantaire was one of these men. He was the obverse of Enjolras.

One might almost say that affinities begin with the letters of the alphabet. In the series O and P are inseparable. You can, at will, pronounce O and P or Orestes and Pylades.

Grantaire, Enjolras' true satellite, inhabited this circle of young men; he lived there, he took no pleasure anywhere but there; he followed them everywhere. His joy was to see these forms go and come through the fumes of wine. They tolerated him on account of his good humor.

Enjolras, the believer, disdained this sceptic; and, a sober man himself, scorned this drunkard. He accorded him a little lofty pity. Grantaire was an unaccepted Pylades. Always harshly treated by Enjolras, roughly repulsed, rejected yet ever returning to the charge, he said of Enjolras: "What fine marble!"

II

Blondeau's Funeral Oration by Bossuet

On a certain afternoon, which had, as will be seen hereafter, some coincidence with the events heretofore related, Laigle de Meaux was to be seen leaning in a sensual manner against the doorpost of the Café Musain. He had the air of a caryatid on a vacation; he carried nothing but his reverie, however. He was staring at the Place Saint-Michel. To lean one's back against a thing is equivalent to lying down while standing erect, which attitude is not hated by thinkers. Laigle de Meaux was pondering without melancholy, over a little misadventure which had befallen him two days previously at the law-school, and which had modified his personal plans for the future, plans which were rather indistinct in any case.

Reverie does not prevent a cab from passing by, nor the dreamer from taking note of that cab. Laigle de Meaux, whose eyes were straying about in a sort of diffuse lounging, perceived, athwart his somnambulism, a two-wheeled vehicle proceeding through the place, at a foot pace and apparently in indecision. For whom was this cabriolet? Why was it driving at a walk? Laigle took a survey. In it, beside the coachman, sat a young man, and in front of the young man lay a rather bulky hand-bag. The bag displayed to passers-by the following name inscribed in large black letters on a card which was sewn to the stuff: Marius Pontmercy.

This name caused Laigle to change his attitude. He drew himself up and hurled this apostrophe at the young man in the cabriolet:—

"Monsieur Marius Pontmercy!"

The cabriolet thus addressed came to a halt.

The young man, who also seemed deeply buried in thought, raised his eyes:—

"Hey?" said he.

"You are M. Marius Pontmercy?"

"Certainly."

"I was looking for you," resumed Laigle de Meaux.

"How so?" demanded Marius; for it was he: in fact, he had just quitted his grandfather's, and had before him a face which he now beheld for the first time. "I do not know you."

"Neither do I know you," responded Laigle.

Marius thought he had encountered a wag, the beginning of a mystification in the open street. He was not in a very good humor at the moment. He frowned. Laigle de Meaux went on imperturbably:—

"You were not at the school day before yesterday."

"That is possible."

"That is certain."

"You are a student?" demanded Marius.

"Yes, sir. Like yourself. Day before yesterday, I entered the school, by chance. You know, one does have such freaks sometimes. The professor was just calling the roll. You are not unaware that they are very ridiculous on such occasions. At the third call, unanswered, your name is erased from the list. Sixty francs in the gulf."

Marius began to listen.

"It was Blondeau who was making the call. You know Blondeau, he has a very pointed and very malicious nose, and he delights to scent out the absent. He slyly began with the letter P. I was not listening, not being compromised by that letter. The call was not going badly. No erasures; the universe was present. Blondeau was grieved. I said to myself: 'Blondeau, my love, you will not get the very smallest sort of an execution to-day.' All at once Blondeau calls, 'Marius Pontmercy!' No one answers. Blondeau, filled with hope, repeats more loudly: 'Marius Pontmercy!' And he takes his pen. Monsieur, I have bowels of compassion. I said to myself hastily: 'Here's a brave fellow who is going to get scratched out. Attention. Here is a veritable mortal who is not exact. He's not a good student. Here is none of your heavy-sides, a student who studies, a greenhorn pedant, strong on letters, theology, science, and sapience, one of those dull wits cut by the square; a pin by profession. He is an honorable idler who lounges, who practises country jaunts, who cultivates the grisette, who pays court to the fair sex, who is at this very moment, perhaps, with my mistress. Let us save him. Death to Blondeau!' At that moment, Blondeau dipped his pen in, all black with erasures in the ink, cast his yellow eyes round the audience room, and repeated for the third time: 'Marius Pontmercy!' I replied: 'Present!' This is why you were not crossed off."

"Monsieur!—" said Marius.

"And why I was," added Laigle de Meaux.

"I do not understand you," said Marius.

Laigle resumed:—

"Nothing is more simple. I was close to the desk to reply, and close to the door for the purpose of flight. The professor gazed at me with a certain intensity. All of a sudden, Blondeau, who must be the malicious nose alluded to by Boileau, skipped to the letter L. L is my letter. I am from Meaux, and my name is Lesgle."

"L'Aigle!" interrupted Marius, "what fine name!"

"Monsieur, Blondeau came to this fine name, and called: 'Laigle!' I reply: 'Present!' Then Blondeau gazes at me, with the gentleness of a tiger, and says to me: 'If you are Pontmercy, you are not Laigle.' A phrase which has a disobliging air for you, but which was lugubrious only for me. That said, he crossed me off."

Marius exclaimed:—

"I am mortified, sir—"

"First of all," interposed Laigle, "I demand permission to embalm Blondeau in a few phrases of deeply felt eulogium. I will assume that he is dead. There will be no great change required in his gauntness, in his pallor, in his coldness, and in his smell. And I say: '*Erudimini qui judicatis terram*. Here lies Blondeau, Blondeau the Nose, Blondeau Nasica, the ox of discipline, *bos disciplinæ*, the bloodhound of the password, the angel of the roll-call, who was upright, square, exact, rigid, honest, and hideous. God crossed him off as he crossed me off.'"

Marius resumed:—

"I am very sorry—"

"Young man," said Laigle de Meaux, "let this serve you as a lesson. In future, be exact."

"I really beg you a thousand pardons."

"Do not expose your neighbor to the danger of having his name erased again."

"I am extremely sorry—"

Laigle burst out laughing.

"And I am delighted. I was on the brink of becoming a lawyer. This erasure saves me. I renounce the triumphs of the bar. I shall not defend the widow, and I shall not attack the orphan. No more toga, no more stage. Here is my erasure all ready for me. It is to you that I am indebted for it, Monsieur Pontmercy. I intend to pay a solemn call of thanks upon you. Where do you live?"

"In this cab," said Marius.

"A sign of opulence," retorted Laigle calmly. "I congratulate you. You have there a rent of nine thousand francs per annum."

At that moment, Courfeyrac emerged from the café.

Marius smiled sadly.

"I have paid this rent for the last two hours, and I aspire to get rid of it; but there is a sort of history attached to it, and I don't know where to go."

"Come to my place, sir," said Courfeyrac.

"I have the priority," observed Laigle, "but I have no home."

"Hold your tongue, Bossuet," said Courfeyrac.

"Bossuet," said Marius, "but I thought that your name was Laigle."

"De Meaux," replied Laigle; "by metaphor, Bossuet."

Courfeyrac entered the cab.

"Coachman," said he, "hotel de la Porte-Saint-Jacques."

And that very evening, Marius found himself installed in a chamber of the hotel de la Porte-Saint-Jacques side by side with Courfeyrac.

III

Marius' Astonishments

In a few days, Marius had become Courfeyrac's friend. Youth is the season for prompt welding and the rapid healing of scars. Marius breathed freely in Courfeyrac's society, a decidedly new thing for him. Courfeyrac put no questions to him. He did not even think of such a thing. At that age, faces disclose everything on the spot. Words are superfluous. There are young men of whom it can be said that their countenances chatter. One looks at them and one knows them.

One morning, however, Courfeyrac abruptly addressed this interrogation to him:—

"By the way, have you any political opinions?"

"The idea!" said Marius, almost affronted by the question.

"What are you?"

"A democrat-Bonapartist."

"The gray hue of a reassured rat," said Courfeyrac.

On the following day, Courfeyrac introduced Marius at the Café Musain. Then he whispered in his ear, with a smile: "I must give you your entry to the revolution." And he led him to the hall of the Friends of the A B C. He presented him to the other comrades, saying this simple word which Marius did not understand: "A pupil."

Marius had fallen into a wasps'-nest of wits. However, although he was silent and grave, he was, nonetheless, both winged and armed.

Marius, up to that time solitary and inclined to soliloquy, and to asides, both by habit and by taste, was a little fluttered by this covey of young men around him. All these various initiatives solicited his attention at once, and pulled him about. The tumultuous movements of these minds at liberty and at work set his ideas in a whirl. Sometimes, in his trouble, they fled so far from him, that he had difficulty in recovering them. He heard them talk of philosophy, of literature, of art, of history, of religion, in unexpected fashion. He caught glimpses of strange aspects; and, as he did not place them in proper perspective, he was not altogether sure that it was not chaos that he grasped. On abandoning his grandfather's opinions for the opinions of his father, he had supposed himself fixed; he now suspected, with uneasiness, and without daring to avow it to himself, that he was not. The angle at which he saw everything began to be displaced anew. A certain oscillation set all the horizons of his brains in motion. An odd internal upsetting. He almost suffered from it.

It seemed as though there were no "consecrated things" for those young men. Marius heard singular propositions on every sort of subject, which embarrassed his still timid mind.

A theatre poster presented itself, adorned with the title of a tragedy from the ancient repertory called classic: "Down with tragedy dear to the bourgeois!" cried Bahorel. And Marius heard Combeferre reply:—

"You are wrong, Bahorel. The bourgeoisie loves tragedy, and the bourgeoisie must be left at peace on that score. Bewigged tragedy has a reason for its existence, and I am not one of those who, by order of Æschylus, contest its right to existence. There are rough outlines in nature; there are, in creation, ready-made parodies; a beak which is not a beak, wings which are not wings, gills which are not gills, paws which are not paws, a cry of pain which arouses a desire to laugh, there is the duck. Now, since poultry exists by the side of the bird, I do not see why classic tragedy should not exist in the face of antique tragedy."

Or chance decreed that Marius should traverse Rue Jean-Jacques Rousseau between Enjolras and Courfeyrac.

Courfeyrac took his arm:—

"Pay attention. This is the Rue Plâtrière, now called Rue Jean-Jacques Rousseau, on account of a singular household which lived in it sixty years ago. This consisted of Jean-Jacques and Thérèse. From time to time, little beings were born there. Thérèse gave birth to them, Jean-Jacques represented them as foundlings."

And Enjolras addressed Courfeyrac roughly:—

"Silence in the presence of Jean-Jacques! I admire that man. He denied his own children, that may be; but he adopted the people."

Not one of these young men articulated the word: The Emperor. Jean Prouvaire alone sometimes said Napoleon; all the others said "Bonaparte." Enjolras pronounced it "Buonaparte."

Marius was vaguely surprised. *Initium sapientiæ.*

IV

The Back Room of the Café Musain

One of the conversations among the young men, at which Marius was present and in which he sometimes joined, was a veritable shock to his mind.

This took place in the back room of the Café Musain. Nearly all the Friends of the A B C had convened that evening. The argand lamp was solemnly lighted. They talked of one thing and another, without passion and with noise. With the exception of Enjolras and Marius, who held their peace, all were haranguing rather at hap-hazard. Conversations between comrades sometimes are subject to these peaceable tumults. It was a game and an uproar as much as a conversation. They tossed words to each other and caught them up in turn. They were chattering in all quarters.

No woman was admitted to this back room, except Louison, the dish-washer of the café, who passed through it from time to time, to go to her washing in the "lavatory."

Grantaire, thoroughly drunk, was deafening the corner of which he had taken possession, reasoning and contradicting at the top of his lungs, and shouting:—

"I am thirsty. Mortals, I am dreaming: that the tun of Heidelberg has an attack of apoplexy, and that I am one of the dozen leeches which will be applied to it. I want a drink. I desire to forget life. Life is a hideous invention of I know not whom. It lasts no time at all, and is worth nothing. One breaks one's neck in living. Life is a theatre set in which there are but few practicable entrances. Happiness is an antique reliquary painted on one side only. Ecclesiastes says: 'All is vanity.' I agree with that good man, who never existed, perhaps. Zero not wishing to go stark naked, clothed himself in vanity. O vanity! The patching up of everything with big words! a kitchen is a laboratory, a dancer is a professor, an acrobat is a gymnast, a boxer is a pugilist, an apothecary is a chemist, a wigmaker is an artist, a hodman is an architect, a jockey is a sportsman, a wood-louse is a pterigybranche. Vanity has a right and a wrong side; the right side is stupid, it is the negro with his glass beads; the wrong side is foolish, it is the philosopher with his rags. I weep over the one and I laugh over the other. What are called honors and dignities, and even dignity and honor, are generally of pinchbeck. Kings make playthings of human pride. Caligula made a horse a consul; Charles II made a knight of a sirloin. Wrap yourself up now, then, between Consul Incitatus and Baronet Roastbeef. As for the intrinsic value of people, it is no longer respectable in the least. Listen to the panegyric which neighbor makes of neighbor. White on white is ferocious; if the lily could speak, what a setting down it would give the dove! A bigoted woman prating of a devout woman is more venomous than the asp and the cobra. It is a shame that I am ignorant, otherwise I would quote to you a mass of things; but I know nothing. For instance, I have always been witty; when I was a pupil of Gros, instead of daubing wretched little pictures, I passed my time in pilfering apples; *rapin* is the masculine of *rapine*. So much for myself; as for the rest of you, you are worth no more than I am. I scoff at your perfections, excellencies, and qualities. Every good quality tends towards a defect; economy borders on avarice, the generous man is next door to the prodigal, the brave man rubs elbows with the braggart; he who says very pious says a trifle bigoted; there are just as many vices in virtue as there are holes in Diogenes' cloak. Whom do you admire, the slain or the slayer, Cæsar or Brutus? Generally men are in favor of the slayer. Long live Brutus, he has slain! There lies the virtue. Virtue, granted, but madness also. There are queer spots on those great men. The Brutus who killed Cæsar was in love with the statue of a little boy. This statue was from the hand of the Greek sculptor Strongylion, who also carved that figure of an Amazon known as the Beautiful Leg, Eucnemos, which Nero carried with him in his travels. This Strongylion left but two statues which placed Nero and Brutus in accord. Brutus was in love with the one, Nero with the other. All history is nothing but wearisome repetition. One century is the plagiarist of the other. The battle of Marengo copies the battle of Pydna; the Tolbiac of Clovis and the Austerlitz of Napoleon are as like each other as two drops of water. I don't attach much importance to victory. Nothing is so stupid as to conquer; true glory lies in convincing. But try to prove something! If you are content with success, what mediocrity, and with conquering, what wretchedness! Alas, vanity and cowardice everywhere. Everything obeys success, even grammar. *Si volet usus*, says Horace. Therefore I disdain the human race. Shall we descend to the party at all? Do you wish me to begin admiring the peoples? What people, if you please? Shall it be Greece? The Athenians, those Parisians of days gone by, slew Phocion, as we might say Coligny, and fawned upon tyrants to such an extent that Anacephorus said of Pisistratus: "His urine attracts the bees." The most prominent man in Greece for fifty years was that grammarian Philetas, who was so small and so thin that he was obliged to load his shoes with lead in order not to be blown away by the wind. There stood on the great square in Corinth a statue carved by Silanion and catalogued by Pliny; this statue represented Episthates. What did Episthates do? He invented a trip. That sums up Greece and glory. Let us pass on to others. Shall I admire England? Shall I admire France? France? Why? Because of Paris? I have just told you my opinion of Athens. England? Why? Because of London? I hate Carthage. And then, London, the metropolis of luxury, is the headquarters of wretchedness. There are a hundred deaths a year of hunger in the parish of Charing-Cross alone. Such is Albion. I add, as the climax, that I have seen an Englishwoman dancing in a wreath of roses and blue spectacles. A fig then for England! If I do not admire John Bull, shall I admire Brother Jonathan? I have but little taste for that slave-holding brother. Take away *Time is money*, what remains of England? Take away *Cotton is king*, what remains of America? Germany is the lymph, Italy is the bile. Shall we go into ecstasies over Russia? Voltaire admired it. He also admired China. I admit that Russia has its beauties, among others, a stout despotism; but I pity the despots. Their health is delicate. A decapitated Alexis, a poignarded Peter, a strangled Paul, another Paul crushed flat with kicks, divers Ivans strangled, with their throats cut, numerous Nicholases and Basils poisoned, all this indicates that the palace of the Emperors of Russia is in a condition of flagrant insalubrity. All civilized peoples offer this detail to the admiration of the thinker; war; now, war, civilized war, exhausts and sums up all the forms of ruffianism, from the brigandage of the Trabuceros in the gorges of Mont Jaxa to the marauding of the Comanche Indians in the Doubtful Pass. 'Bah!' you will say to me, 'but Europe is certainly better than Asia?' I admit that Asia is a farce; but I do not precisely see what you find to laugh at in the Grand Lama, you peoples of the west, who have mingled with your fashions and your elegances all the complicated filth of majesty, from the dirty chemise of Queen Isabella to the chamber-chair of the Dauphin. Gentlemen of the human race, I tell you, not a bit of it! It is at Brussels that the most beer is consumed, at Stockholm the most brandy, at Madrid the most chocolate, at Amsterdam the most gin, at London the most wine, at Constantinople the most coffee, at Paris the most absinthe; there are all the useful notions. Paris carries the day, in short. In Paris, even the rag-pickers are sybarites; Diogenes would have loved to be a rag-picker of the Place Maubert better than to be a philosopher at the Piræus. Learn this in addition; the wineshops of the rag-pickers are called *bibines*; the most celebrated are the *Saucepan* and *The Slaughter-House*. Hence, tea-gardens, goguettes, caboulots, bouibuis, mastroquets, bastringues, manezingues, bibines of the rag-pickers, caravanseries of the caliphs, I certify to you, I am a voluptuary, I eat at Richard's at forty sous a head, I must have Persian carpets to roll naked Cleopatra in! Where is Cleopatra? Ah! So it is you, Louison. Good day."

Thus did Grantaire, more than intoxicated, launch into speech, catching at the dish-washer in her passage, from his corner in the back room of the Café Musain.

Bossuet, extending his hand towards him, tried to impose silence on him, and Grantaire began again worse than ever:—

"Aigle de Meaux, down with your paws. You produce on me no effect with your gesture of Hippocrates refusing Artaxerxes' bric-à-brac. I excuse you from the task of soothing me. Moreover, I am sad. What do you wish me to say to you? Man is evil, man is deformed; the butterfly is a success, man is a failure. God made a mistake with that animal. A crowd offers a choice of ugliness. The first comer is a wretch, *Femme*— woman—rhymes with *infâme*,—infamous. Yes, I have the spleen, complicated with melancholy, with homesickness, plus hypochondria, and I am vexed and I rage, and I yawn, and I am bored, and I am tired to death, and I am stupid! Let God go to the devil!"

"Silence then, capital R!" resumed Bossuet, who was discussing a point of law behind the scenes, and who was plunged more than waist high in a phrase of judicial slang, of which this is the conclusion:—

"—And as for me, although I am hardly a legist, and at the most, an amateur attorney, I maintain this: that, in accordance with the terms of the customs of Normandy, at Saint-Michel, and for each year, an equivalent must be paid to the profit of the lord of the manor, saving the rights of others, and by all and several, the proprietors as well as those seized with inheritance, and that, for all emphyteuses, leases, freeholds, contracts of domain, mortgages—"

"Echo, plaintive nymph," hummed Grantaire.

Near Grantaire, an almost silent table, a sheet of paper, an inkstand and a pen between two glasses of brandy, announced that a vaudeville was being sketched out.

This great affair was being discussed in a low voice, and the two heads at work touched each other: "Let us begin by finding names. When one has the names, one finds the subject."

"That is true. Dictate. I will write."

"Monsieur Dorimon."

"An independent gentleman?"

"Of course."

"His daughter, Célestine."

"—tine. What next?"

"Colonel Sainval."

"Sainval is stale. I should say Valsin."

Beside the vaudeville aspirants, another group, which was also taking advantage of the uproar to talk low, was discussing a duel. An old fellow of thirty was counselling a young one of eighteen, and explaining to him what sort of an adversary he had to deal with.

"The deuce! Look out for yourself. He is a fine swordsman. His play is neat. He has the attack, no wasted feints, wrist, dash, lightning, a just parade, mathematical parries, *bigre!* and he is left-handed."

In the angle opposite Grantaire, Joly and Bahorel were playing dominoes, and talking of love.

"You are in luck, that you are," Joly was saying. "You have a mistress who is always laughing."

"That is a fault of hers," returned Bahorel. "One's mistress does wrong to laugh. That encourages one to deceive her. To see her gay removes your remorse; if you see her sad, your conscience pricks you."

"Ingrate! a woman who laughs is such a good thing! And you never quarrel!"

"That is because of the treaty which we have made. On forming our little Holy Alliance we assigned ourselves each our frontier, which we never cross. What is situated on the side of winter belongs to Vaud, on the side of the wind to Gex. Hence the peace."

"Peace is happiness digesting."

"And you, Jolllly, where do you stand in your entanglement with Mamselle—you know whom I mean?"

"She sulks at me with cruel patience."

"Yet you are a lover to soften the heart with gauntness."

"Alas!"

"In your place, I would let her alone."

"That is easy enough to say."

"And to do. Is not her name Musichetta?"

"Yes. Ah! my poor Bahorel, she is a superb girl, very literary, with tiny feet, little hands, she dresses well, and is white and dimpled, with the eyes of a fortune-teller. I am wild over her."

"My dear fellow, then in order to please her, you must be elegant, and produce effects with your knees. Buy a good pair of trousers of double-milled cloth at Staub's. That will assist."

"At what price?" shouted Grantaire.

The third corner was delivered up to a poetical discussion. Pagan mythology was giving battle to Christian mythology. The question was about Olympus, whose part was taken by Jean Prouvaire, out of pure romanticism.

Jean Prouvaire was timid only in repose. Once excited, he burst forth, a sort of mirth accentuated his enthusiasm, and he was at once both laughing and lyric.

"Let us not insult the gods," said he. "The gods may not have taken their departure. Jupiter does not impress me as dead. The gods are dreams, you say. Well, even in nature, such as it is to-day, after the flight of these dreams, we still find all the grand old pagan myths. Such and such a mountain with the profile of a citadel, like the Vignemale, for example, is still to me the headdress of Cybele; it has not been proved to me that Pan does not come at night to breathe into the hollow trunks of the willows, stopping up the holes in turn with his fingers, and I have always believed that Io had something to do with the cascade of Pissevache."

In the last corner, they were talking politics. The Charter which had been granted was getting roughly handled. Combeferre was upholding it weakly. Courfeyrac was energetically making a breach in it. On the table lay an unfortunate copy of the famous Touquet Charter. Courfeyrac had seized it, and was brandishing it, mingling with his arguments the rattling of this sheet of paper.

"In the first place, I won't have any kings; if it were only from an economical point of view, I don't want any; a king is a parasite. One does not have kings gratis. Listen to this: the dearness of kings. At the death of François I, the national debt of France amounted to an income of thirty thousand livres; at the death of Louis XIV it was two milliards, six hundred millions, at twenty-eight livres the mark, which was equivalent in 1760, according to Desmarets, to four milliards, five hundred millions, which would to-day be equivalent to twelve milliards. In the second place, and no offence to Combeferre, a charter granted is but a poor expedient of civilization. To save the transition, to soften the passage, to deaden the shock, to cause the nation to pass insensibly from the monarchy to democracy by the practice of constitutional fictions,—what detestable reasons all those are! No! no! let us never enlighten the people with false daylight. Principles dwindle and pale in your constitutional cellar. No illegitimacy, no compromise, no grant from the king to the people. In all such grants there is an Article 14. By the side of the hand which gives there is the claw which snatches back. I refuse your charter point-blank. A charter is a mask; the lie lurks beneath it. A people which accepts a charter abdicates. The law is only the law when entire. No! no charter!"

It was winter; a couple of fagots were crackling in the fireplace. This was tempting, and Courfeyrac could not resist. He crumpled the poor Touquet Charter in his fist, and flung it in the fire. The paper flashed up. Combeferre watched the masterpiece of Louis XVIII burn philosophically, and contented himself with saying:—

"The charter metamorphosed into flame."

And sarcasms, sallies, jests, that French thing which is called *entrain*, and that English thing which is called humor, good and bad taste, good and bad reasons, all the wild pyrotechnics of dialogue, mounting together and crossing from all points of the room, produced a sort of merry bombardment over their heads.

V

ENLARGEMENT OF HORIZON

The shocks of youthful minds among themselves have this admirable property, that one can never foresee the spark, nor divine the lightning flash. What will dart out presently? No one knows. The burst of laughter starts from a tender feeling.

At the moment of jest, the serious makes its entry. Impulses depend on the first chance word. The spirit of each is sovereign, jest suffices to open the field to the unexpected. These are conversations with abrupt turns, in which the perspective changes suddenly. Chance is the stage-manager of such conversations.

A severe thought, starting oddly from a clash of words, suddenly traversed the conflict of quips in which Grantaire, Bahorel, Prouvaire, Bossuet, Combeferre, and Courfeyrac were confusedly fencing.

How does a phrase crop up in a dialogue? Whence comes it that it suddenly impresses itself on the attention of those who hear it? We have just said, that no one knows anything about it. In the midst of the uproar, Bossuet all at once terminated some apostrophe to Combeferre, with this date:—

"June 18th, 1815, Waterloo."

At this name of Waterloo, Marius, who was leaning his elbows on a table, beside a glass of water, removed his wrist from beneath his chin, and began to gaze fixedly at the audience.

"Pardieu!" exclaimed Courfeyrac ("Parbleu" was falling into disuse at this period), "that number 18 is strange and strikes me. It is Bonaparte's fatal number. Place Louis in front and Brumaire behind, you have the whole destiny of the man, with this significant peculiarity, that the end treads close on the heels of the commencement."

Enjolras, who had remained mute up to that point, broke the silence and addressed this remark to Combeferre:—

"You mean to say, the crime and the expiation."

This word *crime* overpassed the measure of what Marius, who was already greatly agitated by the abrupt evocation of Waterloo, could accept.

He rose, walked slowly to the map of France spread out on the wall, and at whose base an island was visible in a separate compartment, laid his finger on this compartment and said:—

"Corsica, a little island which has rendered France very great."

This was like a breath of icy air. All ceased talking. They felt that something was on the point of occurring.

Bahorel, replying to Bossuet, was just assuming an attitude of the torso to which he was addicted. He gave it up to listen.

Enjolras, whose blue eye was not fixed on any one, and who seemed to be gazing at space, replied, without glancing at Marius:—

"France needs no Corsica to be great. France is great because she is France. *Quia nomina leo.*"

Marius felt no desire to retreat; he turned towards Enjolras, and his voice burst forth with a vibration which came from a quiver of his very being:—

"God forbid that I should diminish France! But amalgamating Napoleon with her is not diminishing her. Come! let us argue the question. I am a newcomer among you, but I will confess that you amaze me. Where do we stand? Who are we? Who are you? Who am I? Let us come to an explanation about the Emperor. I hear you say *Buonaparte*, accenting the *u* like the Royalists. I warn you that my grandfather does better still; he says *Buonaparté*. I thought you were young men. Where, then, is your enthusiasm? And what are you doing with it? Whom do you admire, if you do not admire the Emperor? And what more do you want? If you will have none of that great man, what great men would you like? He had everything. He was complete. He had in his brain the sum of human faculties. He made codes like Justinian, he dictated like Cæsar, his conversation was mingled with the lightning-flash of Pascal, with the thunderclap of Tacitus, he made history and he wrote it, his bulletins are Iliads, he combined the cipher of Newton with the metaphor of Mahomet, he left behind him in the East words as great as the pyramids, at Tilsit he taught Emperors majesty, at the Academy of Sciences he replied to Laplace, in the Council of State he held his own against Merlin, he gave a soul to the geometry of the first, and to the chicanery of the last, he was a legist with the attorneys and sidereal with the astronomers; like Cromwell blowing out one of two candles, he went to the Temple to bargain for a curtain tassel; he saw everything; he knew everything; which did not prevent him from laughing good-naturedly beside the cradle of his little child; and all at once, frightened Europe lent an ear, armies put themselves in motion, parks of artillery rumbled, pontoons stretched over the rivers, clouds of cavalry galloped in the storm, cries, trumpets, a trembling of thrones in every direction, the frontiers of kingdoms oscillated on the map, the sound of a superhuman sword was heard, as it was drawn from its sheath; they beheld him, him, rise erect on the horizon with a blazing brand in his hand, and a glow in his eyes, unfolding amid the thunder, his two wings, the grand army and the old guard, and he was the archangel of war!"

All held their peace, and Enjolras bowed his head. Silence always produces somewhat the effect of acquiescence, of the enemy being driven to the wall. Marius continued with increased enthusiasm, and almost without pausing for breath:—

"Let us be just, my friends! What a splendid destiny for a nation to be the Empire of such an Emperor, when that nation is France and when it adds its own genius to the genius of that man! To appear and to reign, to march and to triumph, to have for halting-places all capitals, to take his grenadiers and to make kings of them, to decree the falls of dynasties, and to transfigure Europe at the pace of a charge; to make you feel that when you threaten you lay your hand on the hilt of the sword of God; to follow in a single man, Hannibal, Cæsar, Charlemagne; to be the people of some one who mingles with your dawns the startling announcement of a battle won, to have the cannon of the Invalides to rouse you in the morning, to hurl into abysses of light prodigious words which flame forever, Marengo, Arcola, Austerlitz, Jena, Wagram! To cause constellations of victories to flash forth at each instant from the zenith of the centuries, to make the French Empire a pendant to the Roman Empire, to be the great nation and to give birth to the grand army, to make its legions fly forth over all the earth, as a mountain sends out its eagles on all sides to conquer, to dominate, to strike with lightning, to be in Europe a sort of nation gilded through glory, to sound athwart the centuries a trumpet-blast of Titans, to conquer the world twice, by conquest and by dazzling, that is sublime; and what greater thing is there?"

"To be free," said Combeferre.

Marius lowered his head in his turn; that cold and simple word had traversed his epic effusion like a blade of steel, and he felt it vanishing within him. When he raised his eyes, Combeferre was no longer there. Probably satisfied with his reply to the apotheosis, he had just taken his departure, and all, with the exception of Enjolras, had followed him. The room had been emptied. Enjolras, left alone with Marius, was gazing gravely at him. Marius, however, having rallied his ideas to some extent, did not consider himself beaten; there lingered in him a trace of inward fermentation which was on the point, no doubt, of translating itself into syllogisms arrayed against Enjolras, when all of a sudden, they heard some one singing on the stairs as he went. It was Combeferre, and this is what he was singing:—

> *"Si César m'avait donné*
> *La gloire et la guerre,*
> *Et qu'il me fallait quitter*
> *L'amour de ma mère,*
> *Je dirais au grand César:*
> *Reprends ton sceptre et ton char,*
> *J'aime mieux ma mère, ô gué!*
> *J'aime mieux ma mère!"*

The wild and tender accents with which Combeferre sang communicated to this couplet a sort of strange grandeur. Marius, thoughtfully, and with his eyes diked on the ceiling, repeated almost mechanically: "My mother?—"

At that moment, he felt Enjolras' hand on his shoulder.

"Citizen," said Enjolras to him, "my mother is the Republic."

VI

Res Angusta

That evening left Marius profoundly shaken, and with a melancholy shadow in his soul. He felt what the earth may possibly feel, at the moment when it is torn open with the iron, in order that grain may be deposited within it; it feels only the wound; the quiver of the germ and the joy of the fruit only arrive later.

Marius was gloomy. He had but just acquired a faith; must he then reject it already? He affirmed to himself that he would not. He declared to himself that he would not doubt, and he began to doubt in spite of himself. To stand between two religions, from one of which you have not as yet emerged, and another into which you have not yet entered, is intolerable; and twilight is pleasing only to bat-like souls. Marius was clear-eyed, and he required the true light. The half-lights of doubt pained him. Whatever may have been his desire to remain where he was, he could not halt there, he was irresistibly constrained to continue, to advance, to examine, to think, to march further. Whither would this lead him? He feared, after having taken so many steps which had brought him nearer to his father, to now take a step which should estrange him from that father. His discomfort was augmented by all the reflections which occurred to him. An escarpment rose around him. He was in accord neither with his grandfather nor with his friends; daring in the eyes of the one, he was behind the times in the eyes of the others, and he recognized the fact that he was doubly isolated, on the side of age and on the side of youth. He ceased to go to the Café Musain.

In the troubled state of his conscience, he no longer thought of certain serious sides of existence. The realities of life do not allow themselves to be forgotten. They soon elbowed him abruptly.

One morning, the proprietor of the hotel entered Marius' room and said to him:—

"Monsieur Courfeyrac answered for you."

"Yes."

"But I must have my money."

"Request Courfeyrac to come and talk with me," said Marius.

Courfeyrac having made his appearance, the host left them. Marius then told him what it had not before occurred to him to relate, that he was the same as alone in the world, and had no relatives.

"What is to become of you?" said Courfeyrac.

"I do not know in the least," replied Marius.

"What are you going to do?"

"I do not know."

"Have you any money?"

"Fifteen francs."

"Do you want me to lend you some?"

"Never."

"Have you clothes?"

"Here is what I have."

"Have you trinkets?"

"A watch."

"Silver?"

"Gold; here it is."

"I know a clothes-dealer who will take your frock-coat and a pair of trousers."

"That is good."

"You will then have only a pair of trousers, a waistcoat, a hat and a coat."

"And my boots."

"What! you will not go barefoot? What opulence!"

"That will be enough."

"I know a watchmaker who will buy your watch."

"That is good."

"No; it is not good. What will you do after that?"

"Whatever is necessary. Anything honest, that is to say."

"Do you know English?"

"No."

"Do you know German?"

"No."

"So much the worse."

"Why?"

"Because one of my friends, a publisher, is getting up a sort of an encyclopædia, for which you might have translated English or German articles. It is badly paid work, but one can live by it."

"I will learn English and German."

"And in the meanwhile?"

"In the meanwhile I will live on my clothes and my watch."

The clothes-dealer was sent for. He paid twenty francs for the cast-off garments. They went to the watchmaker's. He bought the watch for forty-five francs.

"That is not bad," said Marius to Courfeyrac, on their return to the hotel, "with my fifteen francs, that makes eighty."

"And the hotel bill?" observed Courfeyrac.

"Hello, I had forgotten that," said Marius.

The landlord presented his bill, which had to be paid on the spot. It amounted to seventy francs.

"I have ten francs left," said Marius.

"The deuce," exclaimed Courfeyrac, "you will eat up five francs while you are learning English, and five while learning German. That will be swallowing a tongue very fast, or a hundred sous very slowly."

In the meantime Aunt Gillenormand, a rather good-hearted person at bottom in difficulties, had finally hunted up Marius' abode.

One morning, on his return from the law-school, Marius found a letter from his aunt, and the *sixty pistoles*, that is to say, six hundred francs in gold, in a sealed box.

Marius sent back the thirty louis to his aunt, with a respectful letter, in which he stated that he had sufficient means of subsistence and that he should be able thenceforth to supply all his needs. At that moment, he had three francs left.

His aunt did not inform his grandfather of this refusal for fear of exasperating him. Besides, had he not said: "Let me never hear the name of that blood-drinker again!"

Marius left the hotel de la Porte Saint-Jacques, as he did not wish to run in debt there.

BOOK FIFTH
THE EXCELLENCE OF MISFORTUNE

I

MARIUS INDIGENT

Life became hard for Marius. It was nothing to eat his clothes and his watch. He ate of that terrible, inexpressible thing that is called *de la vache enragé*; that is to say, he endured great hardships and privations. A terrible thing it is, containing days without bread, nights without sleep, evenings without a candle, a hearth without a fire, weeks without work, a future without hope, a coat out at the elbows, an old hat which evokes the laughter of young girls, a door which one finds locked on one at night because one's rent is not paid, the insolence of the porter and the cook-shop man, the sneers of neighbors, humiliations, dignity trampled on, work of whatever nature accepted, disgusts, bitterness, despondency. Marius learned how all this is eaten, and how such are often the only things which one has to devour. At that moment of his existence when a man needs his pride, because he needs love, he felt that he was jeered at because he was badly dressed, and ridiculous because he was poor. At the age when youth swells the heart with imperial pride, he dropped his eyes more than once on his dilapidated boots, and he knew the unjust shame and the poignant blushes of wretchedness. Admirable and terrible trial from which the feeble emerge base, from which the strong emerge sublime. A crucible into which destiny casts a man, whenever it desires a scoundrel or a demi-god.

For many great deeds are performed in petty combats. There are instances of bravery ignored and obstinate, which defend themselves step by step in that fatal onslaught of necessities and turpitudes. Noble and mysterious triumphs which no eye beholds, which are requited with no renown, which are saluted with no trumpet blast. Life, misfortune, isolation, abandonment, poverty, are the fields of battle which have their heroes; obscure heroes, who are, sometimes, grander than the heroes who win renown.

Firm and rare natures are thus created; misery, almost always a step-mother, is sometimes a mother; destitution gives birth to might of soul and spirit; distress is the nurse of pride; unhappiness is a good milk for the magnanimous.

There came a moment in Marius' life, when he swept his own landing, when he bought his sou's worth of Brie cheese at the fruiterer's, when he waited until twilight had fallen to slip into the baker's and purchase a loaf, which he carried off furtively to his attic as though he had stolen it. Sometimes there could be seen gliding into the butcher's shop on the corner, in the midst of the bantering cooks who elbowed him, an awkward young man, carrying big books under his arm, who had a timid yet angry air, who, on entering, removed his hat from a brow whereon stood drops of perspiration, made a profound bow to the butcher's astonished wife, asked for a mutton cutlet, paid six or seven sous for it, wrapped it up in a paper, put it under his arm, between two books, and went away. It was Marius. On this cutlet, which he cooked for himself, he lived for three days.

On the first day he ate the meat, on the second he ate the fat, on the third he gnawed the bone. Aunt Gillenormand made repeated attempts, and sent him the sixty pistoles several times. Marius returned them on every occasion, saying that he needed nothing.

He was still in mourning for his father when the revolution which we have just described was effected within him. From that time forth, he had not put off his black garments. But his garments were quitting him. The day came when he had no longer a coat. The trousers would go next. What was to be done? Courfeyrac, to whom he had, on his side, done some good turns, gave him an old coat. For thirty sous, Marius got it turned by some porter or other, and it was a new coat. But this coat was green. Then Marius ceased to go out until after nightfall. This made his coat black. As he wished always to appear in mourning, he clothed himself with the night.

In spite of all this, he got admitted to practice as a lawyer. He was supposed to live in Courfeyrac's room, which was decent, and where a certain number of law-books backed up and completed by several dilapidated volumes of romance, passed as the library required by the regulations. He had his letters addressed to Courfeyrac's quarters.

When Marius became a lawyer, he informed his grandfather of the fact in a letter which was cold but full of submission and respect. M. Gillenormand trembled as he took the letter, read it, tore it in four pieces, and threw it into the waste-basket. Two or three days later, Mademoiselle Gillenormand heard her father, who was alone in his room, talking aloud to himself. He always did this whenever he was greatly agitated. She listened, and the old man was saying: "If you were not a fool, you would know that one cannot be a baron and a lawyer at the same time."

II

Marius Poor

It is the same with wretchedness as with everything else. It ends by becoming bearable. It finally assumes a form, and adjusts itself. One vegetates, that is to say, one develops in a certain meagre fashion, which is, however, sufficient for life. This is the mode in which the existence of Marius Pontmercy was arranged:

He had passed the worst straits; the narrow pass was opening out a little in front of him. By dint of toil, perseverance, courage, and will, he had managed to draw from his work about seven hundred francs a year. He had learned German and English; thanks to Courfeyrac, who had put him in communication with his friend the publisher, Marius filled the modest post of utility man in the literature of the publishing house. He drew up prospectuses, translated newspapers, annotated editions, compiled biographies, etc.; net product, year in and year out, seven hundred francs. He lived on it. How? Not so badly. We will explain.

Marius occupied in the Gorbeau house, for an annual sum of thirty francs, a den minus a fireplace, called a cabinet, which contained only the most indispensable articles of furniture. This furniture belonged to him. He gave three francs a month to the old *principal tenant* to come and sweep his hole, and to bring him a little hot water every morning, a fresh egg, and a penny roll. He breakfasted on this egg and roll. His breakfast varied in cost from two to four sous, according as eggs were dear or cheap. At six o'clock in the evening he descended the Rue Saint-Jacques to dine at Rousseau's, opposite Basset's, the stamp-dealer's, on the corner of the Rue des Mathurins. He ate no soup. He took a six-sou plate of meat, a half-portion of vegetables for three sous, and a three-sou dessert. For three sous he got as much bread as he wished. As for wine, he drank water. When he paid at the desk where Madam Rousseau, at that period still plump and rosy majestically presided, he gave a sou to the waiter, and Madam Rousseau gave him a smile. Then he went away. For sixteen sous he had a smile and a dinner.

This Restaurant Rousseau, where so few bottles and so many water carafes were emptied, was a calming potion rather than a restaurant.

It no longer exists. The proprietor had a fine nickname: he was called *Rousseau the Aquatic*.

Thus, breakfast four sous, dinner sixteen sous; his food cost him twenty sous a day; which made three hundred and sixty-five francs a year. Add the thirty francs for rent, and the thirty-six francs to the old woman, plus a few trifling expenses; for four hundred and fifty francs, Marius was fed, lodged, and waited on. His clothing cost him a hundred francs, his linen fifty francs, his washing fifty francs; the whole did not exceed six hundred and fifty francs. He was rich. He sometimes lent ten francs to a friend. Courfeyrac had once been able to borrow sixty francs of him. As far as fire was concerned, as Marius had no fireplace, he had "simplified matters."

Marius always had two complete suits of clothes, the one old, "for every day"; the other, brand new for special occasions. Both were black. He had but three shirts, one on his person, the second in the commode, and the third in the washerwoman's hands. He renewed them as they wore out. They were always ragged, which caused him to button his coat to the chin.

It had required years for Marius to attain to this flourishing condition. Hard years; difficult, some of them, to traverse, others to climb. Marius had not failed for a single day. He had endured everything in the way of destitution; he had done everything except contract debts. He did himself the justice to say that he had never owed any one a sou. A debt was, to him, the beginning of slavery. He even said to himself, that a creditor is worse than a master; for the master possesses only your person, a creditor possesses your dignity and can administer to it a box on the ear. Rather than borrow, he went without food. He had passed many a day fasting. Feeling that all extremes meet, and that, if one is not on one's guard, lowered fortunes may lead to baseness of soul, he kept a jealous watch on his pride. Such and such a formality or action, which, in any other situation would have appeared merely a deference to him, now seemed insipidity, and he nerved himself against it. His face wore a sort of severe flush. He was timid even to rudeness.

During all these trials he had felt himself encouraged and even uplifted, at times, by a secret force that he possessed within himself. The soul aids the body, and at certain moments, raises it. It is the only bird which bears up its own cage.

Besides his father's name, another name was graven in Marius' heart, the name of Thénardier. Marius, with his grave and enthusiastic nature, surrounded with a sort of aureole the man to whom, in his thoughts, he owed his father's life,—that intrepid sergeant who had saved the colonel amid the bullets and the cannon-balls of Waterloo. He never separated the memory of this man from the memory of his father, and he associated them in his veneration. It was a sort of worship in two steps, with the grand altar for the colonel and the lesser one for Thénardier. What redoubled the tenderness of his gratitude towards Thénardier, was the idea of the distress into which he knew that Thénardier had fallen, and which had engulfed the latter. Marius had learned at Montfermeil of the ruin and bankruptcy of the unfortunate inn-keeper. Since that time, he had made unheard-of efforts to find traces of him and to reach him in that dark abyss of misery in which Thénardier had disappeared. Marius had beaten the whole country; he had gone to Chelles, to Bondy, to Gourney, to Nogent, to Lagny. He had persisted for three years, expending in these explorations the little money which he had laid by. No one had been able to give him any news of Thénardier: he was supposed to have gone abroad. His creditors had also sought him, with less love than Marius, but with as much assiduity, and had not been able to lay their hands on him. Marius blamed himself, and was almost angry with himself for his lack of success in his researches. It was the only debt left him by the colonel, and Marius made it a matter of honor to pay it. "What," he thought, "when my father lay dying on the field of battle, did Thénardier contrive to find him amid the smoke and the grape-shot, and bear him off on his shoulders, and yet he owed him nothing, and I, who owe so much to Thénardier, cannot join him in this shadow where he is lying in the pangs of death, and in my turn bring him back from death to life! Oh! I will find him!" To find Thénardier, in fact, Marius would have given one of his arms, to rescue him from his misery, he would have sacrificed all his blood. To see Thénardier, to render Thénardier some service, to say to him: "You do not know me; well, I do know you! Here I am. Dispose of me!" This was Marius' sweetest and most magnificent dream.

III

MARIUS GROWN UP

At this epoch, Marius was twenty years of age. It was three years since he had left his grandfather. Both parties had remained on the same terms, without attempting to approach each other, and without seeking to see each other. Besides, what was the use of seeing each other? Marius was the brass vase, while Father Gillenormand was the iron pot.

We admit that Marius was mistaken as to his grandfather's heart. He had imagined that M. Gillenormand had never loved him, and that that crusty, harsh, and smiling old fellow who cursed, shouted, and stormed and brandished his cane, cherished for him, at the most, only that affection, which is at once slight and severe, of the dotards of comedy. Marius was in error. There are fathers who do not love their children; there exists no grandfather who does not adore his grandson. At bottom, as we have said, M. Gillenormand idolized Marius. He idolized him after his own fashion, with an accompaniment of snappishness and boxes on the ear; but, this child once gone, he felt a black void in his heart; he would allow no one to mention the child to him, and all the while secretly regretted that he was so well obeyed. At first, he hoped that this Buonapartist, this Jacobin, this terrorist, this Septembrist, would return. But the weeks passed by, years passed; to M. Gillenormand's great despair, the "blood-drinker" did not make his appearance. "I could not do otherwise than turn him out," said the grandfather to himself, and he asked himself: "If the thing were to do over again, would I do it?" His pride instantly answered "yes," but his aged head, which he shook in silence, replied sadly "no." He had his hours of depression. He missed Marius. Old men need affection as they need the sun. It is warmth. Strong as his nature was, the absence of Marius had wrought some change in him. Nothing in the world could have induced him to take a step towards "that rogue"; but he suffered. He never inquired about him, but he thought of him incessantly. He lived in the Marais in a more and more retired manner; he was still merry and violent as of old, but his merriment had a convulsive harshness, and his violences always terminated in a sort of gentle and gloomy dejection.

He sometimes said: "Oh! if he only would return, what a good box on the ear I would give him!"

As for his aunt, she thought too little to love much; Marius was no longer for her much more than a vague black form; and she eventually came to occupy herself with him much less than with the cat or the paroquet which she probably had. What augmented Father Gillenormand's secret suffering was, that he locked it all up within his breast, and did not allow its existence to be divined. His sorrow was like those recently invented furnaces which consume their own smoke. It sometimes happened that officious busybodies spoke to him of Marius, and asked him: "What is your grandson doing?" "What has become of him?" The old bourgeois replied with a sigh, that he was a sad case, and giving a fillip to his cuff, if he wished to appear gay: "Monsieur le Baron de Pontmercy is practising pettifogging in some corner or other."

While the old man regretted, Marius applauded himself. As is the case with all good-hearted people, misfortune had eradicated his bitterness. He only thought of M. Gillenormand in an amiable light, but he had set his mind on not receiving anything more from the man who *had been unkind to his father*. This was the mitigated translation of his first indignation. Moreover, he was happy at having suffered, and at suffering still. It was for his father's sake. The hardness of his life satisfied and pleased him. He said to himself with a sort of joy that—*it was certainly the least he could do*; that it was an expiation;—that, had it not been for that, he would have been punished in some other way and later on for his impious indifference towards his father, and such a father! that it would not have been just that his father should have all the suffering, and he none of it; and that, in any case, what were his toils and his destitution compared with the colonel's heroic life? that, in short, the only way for him to approach his father and resemble him, was to be brave in the face of indigence, as the other had been valiant before the enemy; and that that was, no doubt, what the colonel had meant to imply by the words: "He will be worthy of it." Words which Marius continued to wear, not on his breast, since the colonel's writing had disappeared, but in his heart.

And then, on the day when his grandfather had turned him out of doors, he had been only a child, now he was a man. He felt it. Misery, we repeat, had been good for him. Poverty in youth, when it succeeds, has this magnificent property about it, that it turns the whole will towards effort, and the whole soul towards aspiration. Poverty instantly lays material life bare and renders it hideous; hence inexpressible bounds towards the ideal life. The wealthy young man has a hundred coarse and brilliant distractions, horse races, hunting, dogs, tobacco, gaming, good repasts, and all the rest of it; occupations for the baser side of the soul, at the expense of the loftier and more delicate sides. The poor young man wins his bread with difficulty; he eats; when he has eaten, he has nothing more but meditation. He goes to the spectacles which God furnishes gratis; he gazes at the sky, space, the stars, flowers, children, the humanity among which he is suffering, the creation amid which he beams. He gazes so much on humanity that he perceives its soul, he gazes upon creation to such an extent that he beholds God. He dreams, he feels himself great; he dreams on, and feels himself tender. From the egotism of the man who suffers he passes to the compassion of the man who meditates. An admirable sentiment breaks forth in him, forgetfulness of self and pity for all. As he thinks of the innumerable enjoyments which nature offers, gives, and lavishes to souls which stand open, and refuses to souls that are closed, he comes to pity, he the millionnaire of the mind, the millionnaire of money. All hatred departs from his heart, in proportion as light penetrates his spirit. And is he unhappy? No. The misery of a young man is never miserable. The first young lad who comes to hand, however poor he may be, with his strength, his health, his rapid walk, his brilliant eyes, his warmly circulating blood, his black hair, his red lips, his white teeth, his pure breath, will always arouse the envy of an aged emperor. And then, every morning, he sets himself afresh to the task of earning his bread; and while his hands earn his bread, his dorsal column gains pride, his brain gathers ideas. His task finished, he returns to ineffable ecstasies, to contemplation, to joys; he beholds his feet set in afflictions, in obstacles, on the pavement, in the nettles, sometimes in the mire; his head in the light. He is firm, serene, gentle, peaceful, attentive, serious, content with little, kindly; and he thanks God for having bestowed on him those two forms of riches which many a rich man lacks: work, which makes him free; and thought, which makes him dignified.

This is what had happened with Marius. To tell the truth, he inclined a little too much to the side of contemplation. From the day when he had succeeded in earning his living with some approach to certainty, he had stopped, thinking it good to be poor, and retrenching time from his work to give to thought; that is to say, he sometimes passed entire days in meditation, absorbed, engulfed, like a visionary, in the mute voluptuousness of ecstasy and inward radiance. He had thus propounded the problem of his life: to toil as little as possible at material labor, in order to toil as much as possible at the labor which is impalpable; in other words, to bestow a few hours on real life, and to cast the rest to the infinite. As he believed that he lacked nothing, he did not perceive that contemplation, thus understood, ends by becoming one of the forms of idleness; that he was contenting himself with conquering the first necessities of life, and that he was resting from his labors too soon.

It was evident that, for this energetic and enthusiastic nature, this could only be a transitory state, and that, at the first shock against the inevitable complications of destiny, Marius would awaken.

In the meantime, although he was a lawyer, and whatever Father Gillenormand thought about the matter, he was not practising, he was not even pettifogging. Meditation had turned him aside from pleading. To haunt attorneys, to follow the court, to hunt up cases—what a bore! Why should he do it? He saw no reason for changing the manner of gaining his livelihood! The obscure and ill-paid publishing establishment had come to mean for him a sure source of work which did not involve too much labor, as we have explained, and which sufficed for his wants.

One of the publishers for whom he worked, M. Magimel, I think, offered to take him into his own house, to lodge him well, to furnish him with regular occupation, and to give him fifteen hundred francs a year. To be well lodged! Fifteen hundred francs! No doubt. But renounce his liberty! Be on fixed wages! A sort of hired man of letters! According to Marius' opinion, if he accepted, his position would become both better and worse at the same time, he acquired comfort, and lost his dignity; it was a fine and complete unhappiness converted into a repulsive and ridiculous state of torture: something like the case of a blind man who should recover the sight of one eye. He refused.

Marius dwelt in solitude. Owing to his taste for remaining outside of everything, and through having been too much alarmed, he had not entered decidedly into the group presided over by Enjolras. They had remained good friends; they were ready to assist each other on occasion in every possible way; but nothing more. Marius had two friends: one young, Courfeyrac; and one old, M. Mabeuf. He inclined more to the old man. In the first place, he owed to him the revolution which had taken place within him; to him he was indebted for having known and loved his father. "He operated on me for a cataract," he said.

The churchwarden had certainly played a decisive part.

It was not, however, that M. Mabeuf had been anything but the calm and impassive agent of Providence in this connection. He had enlightened Marius by chance and without being aware of the fact, as does a candle which some one brings; he had been the candle and not the some one.

As for Marius' inward political revolution, M. Mabeuf was totally incapable of comprehending it, of willing or of directing it.

As we shall see M. Mabeuf again, later on, a few words will not be superfluous.

IV

M. MABEUF

On the day when M. Mabeuf said to Marius: "Certainly I approve of political opinions," he expressed the real state of his mind. All political opinions were matters of indifference to him, and he approved them all, without distinction, provided they left him in peace, as the Greeks called the Furies "the beautiful, the good, the charming," the Eumenides. M. Mabeuf's political opinion consisted in a passionate love for plants, and, above all, for books. Like all the rest of the world, he possessed the termination in *ist*, without which no one could exist at that time, but he was neither a Royalist, a Bonapartist, a Chartist, an Orleanist, nor an Anarchist; he was a *bouquinist*, a collector of old books. He did not understand how men could busy themselves with hating each other because of silly stuff like the charter, democracy, legitimacy, monarchy, the republic, etc., when there were in the world all sorts of mosses, grasses, and shrubs which they might be looking at, and heaps of folios, and even of 32mos, which they might turn over. He took good care not to become useless; having books did not prevent his reading, being a botanist did not prevent his being a gardener. When he made Pontmercy's acquaintance, this sympathy had existed between the colonel and himself—that what the colonel did for flowers, he did for fruits. M. Mabeuf had succeeded in producing seedling pears as savory as the pears of St. Germain; it is from one of his combinations, apparently, that the October Mirabelle, now celebrated and no less perfumed than the summer Mirabelle, owes its origin. He went to mass rather from gentleness than from piety, and because, as he loved the faces of men, but hated their noise, he found them assembled and silent only in church. Feeling that he must be something in the State, he had chosen the career of warden. However, he had never succeeded in loving any woman as much as a tulip bulb, nor any man as much as an Elzevir. He had long passed sixty, when, one day, some one asked him: "Have you never been married?" "I have forgotten," said he. When it sometimes happened to him—and to whom does it not happen?—to say: "Oh! if I were only rich!" it was not when ogling a pretty girl, as was the case with Father Gillenormand, but when contemplating an old book. He lived alone with an old housekeeper. He was somewhat gouty, and when he was asleep, his aged fingers, stiffened with rheumatism, lay crooked up in the folds of his sheets. He had composed and published a *Flora of the Environs of Cauteretz*, with colored plates, a work which enjoyed a tolerable measure of esteem and which sold well. People rang his bell, in the Rue Mésières, two or three times a day, to ask for it. He drew as much as two thousand francs a year from it; this constituted nearly the whole of his fortune. Although poor, he had had the talent to form for himself, by dint of patience, privations, and time, a precious collection of rare copies of every sort. He never went out without a book under his arm, and he often returned with two. The sole decoration of the four rooms on the ground floor, which composed his lodgings, consisted of framed herbariums, and engravings of the old masters. The sight of a sword or a gun chilled his blood. He had never approached a cannon in his life, even at the Invalides. He had a passable stomach, a brother who was a curé, perfectly white hair, no teeth, either in his mouth or his mind, a trembling in every limb, a Picard accent, an infantile laugh, the air of an old sheep, and he was easily frightened. Add to this, that he had no other friendship, no other acquaintance among the living, than an old bookseller of the Porte-Saint-Jacques, named Royal. His dream was to naturalize indigo in France.

His servant was also a sort of innocent. The poor good old woman was a spinster. Sultan, her cat, which might have mewed Allegri's miserere in the Sixtine Chapel, had filled her heart and sufficed for the quantity of passion which existed in her. None of her dreams had ever proceeded as far as man. She had never been able to get further than her cat. Like him, she had a moustache. Her glory consisted in her caps, which were always white. She passed her time, on Sundays, after mass, in counting over the linen in her chest, and in spreading out on her bed the dresses in the piece which she bought and never had made up. She knew how to read. M. Mabeuf had nicknamed her Mother Plutarque.

M. Mabeuf had taken a fancy to Marius, because Marius, being young and gentle, warmed his age without startling his timidity. Youth combined with gentleness produces on old people the effect of the sun without wind. When Marius was saturated with military glory, with gunpowder, with marches and countermarches, and with all those prodigious battles in which his father had given and received such tremendous blows of the sword, he went to see M. Mabeuf, and M. Mabeuf talked to him of his hero from the point of view of flowers.

His brother the curé died about 1830, and almost immediately, as when the night is drawing on, the whole horizon grew dark for M. Mabeuf. A notary's failure deprived him of the sum of ten thousand francs, which was all that he possessed in his brother's right and his own. The Revolution of July brought a crisis to publishing. In a period of embarrassment, the first thing which does not sell is a *Flora. The Flora of the Environs of Cauteretz* stopped short. Weeks passed by without a single purchaser. Sometimes M. Mabeuf started at the sound of the bell. "Monsieur," said Mother Plutarque sadly, "it is the water-carrier." In short, one day, M. Mabeuf quitted the Rue Mésières, abdicated the functions of warden, gave up Saint-Sulpice, sold not a part of his books, but of his prints,—that to which he was the least attached,— and installed himself in a little house on the Rue Montparnasse, where, however, he remained but one quarter for two reasons: in the first place, the ground floor and the garden cost three hundred francs, and he dared not spend more than two hundred francs on his rent; in the second, being near Faton's shooting-gallery, he could hear the pistol-shots; which was intolerable to him.

He carried off his *Flora*, his copper-plates, his herbariums, his portfolios, and his books, and established himself near the Salpêtrière, in a sort of thatched cottage of the village of Austerlitz, where, for fifty crowns a year, he got three rooms and a garden enclosed by a hedge, and containing a well. He took advantage of this removal to sell off nearly all his furniture. On the day of his entrance into his new quarters, he was very gay, and drove the nails on which his engravings and herbariums were to hang, with his own hands, dug in his garden the rest of the day, and at night, perceiving that Mother Plutarque had a melancholy air, and was very thoughtful, he tapped her on the shoulder and said to her with a smile: "We have the indigo!"

Only two visitors, the bookseller of the Porte-Saint-Jacques and Marius, were admitted to view the thatched cottage at Austerlitz, a brawling name which was, to tell the truth, extremely disagreeable to him.

However, as we have just pointed out, brains which are absorbed in some bit of wisdom, or folly, or, as it often happens, in both at once, are but slowly accessible to the things of actual life. Their own destiny is a far-off thing to them. There results from such concentration a passivity, which, if it were the outcome of reasoning, would resemble philosophy. One declines, descends, trickles away, even crumbles away, and yet is hardly conscious of it one's self. It always ends, it is true, in an awakening, but the awakening is tardy. In the meantime, it seems as though we held ourselves neutral in the game which is going on between our happiness and our unhappiness. We are the stake, and we look on at the game with indifference.

It is thus that, athwart the cloud which formed about him, when all his hopes were extinguished one after the other, M. Mabeuf remained rather puerilely, but profoundly serene. His habits of mind had the regular swing of a pendulum. Once mounted on an illusion, he went for a very long time, even after the illusion had disappeared. A clock does not stop short at the precise moment when the key is lost.

M. Mabeuf had his innocent pleasures. These pleasures were inexpensive and unexpected; the merest chance furnished them. One day, Mother Plutarque was reading a romance in one corner of the room. She was reading aloud, finding that she understood better thus. To read aloud is to assure one's self of what one is reading. There are people who read very loud, and who have the appearance of giving themselves their word of honor as to what they are perusing.

It was with this sort of energy that Mother Plutarque was reading the romance which she had in hand. M. Mabeuf heard her without listening to her.

In the course of her reading, Mother Plutarque came to this phrase. It was a question of an officer of dragoons and a beauty:—

"—The beauty pouted, and the dragoon—"

Here she interrupted herself to wipe her glasses.

"Bouddha and the Dragon," struck in M. Mabeuf in a low voice. "Yes, it is true that there was a dragon, which, from the depths of its cave, spouted flame through his maw and set the heavens on fire. Many stars had already been consumed by this monster, which, besides, had the claws of a tiger. Bouddha went into its den and succeeded in converting the dragon. That is a good book that you are reading, Mother Plutarque. There is no more beautiful legend in existence."

And M. Mabeuf fell into a delicious reverie.

V

Poverty a Good Neighbor for Misery

Marius liked this candid old man who saw himself gradually falling into the clutches of indigence, and who came to feel astonishment, little by little, without, however, being made melancholy by it. Marius met Courfeyrac and sought out M. Mabeuf. Very rarely, however; twice a month at most.

Marius' pleasure consisted in taking long walks alone on the outer boulevards, or in the Champs-de-Mars, or in the least frequented alleys of the Luxembourg. He often spent half a day in gazing at a market garden, the beds of lettuce, the chickens on the dung-heap, the horse turning the water-wheel. The passers-by stared at him in surprise, and some of them thought his attire suspicious and his mien sinister. He was only a poor young man dreaming in an objectless way.

It was during one of his strolls that he had hit upon the Gorbeau house, and, tempted by its isolation and its cheapness, had taken up his abode there. He was known there only under the name of M. Marius.

Some of his father's old generals or old comrades had invited him to go and see them, when they learned about him. Marius had not refused their invitations. They afforded opportunities of talking about his father. Thus he went from time to time, to Comte Pajol, to General Bellavesne, to General Fririon, to the Invalides. There was music and dancing there. On such evenings, Marius put on his new coat. But he never went to these evening parties or balls except on days when it was freezing cold, because he could not afford a carriage, and he did not wish to arrive with boots otherwise than like mirrors.

He said sometimes, but without bitterness: "Men are so made that in a drawing-room you may be soiled everywhere except on your shoes. In order to insure a good reception there, only one irreproachable thing is asked of you; your conscience? No, your boots."

All passions except those of the heart are dissipated by reverie. Marius' political fevers vanished thus. The Revolution of 1830 assisted in the process, by satisfying and calming him. He remained the same, setting aside his fits of wrath. He still held the same opinions. Only, they had been tempered. To speak accurately, he had no longer any opinions, he had sympathies. To what party did he belong? To the party of humanity. Out of humanity he chose France; out of the Nation he chose the people; out of the people he chose the woman. It was to that point above all, that his pity was directed. Now he preferred an idea to a deed, a poet to a hero, and he admired a book like Job more than an event like Marengo. And then, when, after a day spent in meditation, he returned in the evening through the boulevards, and caught a glimpse through the branches of the trees of the fathomless space beyond, the nameless gleams, the abyss, the shadow, the mystery, all that which is only human seemed very pretty indeed to him.

He thought that he had, and he really had, in fact, arrived at the truth of life and of human philosophy, and he had ended by gazing at nothing but heaven, the only thing which Truth can perceive from the bottom of her well.

This did not prevent him from multiplying his plans, his combinations, his scaffoldings, his projects for the future. In this state of reverie, an eye which could have cast a glance into Marius' interior would have been dazzled with the purity of that soul. In fact, had it been given to our eyes of the flesh to gaze into the consciences of others, we should be able to judge a man much more surely according to what he dreams, than according to what he thinks. There is will in thought, there is none in dreams. Reverie, which is utterly spontaneous, takes and keeps, even in the gigantic and the ideal, the form of our spirit. Nothing proceeds more directly and more sincerely from the very depth of our soul, than our unpremeditated and boundless aspirations towards the splendors of destiny. In these aspirations, much more than in deliberate, rational co-ordinated ideas, is the real character of a man to be found. Our chimæras are the things which the most resemble us. Each one of us dreams of the unknown and the impossible in accordance with his nature.

Towards the middle of this year 1831, the old woman who waited on Marius told him that his neighbors, the wretched Jondrette family, had been turned out of doors. Marius, who passed nearly the whole of his days out of the house, hardly knew that he had any neighbors.

"Why are they turned out?" he asked.

"Because they do not pay their rent; they owe for two quarters."

"How much is it?"

"Twenty francs," said the old woman.

Marius had thirty francs saved up in a drawer.

"Here," he said to the old woman, "take these twenty-five francs. Pay for the poor people and give them five francs, and do not tell them that it was I."

VI

THE SUBSTITUTE

It chanced that the regiment to which Lieutenant Théodule belonged came to perform garrison duty in Paris. This inspired Aunt Gillenormand with a second idea. She had, on the first occasion, hit upon the plan of having Marius spied upon by Théodule; now she plotted to have Théodule take Marius' place.

At all events and in case the grandfather should feel the vague need of a young face in the house,—these rays of dawn are sometimes sweet to ruin,—it was expedient to find another Marius. "Take it as a simple erratum," she thought, "such as one sees in books. For Marius, read Théodule."

A grandnephew is almost the same as a grandson; in default of a lawyer one takes a lancer.

One morning, when M. Gillenormand was about to read something in the *Quotidienne*, his daughter entered and said to him in her sweetest voice; for the question concerned her favorite:—

"Father, Théodule is coming to present his respects to you this morning."

"Who's Théodule?"

"Your grandnephew."

"Ah!" said the grandfather.

Then he went back to his reading, thought no more of his grandnephew, who was merely some Théodule or other, and soon flew into a rage, which almost always happened when he read. The "sheet" which he held, although Royalist, of course, announced for the following day, without any softening phrases, one of these little events which were of daily occurrence at that date in Paris: "That the students of the schools of law and medicine were to assemble on the Place du Panthéon, at midday,—to deliberate." The discussion concerned one of the questions of the moment, the artillery of the National Guard, and a conflict between the Minister of War and "the citizen's militia," on the subject of the cannon parked in the courtyard of the Louvre. The students were to "deliberate" over this. It did not take much more than this to swell M. Gillenormand's rage.

He thought of Marius, who was a student, and who would probably go with the rest, to "deliberate, at midday, on the Place du Panthéon."

As he was indulging in this painful dream, Lieutenant Théodule entered clad in plain clothes as a bourgeois, which was clever of him, and was discreetly introduced by Mademoiselle Gillenormand. The lancer had reasoned as follows: "The old druid has not sunk all his money in a life pension. It is well to disguise one's self as a civilian from time to time."

Mademoiselle Gillenormand said aloud to her father:—

"Théodule, your grandnephew."

And in a low voice to the lieutenant:—

"Approve of everything."

And she withdrew.

The lieutenant, who was but little accustomed to such venerable encounters, stammered with some timidity: "Good day, uncle,"—and made a salute composed of the involuntary and mechanical outline of the military salute finished off as a bourgeois salute.

"Ah! so it's you; that is well, sit down," said the old gentleman.

That said, he totally forgot the lancer.

Théodule seated himself, and M. Gillenormand rose.

M. Gillenormand began to pace back and forth, his hands in his pockets, talking aloud, and twitching, with his irritated old fingers, at the two watches which he wore in his two fobs.

"That pack of brats! they convene on the Place du Panthéon! by my life! urchins who were with their nurses but yesterday! If one were to squeeze their noses, milk would burst out. And they deliberate to-morrow, at midday. What are we coming to? What are we coming to? It is clear that we are making for the abyss. That is what the *descamisados* have brought us to! To deliberate on the citizen artillery! To go and jabber in the open air over the jibes of the National Guard! And with whom are they to meet there? Just see whither Jacobinism leads. I will bet anything you like, a million against a counter, that there will be no one there but returned convicts and released galley-slaves. The Republicans and the galley-slaves,—they form but one nose and one handkerchief. Carnot used to say: 'Where would you have me go, traitor?' Fouché replied: 'Wherever you please, imbecile!' That's what the Republicans are like."

"That is true," said Théodule.

M. Gillenormand half turned his head, saw Théodule, and went on:—

"When one reflects that that scoundrel was so vile as to turn carbonaro! Why did you leave my house? To go and become a Republican! Pssst! In the first place, the people want none of your republic, they have common sense, they know well that there always have been kings, and that there always will be; they know well that the people are only the people, after all, they make sport of it, of your republic—do you understand, idiot? Is it not a horrible caprice? To fall in love with Père Duchesne, to make sheep's-eyes at the guillotine, to sing romances, and play on the guitar under the balcony of '93—it's enough to make one spit on all these young fellows, such fools are they! They are all alike. Not one escapes. It suffices for them to breathe the air which blows through the street to lose their senses. The nineteenth century is poison. The first scamp that happens along lets his beard grow like a goat's, thinks himself a real scoundrel, and abandons his old relatives. He's a Republican, he's a romantic. What does that mean, romantic? Do me the favor to tell me what it is. All possible follies. A year ago, they ran to *Hernani*. Now, I just ask you, *Hernani!* antitheses! abominations which are not even written in French! And then, they have cannons in the courtyard of the Louvre. Such are the rascalities of this age!"

"You are right, uncle," said Théodule.

M. Gillenormand resumed:—

"Cannons in the courtyard of the Museum! For what purpose? Do you want to fire grape-shot at the Apollo Belvedere? What have those cartridges to do with the Venus de Medici? Oh! the young men of the present day are all blackguards! What a pretty creature is their Benjamin Constant! And those who are not rascals are simpletons! They do all they can to make themselves ugly, they are badly dressed, they are afraid of women, in the presence of petticoats they have a mendicant air which sets the girls into fits of laughter; on my word of honor, one would say the poor creatures were ashamed of love. They are deformed, and they complete themselves by being stupid; they repeat the puns of Tiercelin and Potier, they have sack coats, stablemen's waistcoats, shirts of coarse linen, trousers of coarse cloth, boots of coarse leather, and their rigmarole resembles their plumage. One might make use of their jargon to put new soles on their old shoes. And all this awkward batch of brats has political opinions, if you please. Political opinions should be strictly forbidden. They fabricate systems, they recast society, they demolish the monarchy, they fling all laws to the earth, they put the attic in the cellar's place and my porter in the place of the King, they turn Europe topsy-turvy, they

VICTOR HUGO

reconstruct the world, and all their love affairs consist in staring slily at the ankles of the laundresses as these women climb into their carts. Ah! Marius! Ah! you blackguard! to go and vociferate on the public place! to discuss, to debate, to take measures! They call that measures, just God! Disorder humbles itself and becomes silly. I have seen chaos, I now see a mess. Students deliberating on the National Guard,—such a thing could not be seen among the Ogibewas nor the Cadodaches! Savages who go naked, with their noddles dressed like a shuttlecock, with a club in their paws, are less of brutes than those bachelors of arts! The four-penny monkeys! And they set up for judges! Those creatures deliberate and ratiocinate! The end of the world is come! This is plainly the end of this miserable terraqueous globe! A final hiccough was required, and France has emitted it. Deliberate, my rascals! Such things will happen so long as they go and read the newspapers under the arcades of the Odéon. That costs them a sou, and their good sense, and their intelligence, and their heart and their soul, and their wits. They emerge thence, and decamp from their families. All newspapers are pests; all, even the *Drapeau Blanc!* At bottom, Martainville was a Jacobin. Ah! just Heaven! you may boast of having driven your grandfather to despair, that you may!"

"That is evident," said Théodule.

And profiting by the fact that M. Gillenormand was taking breath, the lancer added in a magisterial manner:—

"There should be no other newspaper than the *Moniteur*, and no other book than the *Annuaire Militaire*."

M. Gillenormand continued:—

"It is like their Sieyès! A regicide ending in a senator; for that is the way they always end. They give themselves a scar with the address of *thou* as citizens, in order to get themselves called, eventually, *Monsieur le Comte*. Monsieur le Comte as big as my arm, assassins of September. The philosopher Sieyès! I will do myself the justice to say, that I have never had any better opinion of the philosophies of all those philosophers, than of the spectacles of the grimacer of Tivoli! One day I saw the Senators cross the Quai Malplaquet in mantles of violet velvet sown with bees, with hats à la Henri IV. They were hideous. One would have pronounced them monkeys from the tiger's court. Citizens, I declare to you, that your progress is madness, that your humanity is a dream, that your revolution is a crime, that your republic is a monster, that your young and virgin France comes from the brothel, and I maintain it against all, whoever you may be, whether journalists, economists, legists, or even were you better judges of liberty, of equality, and fraternity than the knife of the guillotine! And that I announce to you, my fine fellows!"

"Parbleu!" cried the lieutenant, "that is wonderfully true."

M. Gillenormand paused in a gesture which he had begun, wheeled round, stared Lancer Théodule intently in the eyes, and said to him:—

"You are a fool."

BOOK SIXTH
THE CONJUNCTION OF TWO STARS

I

THE SOBRIQUET: MODE OF FORMATION OF FAMILY NAMES

Marius was, at this epoch, a handsome young man, of medium stature, with thick and intensely black hair, a lofty and intelligent brow, well-opened and passionate nostrils, an air of calmness and sincerity, and with something indescribably proud, thoughtful, and innocent over his whole countenance. His profile, all of whose lines were rounded, without thereby losing their firmness, had a certain Germanic sweetness, which has made its way into the French physiognomy by way of Alsace and Lorraine, and that complete absence of angles which rendered the Sicambres so easily recognizable among the Romans, and which distinguishes the leonine from the aquiline race. He was at that period of life when the mind of men who think is composed, in nearly equal parts, of depth and ingenuousness. A grave situation being given, he had all that is required to be stupid: one more turn of the key, and he might be sublime. His manners were reserved, cold, polished, not very genial. As his mouth was charming, his lips the reddest, and his teeth the whitest in the world, his smile corrected the severity of his face, as a whole. At certain moments, that pure brow and that voluptuous smile presented a singular contrast. His eyes were small, but his glance was large.

At the period of his most abject misery, he had observed that young girls turned round when he passed by, and he fled or hid, with death in his soul. He thought that they were staring at him because of his old clothes, and that they were laughing at them; the fact is, that they stared at him because of his grace, and that they dreamed of him.

This mute misunderstanding between him and the pretty passers-by had made him shy. He chose none of them for the excellent reason that he fled from all of them. He lived thus indefinitely,—stupidly, as Courfeyrac said.

Courfeyrac also said to him: "Do not aspire to be venerable" (they called each other *thou*; it is the tendency of youthful friendships to slip into this mode of address). "Let me give you a piece of advice, my dear fellow. Don't read so many books, and look a little more at the lasses.

The jades have some good points about them, O Marius! By dint of fleeing and blushing, you will become brutalized."

On other occasions, Courfeyrac encountered him and said:—"Good morning, Monsieur l'Abbé!"

When Courfeyrac had addressed to him some remark of this nature, Marius avoided women, both young and old, more than ever for a week to come, and he avoided Courfeyrac to boot.

Nevertheless, there existed in all the immensity of creation, two women whom Marius did not flee, and to whom he paid no attention whatever. In truth, he would have been very much amazed if he had been informed that they were women. One was the bearded old woman who swept out his chamber, and caused Courfeyrac to say: "Seeing that his servant woman wears his beard, Marius does not wear his own beard." The other was a sort of little girl whom he saw very often, and whom he never looked at.

For more than a year, Marius had noticed in one of the walks of the Luxembourg, the one which skirts the parapet of the Pépinière, a man and a very young girl, who were almost always seated side by side on the same bench, at the most solitary end of the alley, on the Rue de l'Ouest side. Every time that that chance which meddles with the strolls of persons whose gaze is turned inwards, led Marius to that walk,—and it was nearly every day,—he found this couple there. The man appeared to be about sixty years of age; he seemed sad and serious; his whole person presented the robust and weary aspect peculiar to military men who have retired from the service. If he had worn a decoration, Marius would have said: "He is an ex-officer." He had a kindly but unapproachable air, and he never let his glance linger on the eyes of any one. He wore blue trousers, a blue frock coat and a broad-brimmed hat, which always appeared to be new, a black cravat, a quaker shirt, that is to say, it was dazzlingly white, but of coarse linen. A grisette who passed near him one day, said: "Here's a very tidy widower." His hair was very white.

The first time that the young girl who accompanied him came and seated herself on the bench which they seemed to have adopted, she was a sort of child thirteen or fourteen years of age, so thin as to be almost homely, awkward, insignificant, and with a possible promise of handsome eyes. Only, they were always raised with a sort of displeasing assurance. Her dress was both aged and childish, like the dress of the scholars in a convent; it consisted of a badly cut gown of black merino. They had the air of being father and daughter.

Marius scanned this old man, who was not yet aged, and this little girl, who was not yet a person, for a few days, and thereafter paid no attention to them. They, on their side, did not appear even to see him. They conversed together with a peaceful and indifferent air. The girl chattered incessantly and merrily. The old man talked but little, and, at times, he fixed on her eyes overflowing with an ineffable paternity.

Marius had acquired the mechanical habit of strolling in that walk. He invariably found them there.

This is the way things went:—

Marius liked to arrive by the end of the alley which was furthest from their bench; he walked the whole length of the alley, passed in front of them, then returned to the extremity whence he had come, and began again. This he did five or six times in the course of his promenade, and the promenade was taken five or six times a week, without its having occurred to him or to these people to exchange a greeting. That personage, and that young girl, although they appeared,—and perhaps because they appeared,—to shun all glances, had, naturally, caused some attention on the part of the five or six students who strolled along the Pépinière from time to time; the studious after their lectures, the others after their game of billiards. Courfeyrac, who was among the last, had observed them several times, but, finding the girl homely, he had speedily and carefully kept out of the way. He had fled, discharging at them a sobriquet, like a Parthian dart. Impressed solely with the child's gown and the old man's hair, he had dubbed the daughter Mademoiselle Lanoire, and the father, Monsieur Leblanc, so that as no one knew them under any other title, this nickname became a law in the default of any other name. The students said: "Ah! Monsieur Leblanc is on his bench." And Marius, like the rest, had found it convenient to call this unknown gentleman Monsieur Leblanc.

We shall follow their example, and we shall say M. Leblanc, in order to facilitate this tale.

So Marius saw them nearly every day, at the same hour, during the first year. He found the man to his taste, but the girl insipid.

II

LUX FACTA EST

During the second year, precisely at the point in this history which the reader has now reached, it chanced that this habit of the Luxembourg was interrupted, without Marius himself being quite aware why, and nearly six months elapsed, during which he did not set foot in the alley. One day, at last, he returned thither once more; it was a serene summer morning, and Marius was in joyous mood, as one is when the weather is fine. It seemed to him that he had in his heart all the songs of the birds that he was listening to, and all the bits of blue sky of which he caught glimpses through the leaves of the trees.

He went straight to "his alley," and when he reached the end of it he perceived, still on the same bench, that well-known couple. Only, when he approached, it certainly was the same man; but it seemed to him that it was no longer the same girl. The person whom he now beheld was a tall and beautiful creature, possessed of all the most charming lines of a woman at the precise moment when they are still combined with all the most ingenuous graces of the child; a pure and fugitive moment, which can be expressed only by these two words,—"fifteen years." She had wonderful brown hair, shaded with threads of gold, a brow that seemed made of marble, cheeks that seemed made of rose-leaf, a pale flush, an agitated whiteness, an exquisite mouth, whence smiles darted like sunbeams, and words like music, a head such as Raphael would have given to Mary, set upon a neck that Jean Goujon would have attributed to a Venus. And, in order that nothing might be lacking to this bewitching face, her nose was not handsome—it was pretty; neither straight nor curved, neither Italian nor Greek; it was the Parisian nose, that is to say, spiritual, delicate, irregular, pure,—which drives painters to despair, and charms poets.

When Marius passed near her, he could not see her eyes, which were constantly lowered. He saw only her long chestnut lashes, permeated with shadow and modesty.

This did not prevent the beautiful child from smiling as she listened to what the white-haired old man was saying to her, and nothing could be more fascinating than that fresh smile, combined with those drooping eyes.

For a moment, Marius thought that she was another daughter of the same man, a sister of the former, no doubt. But when the invariable habit of his stroll brought him, for the second time, near the bench, and he had examined her attentively, he recognized her as the same. In six months the little girl had become a young maiden; that was all. Nothing is more frequent than this phenomenon. There is a moment when girls blossom out in the twinkling of an eye, and become roses all at once. One left them children but yesterday; today, one finds them disquieting to the feelings.

This child had not only grown, she had become idealized. As three days in April suffice to cover certain trees with flowers, six months had sufficed to clothe her with beauty. Her April had arrived.

One sometimes sees people, who, poor and mean, seem to wake up, pass suddenly from indigence to luxury, indulge in expenditures of all sorts, and become dazzling, prodigal, magnificent, all of a sudden. That is the result of having pocketed an income; a note fell due yesterday. The young girl had received her quarterly income.

And then, she was no longer the school-girl with her felt hat, her merino gown, her scholar's shoes, and red hands; taste had come to her with beauty; she was a well-dressed person, clad with a sort of rich and simple elegance, and without affectation. She wore a dress of black damask, a cape of the same material, and a bonnet of white crape. Her white gloves displayed the delicacy of the hand which toyed with the carved, Chinese ivory handle of a parasol, and her silken shoe outlined the smallness of her foot. When one passed near her, her whole toilette exhaled a youthful and penetrating perfume.

As for the man, he was the same as usual.

The second time that Marius approached her, the young girl raised her eyelids; her eyes were of a deep, celestial blue, but in that veiled azure, there was, as yet, nothing but the glance of a child. She looked at Marius indifferently, as she would have stared at the brat running beneath the sycamores, or the marble vase which cast a shadow on the bench, and Marius, on his side, continued his promenade, and thought about something else.

He passed near the bench where the young girl sat, five or six times, but without even turning his eyes in her direction.

On the following days, he returned, as was his wont, to the Luxembourg; as usual, he found there "the father and daughter;" but he paid no further attention to them. He thought no more about the girl now that she was beautiful than he had when she was homely. He passed very near the bench where she sat, because such was his habit.

III

EFFECT OF THE SPRING

One day, the air was warm, the Luxembourg was inundated with light and shade, the sky was as pure as though the angels had washed it that morning, the sparrows were giving vent to little twitters in the depths of the chestnut-trees. Marius had thrown open his whole soul to nature, he was not thinking of anything, he simply lived and breathed, he passed near the bench, the young girl raised her eyes to him, the two glances met.

What was there in the young girl's glance on this occasion? Marius could not have told. There was nothing and there was everything. It was a strange flash.

She dropped her eyes, and he pursued his way.

What he had just seen was no longer the ingenuous and simple eye of a child; it was a mysterious gulf which had half opened, then abruptly closed again.

There comes a day when the young girl glances in this manner. Woe to him who chances to be there!

That first gaze of a soul which does not, as yet, know itself, is like the dawn in the sky. It is the awakening of something radiant and strange. Nothing can give any idea of the dangerous charm of that unexpected gleam, which flashes suddenly and vaguely forth from adorable shadows, and which is composed of all the innocence of the present, and of all the passion of the future. It is a sort of undecided tenderness which reveals itself by chance, and which waits. It is a snare which the innocent maiden sets unknown to herself, and in which she captures hearts without either wishing or knowing it. It is a virgin looking like a woman.

It is rare that a profound reverie does not spring from that glance, where it falls. All purities and all candors meet in that celestial and fatal gleam which, more than all the best-planned tender glances of coquettes, possesses the magic power of causing the sudden blossoming, in the depths of the soul, of that sombre flower, impregnated with perfume and with poison, which is called love.

That evening, on his return to his garret, Marius cast his eyes over his garments, and perceived, for the first time, that he had been so slovenly, indecorous, and inconceivably stupid as to go for his walk in the Luxembourg with his "every-day clothes," that is to say, with a hat battered near the band, coarse carter's boots, black trousers which showed white at the knees, and a black coat which was pale at the elbows.

IV

Beginning of a Great Malady

On the following day, at the accustomed hour, Marius drew from his wardrobe his new coat, his new trousers, his new hat, and his new boots; he clothed himself in this complete panoply, put on his gloves, a tremendous luxury, and set off for the Luxembourg.

On the way thither, he encountered Courfeyrac, and pretended not to see him. Courfeyrac, on his return home, said to his friends:—

"I have just met Marius' new hat and new coat, with Marius inside them. He was going to pass an examination, no doubt. He looked utterly stupid."

On arriving at the Luxembourg, Marius made the tour of the fountain basin, and stared at the swans; then he remained for a long time in contemplation before a statue whose head was perfectly black with mould, and one of whose hips was missing. Near the basin there was a bourgeois forty years of age, with a prominent stomach, who was holding by the hand a little urchin of five, and saying to him: "Shun excess, my son, keep at an equal distance from despotism and from anarchy." Marius listened to this bourgeois. Then he made the circuit of the basin once more. At last he directed his course towards "his alley," slowly, and as if with regret. One would have said that he was both forced to go there and withheld from doing so. He did not perceive it himself, and thought that he was doing as he always did.

On turning into the walk, he saw M. Leblanc and the young girl at the other end, "on their bench." He buttoned his coat up to the very top, pulled it down on his body so that there might be no wrinkles, examined, with a certain complaisance, the lustrous gleams of his trousers, and marched on the bench. This march savored of an attack, and certainly of a desire for conquest. So I say that he marched on the bench, as I should say: "Hannibal marched on Rome."

However, all his movements were purely mechanical, and he had interrupted none of the habitual preoccupations of his mind and labors. At that moment, he was thinking that the *Manuel du Baccalauréat* was a stupid book, and that it must have been drawn up by rare idiots, to allow of three tragedies of Racine and only one comedy of Molière being analyzed therein as masterpieces of the human mind. There was a piercing whistling going on in his ears. As he approached the bench, he held fast to the folds in his coat, and fixed his eyes on the young girl. It seemed to him that she filled the entire extremity of the alley with a vague blue light.

In proportion as he drew near, his pace slackened more and more. On arriving at some little distance from the bench, and long before he had reached the end of the walk, he halted, and could not explain to himself why he retraced his steps. He did not even say to himself that he would not go as far as the end. It was only with difficulty that the young girl could have perceived him in the distance and noted his fine appearance in his new clothes. Nevertheless, he held himself very erect, in case any one should be looking at him from behind.

He attained the opposite end, then came back, and this time he approached a little nearer to the bench. He even got to within three intervals of trees, but there he felt an indescribable impossibility of proceeding further, and he hesitated. He thought he saw the young girl's face bending towards him. But he exerted a manly and violent effort, subdued his hesitation, and walked straight ahead. A few seconds later, he rushed in front of the bench, erect and firm, reddening to the very ears, without daring to cast a glance either to the right or to the left, with his hand thrust into his coat like a statesman. At the moment when he passed,—under the cannon of the place,—he felt his heart beat wildly. As on the preceding day, she wore her damask gown and her crape bonnet. He heard an ineffable voice, which must have been "her voice." She was talking tranquilly. She was very pretty. He felt it, although he made no attempt to see her. "She could not, however," he thought, "help feeling esteem and consideration for me, if she only knew that I am the veritable author of the dissertation on Marcos Obrégon de la Ronde, which M. François de Neufchâteau put, as though it were his own, at the head of his edition of *Gil Blas*." He went beyond the bench as far as the extremity of the walk, which was very near, then turned on his heel and passed once more in front of the lovely girl. This time, he was very pale. Moreover, all his emotions were disagreeable. As he went further from the bench and the young girl, and while his back was turned to her, he fancied that she was gazing after him, and that made him stumble.

He did not attempt to approach the bench again; he halted near the middle of the walk, and there, a thing which he never did, he sat down, and reflecting in the most profoundly indistinct depths of his spirit, that after all, it was hard that persons whose white bonnet and black gown he admired should be absolutely insensible to his splendid trousers and his new coat.

At the expiration of a quarter of an hour, he rose, as though he were on the point of again beginning his march towards that bench which was surrounded by an aureole. But he remained standing there, motionless. For the first time in fifteen months, he said to himself that that gentleman who sat there every day with his daughter, had, on his side, noticed him, and probably considered his assiduity singular.

For the first time, also, he was conscious of some irreverence in designating that stranger, even in his secret thoughts, by the sobriquet of M. Leblanc.

He stood thus for several minutes, with drooping head, tracing figures in the sand, with the cane which he held in his hand.

Then he turned abruptly in the direction opposite to the bench, to M. Leblanc and his daughter, and went home.

That day he forgot to dine. At eight o'clock in the evening he perceived this fact, and as it was too late to go down to the Rue Saint-Jacques, he said: "Never mind!" and ate a bit of bread.

He did not go to bed until he had brushed his coat and folded it up with great care.

V

Divers Claps of Thunder Fall on Ma'am Bougon

On the following day, Ma'am Bougon, as Courfeyrac styled the old portress-principal-tenant, housekeeper of the Gorbeau hovel, Ma'am Bougon, whose name was, in reality, Madame Burgon, as we have found out, but this iconoclast, Courfeyrac, respected nothing,— Ma'am Bougon observed, with stupefaction, that M. Marius was going out again in his new coat.

He went to the Luxembourg again, but he did not proceed further than his bench midway of the alley. He seated himself there, as on the preceding day, surveying from a distance, and clearly making out, the white bonnet, the black dress, and above all, that blue light. He did not stir from it, and only went home when the gates of the Luxembourg closed. He did not see M. Leblanc and his daughter retire. He concluded that they had quitted the garden by the gate on the Rue de l'Ouest. Later on, several weeks afterwards, when he came to think it over, he could never recall where he had dined that evening.

On the following day, which was the third, Ma'am Bougon was thunderstruck. Marius went out in his new coat. "Three days in succession!" she exclaimed.

She tried to follow him, but Marius walked briskly, and with immense strides; it was a hippopotamus undertaking the pursuit of a chamois. She lost sight of him in two minutes, and returned breathless, three-quarters choked with asthma, and furious. "If there is any sense," she growled, "in putting on one's best clothes every day, and making people run like this!"

Marius betook himself to the Luxembourg.

The young girl was there with M. Leblanc. Marius approached as near as he could, pretending to be busy reading a book, but he halted afar off, then returned and seated himself on his bench, where he spent four hours in watching the house-sparrows who were skipping about the walk, and who produced on him the impression that they were making sport of him.

A fortnight passed thus. Marius went to the Luxembourg no longer for the sake of strolling there, but to seat himself always in the same spot, and that without knowing why. Once arrived there, he did not stir. He put on his new coat every morning, for the purpose of not showing himself, and he began all over again on the morrow.

She was decidedly a marvellous beauty. The only remark approaching a criticism, that could be made, was, that the contradiction between her gaze, which was melancholy, and her smile, which was merry, gave a rather wild effect to her face, which sometimes caused this sweet countenance to become strange without ceasing to be charming.

VI

Taken Prisoner

On one of the last days of the second week, Marius was seated on his bench, as usual, holding in his hand an open book, of which he had not turned a page for the last two hours. All at once he started. An event was taking place at the other extremity of the walk. Leblanc and his daughter had just left their seat, and the daughter had taken her father's arm, and both were advancing slowly, towards the middle of the alley where Marius was. Marius closed his book, then opened it again, then forced himself to read; he trembled; the aureole was coming straight towards him. "Ah! good Heavens!" thought he, "I shall not have time to strike an attitude." Still the white-haired man and the girl advanced. It seemed to him that this lasted for a century, and that it was but a second. "What are they coming in this direction for?" he asked himself. "What! She will pass here? Her feet will tread this sand, this walk, two paces from me?" He was utterly upset, he would have liked to be very handsome, he would have liked to own the cross. He heard the soft and measured sound of their approaching footsteps. He imagined that M. Leblanc was darting angry glances at him. "Is that gentleman going to address me?" he thought to himself. He dropped his head; when he raised it again, they were very near him. The young girl passed, and as she passed, she glanced at him. She gazed steadily at him, with a pensive sweetness which thrilled Marius from head to foot. It seemed to him that she was reproaching him for having allowed so long a time to elapse without coming as far as her, and that she was saying to him: "I am coming myself." Marius was dazzled by those eyes fraught with rays and abysses.

He felt his brain on fire. She had come to him, what joy! And then, how she had looked at him! She appeared to him more beautiful than he had ever seen her yet. Beautiful with a beauty which was wholly feminine and angelic, with a complete beauty which would have made Petrarch sing and Dante kneel. It seemed to him that he was floating free in the azure heavens. At the same time, he was horribly vexed because there was dust on his boots.

He thought he felt sure that she had looked at his boots too.

He followed her with his eyes until she disappeared. Then he started up and walked about the Luxembourg garden like a madman. It is possible that, at times, he laughed to himself and talked aloud. He was so dreamy when he came near the children's nurses, that each one of them thought him in love with her.

He quitted the Luxembourg, hoping to find her again in the street.

He encountered Courfeyrac under the arcades of the Odéon, and said to him: "Come and dine with me." They went off to Rousseau's and spent six francs. Marius ate like an ogre. He gave the waiter six sous. At dessert, he said to Courfeyrac. "Have you read the paper? What a fine discourse Audry de Puyraveau delivered!"

He was desperately in love.

After dinner, he said to Courfeyrac: "I will treat you to the play." They went to the Porte-Sainte-Martin to see Frédérick in *l'Auberge des Adrets*. Marius was enormously amused.

At the same time, he had a redoubled attack of shyness. On emerging from the theatre, he refused to look at the garter of a modiste who was stepping across a gutter, and Courfeyrac, who said: "I should like to put that woman in my collection," almost horrified him.

Courfeyrac invited him to breakfast at the Café Voltaire on the following morning. Marius went thither, and ate even more than on the preceding evening. He was very thoughtful and very merry. One would have said that he was taking advantage of every occasion to laugh uproariously. He tenderly embraced some man or other from the provinces, who was presented to him. A circle of students formed round the table, and they spoke of the nonsense paid for by the State which was uttered from the rostrum in the Sorbonne, then the conversation fell upon the faults and omissions in Guicherat's dictionaries and grammars. Marius interrupted the discussion to exclaim: "But it is very agreeable, all the same to have the cross!"

"That's queer!" whispered Courfeyrac to Jean Prouvaire.

"No," responded Prouvaire, "that's serious."

It was serious; in fact, Marius had reached that first violent and charming hour with which grand passions begin.

A glance had wrought all this.

When the mine is charged, when the conflagration is ready, nothing is more simple. A glance is a spark.

It was all over with him. Marius loved a woman. His fate was entering the unknown.

The glance of women resembles certain combinations of wheels, which are tranquil in appearance yet formidable. You pass close to them every day, peaceably and with impunity, and without a suspicion of anything. A moment arrives when you forget that the thing is there. You go and come, dream, speak, laugh. All at once you feel yourself clutched; all is over. The wheels hold you fast, the glance has ensnared you. It has caught you, no matter where or how, by some portion of your thought which was fluttering loose, by some distraction which had attacked you. You are lost. The whole of you passes into it. A chain of mysterious forces takes possession of you. You struggle in vain; no more human succor is possible. You go on falling from gearing to gearing, from agony to agony, from torture to torture, you, your mind, your fortune, your future, your soul; and, according to whether you are in the power of a wicked creature, or of a noble heart, you will not escape from this terrifying machine otherwise than disfigured with shame, or transfigured by passion.

VII

ADVENTURES OF THE LETTER U DELIVERED OVER TO CONJECTURES

Isolation, detachment, from everything, pride, independence, the taste of nature, the absence of daily and material activity, the life within himself, the secret conflicts of chastity, a benevolent ecstasy towards all creation, had prepared Marius for this possession which is called passion. His worship of his father had gradually become a religion, and, like all religions, it had retreated to the depths of his soul. Something was required in the foreground. Love came.

A full month elapsed, during which Marius went every day to the Luxembourg. When the hour arrived, nothing could hold him back.—"He is on duty," said Courfeyrac. Marius lived in a state of delight. It is certain that the young girl did look at him.

He had finally grown bold, and approached the bench. Still, he did not pass in front of it any more, in obedience to the instinct of timidity and to the instinct of prudence common to lovers. He considered it better not to attract "the attention of the father." He combined his stations behind the trees and the pedestals of the statues with a profound diplomacy, so that he might be seen as much as possible by the young girl and as little as possible by the old gentleman. Sometimes, he remained motionless by the half-hour together in the shade of a Leonidas or a Spartacus, holding in his hand a book, above which his eyes, gently raised, sought the beautiful girl, and she, on her side, turned her charming profile towards him with a vague smile. While conversing in the most natural and tranquil manner in the world with the white-haired man, she bent upon Marius all the reveries of a virginal and passionate eye. Ancient and time-honored manœuvre which Eve understood from the very first day of the world, and which every woman understands from the very first day of her life! her mouth replied to one, and her glance replied to another.

It must be supposed, that M. Leblanc finally noticed something, for often, when Marius arrived, he rose and began to walk about. He had abandoned their accustomed place and had adopted the bench by the Gladiator, near the other end of the walk, as though with the object of seeing whether Marius would pursue them thither. Marius did not understand, and committed this error. "The father" began to grow inexact, and no longer brought "his daughter" every day. Sometimes, he came alone. Then Marius did not stay. Another blunder.

Marius paid no heed to these symptoms. From the phase of timidity, he had passed, by a natural and fatal progress, to the phase of blindness. His love increased. He dreamed of it every night. And then, an unexpected bliss had happened to him, oil on the fire, a redoubling of the shadows over his eyes. One evening, at dusk, he had found, on the bench which "M. Leblanc and his daughter" had just quitted, a handkerchief, a very simple handkerchief, without embroidery, but white, and fine, and which seemed to him to exhale ineffable perfume. He seized it with rapture. This handkerchief was marked with the letters U. F. Marius knew nothing about this beautiful child,—neither her family name, her Christian name nor her abode; these two letters were the first thing of her that he had gained possession of, adorable initials, upon which he immediately began to construct his scaffolding. U was evidently the Christian name. "Ursule!" he thought, "what a delicious name!" He kissed the handkerchief, drank it in, placed it on his heart, on his flesh, during the day, and at night, laid it beneath his lips that he might fall asleep on it.

"I feel that her whole soul lies within it!" he exclaimed.

This handkerchief belonged to the old gentleman, who had simply let it fall from his pocket.

In the days which followed the finding of this treasure, he only displayed himself at the Luxembourg in the act of kissing the handkerchief and laying it on his heart. The beautiful child understood nothing of all this, and signified it to him by imperceptible signs.

"O modesty!" said Marius.

VIII

The Veterans Themselves Can Be Happy

Since we have pronounced the word modesty, and since we conceal nothing, we ought to say that once, nevertheless, in spite of his ecstasies, "his Ursule" caused him very serious grief. It was on one of the days when she persuaded M. Leblanc to leave the bench and stroll along the walk. A brisk May breeze was blowing, which swayed the crests of the plaintain-trees. The father and daughter, arm in arm, had just passed Marius' bench. Marius had risen to his feet behind them, and was following them with his eyes, as was fitting in the desperate situation of his soul.

All at once, a gust of wind, more merry than the rest, and probably charged with performing the affairs of Springtime, swept down from the nursery, flung itself on the alley, enveloped the young girl in a delicious shiver, worthy of Virgil's nymphs, and the fawns of Theocritus, and lifted her dress, the robe more sacred than that of Isis, almost to the height of her garter. A leg of exquisite shape appeared. Marius saw it. He was exasperated and furious.

The young girl had hastily thrust down her dress, with a divinely troubled motion, but he was nonetheless angry for all that. He was alone in the alley, it is true. But there might have been some one there. And what if there had been some one there! Can any one comprehend such a thing? What she had just done is horrible!—Alas, the poor child had done nothing; there had been but one culprit, the wind; but Marius, in whom quivered the Bartholo who exists in Cherubin, was determined to be vexed, and was jealous of his own shadow. It is thus, in fact, that the harsh and capricious jealousy of the flesh awakens in the human heart, and takes possession of it, even without any right. Moreover, setting aside even that jealousy, the sight of that charming leg had contained nothing agreeable for him; the white stocking of the first woman he chanced to meet would have afforded him more pleasure.

When "his Ursule," after having reached the end of the walk, retraced her steps with M. Leblanc, and passed in front of the bench on which Marius had seated himself once more, Marius darted a sullen and ferocious glance at her. The young girl gave way to that slight straightening up with a backward movement, accompanied by a raising of the eyelids, which signifies: "Well, what is the matter?"

This was "their first quarrel."

Marius had hardly made this scene at her with his eyes, when some one crossed the walk. It was a veteran, very much bent, extremely wrinkled, and pale, in a uniform of the Louis XV pattern, bearing on his breast the little oval plaque of red cloth, with the crossed swords, the soldier's cross of Saint-Louis, and adorned, in addition, with a coat-sleeve, which had no arm within it, with a silver chin and a wooden leg. Marius thought he perceived that this man had an extremely well satisfied air. It even struck him that the aged cynic, as he hobbled along past him, addressed to him a very fraternal and very merry wink, as though some chance had created an understanding between them, and as though they had shared some piece of good luck together. What did that relic of Mars mean by being so contented? What had passed between that wooden leg and the other? Marius reached a paroxysm of jealousy.—"Perhaps he was there!" he said to himself; "perhaps he saw!"—And he felt a desire to exterminate the veteran.

With the aid of time, all points grow dull. Marius' wrath against "Ursule," just and legitimate as it was, passed off. He finally pardoned her; but this cost him a great effort; he sulked for three days.

Nevertheless, in spite of all this, and because of all this, his passion augmented and grew to madness.

IX

ECLIPSE

The reader has just seen how Marius discovered, or thought that he discovered, that *She* was named Ursule.

Appetite grows with loving. To know that her name was Ursule was a great deal; it was very little. In three or four weeks, Marius had devoured this bliss. He wanted another. He wanted to know where she lived.

He had committed his first blunder, by falling into the ambush of the bench by the Gladiator. He had committed a second, by not remaining at the Luxembourg when M. Leblanc came thither alone. He now committed a third, and an immense one. He followed "Ursule."

She lived in the Rue de l'Ouest, in the most unfrequented spot, in a new, three-story house, of modest appearance.

From that moment forth, Marius added to his happiness of seeing her at the Luxembourg the happiness of following her home.

His hunger was increasing. He knew her first name, at least, a charming name, a genuine woman's name; he knew where she lived; he wanted to know who she was.

One evening, after he had followed them to their dwelling, and had seen them disappear through the carriage gate, he entered in their train and said boldly to the porter:—

"Is that the gentleman who lives on the first floor, who has just come in?"

"No," replied the porter. "He is the gentleman on the third floor."

Another step gained. This success emboldened Marius.

"On the front?" he asked.

"Parbleu!" said the porter, "the house is only built on the street."

"And what is that gentleman's business?" began Marius again.

"He is a gentleman of property, sir. A very kind man who does good to the unfortunate, though not rich himself."

"What is his name?" resumed Marius.

The porter raised his head and said:—

"Are you a police spy, sir?"

Marius went off quite abashed, but delighted. He was getting on.

"Good," thought he, "I know that her name is Ursule, that she is the daughter of a gentleman who lives on his income, and that she lives there, on the third floor, in the Rue de l'Ouest."

On the following day, M. Leblanc and his daughter made only a very brief stay in the Luxembourg; they went away while it was still broad daylight. Marius followed them to the Rue de l'Ouest, as he had taken up the habit of doing. On arriving at the carriage entrance M. Leblanc made his daughter pass in first, then paused, before crossing the threshold, and stared intently at Marius.

On the next day they did not come to the Luxembourg. Marius waited for them all day in vain.

At nightfall, he went to the Rue de l'Ouest, and saw a light in the windows of the third story.

He walked about beneath the windows until the light was extinguished.

The next day, no one at the Luxembourg. Marius waited all day, then went and did sentinel duty under their windows. This carried him on to ten o'clock in the evening.

His dinner took care of itself. Fever nourishes the sick man, and love the lover.

He spent a week in this manner. M. Leblanc no longer appeared at the Luxembourg.

Marius indulged in melancholy conjectures; he dared not watch the porte-cochère during the day; he contented himself with going at night to gaze upon the red light of the windows. At times he saw shadows flit across them, and his heart began to beat.

On the eighth day, when he arrived under the windows, there was no light in them.

"Hello!" he said, "the lamp is not lighted yet. But it is dark. Can they have gone out?" He waited until ten o'clock. Until midnight. Until one in the morning. Not a light appeared in the windows of the third story, and no one entered the house.

He went away in a very gloomy frame of mind.

On the morrow,—for he only existed from morrow to morrow, there was, so to speak, no to-day for him,—on the morrow, he found no one at the Luxembourg; he had expected this. At dusk, he went to the house.

No light in the windows; the shades were drawn; the third floor was totally dark.

Marius rapped at the porte-cochère, entered, and said to the porter:—

"The gentleman on the third floor?"

"Has moved away," replied the porter.

Marius reeled and said feebly:—

"How long ago?"

"Yesterday."

"Where is he living now?"

"I don't know anything about it."

"So he has not left his new address?"

"No."

And the porter, raising his eyes, recognized Marius.

"Come! So it's you!" said he; "but you are decidedly a spy then?"

BOOK SEVENTH
PATRON MINETTE

I

MINES AND MINERS

H uman societies all have what is called in theatrical parlance, *a third lower floor*. The social soil is everywhere undermined, sometimes for good, sometimes for evil. These works are superposed one upon the other. There are superior mines and inferior mines. There is a top and a bottom in this obscure sub-soil, which sometimes gives way beneath civilization, and which our indifference and heedlessness trample under foot. The Encyclopedia, in the last century, was a mine that was almost open to the sky. The shades, those sombre hatchers of primitive Christianity, only awaited an opportunity to bring about an explosion under the Cæsars and to inundate the human race with light. For in the sacred shadows there lies latent light. Volcanoes are full of a shadow that is capable of flashing forth. Every form begins by being night. The catacombs, in which the first mass was said, were not alone the cellar of Rome, they were the vaults of the world.

Beneath the social construction, that complicated marvel of a structure, there are excavations of all sorts. There is the religious mine, the philosophical mine, the economic mine, the revolutionary mine. Such and such a pick-axe with the idea, such a pick with ciphers. Such another with wrath. People hail and answer each other from one catacomb to another. Utopias travel about underground, in the pipes. There they branch out in every direction. They sometimes meet, and fraternize there. Jean-Jacques lends his pick to Diogenes, who lends him his lantern. Sometimes they enter into combat there. Calvin seizes Socinius by the hair. But nothing arrests nor interrupts the tension of all these energies toward the goal, and the vast, simultaneous activity, which goes and comes, mounts, descends, and mounts again in these obscurities, and which immense unknown swarming slowly transforms the top and the bottom and the inside and the outside. Society hardly even suspects this digging which leaves its surface intact and changes its bowels. There are as many different subterranean stages as there are varying works, as there are extractions. What emerges from these deep excavations? The future.

The deeper one goes, the more mysterious are the toilers. The work is good, up to a degree which the social philosophies are able to recognize;

beyond that degree it is doubtful and mixed; lower down, it becomes terrible. At a certain depth, the excavations are no longer penetrable by the spirit of civilization, the limit breathable by man has been passed; a beginning of monsters is possible.

The descending scale is a strange one; and each one of the rungs of this ladder corresponds to a stage where philosophy can find foothold, and where one encounters one of these workmen, sometimes divine, sometimes misshapen. Below John Huss, there is Luther; below Luther, there is Descartes; below Descartes, there is Voltaire; below Voltaire, there is Condorcet; below Condorcet, there is Robespierre; below Robespierre, there is Marat; below Marat there is Babeuf. And so it goes on. Lower down, confusedly, at the limit which separates the indistinct from the invisible, one perceives other gloomy men, who perhaps do not exist as yet. The men of yesterday are spectres; those of to-morrow are forms. The eye of the spirit distinguishes them but obscurely. The embryonic work of the future is one of the visions of philosophy.

A world in limbo, in the state of fœtus, what an unheard-of spectre!

Saint-Simon, Owen, Fourier, are there also, in lateral galleries.

Surely, although a divine and invisible chain unknown to themselves, binds together all these subterranean pioneers who, almost always, think themselves isolated, and who are not so, their works vary greatly, and the light of some contrasts with the blaze of others. The first are paradisiacal, the last are tragic. Nevertheless, whatever may be the contrast, all these toilers, from the highest to the most nocturnal, from the wisest to the most foolish, possess one likeness, and this is it: disinterestedness. Marat forgets himself like Jesus. They throw themselves on one side, they omit themselves, they think not of themselves. They have a glance, and that glance seeks the absolute. The first has the whole heavens in his eyes; the last, enigmatical though he may be, has still, beneath his eyelids, the pale beam of the infinite. Venerate the man, whoever he may be, who has this sign—the starry eye.

The shadowy eye is the other sign.

With it, evil commences. Reflect and tremble in the presence of any one who has no glance at all. The social order has its black miners.

There is a point where depth is tantamount to burial, and where light becomes extinct.

Below all these mines which we have just mentioned, below all these galleries, below this whole immense, subterranean, venous system of progress and utopia, much further on in the earth, much lower than Marat, lower than Babeuf, lower, much lower, and without any connection with the upper levels, there lies the last mine. A formidable spot. This is what we have designated as the *le troisième dessous*. It is the grave of shadows. It is the cellar of the blind. *Inferi*.

This communicates with the abyss.

II

The Lowest Depths

There disinterestedness vanishes. The demon is vaguely outlined; each one is for himself. The *I* in the eyes howls, seeks, fumbles, and gnaws. The social Ugolino is in this gulf.

The wild spectres who roam in this grave, almost beasts, almost phantoms, are not occupied with universal progress; they are ignorant both of the idea and of the word; they take no thought for anything but the satisfaction of their individual desires. They are almost unconscious, and there exists within them a sort of terrible obliteration. They have two mothers, both step-mothers, ignorance and misery. They have a guide, necessity; and for all forms of satisfaction, appetite. They are brutally voracious, that is to say, ferocious, not after the fashion of the tyrant, but after the fashion of the tiger. From suffering these spectres pass to crime; fatal affiliation, dizzy creation, logic of darkness. That which crawls in the social third lower level is no longer complaint stifled by the absolute; it is the protest of matter, Man there becomes a dragon. To be hungry, to be thirsty—that is the point of departure; to be Satan—that is the point reached. From that vault Lacenaire emerges.

We have just seen, in Book Fourth, one of the compartments of the upper mine, of the great political, revolutionary, and philosophical excavation. There, as we have just said, all is pure, noble, dignified, honest. There, assuredly, one might be misled; but error is worthy of veneration there, so thoroughly does it imply heroism. The work there effected, taken as a whole has a name: Progress.

The moment has now come when we must take a look at other depths, hideous depths. There exists beneath society, we insist upon this point, and there will exist, until that day when ignorance shall be dissipated, the great cavern of evil.

This cavern is below all, and is the foe of all. It is hatred, without exception. This cavern knows no philosophers; its dagger has never cut a pen. Its blackness has no connection with the sublime blackness of the inkstand. Never have the fingers of night which contract beneath this stifling ceiling, turned the leaves of a book nor unfolded a newspaper. Babeuf is a speculator to Cartouche; Marat is an aristocrat to Schinderhannes. This cavern has for its object the destruction of everything.

Of everything. Including the upper superior mines, which it execrates. It not only undermines, in its hideous swarming, the actual social order; it undermines philosophy, it undermines human thought, it undermines civilization, it undermines revolution, it undermines progress. Its name is simply theft, prostitution, murder, assassination. It is darkness, and it desires chaos. Its vault is formed of ignorance.

All the others, those above it, have but one object—to suppress it. It is to this point that philosophy and progress tend, with all their organs simultaneously, by their amelioration of the real, as well as by their contemplation of the absolute. Destroy the cavern Ignorance and you destroy the lair Crime.

Let us condense, in a few words, a part of what we have just written. The only social peril is darkness.

Humanity is identity. All men are made of the same clay. There is no difference, here below, at least, in predestination. The same shadow in front, the same flesh in the present, the same ashes afterwards. But ignorance, mingled with the human paste, blackens it. This incurable blackness takes possession of the interior of a man and is there converted into evil.

III

Babet, Gueulemer, Claquesous,
and Montparnasse

A quartette of ruffians, Claquesous, Gueulemer, Babet, and Montparnasse governed the third lower floor of Paris, from 1830 to 1835.

Gueulemer was a Hercules of no defined position. For his lair he had the sewer of the Arche-Marion. He was six feet high, his pectoral muscles were of marble, his biceps of brass, his breath was that of a cavern, his torso that of a colossus, his head that of a bird. One thought one beheld the Farnese Hercules clad in duck trousers and a cotton velvet waistcoat. Gueulemer, built after this sculptural fashion, might have subdued monsters; he had found it more expeditious to be one. A low brow, large temples, less than forty years of age, but with crow's-feet, harsh, short hair, cheeks like a brush, a beard like that of a wild boar; the reader can see the man before him. His muscles called for work, his stupidity would have none of it. He was a great, idle force. He was an assassin through coolness. He was thought to be a creole. He had, probably, somewhat to do with Marshal Brune, having been a porter at Avignon in 1815. After this stage, he had turned ruffian.

The diaphaneity of Babet contrasted with the grossness of Gueulemer. Babet was thin and learned. He was transparent but impenetrable. Daylight was visible through his bones, but nothing through his eyes. He declared that he was a chemist. He had been a jack of all trades. He had played in vaudeville at Saint-Mihiel. He was a man of purpose, a fine talker, who underlined his smiles and accentuated his gestures. His occupation consisted in selling, in the open air, plaster busts and portraits of "the head of the State." In addition to this, he extracted teeth. He had exhibited phenomena at fairs, and he had owned a booth with a trumpet and this poster: "Babet, Dental Artist, Member of the Academies, makes physical experiments on metals and metalloids, extracts teeth, undertakes stumps abandoned by his brother practitioners. Price: one tooth, one franc, fifty centimes; two teeth, two francs; three teeth, two francs, fifty. Take advantage of this opportunity." This *Take advantage of this opportunity* meant: Have as many teeth extracted as possible. He had been married and had had children. He did not know what had become of his wife and children. He had lost them as one loses his handkerchief. Babet read the papers, a striking exception in the world to which he belonged. One day, at the period when he had his family with him in his booth on wheels, he had read in the *Messager*, that a woman had just given birth to a child, who was doing well, and had a calf's muzzle, and he exclaimed: "There's a fortune! my wife has not the wit to present me with a child like that!"

Later on he had abandoned everything, in order to "undertake Paris." This was his expression.

Who was Claquesous? He was night. He waited until the sky was daubed with black, before he showed himself. At nightfall he emerged from the hole whither he returned before daylight. Where was this hole? No one knew. He only addressed his accomplices in the most absolute darkness, and with his back turned to them. Was his name Claquesous? Certainly not. If a candle was brought, he put on a mask. He was a ventriloquist. Babet said: "Claquesous is a nocturne for two voices." Claquesous was vague, terrible, and a roamer. No one was sure whether he had a name, Claquesous being a sobriquet; none was sure that he had a voice, as his stomach spoke more frequently than his voice; no one was sure that he had a face, as he was never seen without his mask. He disappeared as though he had vanished into thin air; when he appeared, it was as though he sprang from the earth.

A lugubrious being was Montparnasse. Montparnasse was a child; less than twenty years of age, with a handsome face, lips like cherries, charming black hair, the brilliant light of springtime in his eyes; he had all vices and aspired to all crimes.

The digestion of evil aroused in him an appetite for worse. It was the street boy turned pickpocket, and a pickpocket turned garroter. He was genteel, effeminate, graceful, robust, sluggish, ferocious. The rim of his hat was curled up on the left side, in order to make room for a tuft of hair, after the style of 1829. He lived by robbery with violence. His coat was of the best cut, but threadbare. Montparnasse was a fashion-plate in misery and given to the commission of murders. The cause of all this youth's crimes was the desire to be well-dressed. The first grisette who had said to him: "You are handsome!" had cast the stain of darkness into his heart, and had made a Cain of this Abel. Finding that he was handsome, he desired to be elegant: now, the height of elegance is idleness; idleness in a poor man means crime. Few prowlers were so dreaded as Montparnasse. At eighteen, he had already numerous corpses in his past. More than one passer-by lay with outstretched arms in the presence of this wretch, with his face in a pool of blood. Curled, pomaded, with laced waist, the hips of a woman, the bust of a Prussian officer, the murmur of admiration from the boulevard wenches surrounding him, his cravat knowingly tied, a bludgeon in his pocket, a flower in his buttonhole; such was this dandy of the sepulchre.

IV

COMPOSITION OF THE TROUPE

These four ruffians formed a sort of Proteus, winding like a serpent among the police, and striving to escape Vidocq's indiscreet glances "under divers forms, tree, flame, fountain," lending each other their names and their traps, hiding in their own shadows, boxes with secret compartments and refuges for each other, stripping off their personalities, as one removes his false nose at a masked ball, sometimes simplifying matters to the point of consisting of but one individual, sometimes multiplying themselves to such a point that Coco-Latour himself took them for a whole throng.

These four men were not four men; they were a sort of mysterious robber with four heads, operating on a grand scale on Paris; they were that monstrous polyp of evil, which inhabits the crypt of society.

Thanks to their ramifications, and to the network underlying their relations, Babet, Gueulemer, Claquesous, and Montparnasse were charged with the general enterprise of the ambushes of the department of the Seine. The inventors of ideas of that nature, men with nocturnal imaginations, applied to them to have their ideas executed. They furnished the canvas to the four rascals, and the latter undertook the preparation of the scenery. They labored at the stage setting. They were always in a condition to lend a force proportioned and suitable to all crimes which demanded a lift of the shoulder, and which were sufficiently lucrative. When a crime was in quest of arms, they under-let their accomplices. They kept a troupe of actors of the shadows at the disposition of all underground tragedies.

They were in the habit of assembling at nightfall, the hour when they woke up, on the plains which adjoin the Salpêtrière. There they held their conferences. They had twelve black hours before them; they regulated their employment accordingly.

Patron-Minette,—such was the name which was bestowed in the subterranean circulation on the association of these four men. In the fantastic, ancient, popular parlance, which is vanishing day by day, *Patron-Minette* signifies the morning, the same as *entre chien et loup*—between dog and wolf—signifies the evening. This appellation, *Patron-Minette*, was probably derived from the hour at which their work ended, the dawn being the vanishing moment for phantoms and for the separation of ruffians. These four men were known under this title. When the President of the Assizes visited Lacenaire in his prison, and questioned him concerning a misdeed which Lacenaire denied, "Who did it?" demanded the President. Lacenaire made this response, enigmatical so far as the magistrate was concerned, but clear to the police: "Perhaps it was Patron-Minette."

A piece can sometimes be divined on the enunciation of the personages; in the same manner a band can almost be judged from the list of ruffians composing it. Here are the appellations to which the principal members of Patron-Minette answered,—for the names have survived in special memoirs.

Panchaud, alias Printanier, alias Bigrenaille.

Brujon. (There was a Brujon dynasty; we cannot refrain from interpolating this word.)

Boulatruelle, the road-mender already introduced.

Laveuve.

Finistère.

Homère-Hogu, a negro.

Mardisoir. (Tuesday evening.)

Dépêche. (Make haste.)

Fauntleroy, alias Bouquetière (the Flower Girl).

Glorieux, a discharged convict.

Barrecarrosse (Stop-carriage), called Monsieur Dupont.

L'Esplanade-du-Sud.

Poussagrive.

Carmagnolet.

Kruideniers, called Bizarro.

Mangedentelle. (Lace-eater.)

Les-pieds-en-l'Air. (Feet in the air.)

Demi-Liard, called Deux-Milliards.

Etc., etc.

We pass over some, and not the worst of them. These names have faces attached. They do not express merely beings, but species. Each one of these names corresponds to a variety of those misshapen fungi from the under side of civilization.

Those beings, who were not very lavish with their countenances, were not among the men whom one sees passing along the streets. Fatigued by the wild nights which they passed, they went off by day to sleep, sometimes in the lime-kilns, sometimes in the abandoned quarries of Montmatre or Montrouge, sometimes in the sewers. They ran to earth.

What became of these men? They still exist. They have always existed. Horace speaks of them: *Ambubaiarum collegia, pharmacopolæ, mendici, mimæ*; and so long as society remains what it is, they will remain what they are. Beneath the obscure roof of their cavern, they are continually born again from the social ooze. They return, spectres, but always identical; only, they no longer bear the same names and they are no longer in the same skins. The individuals extirpated, the tribe subsists.

They always have the same faculties. From the vagrant to the tramp, the race is maintained in its purity. They divine purses in pockets, they scent out watches in fobs. Gold and silver possess an odor for them. There exist ingenuous bourgeois, of whom it might be said, that they have a "stealable" air. These men patiently pursue these bourgeois. They experience the quivers of a spider at the passage of a stranger or of a man from the country.

These men are terrible, when one encounters them, or catches a glimpse of them, towards midnight, on a deserted boulevard. They do not seem to be men but forms composed of living mists; one would say that they habitually constitute one mass with the shadows, that they are in no wise distinct from them, that they possess no other soul than the darkness, and that it is only momentarily and for the purpose of living for a few minutes a monstrous life, that they have separated from the night.

What is necessary to cause these spectres to vanish? Light. Light in floods. Not a single bat can resist the dawn. Light up society from below.

BOOK EIGHTH
THE WICKED POOR MAN

I

Marius, While Seeking a Girl in a Bonnet, Encounters a Man in a Cap

Summer passed, then the autumn; winter came. Neither M. Leblanc nor the young girl had again set foot in the Luxembourg garden. Thenceforth, Marius had but one thought,—to gaze once more on that sweet and adorable face. He sought constantly, he sought everywhere; he found nothing. He was no longer Marius, the enthusiastic dreamer, the firm, resolute, ardent man, the bold defier of fate, the brain which erected future on future, the young spirit encumbered with plans, with projects, with pride, with ideas and wishes; he was a lost dog. He fell into a black melancholy. All was over. Work disgusted him, walking tired him. Vast nature, formerly so filled with forms, lights, voices, counsels, perspectives, horizons, teachings, now lay empty before him. It seemed to him that everything had disappeared.

He thought incessantly, for he could not do otherwise; but he no longer took pleasure in his thoughts. To everything that they proposed to him in a whisper, he replied in his darkness: "What is the use?"

He heaped a hundred reproaches on himself. "Why did I follow her? I was so happy at the mere sight of her! She looked at me; was not that immense? She had the air of loving me. Was not that everything? I wished to have, what? There was nothing after that. I have been absurd. It is my own fault," etc., etc. Courfeyrac, to whom he confided nothing,—it was his nature,—but who made some little guess at everything,—that was his nature,—had begun by congratulating him on being in love, though he was amazed at it; then, seeing Marius fall into this melancholy state, he ended by saying to him: "I see that you have been simply an animal. Here, come to the Chaumière."

Once, having confidence in a fine September sun, Marius had allowed himself to be taken to the ball at Sceaux by Courfeyrac, Bossuet, and Grantaire, hoping, what a dream! that he might, perhaps, find her there. Of course he did not see the one he sought.—"But this is the place, all the same, where all lost women are found," grumbled Grantaire in an aside. Marius left his friends at the ball and returned home on foot, alone, through the night, weary, feverish, with sad and troubled eyes, stunned by the noise and dust of the merry wagons filled with singing creatures on their way home from the feast, which passed close to him, as he, in his discouragement, breathed in the acrid scent of the walnut-trees, along the road, in order to refresh his head.

He took to living more and more alone, utterly overwhelmed, wholly given up to his inward anguish, going and coming in his pain like the wolf in the trap, seeking the absent one everywhere, stupefied by love.

On another occasion, he had an encounter which produced on him a singular effect. He met, in the narrow streets in the vicinity of the Boulevard des Invalides, a man dressed like a workingman and wearing a cap with a long visor, which allowed a glimpse of locks of very white hair. Marius was struck with the beauty of this white hair, and scrutinized the man, who was walking slowly and as though absorbed in painful meditation. Strange to say, he thought that he recognized M. Leblanc. The hair was the same, also the profile, so far as the cap permitted a view of it, the mien identical, only more depressed. But why these workingman's clothes? What was the meaning of this? What signified that disguise? Marius was greatly astonished. When he recovered himself, his first impulse was to follow the man; who knows whether he did not hold at last the clue which he was seeking? In any case, he must see the man near at hand, and clear up the mystery. But the idea occurred to him too late, the man was no longer there. He had turned into some little side street, and Marius could not find him. This encounter occupied his mind for three days and then was effaced. "After all," he said to himself, "it was probably only a resemblance."

II

Treasure Trove

Marius had not left the Gorbeau house. He paid no attention to any one there.

At that epoch, to tell the truth, there were no other inhabitants in the house, except himself and those Jondrettes whose rent he had once paid, without, moreover, ever having spoken to either father, mother, or daughters. The other lodgers had moved away or had died, or had been turned out in default of payment.

One day during that winter, the sun had shown itself a little in the afternoon, but it was the 2d of February, that ancient Candlemas day whose treacherous sun, the precursor of a six weeks' cold spell, inspired Mathieu Laensberg with these two lines, which have with justice remained classic:—

> *Qu'il luise ou qu'il luiserne,*
> *L'ours rentre dans en sa caverne.*

Marius had just emerged from his: night was falling. It was the hour for his dinner; for he had been obliged to take to dining again, alas! oh, infirmities of ideal passions!

He had just crossed his threshold, where Ma'am Bougon was sweeping at the moment, as she uttered this memorable monologue:—

"What is there that is cheap now? Everything is dear. There is nothing in the world that is cheap except trouble; you can get that for nothing, the trouble of the world!"

Marius slowly ascended the boulevard towards the barrier, in order to reach the Rue Saint-Jacques. He was walking along with drooping head.

All at once, he felt some one elbow him in the dusk; he wheeled round, and saw two young girls clad in rags, the one tall and slim, the other a little shorter, who were passing rapidly, all out of breath, in terror, and with the appearance of fleeing; they had been coming to meet him, had not seen him, and had jostled him as they passed. Through the twilight, Marius could distinguish their livid faces, their wild heads, their dishevelled hair, their hideous bonnets, their ragged petticoats, and their bare feet. They were talking as they ran. The taller said in a very low voice:—

"The bobbies have come. They came near nabbing me at the half-circle." The other answered: "I saw them. I bolted, bolted, bolted!"

Through this repulsive slang, Marius understood that gendarmes or the police had come near apprehending these two children, and that the latter had escaped.

They plunged among the trees of the boulevard behind him, and there created, for a few minutes, in the gloom, a sort of vague white spot, then disappeared.

Marius had halted for a moment.

He was about to pursue his way, when his eye lighted on a little grayish package lying on the ground at his feet. He stooped and picked it up. It was a sort of envelope which appeared to contain papers.

"Good," he said to himself, "those unhappy girls dropped it."

He retraced his steps, he called, he did not find them; he reflected that they must already be far away, put the package in his pocket, and went off to dine.

On the way, he saw in an alley of the Rue Mouffetard, a child's coffin, covered with a black cloth resting on three chairs, and illuminated by a candle. The two girls of the twilight recurred to his mind.

"Poor mothers!" he thought. "There is one thing sadder than to see one's children die; it is to see them leading an evil life."

Then those shadows which had varied his melancholy vanished from his thoughts, and he fell back once more into his habitual preoccupations. He fell to thinking once more of his six months of love and happiness in the open air and the broad daylight, beneath the beautiful trees of Luxembourg.

"How gloomy my life has become!" he said to himself. "Young girls are always appearing to me, only formerly they were angels and now they are ghouls."

III

Quadrifrons

That evening, as he was undressing preparatory to going to bed, his hand came in contact, in the pocket of his coat, with the packet which he had picked up on the boulevard. He had forgotten it. He thought that it would be well to open it, and that this package might possibly contain the address of the young girls, if it really belonged to them, and, in any case, the information necessary to a restitution to the person who had lost it.

He opened the envelope.

It was not sealed and contained four letters, also unsealed.

They bore addresses.

All four exhaled a horrible odor of tobacco.

The first was addressed: *"To Madame, Madame la Marquise de Grucheray, the place opposite the Chamber of Deputies, No.—"*

Marius said to himself, that he should probably find in it the information which he sought, and that, moreover, the letter being open, it was probable that it could be read without impropriety.

It was conceived as follows:—

Madame la Marquise

The virtue of clemency and piety is that which most closely unites sosiety. Turn your Christian spirit and cast a look of compassion on this unfortunate Spanish victim of loyalty and attachment to the sacred cause of legitimacy, who has given with his blood, consecrated his fortune, evverything, to defend that cause, and to-day finds himself in the greatest missery. He doubts not that your honorable person will grant succor to preserve an existence exteremely painful for a military man of education and honor full of wounds, counts in advance on the humanity which animates you and on the interest which Madame la Marquise bears to a nation so unfortunate. Their prayer will not be in vain, and their gratitude will preserve theirs charming souvenir.

My respectful sentiments, with which I have the honor
to be Madame, Don Alvarès, Spanish Captain of Cavalry, a
royalist who has take refuge in France, who finds himself on
travells for his country, and the resources are lacking him to
continue his travells.

No address was joined to the signature. Marius hoped to find the
address in the second letter, whose superscription read: *À Madame,
Madame la Comtesse de Montvernet, Rue Cassette, No. 9*. This is what
Marius read in it:—

Madame la Comtesse
    It is an unhappy mother of a family of six children the
last of which is only eight months old. I sick since my last
confinement, abandoned by my husband five months ago,
haveing no resources in the world the most frightful indigance.
    In the hope of Madame la Comtesse, she has the honor
to be,

Madame, with profound respect,
Mistress Balizard

Marius turned to the third letter, which was a petition like the
preceding; he read:—

Monsieur Pabourgeot, Elector, wholesale stocking merchant,
Rue Saint-Denis on the corner of the Rue aux Fers.
    I permit myself to address you this letter to beg you to
grant me the pretious favor of your simpaties and to interest
yourself in a man of letters who has just sent a drama to the
Théâtre-Français. The subject is historical, and the action takes
place in Auvergne in the time of the Empire; the style, I think,
is natural, laconic, and may have some merit. There are
couplets to be sung in four places. The comic, the serious, the
unexpected, are mingled in a variety of characters, and a tinge
of romanticism lightly spread through all the intrigue which
proceeds misteriously, and ends, after striking altarations, in
the midst of many beautiful strokes of brilliant scenes.
    My principal object is to satisfi the desire which
progressively animates the man of our century, that is to say,

the fashion, that capritious and bizarre weathervane which changes at almost every new wind.

In spite of these qualities I have reason to fear that jealousy, the egotism of priviliged authors, may obtaine my exclusion from the theatre, for I am not ignorant of the mortifications with which newcomers are treated.

Monsiuer Pabourgeot, your just reputation as an enlightened protector of men of litters emboldens me to send you my daughter who will explain our indigant situation to you, lacking bread and fire in this wynter season. When I say to you that I beg you to accept the dedication of my drama which I desire to make to you and of all those that I shall make, is to prove to you how great is my ambition to have the honor of sheltering myself under your protection, and of adorning my writings with your name. If you deign to honor me with the most modest offering, I shall immediately occupy myself in making a piesse of verse to pay you my tribute of gratitude. Which I shall endeavor to render this piesse as perfect as possible, will be sent to you before it is inserted at the beginning of the drama and delivered on the stage.

To Monsieur and Madame Pabourgeot,

My most respectful complements,
Genflot, man of letters

P. S. Even if it is only forty sous.

Excuse me for sending my daughter and not presenting myself, but sad motives connected with the toilet do not permit me, alas! to go out.

Finally, Marius opened the fourth letter. The address ran: *To the benevolent Gentleman of the church of Saint-Jacques-du-haut-Pas*. It contained the following lines:—

Benevolent Man: If you deign to accompany my daughter, you will behold a misserable calamity, and I will show you my certificates.

At the aspect of these writings your generous soul will be moved with a sentiment of obvious benevolence, for true philosophers always feel lively emotions.

Admit, compassionate man, that it is necessary to suffer the most cruel need, and that it is very painful, for the sake of obtaining a little relief, to get oneself attested by the authorities as though one were not free to suffer and to die of inanition while waiting to have our misery relieved. Destinies are very fatal for several and too prodigal or too protecting for others.

I await your presence or your offering, if you deign to make one, and I beseech you to accept the respectful sentiments with which I have the honor to be, truly magnanimous man,

your very humble and very obedient servant,

P. Fabantou, dramatic artist

After perusing these four letters, Marius did not find himself much further advanced than before.

In the first place, not one of the signers gave his address.

Then, they seemed to come from four different individuals, Don Alvarès, Mistress Balizard, the poet Genflot, and dramatic artist Fabantou; but the singular thing about these letters was, that all four were written by the same hand.

What conclusion was to be drawn from this, except that they all come from the same person?

Moreover, and this rendered the conjecture all the more probable, the coarse and yellow paper was the same in all four, the odor of tobacco was the same, and, although an attempt had been made to vary the style, the same orthographical faults were reproduced with the greatest tranquillity, and the man of letters Genflot was no more exempt from them than the Spanish captain.

It was waste of trouble to try to solve this petty mystery. Had it not been a chance find, it would have borne the air of a mystification. Marius was too melancholy to take even a chance pleasantry well, and to lend himself to a game which the pavement of the street seemed desirous of playing with him. It seemed to him that he was playing the part of the blind man in blind man's buff between the four letters, and that they were making sport of him.

Nothing, however, indicated that these letters belonged to the two young girls whom Marius had met on the boulevard. After all, they were evidently papers of no value. Marius replaced them in their envelope, flung the whole into a corner and went to bed. About seven o'clock in the morning, he had just risen and breakfasted, and was trying to settle down to work, when there came a soft knock at his door.

As he owned nothing, he never locked his door, unless occasionally, though very rarely, when he was engaged in some pressing work. Even when absent he left his key in the lock. "You will be robbed," said Ma'am Bougon. "Of what?" said Marius. The truth is, however, that he had, one day, been robbed of an old pair of boots, to the great triumph of Ma'am Bougon.

There came a second knock, as gentle as the first.

"Come in," said Marius.

The door opened.

"What do you want, Ma'am Bougon?" asked Marius, without raising his eyes from the books and manuscripts on his table.

A voice which did not belong to Ma'am Bougon replied:—

"Excuse me, sir—"

It was a dull, broken, hoarse, strangled voice, the voice of an old man, roughened with brandy and liquor.

Marius turned round hastily, and beheld a young girl.

IV

A Rose in Misery

A very young girl was standing in the half-open door. The dormer window of the garret, through which the light fell, was precisely opposite the door, and illuminated the figure with a wan light. She was a frail, emaciated, slender creature; there was nothing but a chemise and a petticoat upon that chilled and shivering nakedness. Her girdle was a string, her head ribbon a string, her pointed shoulders emerged from her chemise, a blond and lymphatic pallor, earth-colored collar-bones, red hands, a half-open and degraded mouth, missing teeth, dull, bold, base eyes; she had the form of a young girl who has missed her youth, and the look of a corrupt old woman; fifty years mingled with fifteen; one of those beings which are both feeble and horrible, and which cause those to shudder whom they do not cause to weep.

Marius had risen, and was staring in a sort of stupor at this being, who was almost like the forms of the shadows which traverse dreams.

The most heart-breaking thing of all was, that this young girl had not come into the world to be homely. In her early childhood she must even have been pretty. The grace of her age was still struggling against the hideous, premature decrepitude of debauchery and poverty. The remains of beauty were dying away in that face of sixteen, like the pale sunlight which is extinguished under hideous clouds at dawn on a winter's day.

That face was not wholly unknown to Marius. He thought he remembered having seen it somewhere.

"What do you wish, Mademoiselle?" he asked.

The young girl replied in her voice of a drunken convict:—

"Here is a letter for you, Monsieur Marius."

She called Marius by his name; he could not doubt that he was the person whom she wanted; but who was this girl? How did she know his name?

Without waiting for him to tell her to advance, she entered. She entered resolutely, staring, with a sort of assurance that made the heart bleed, at the whole room and the unmade bed. Her feet were bare.

Large holes in her petticoat permitted glimpses of her long legs and her thin knees. She was shivering.

She held a letter in her hand, which she presented to Marius.

Marius, as he opened the letter, noticed that the enormous wafer which sealed it was still moist. The message could not have come from a distance. He read:—

My amiable neighbor, young man: I have learned of your goodness to me, that you paid my rent six months ago. I bless you, young man. My eldest daughter will tell you that we have been without a morsel of bread for two days, four persons and my spouse ill. If I am not deseaved in my opinion, I think I may hope that your generous heart will melt at this statement and the desire will subjugate you to be propitious to me by daigning to lavish on me a slight favor.

I am with the distinguished consideration which is due to the benefactors of humanity,—

Jondrette

P.S. My eldest daughter will await your orders, dear Monsieur Marius.

This letter, coming in the very midst of the mysterious adventure which had occupied Marius' thoughts ever since the preceding evening, was like a candle in a cellar. All was suddenly illuminated.

This letter came from the same place as the other four. There was the same writing, the same style, the same orthography, the same paper, the same odor of tobacco.

There were five missives, five histories, five signatures, and a single signer. The Spanish Captain Don Alvarès, the unhappy Mistress Balizard, the dramatic poet Genflot, the old comedian Fabantou, were all four named Jondrette, if, indeed, Jondrette himself were named Jondrette.

Marius had lived in the house for a tolerably long time, and he had had, as we have said, but very rare occasion to see, to even catch a glimpse of, his extremely mean neighbors. His mind was elsewhere, and where the mind is, there the eyes are also. He had been obliged more than once to pass the Jondrettes in the corridor or on the stairs; but they were mere forms to him; he had paid so little heed to them, that, on the preceding evening, he had jostled the Jondrette girls on the boulevard, without recognizing them, for it had evidently been they, and it was with great difficulty that the one who had just entered his room had awakened in him, in spite of disgust and pity, a vague recollection of having met her elsewhere.

Now he saw everything clearly. He understood that his neighbor Jondrette, in his distress, exercised the industry of speculating on the charity of benevolent persons, that he procured addresses, and that he wrote under feigned names to people whom he judged to be wealthy and compassionate, letters which his daughters delivered at their risk and peril, for this father had come to such a pass, that he risked his daughters; he was playing a game with fate, and he used them as the stake. Marius understood that probably, judging from their flight on the evening before, from their breathless condition, from their terror and from the words of slang which he had overheard, these unfortunate creatures were plying some inexplicably sad profession, and that the result of the whole was, in the midst of human society, as it is now constituted, two miserable beings who were neither girls nor women, a species of impure and innocent monsters produced by misery.

Sad creatures, without name, or sex, or age, to whom neither good nor evil were any longer possible, and who, on emerging from childhood, have already nothing in this world, neither liberty, nor virtue, nor responsibility. Souls which blossomed out yesterday, and are faded to-day, like those flowers let fall in the streets, which are soiled with every sort of mire, while waiting for some wheel to crush them. Nevertheless, while Marius bent a pained and astonished gaze on her, the young girl was wandering back and forth in the garret with the audacity of a spectre. She kicked about, without troubling herself as to her nakedness. Occasionally her chemise, which was untied and torn, fell almost to her waist. She moved the chairs about, she disarranged the toilet articles which stood on the commode, she handled Marius' clothes, she rummaged about to see what there was in the corners.

"Hullo!" said she, "you have a mirror!"

And she hummed scraps of vaudevilles, as though she had been alone, frolicsome refrains which her hoarse and guttural voice rendered lugubrious.

An indescribable constraint, weariness, and humiliation were perceptible beneath this hardihood. Effrontery is a disgrace.

Nothing could be more melancholy than to see her sport about the room, and, so to speak, flit with the movements of a bird which is frightened by the daylight, or which has broken its wing. One felt that under other conditions of education and destiny, the gay and over-free mien of this young girl might have turned out sweet and charming. Never, even among animals, does the creature born to be a dove change into an osprey. That is only to be seen among men.

Marius reflected, and allowed her to have her way.

She approached the table.

"Ah!" said she, "books!"

A flash pierced her glassy eye. She resumed, and her accent expressed the happiness which she felt in boasting of something, to which no human creature is insensible:—

"I know how to read, I do!"

She eagerly seized a book which lay open on the table, and read with tolerable fluency:—

"—General Bauduin received orders to take the château of Hougomont which stands in the middle of the plain of Waterloo, with five battalions of his brigade."

She paused.

"Ah! Waterloo! I know about that. It was a battle long ago. My father was there. My father has served in the armies. We are fine Bonapartists in our house, that we are! Waterloo was against the English."

She laid down the book, caught up a pen, and exclaimed:—

"And I know how to write, too!"

She dipped her pen in the ink, and turning to Marius:—

"Do you want to see? Look here, I'm going to write a word to show you."

And before he had time to answer, she wrote on a sheet of white paper, which lay in the middle of the table: "The bobbies are here."

Then throwing down the pen:—

"There are no faults of orthography. You can look. We have received an education, my sister and I. We have not always been as we are now. We were not made—"

Here she paused, fixed her dull eyes on Marius, and burst out laughing, saying, with an intonation which contained every form of anguish, stifled by every form of cynicism:—

"Bah!"

And she began to hum these words to a gay air:—

"J'ai faim, mon père."	*I am hungry, father.*
Pas de fricot.	*I have no food.*
J'ai froid, ma mère.	*I am cold, mother.*
Pas de tricot.	*I have no clothes.*
Grelotte,	*Lolotte!*
Lolotte!	*Shiver,*
Sanglote,	*Sob,*
Jacquot!"	*Jacquot!"*

She had hardly finished this couplet, when she exclaimed:—

"Do you ever go to the play, Monsieur Marius? I do. I have a little brother who is a friend of the artists, and who gives me tickets sometimes. But I don't like the benches in the galleries. One is cramped and uncomfortable there. There are rough people there sometimes; and people who smell bad."

Then she scrutinized Marius, assumed a singular air and said:—

"Do you know, Mr. Marius, that you are a very handsome fellow?"

And at the same moment the same idea occurred to them both, and made her smile and him blush. She stepped up to him, and laid her hand on his shoulder: "You pay no heed to me, but I know you, Mr. Marius. I meet you here on the staircase, and then I often see you going to a person named Father Mabeuf who lives in the direction of Austerlitz, sometimes when I have been strolling in that quarter. It is very becoming to you to have your hair tumbled thus."

She tried to render her voice soft, but only succeeded in making it very deep. A portion of her words was lost in the transit from her larynx to her lips, as though on a piano where some notes are missing.

Marius had retreated gently.

"Mademoiselle," said he, with his cool gravity, "I have here a package which belongs to you, I think. Permit me to return it to you."

And he held out the envelope containing the four letters.

She clapped her hands and exclaimed:—

"We have been looking everywhere for that!"

Then she eagerly seized the package and opened the envelope, saying as she did so:—

"Dieu de Dieu! how my sister and I have hunted! And it was you who found it! On the boulevard, was it not? It must have been on the boulevard? You see, we let it fall when we were running. It was that brat of a sister of mine who was so stupid. When we got home, we could not find it anywhere. As we did not wish to be beaten, as that is useless, as that is entirely useless, as that is absolutely useless, we said that we had carried the letters to the proper persons, and that they had said to us: 'Nix.' So here they are, those poor letters! And how did you find out that they belonged to me? Ah! yes, the writing. So it was you that we jostled as we passed last night. We couldn't see. I said to my sister: 'Is it a gentleman?' My sister said to me: 'I think it is a gentleman.'"

In the meanwhile she had unfolded the petition addressed to "the benevolent gentleman of the church of Saint-Jacques-du-Haut-Pas."

"Here!" said she, "this is for that old fellow who goes to mass. By the way, this is his hour. I'll go and carry it to him. Perhaps he will give us something to breakfast on."

Then she began to laugh again, and added:—

"Do you know what it will mean if we get a breakfast today? It will mean that we shall have had our breakfast of the day before yesterday, our breakfast of yesterday, our dinner of to-day, and all that at once, and this morning. Come! Parbleu! if you are not satisfied, dogs, burst!"

This reminded Marius of the wretched girl's errand to himself. He fumbled in his waistcoat pocket, and found nothing there.

The young girl went on, and seemed to have no consciousness of Marius' presence.

"I often go off in the evening. Sometimes I don't come home again. Last winter, before we came here, we lived under the arches of the bridges. We huddled together to keep from freezing. My little sister cried. How melancholy the water is! When I thought of drowning myself, I said to myself: 'No, it's too cold.' I go out alone, whenever I choose, I sometimes sleep in the ditches. Do you know, at night, when I walk along the boulevard, I see the trees like forks, I see houses, all black and as big as Notre Dame, I fancy that the white walls are the river, I say to myself: 'Why, there's water there!' The stars are like the lamps in illuminations, one would say that they smoked and that the wind blew them out, I am bewildered, as though horses were breathing in my ears; although it is night, I hear hand-organs and spinning-machines, and I don't know what all. I think people are flinging stones at me, I flee without knowing whither, everything whirls and whirls. You feel very queer when you have had no food."

And then she stared at him with a bewildered air.

By dint of searching and ransacking his pockets, Marius had finally collected five francs sixteen sous. This was all he owned in the world for the moment. "At all events," he thought, "there is my dinner for to-day, and to-morrow we will see." He kept the sixteen sous, and handed the five francs to the young girl.

She seized the coin.

"Good!" said she, "the sun is shining!"

And, as though the sun had possessed the property of melting the avalanches of slang in her brain, she went on:—

"Five francs! the shiner! a monarch! in this hole! Ain't this fine! You're a jolly thief! I'm your humble servant! Bravo for the good fellows! Two days' wine! and meat! and stew! we'll have a royal feast! and a good fill!"

She pulled her chemise up on her shoulders, made a low bow to Marius, then a familiar sign with her hand, and went towards the door, saying:—

"Good morning, sir. It's all right. I'll go and find my old man."

As she passed, she caught sight of a dry crust of bread on the commode, which was moulding there amid the dust; she flung herself upon it and bit into it, muttering:—

"That's good! it's hard! it breaks my tooth!"

Then she departed.

V

A Providential Peep-Hole

Marius had lived for five years in poverty, in destitution, even in distress, but he now perceived that he had not known real misery. True misery he had but just had a view of. It was its spectre which had just passed before his eyes. In fact, he who has only beheld the misery of man has seen nothing; the misery of woman is what he must see; he who has seen only the misery of woman has seen nothing; he must see the misery of the child.

When a man has reached his last extremity, he has reached his last resources at the same time. Woe to the defenceless beings who surround him! Work, wages, bread, fire, courage, good will, all fail him simultaneously. The light of day seems extinguished without, the moral light within; in these shadows man encounters the feebleness of the woman and the child, and bends them violently to ignominy.

Then all horrors become possible. Despair is surrounded with fragile partitions which all open on either vice or crime.

Health, youth, honor, all the shy delicacies of the young body, the heart, virginity, modesty, that epidermis of the soul, are manipulated in sinister wise by that fumbling which seeks resources, which encounters opprobrium, and which accommodates itself to it. Fathers, mothers, children, brothers, sisters, men, women, daughters, adhere and become incorporated, almost like a mineral formation, in that dusky promiscuousness of sexes, relationships, ages, infamies, and innocences. They crouch, back to back, in a sort of hut of fate. They exchange woebegone glances. Oh, the unfortunate wretches! How pale they are! How cold they are! It seems as though they dwelt in a planet much further from the sun than ours.

This young girl was to Marius a sort of messenger from the realm of sad shadows. She revealed to him a hideous side of the night.

Marius almost reproached himself for the preoccupations of reverie and passion which had prevented his bestowing a glance on his neighbors up to that day. The payment of their rent had been a mechanical movement, which any one would have yielded to; but he, Marius, should have done better than that. What! only a wall separated him from those abandoned beings who lived gropingly in the dark outside the pale of the rest of the world, he was elbow to elbow with them, he was, in some sort, the last link of the human race which they touched, he heard them live, or rather, rattle in the death agony beside him, and he paid no heed to them! Every day, every instant, he heard them walking on the other side of the wall, he heard them go, and come, and speak, and he did not even lend an ear! And groans lay in those words, and he did not even listen to them, his thoughts were elsewhere, given up to dreams, to impossible radiances, to loves in the air, to follies; and all the while, human creatures, his brothers in Jesus Christ, his brothers in the people, were agonizing in vain beside him! He even formed a part of their misfortune, and he aggravated it. For if they had had another neighbor who was less chimerical and more attentive, any ordinary and charitable man, evidently their indigence would have been noticed, their signals of distress would have been perceived, and they would have been taken hold of and rescued! They appeared very corrupt and very depraved, no doubt, very vile, very odious even; but those who fall without becoming degraded are rare; besides, there is a point where the unfortunate and the infamous unite and are confounded in a single word, a fatal word, *les misérables*; whose fault is this? And then should not the charity be all the more profound, in proportion as the fall is great?

While reading himself this moral lesson, for there were occasions on which Marius, like all truly honest hearts, was his own pedagogue and scolded himself more than he deserved, he stared at the wall which separated him from the Jondrettes, as though he were able to make his gaze, full of pity, penetrate that partition and warm these wretched people. The wall was a thin layer of plaster upheld by lathes and beams, and, as the reader had just learned, it allowed the sound of voices and words to be clearly distinguished. Only a man as dreamy as Marius could have failed to perceive this long before. There was no paper pasted on the wall, either on the side of the Jondrettes or on that of Marius; the coarse construction was visible in its nakedness. Marius examined the partition, almost unconsciously; sometimes reverie examines, observes, and scrutinizes as thought would. All at once he sprang up; he had just perceived, near the top, close to the ceiling, a triangular hole, which resulted from the space between three lathes. The plaster which should have filled this cavity was missing, and by mounting on the commode, a view could be had through this aperture into the Jondrettes' attic.

Commiseration has, and should have, its curiosity. This aperture formed a sort of peep-hole. It is permissible to gaze at misfortune like a traitor in order to succor it.

"Let us get some little idea of what these people are like," thought Marius, "and in what condition they are."

He climbed upon the commode, put his eye to the crevice, and looked.

VI

The Wild Man in his Lair

Cities, like forests, have their caverns in which all the most wicked and formidable creatures which they contain conceal themselves. Only, in cities, that which thus conceals itself is ferocious, unclean, and petty, that is to say, ugly; in forests, that which conceals itself is ferocious, savage, and grand, that is to say, beautiful. Taking one lair with another, the beast's is preferable to the man's. Caverns are better than hovels.

What Marius now beheld was a hovel.

Marius was poor, and his chamber was poverty-stricken, but as his poverty was noble, his garret was neat. The den upon which his eye now rested was abject, dirty, fetid, pestiferous, mean, sordid. The only furniture consisted of a straw chair, an infirm table, some old bits of crockery, and in two of the corners, two indescribable pallets; all the light was furnished by a dormer window of four panes, draped with spiders' webs. Through this aperture there penetrated just enough light to make the face of a man appear like the face of a phantom. The walls had a leprous aspect, and were covered with seams and scars, like a visage disfigured by some horrible malady; a repulsive moisture exuded from them. Obscene sketches roughly sketched with charcoal could be distinguished upon them.

The chamber which Marius occupied had a dilapidated brick pavement; this one was neither tiled nor planked; its inhabitants stepped directly on the antique plaster of the hovel, which had grown black under the long-continued pressure of feet. Upon this uneven floor, where the dirt seemed to be fairly incrusted, and which possessed but one virginity, that of the broom, were capriciously grouped constellations of old shoes, socks, and repulsive rags; however, this room had a fireplace, so it was let for forty francs a year. There was every sort of thing in that fireplace, a brazier, a pot, broken boards, rags suspended from nails, a bird-cage, ashes, and even a little fire. Two brands were smouldering there in a melancholy way.

One thing which added still more to the horrors of this garret was, that it was large. It had projections and angles and black holes, the lower sides of roofs, bays, and promontories. Hence horrible, unfathomable nooks where it seemed as though spiders as big as one's fist, wood-lice as large as one's foot, and perhaps even—who knows?—some monstrous human beings, must be hiding.

One of the pallets was near the door, the other near the window. One end of each touched the fireplace and faced Marius. In a corner near the aperture through which Marius was gazing, a colored engraving in a black frame was suspended to a nail on the wall, and at its bottom, in large letters, was the inscription: THE DREAM. This represented a sleeping woman, and a child, also asleep, the child on the woman's lap, an eagle in a cloud, with a crown in his beak, and the woman thrusting the crown away from the child's head, without awaking the latter; in the background, Napoleon in a glory, leaning on a very blue column with a yellow capital ornamented with this inscription:

MARINGO
AUSTERLITS
IENA
WAGRAMME
ELOT

Beneath this frame, a sort of wooden panel, which was no longer than it was broad, stood on the ground and rested in a sloping attitude against the wall. It had the appearance of a picture with its face turned to the wall, of a frame probably showing a daub on the other side, of some pier-glass detached from a wall and lying forgotten there while waiting to be rehung.

Near the table, upon which Marius descried a pen, ink, and paper, sat a man about sixty years of age, small, thin, livid, haggard, with a cunning, cruel, and uneasy air; a hideous scoundrel.

If Lavater had studied this visage, he would have found the vulture mingled with the attorney there, the bird of prey and the pettifogger rendering each other mutually hideous and complementing each other; the pettifogger making the bird of prey ignoble, the bird of prey making the pettifogger horrible.

This man had a long gray beard. He was clad in a woman's chemise, which allowed his hairy breast and his bare arms, bristling with gray hair, to be seen. Beneath this chemise, muddy trousers and boots through which his toes projected were visible.

He had a pipe in his mouth and was smoking. There was no bread in the hovel, but there was still tobacco.

He was writing probably some more letters like those which Marius had read.

On the corner of the table lay an ancient, dilapidated, reddish volume, and the size, which was the antique 12mo of reading-rooms, betrayed a romance. On the cover sprawled the following title, printed in large capitals: GOD; THE KING; HONOR AND THE LADIES; BY DUCRAY DUMINIL, 1814.

As the man wrote, he talked aloud, and Marius heard his words:—

"The idea that there is no equality, even when you are dead! Just look at Père-Lachaise! The great, those who are rich, are up above, in the acacia alley, which is paved. They can reach it in a carriage. The little people, the poor, the unhappy, well, what of them? they are put down below, where the mud is up to your knees, in the damp places. They are put there so that they will decay the sooner! You cannot go to see them without sinking into the earth."

He paused, smote the table with his fist, and added, as he ground his teeth:—

"Oh! I could eat the whole world!"

A big woman, who might be forty years of age, or a hundred, was crouching near the fireplace on her bare heels.

She, too, was clad only in a chemise and a knitted petticoat patched with bits of old cloth. A coarse linen apron concealed the half of her petticoat. Although this woman was doubled up and bent together, it could be seen that she was of very lofty stature. She was a sort of giant, beside her husband. She had hideous hair, of a reddish blond which was turning gray, and which she thrust back from time to time, with her enormous shining hands, with their flat nails.

Beside her, on the floor, wide open, lay a book of the same form as the other, and probably a volume of the same romance.

On one of the pallets, Marius caught a glimpse of a sort of tall pale young girl, who sat there half naked and with pendant feet, and who did not seem to be listening or seeing or living.

No doubt the younger sister of the one who had come to his room.

She seemed to be eleven or twelve years of age. On closer scrutiny it was evident that she really was fourteen. She was the child who had said, on the boulevard the evening before: "I bolted, bolted, bolted!"

She was of that puny sort which remains backward for a long time, then suddenly starts up rapidly. It is indigence which produces these melancholy human plants. These creatures have neither childhood nor youth. At fifteen years of age they appear to be twelve, at sixteen they seem twenty. To-day a little girl, to-morrow a woman. One might say that they stride through life, in order to get through with it the more speedily.

At this moment, this being had the air of a child.

Moreover, no trace of work was revealed in that dwelling; no handicraft, no spinning-wheel, not a tool. In one corner lay some ironmongery of dubious aspect. It was the dull listlessness which follows despair and precedes the death agony.

Marius gazed for a while at this gloomy interior, more terrifying than the interior of a tomb, for the human soul could be felt fluttering there, and life was palpitating there. The garret, the cellar, the lowly ditch where certain indigent wretches crawl at the very bottom of the social edifice, is not exactly the sepulchre, but only its antechamber; but, as the wealthy display their greatest magnificence at the entrance of their palaces, it seems that death, which stands directly side by side with them, places its greatest miseries in that vestibule.

The man held his peace, the woman spoke no word, the young girl did not even seem to breathe. The scratching of the pen on the paper was audible.

The man grumbled, without pausing in his writing. "Canaille! canaille! everybody is canaille!"

This variation to Solomon's exclamation elicited a sigh from the woman.

"Calm yourself, my little friend," she said. "Don't hurt yourself, my dear. You are too good to write to all those people, husband."

Bodies press close to each other in misery, as in cold, but hearts draw apart. This woman must have loved this man, to all appearance, judging from the amount of love within her; but probably, in the daily and reciprocal reproaches of the horrible distress which weighed on the whole group, this had become extinct. There no longer existed in her anything more than the ashes of affection for her husband. Nevertheless, caressing appellations had survived, as is often the case. She called him: *My dear, my little friend, my good man*, etc., with her mouth while her heart was silent.

The man resumed his writing.

VII

STRATEGY AND TACTICS

M arius, with a load upon his breast, was on the point of descending from the species of observatory which he had improvised, when a sound attracted his attention and caused him to remain at his post.

The door of the attic had just burst open abruptly. The eldest girl made her appearance on the threshold. On her feet, she had large, coarse, men's shoes, bespattered with mud, which had splashed even to her red ankles, and she was wrapped in an old mantle which hung in tatters. Marius had not seen it on her an hour previously, but she had probably deposited it at his door, in order that she might inspire the more pity, and had picked it up again on emerging. She entered, pushed the door to behind her, paused to take breath, for she was completely breathless, then exclaimed with an expression of triumph and joy:—

"He is coming!"

The father turned his eyes towards her, the woman turned her head, the little sister did not stir.

"Who?" demanded her father.

"The gentleman!"

"The philanthropist?"

"Yes."

"From the church of Saint-Jacques?"

"Yes."

"That old fellow?"

"Yes."

"And he is coming?"

"He is following me."

"You are sure?"

"I am sure."

"There, truly, he is coming?"

"He is coming in a fiacre."

"In a fiacre. He is Rothschild."

The father rose.

"How are you sure? If he is coming in a fiacre, how is it that you arrive before him? You gave him our address at least? Did you tell him that it was the last door at the end of the corridor, on the right? If he only does not make a mistake! So you found him at the church? Did he read my letter? What did he say to you?"

"Ta, ta, ta," said the girl, "how you do gallop on, my good man! See here: I entered the church, he was in his usual place, I made him a reverence, and I handed him the letter; he read it and said to me: 'Where do you live, my child?' I said: 'Monsieur, I will show you.' He said to me: 'No, give me your address, my daughter has some purchases to make, I will take a carriage and reach your house at the same time that you do.' I gave him the address. When I mentioned the house, he seemed surprised and hesitated for an instant, then he said: 'Never mind, I will come.' When the mass was finished, I watched him leave the church with his daughter, and I saw them enter a carriage. I certainly did tell him the last door in the corridor, on the right."

"And what makes you think that he will come?"

"I have just seen the fiacre turn into the Rue Petit-Banquier. That is what made me run so."

"How do you know that it was the same fiacre?"

"Because I took notice of the number, so there!"

"What was the number?"

"440."

"Good, you are a clever girl."

The girl stared boldly at her father, and showing the shoes which she had on her feet:—

"A clever girl, possibly; but I tell you I won't put these shoes on again, and that I won't, for the sake of my health, in the first place, and for the sake of cleanliness, in the next. I don't know anything more irritating than shoes that squelch, and go *ghi, ghi, ghi,* the whole time. I prefer to go barefoot."

"You are right," said her father, in a sweet tone which contrasted with the young girl's rudeness, "but then, you will not be allowed to enter churches, for poor people must have shoes to do that. One cannot go barefoot to the good God," he added bitterly.

Then, returning to the subject which absorbed him:—

"So you are sure that he will come?"

"He is following on my heels," said she.

The man started up. A sort of illumination appeared on his countenance.

"Wife!" he exclaimed, "you hear. Here is the philanthropist. Extinguish the fire."

The stupefied mother did not stir.

The father, with the agility of an acrobat, seized a broken-nosed jug which stood on the chimney, and flung the water on the brands.

Then, addressing his eldest daughter:—

"Here you! Pull the straw off that chair!"

His daughter did not understand.

He seized the chair, and with one kick he rendered it seatless. His leg passed through it.

As he withdrew his leg, he asked his daughter:—

"Is it cold?"

"Very cold. It is snowing."

The father turned towards the younger girl who sat on the bed near the window, and shouted to her in a thundering voice:—

"Quick! get off that bed, you lazy thing! will you never do anything? Break a pane of glass!"

The little girl jumped off the bed with a shiver.

"Break a pane!" he repeated.

The child stood still in bewilderment.

"Do you hear me?" repeated her father, "I tell you to break a pane!"

The child, with a sort of terrified obedience, rose on tiptoe, and struck a pane with her fist. The glass broke and fell with a loud clatter.

"Good," said the father.

He was grave and abrupt. His glance swept rapidly over all the crannies of the garret. One would have said that he was a general making the final preparation at the moment when the battle is on the point of beginning.

The mother, who had not said a word so far, now rose and demanded in a dull, slow, languid voice, whence her words seemed to emerge in a congealed state:—

"What do you mean to do, my dear?"

"Get into bed," replied the man.

His intonation admitted of no deliberation. The mother obeyed, and threw herself heavily on one of the pallets.

In the meantime, a sob became audible in one corner.

"What's that?" cried the father.

The younger daughter exhibited her bleeding fist, without quitting the corner in which she was cowering. She had wounded herself while breaking the window; she went off, near her mother's pallet and wept silently.

It was now the mother's turn to start up and exclaim:—

"Just see there! What follies you commit! She has cut herself breaking that pane for you!"

"So much the better!" said the man. "I foresaw that."

"What? So much the better?" retorted his wife.

"Peace!" replied the father, "I suppress the liberty of the press."

Then tearing the woman's chemise which he was wearing, he made a strip of cloth with which he hastily swathed the little girl's bleeding wrist.

That done, his eye fell with a satisfied expression on his torn chemise.

"And the chemise too," said he, "this has a good appearance."

An icy breeze whistled through the window and entered the room. The outer mist penetrated thither and diffused itself like a whitish sheet of wadding vaguely spread by invisible fingers. Through the broken pane the snow could be seen falling. The snow promised by the Candlemas sun of the preceding day had actually come.

The father cast a glance about him as though to make sure that he had forgotten nothing. He seized an old shovel and spread ashes over the wet brands in such a manner as to entirely conceal them.

Then drawing himself up and leaning against the chimney-piece:—

"Now," said he, "we can receive the philanthropist."

VIII

The Ray of Light in the Hovel

The big girl approached and laid her hand in her father's.

"Feel how cold I am," said she.

"Bah!" replied the father, "I am much colder than that."

The mother exclaimed impetuously:—

"You always have something better than any one else, so you do! even bad things."

"Down with you!" said the man.

The mother, being eyed after a certain fashion, held her tongue.

Silence reigned for a moment in the hovel. The elder girl was removing the mud from the bottom of her mantle, with a careless air; her younger sister continued to sob; the mother had taken the latter's head between her hands, and was covering it with kisses, whispering to her the while:—

"My treasure, I entreat you, it is nothing of consequence, don't cry, you will anger your father."

"No!" exclaimed the father, "quite the contrary! sob! sob! that's right."

Then turning to the elder:—

"There now! He is not coming! What if he were not to come! I shall have extinguished my fire, wrecked my chair, torn my shirt, and broken my pane all for nothing."

"And wounded the child!" murmured the mother.

"Do you know," went on the father, "that it's beastly cold in this devil's garret! What if that man should not come! Oh! See there, you! He makes us wait! He says to himself: 'Well! they will wait for me! That's what they're there for.' Oh! how I hate them, and with what joy, jubilation, enthusiasm, and satisfaction I could strangle all those rich folks! all those rich folks! These men who pretend to be charitable, who put on airs, who go to mass, who make presents to the priesthood, *preachy, preachy*, in their skullcaps, and who think themselves above us, and who come for the purpose of humiliating us, and to bring us 'clothes,' as they say! old duds that are not worth four sous! And bread! That's not what I want, pack of rascals that they are, it's money! Ah! money! Never!

Because they say that we would go off and drink it up, and that we are drunkards and idlers! And they! What are they, then, and what have they been in their time! Thieves! They never could have become rich otherwise! Oh! Society ought to be grasped by the four corners of the cloth and tossed into the air, all of it! It would all be smashed, very likely, but at least, no one would have anything, and there would be that much gained! But what is that blockhead of a benevolent gentleman doing? Will he come? Perhaps the animal has forgotten the address! I'll bet that that old beast—"

At that moment there came a light tap at the door, the man rushed to it and opened it, exclaiming, amid profound bows and smiles of adoration:—

"Enter, sir! Deign to enter, most respected benefactor, and your charming young lady, also."

A man of ripe age and a young girl made their appearance on the threshold of the attic.

Marius had not quitted his post. His feelings for the moment surpassed the powers of the human tongue.

It was She!

Whoever has loved knows all the radiant meanings contained in those three letters of that word: She.

It was certainly she. Marius could hardly distinguish her through the luminous vapor which had suddenly spread before his eyes. It was that sweet, absent being, that star which had beamed upon him for six months; it was those eyes, that brow, that mouth, that lovely vanished face which had created night by its departure. The vision had been eclipsed, now it reappeared.

It reappeared in that gloom, in that garret, in that misshapen attic, in all that horror.

Marius shuddered in dismay. What! It was she! The palpitations of his heart troubled his sight. He felt that he was on the brink of bursting into tears! What! He beheld her again at last, after having sought her so long! It seemed to him that he had lost his soul, and that he had just found it again.

She was the same as ever, only a little pale; her delicate face was framed in a bonnet of violet velvet, her figure was concealed beneath a pelisse of black satin. Beneath her long dress, a glimpse could be caught of her tiny foot shod in a silken boot.

She was still accompanied by M. Leblanc.

She had taken a few steps into the room, and had deposited a tolerably bulky parcel on the table.

The eldest Jondrette girl had retired behind the door, and was staring with sombre eyes at that velvet bonnet, that silk mantle, and that charming, happy face.

IX

JONDRETTE COMES NEAR WEEPING

The hovel was so dark, that people coming from without felt on entering it the effect produced on entering a cellar. The two newcomers advanced, therefore, with a certain hesitation, being hardly able to distinguish the vague forms surrounding them, while they could be clearly seen and scrutinized by the eyes of the inhabitants of the garret, who were accustomed to this twilight.

M. Leblanc approached, with his sad but kindly look, and said to Jondrette the father:—

"Monsieur, in this package you will find some new clothes and some woollen stockings and blankets."

"Our angelic benefactor overwhelms us," said Jondrette, bowing to the very earth.

Then, bending down to the ear of his eldest daughter, while the two visitors were engaged in examining this lamentable interior, he added in a low and rapid voice:—

"Hey? What did I say? Duds! No money! They are all alike! By the way, how was the letter to that old blockhead signed?"

"Fabantou," replied the girl.

"The dramatic artist, good!"

It was lucky for Jondrette, that this had occurred to him, for at the very moment, M. Leblanc turned to him, and said to him with the air of a person who is seeking to recall a name:—

"I see that you are greatly to be pitied, Monsieur—"

"Fabantou," replied Jondrette quickly.

"Monsieur Fabantou, yes, that is it. I remember."

"Dramatic artist, sir, and one who has had some success."

Here Jondrette evidently judged the moment propitious for capturing the "philanthropist." He exclaimed with an accent which smacked at the same time of the vainglory of the mountebank at fairs, and the humility of the mendicant on the highway:—

"A pupil of Talma! Sir! I am a pupil of Talma! Fortune formerly smiled on me—Alas! Now it is misfortune's turn. You see, my benefactor, no bread, no fire. My poor babes have no fire! My only chair has no seat! A broken pane! And in such weather! My spouse in bed! Ill!"

"Poor woman!" said M. Leblanc.

"My child wounded!" added Jondrette.

The child, diverted by the arrival of the strangers, had fallen to contemplating "the young lady," and had ceased to sob.

"Cry! bawl!" said Jondrette to her in a low voice.

At the same time he pinched her sore hand. All this was done with the talent of a juggler.

The little girl gave vent to loud shrieks.

The adorable young girl, whom Marius, in his heart, called "his Ursule," approached her hastily.

"Poor, dear child!" said she.

"You see, my beautiful young lady," pursued Jondrette "her bleeding wrist! It came through an accident while working at a machine to earn six sous a day. It may be necessary to cut off her arm."

"Really?" said the old gentleman, in alarm.

The little girl, taking this seriously, fell to sobbing more violently than ever.

"Alas! yes, my benefactor!" replied the father.

For several minutes, Jondrette had been scrutinizing "the benefactor" in a singular fashion. As he spoke, he seemed to be examining the other attentively, as though seeking to summon up his recollections. All at once, profiting by a moment when the newcomers were questioning the child with interest as to her injured hand, he passed near his wife, who lay in her bed with a stupid and dejected air, and said to her in a rapid but very low tone:—

"Take a look at that man!"

Then, turning to M. Leblanc, and continuing his lamentations:—

"You see, sir! All the clothing that I have is my wife's chemise! And all torn at that! In the depths of winter! I can't go out for lack of a coat. If I had a coat of any sort, I would go and see Mademoiselle Mars, who knows me and is very fond of me. Does she not still reside in the Rue de la Tour-des-Dames? Do you know, sir? We played together in the provinces. I shared her laurels. Célimène would come to my succor, sir! Elmire would bestow alms on Bélisaire! But no, nothing! And not a sou in the house! My wife ill, and not a sou! My daughter dangerously injured, not a sou! My wife suffers from fits of suffocation. It comes from her age, and besides, her nervous system is affected. She ought to have assistance, and my daughter also! But the doctor! But the apothecary! How am I to pay them? I would kneel to a penny, sir! Such is the condition to which the arts are reduced. And do you know, my charming young lady, and you, my generous protector, do you know, you who breathe forth virtue and goodness, and who perfume that church where my daughter sees you every day when she says her prayers?—For I have brought up my children religiously, sir. I did not want them to take to the theatre. Ah! the hussies! If I catch them tripping! I do not jest, that I don't! I read them lessons on honor, on morality, on virtue! Ask them! They have got to walk straight. They are none of your unhappy wretches who begin by having no family, and end by espousing the public. One is Mamselle Nobody, and one becomes Madame Everybody. Deuce take it! None of that in the Fabantou family! I mean to bring them up virtuously, and they shall be honest, and nice, and believe in God, by the sacred name! Well, sir, my worthy sir, do you know what is going to happen to-morrow? To-morrow is the fourth day of February, the fatal day, the last day of grace allowed me by my landlord; if by this evening I have not paid my rent, to-morrow my oldest daughter, my spouse with her fever, my child with her wound,—we shall all four be turned out of here and thrown into the street, on the boulevard, without shelter, in the rain, in the snow. There, sir. I owe for four quarters—a whole year! that is to say, sixty francs."

Jondrette lied. Four quarters would have amounted to only forty francs, and he could not owe four, because six months had not elapsed since Marius had paid for two.

M. Leblanc drew five francs from his pocket and threw them on the table.

Jondrette found time to mutter in the ear of his eldest daughter:—

"The scoundrel! What does he think I can do with his five francs? That won't pay me for my chair and pane of glass! That's what comes of incurring expenses!"

In the meanwhile, M. Leblanc had removed the large brown great-coat which he wore over his blue coat, and had thrown it over the back of the chair.

"Monsieur Fabantou," he said, "these five francs are all that I have about me, but I shall now take my daughter home, and I will return this evening,—it is this evening that you must pay, is it not?"

Jondrette's face lighted up with a strange expression. He replied vivaciously:—

"Yes, respected sir. At eight o'clock, I must be at my landlord's."

"I will be here at six, and I will fetch you the sixty francs."

"My benefactor!" exclaimed Jondrette, overwhelmed. And he added, in a low tone: "Take a good look at him, wife!"

M. Leblanc had taken the arm of the young girl, once more, and had turned towards the door.

"Farewell until this evening, my friends!" said he.

"Six o'clock?" said Jondrette.

"Six o'clock precisely."

At that moment, the overcoat lying on the chair caught the eye of the elder Jondrette girl.

"You are forgetting your coat, sir," said she.

Jondrette darted an annihilating look at his daughter, accompanied by a formidable shrug of the shoulders.

M. Leblanc turned back and said, with a smile:—

"I have not forgotten it, I am leaving it."

"O my protector!" said Jondrette, "my august benefactor, I melt into tears! Permit me to accompany you to your carriage."

"If you come out," answered M. Leblanc, "put on this coat. It really is very cold."

Jondrette did not need to be told twice. He hastily donned the brown great-coat. And all three went out, Jondrette preceding the two strangers.

X

Tariff of Licensed Cabs: Two Francs an Hour

Marius had lost nothing of this entire scene, and yet, in reality, had seen nothing. His eyes had remained fixed on the young girl, his heart had, so to speak, seized her and wholly enveloped her from the moment of her very first step in that garret. During her entire stay there, he had lived that life of ecstasy which suspends material perceptions and precipitates the whole soul on a single point. He contemplated, not that girl, but that light which wore a satin pelisse and a velvet bonnet. The star Sirius might have entered the room, and he would not have been any more dazzled.

While the young girl was engaged in opening the package, unfolding the clothing and the blankets, questioning the sick mother kindly, and the little injured girl tenderly, he watched her every movement, he sought to catch her words. He knew her eyes, her brow, her beauty, her form, her walk, he did not know the sound of her voice. He had once fancied that he had caught a few words at the Luxembourg, but he was not absolutely sure of the fact. He would have given ten years of his life to hear it, in order that he might bear away in his soul a little of that music. But everything was drowned in the lamentable exclamations and trumpet bursts of Jondrette. This added a touch of genuine wrath to Marius' ecstasy. He devoured her with his eyes. He could not believe that it really was that divine creature whom he saw in the midst of those vile creatures in that monstrous lair. It seemed to him that he beheld a humming-bird in the midst of toads.

When she took her departure, he had but one thought, to follow her, to cling to her trace, not to quit her until he learned where she lived, not to lose her again, at least, after having so miraculously re-discovered her. He leaped down from the commode and seized his hat. As he laid his hand on the lock of the door, and was on the point of opening it, a sudden reflection caused him to pause. The corridor was long, the staircase steep, Jondrette was talkative, M. Leblanc had, no doubt, not yet regained his carriage; if, on turning round in the corridor, or on the staircase, he were to catch sight of him, Marius, in that house, he would, evidently, take the alarm, and find means to escape from him again, and this time it would be final. What was he to do? Should he wait a little? But while he was waiting, the carriage might drive off. Marius was perplexed. At last he accepted the risk and quitted his room.

There was no one in the corridor. He hastened to the stairs. There was no one on the staircase. He descended in all haste, and reached the boulevard in time to see a fiacre turning the corner of the Rue du Petit-Banquier, on its way back to Paris.

Marius rushed headlong in that direction. On arriving at the angle of the boulevard, he caught sight of the fiacre again, rapidly descending the Rue Mouffetard; the carriage was already a long way off, and there was no means of overtaking it; what! run after it? Impossible; and besides, the people in the carriage would assuredly notice an individual running at full speed in pursuit of a fiacre, and the father would recognize him. At that moment, wonderful and unprecedented good luck, Marius perceived an empty cab passing along the boulevard. There was but one thing to be done, to jump into this cab and follow the fiacre. That was sure, efficacious, and free from danger.

Marius made the driver a sign to halt, and called to him:—

"By the hour?"

Marius wore no cravat, he had on his working-coat, which was destitute of buttons, his shirt was torn along one of the plaits on the bosom.

The driver halted, winked, and held out his left hand to Marius, rubbing his forefinger gently with his thumb.

"What is it?" said Marius.

"Pay in advance," said the coachman.

Marius recollected that he had but sixteen sous about him.

"How much?" he demanded.

"Forty sous."

"I will pay on my return."

The driver's only reply was to whistle the air of La Palisse and to whip up his horse.

Marius stared at the retreating cabriolet with a bewildered air. For the lack of four and twenty sous, he was losing his joy, his happiness, his love! He had seen, and he was becoming blind again. He reflected bitterly, and it must be confessed, with profound regret, on the five francs which he had bestowed, that very morning, on that miserable girl. If he had had those five francs, he would have been saved, he would have been born again, he would have emerged from the limbo and darkness, he would have made his escape from isolation and spleen, from his widowed state; he might have re-knotted the black thread of his destiny to that beautiful golden thread, which had just floated before his eyes and had broken at the same instant, once more! He returned to his hovel in despair.

He might have told himself that M. Leblanc had promised to return in the evening, and that all he had to do was to set about the matter more skilfully, so that he might follow him on that occasion; but, in his contemplation, it is doubtful whether he had heard this.

As he was on the point of mounting the staircase, he perceived, on the other side of the boulevard, near the deserted wall skirting the Rue De la Barrière-des-Gobelins, Jondrette, wrapped in the "philanthropist's" great-coat, engaged in conversation with one of those men of disquieting aspect who have been dubbed by common consent, *prowlers of the barriers*; people of equivocal face, of suspicious monologues, who present the air of having evil minds, and who generally sleep in the daytime, which suggests the supposition that they work by night.

These two men, standing there motionless and in conversation, in the snow which was falling in whirlwinds, formed a group that a policeman would surely have observed, but which Marius hardly noticed.

Still, in spite of his mournful preoccupation, he could not refrain from saying to himself that this prowler of the barriers with whom Jondrette was talking resembled a certain Panchaud, alias Printanier, alias Bigrenaille, whom Courfeyrac had once pointed out to him as a very dangerous nocturnal roamer. This man's name the reader has learned in the preceding book. This Panchaud, alias Printanier, alias Bigrenaille, figured later on in many criminal trials, and became a notorious rascal. He was at that time only a famous rascal. To-day he exists in the state of tradition among ruffians and assassins. He was at the head of a school towards the end of the last reign. And in the evening, at nightfall, at the hour when groups form and talk in whispers, he was discussed at La Force in the Fosse-aux-Lions. One might even, in that prison, precisely at the spot where the sewer which served the unprecedented escape, in broad daylight, of thirty prisoners, in 1843, passes under the culvert, read his name, PANCHAUD, audaciously carved by his own hand on the wall of the sewer, during one of his attempts at flight. In 1832, the police already had their eye on him, but he had not as yet made a serious beginning.

XI

OFFERS OF SERVICE FROM MISERY TO WRETCHEDNESS

Marius ascended the stairs of the hovel with slow steps; at the moment when he was about to re-enter his cell, he caught sight of the elder Jondrette girl following him through the corridor. The very sight of this girl was odious to him; it was she who had his five francs, it was too late to demand them back, the cab was no longer there, the fiacre was far away. Moreover, she would not have given them back. As for questioning her about the residence of the persons who had just been there, that was useless; it was evident that she did not know, since the letter signed Fabantou had been addressed "to the benevolent gentleman of the church of Saint-Jacques-du-Haut-Pas."

Marius entered his room and pushed the door to after him.

It did not close; he turned round and beheld a hand which held the door half open.

"What is it?" he asked, "who is there?"

It was the Jondrette girl.

"Is it you?" resumed Marius almost harshly, "still you! What do you want with me?"

She appeared to be thoughtful and did not look at him. She no longer had the air of assurance which had characterized her that morning. She did not enter, but held back in the darkness of the corridor, where Marius could see her through the half-open door.

"Come now, will you answer?" cried Marius. "What do you want with me?"

She raised her dull eyes, in which a sort of gleam seemed to flicker vaguely, and said:—

"Monsieur Marius, you look sad. What is the matter with you?"

"With me!" said Marius.

"Yes, you."

"There is nothing the matter with me."

"Yes, there is!"

"No."

"I tell you there is!"

"Let me alone!"

Marius gave the door another push, but she retained her hold on it.

"Stop," said she, "you are in the wrong. Although you are not rich, you were kind this morning. Be so again now. You gave me something to eat, now tell me what ails you. You are grieved, that is plain. I do not want you to be grieved. What can be done for it? Can I be of any service? Employ me. I do not ask for your secrets, you need not tell them to me, but I may be of use, nevertheless. I may be able to help you, since I help my father. When it is necessary to carry letters, to go to houses, to inquire from door to door, to find out an address, to follow any one, I am of service. Well, you may assuredly tell me what is the matter with you, and I will go and speak to the persons; sometimes it is enough if some one speaks to the persons, that suffices to let them understand matters, and everything comes right. Make use of me."

An idea flashed across Marius' mind. What branch does one disdain when one feels that one is falling?

He drew near to the Jondrette girl.

"Listen—" he said to her.

She interrupted him with a gleam of joy in her eyes.

"Oh yes, do call me *thou!* I like that better."

"Well," he resumed, "thou hast brought hither that old gentleman and his daughter!"

"Yes."

"Dost thou know their address?"

"No."

"Find it for me."

The Jondrette's dull eyes had grown joyous, and they now became gloomy.

"Is that what you want?" she demanded.

"Yes."

"Do you know them?"

"No."

"That is to say," she resumed quickly, "you do not know her, but you wish to know her."

This *them* which had turned into *her* had something indescribably significant and bitter about it.

"Well, can you do it?" said Marius.

"You shall have the beautiful lady's address."

There was still a shade in the words "the beautiful lady" which troubled Marius. He resumed:—

"Never mind, after all, the address of the father and daughter. Their address, indeed!"

She gazed fixedly at him.

"What will you give me?"

"Anything you like."

"Anything I like?"

"Yes."

"You shall have the address."

She dropped her head; then, with a brusque movement, she pulled to the door, which closed behind her.

Marius found himself alone.

He dropped into a chair, with his head and both elbows on his bed, absorbed in thoughts which he could not grasp, and as though a prey to vertigo. All that had taken place since the morning, the appearance of the angel, her disappearance, what that creature had just said to him, a gleam of hope floating in an immense despair,—this was what filled his brain confusedly.

All at once he was violently aroused from his reverie.

He heard the shrill, hard voice of Jondrette utter these words, which were fraught with a strange interest for him:—

"I tell you that I am sure of it, and that I recognized him."

Of whom was Jondrette speaking? Whom had he recognized? M. Leblanc? The father of "his Ursule"? What! Did Jondrette know him? Was Marius about to obtain in this abrupt and unexpected fashion all the information without which his life was so dark to him? Was he about to learn at last who it was that he loved, who that young girl was? Who her father was? Was the dense shadow which enwrapped them on the point of being dispelled? Was the veil about to be rent? Ah! Heavens!

He bounded rather than climbed upon his commode, and resumed his post near the little peep-hole in the partition wall.

Again he beheld the interior of Jondrette's hovel.

XII

The Use Made of M. LeBlanc's Five-Franc Piece

Nothing in the aspect of the family was altered, except that the wife and daughters had levied on the package and put on woollen stockings and jackets. Two new blankets were thrown across the two beds.

Jondrette had evidently just returned. He still had the breathlessness of out of doors. His daughters were seated on the floor near the fireplace, the elder engaged in dressing the younger's wounded hand. His wife had sunk back on the bed near the fireplace, with a face indicative of astonishment. Jondrette was pacing up and down the garret with long strides. His eyes were extraordinary.

The woman, who seemed timid and overwhelmed with stupor in the presence of her husband, turned to say:—

"What, really? You are sure?"

"Sure! Eight years have passed! But I recognize him! Ah! I recognize him. I knew him at once! What! Didn't it force itself on you?"

"No."

"But I told you: 'Pay attention!' Why, it is his figure, it is his face, only older,—there are people who do not grow old, I don't know how they manage it,—it is the very sound of his voice. He is better dressed, that is all! Ah! you mysterious old devil, I've got you, that I have!"

He paused, and said to his daughters:—

"Get out of here, you!—It's queer that it didn't strike you!"

They arose to obey.

The mother stammered:—

"With her injured hand."

"The air will do it good," said Jondrette. "Be off."

It was plain that this man was of the sort to whom no one offers to reply. The two girls departed.

At the moment when they were about to pass through the door, the father detained the elder by the arm, and said to her with a peculiar accent:—

"You will be here at five o'clock precisely. Both of you. I shall need you."

Marius redoubled his attention.

On being left alone with his wife, Jondrette began to pace the room again, and made the tour of it two or three times in silence. Then he spent several minutes in tucking the lower part of the woman's chemise which he wore into his trousers.

All at once, he turned to the female Jondrette, folded his arms and exclaimed:—

"And would you like to have me tell you something? The young lady—"

"Well, what?" retorted his wife, "the young lady?"

Marius could not doubt that it was really she of whom they were speaking. He listened with ardent anxiety. His whole life was in his ears.

But Jondrette had bent over and spoke to his wife in a whisper. Then he straightened himself up and concluded aloud:—

"It is she!"

"That one?" said his wife.

"That very one," said the husband.

No expression can reproduce the significance of the mother's words. Surprise, rage, hate, wrath, were mingled and combined in one monstrous intonation. The pronunciation of a few words, the name, no doubt, which her husband had whispered in her ear, had sufficed to rouse this huge, somnolent woman, and from being repulsive she became terrible.

"It is not possible!" she cried. "When I think that my daughters are going barefoot, and have not a gown to their backs! What! A satin pelisse, a velvet bonnet, boots, and everything; more than two hundred francs' worth of clothes! so that one would think she was a lady! No, you are mistaken! Why, in the first place, the other was hideous, and this one is not so bad-looking! She really is not bad-looking! It can't be she!"

"I tell you that it is she. You will see."

At this absolute assertion, the Jondrette woman raised her large, red, blonde face and stared at the ceiling with a horrible expression. At that moment, she seemed to Marius even more to be feared than her husband. She was a sow with the look of a tigress.

"What!" she resumed, "that horrible, beautiful young lady, who gazed at my daughters with an air of pity,—she is that beggar brat! Oh! I should like to kick her stomach in for her!"

She sprang off of the bed, and remained standing for a moment, her hair in disorder, her nostrils dilating, her mouth half open, her fists clenched and drawn back. Then she fell back on the bed once more. The man paced to and fro and paid no attention to his female.

After a silence lasting several minutes, he approached the female Jondrette, and halted in front of her, with folded arms, as he had done a moment before:—

"And shall I tell you another thing?"

"What is it?" she asked.

He answered in a low, curt voice:—

"My fortune is made."

The woman stared at him with the look that signifies: "Is the person who is addressing me on the point of going mad?"

He went on:—

"Thunder! It was not so very long ago that I was a parishioner of the parish of die-of-hunger-if-you-have-a-fire,-die-of-cold-if-you-have-bread! I have had enough of misery! my share and other people's share! I am not joking any longer, I don't find it comic any more, I've had enough of puns, good God! no more farces, Eternal Father! I want to eat till I am full, I want to drink my fill! to gormandize! to sleep! to do nothing! I want to have my turn, so I do, come now! before I die! I want to be a bit of a millionnaire!"

He took a turn round the hovel, and added:—

"Like other people."

"What do you mean by that?" asked the woman.

He shook his head, winked, screwed up one eye, and raised his voice like a medical professor who is about to make a demonstration:—

"What do I mean by that? Listen!"

"Hush!" muttered the woman, "not so loud! These are matters which must not be overheard."

"Bah! Who's here? Our neighbor? I saw him go out a little while ago. Besides, he doesn't listen, the big booby. And I tell you that I saw him go out."

Nevertheless, by a sort of instinct, Jondrette lowered his voice, although not sufficiently to prevent Marius hearing his words. One favorable circumstance, which enabled Marius not to lose a word of this conversation was the falling snow which deadened the sound of vehicles on the boulevard.

This is what Marius heard:—

"Listen carefully. The Crœsus is caught, or as good as caught! That's all settled already. Everything is arranged. I have seen some people. He will come here this evening at six o'clock. To bring sixty francs, the rascal! Did you notice how I played that game on him, my sixty francs, my landlord, my fourth of February? I don't even owe for one quarter! Isn't he a fool! So he will come at six o'clock! That's the hour when our neighbor goes to his dinner. Mother Bougon is off washing dishes in the city. There's not a soul in the house. The neighbor never comes home until eleven o'clock. The children shall stand on watch. You shall help us. He will give in."

"And what if he does not give in?" demanded his wife.

Jondrette made a sinister gesture, and said:—

"We'll fix him."

And he burst out laughing.

This was the first time Marius had seen him laugh. The laugh was cold and sweet, and provoked a shudder.

Jondrette opened a cupboard near the fireplace, and drew from it an old cap, which he placed on his head, after brushing it with his sleeve.

"Now," said he, "I'm going out. I have some more people that I must see. Good ones. You'll see how well the whole thing will work. I shall be away as short a time as possible, it's a fine stroke of business, do you look after the house."

And with both fists thrust into the pockets of his trousers, he stood for a moment in thought, then exclaimed:—

"Do you know, it's mighty lucky, by the way, that he didn't recognize me! If he had recognized me on his side, he would not have come back again. He would have slipped through our fingers! It was my beard that saved us! my romantic beard! my pretty little romantic beard!"

And again he broke into a laugh.

He stepped to the window. The snow was still falling, and streaking the gray of the sky.

"What beastly weather!" said he.

Then lapping his overcoat across his breast:—

"This rind is too large for me. Never mind," he added, "he did a devilish good thing in leaving it for me, the old scoundrel! If it hadn't been for that, I couldn't have gone out, and everything would have gone wrong! What small points things hang on, anyway!"

And pulling his cap down over his eyes, he quitted the room.

He had barely had time to take half a dozen steps from the door, when the door opened again, and his savage but intelligent face made its appearance once more in the opening.

"I came near forgetting," said he. "You are to have a brazier of charcoal ready."

And he flung into his wife's apron the five-franc piece which the "philanthropist" had left with him.

"A brazier of charcoal?" asked his wife.

"Yes."

"How many bushels?"

"Two good ones."

"That will come to thirty sous. With the rest I will buy something for dinner."

"The devil, no."

"Why?"

"Don't go and spend the hundred-sou piece."

"Why?"

"Because I shall have to buy something, too."

"What?"

"Something."

"How much shall you need?"

"Whereabouts in the neighborhood is there an ironmonger's shop?"

"Rue Mouffetard."

"Ah! yes, at the corner of a street; I can see the shop."

"But tell me how much you will need for what you have to purchase?"

"Fifty sous—three francs."

"There won't be much left for dinner."

"Eating is not the point to-day. There's something better to be done."

"That's enough, my jewel."

At this word from his wife, Jondrette closed the door again, and this time, Marius heard his step die away in the corridor of the hovel, and descend the staircase rapidly.

At that moment, one o'clock struck from the church of Saint-Médard.

XIII

Solus Cum Solo, In Loco Remoto, Non Cogitabuntur Orare Pater Noster

Marius, dreamer as he was, was, as we have said, firm and energetic by nature. His habits of solitary meditation, while they had developed in him sympathy and compassion, had, perhaps, diminished the faculty for irritation, but had left intact the power of waxing indignant; he had the kindliness of a brahmin, and the severity of a judge; he took pity upon a toad, but he crushed a viper. Now, it was into a hole of vipers that his glance had just been directed, it was a nest of monsters that he had beneath his eyes.

"These wretches must be stamped upon," said he.

Not one of the enigmas which he had hoped to see solved had been elucidated; on the contrary, all of them had been rendered more dense, if anything; he knew nothing more about the beautiful maiden of the Luxembourg and the man whom he called M. Leblanc, except that Jondrette was acquainted with them. Athwart the mysterious words which had been uttered, the only thing of which he caught a distinct glimpse was the fact that an ambush was in course of preparation, a dark but terrible trap; that both of them were incurring great danger, she probably, her father certainly; that they must be saved; that the hideous plots of the Jondrettes must be thwarted, and the web of these spiders broken.

He scanned the female Jondrette for a moment. She had pulled an old sheet-iron stove from a corner, and she was rummaging among the old heap of iron.

He descended from the commode as softly as possible, taking care not to make the least noise. Amid his terror as to what was in preparation, and in the horror with which the Jondrettes had inspired him, he experienced a sort of joy at the idea that it might be granted to him perhaps to render a service to the one whom he loved.

But how was it to be done? How warn the persons threatened? He did not know their address. They had reappeared for an instant before his eyes, and had then plunged back again into the immense depths of Paris. Should he wait for M. Leblanc at the door that evening at six o'clock, at the moment of his arrival, and warn him of the trap? But Jondrette and his men would see him on the watch, the spot was lonely, they were stronger than he, they would devise means to seize him or to get him away, and the man whom Marius was anxious to save would be lost. One o'clock had just struck, the trap was to be sprung at six. Marius had five hours before him.

There was but one thing to be done.

He put on his decent coat, knotted a silk handkerchief round his neck, took his hat, and went out, without making any more noise than if he had been treading on moss with bare feet.

Moreover, the Jondrette woman continued to rummage among her old iron.

Once outside of the house, he made for the Rue du Petit-Banquier.

He had almost reached the middle of this street, near a very low wall which a man can easily step over at certain points, and which abuts on a waste space, and was walking slowly, in consequence of his preoccupied condition, and the snow deadened the sound of his steps; all at once he heard voices talking very close by. He turned his head, the street was deserted, there was not a soul in it, it was broad daylight, and yet he distinctly heard voices.

It occurred to him to glance over the wall which he was skirting.

There, in fact, sat two men, flat on the snow, with their backs against the wall, talking together in subdued tones.

These two persons were strangers to him; one was a bearded man in a blouse, and the other a long-haired individual in rags. The bearded man had on a fez, the other's head was bare, and the snow had lodged in his hair.

By thrusting his head over the wall, Marius could hear their remarks.

The hairy one jogged the other man's elbow and said:—

"—With the assistance of Patron-Minette, it can't fail."

"Do you think so?" said the bearded man.

And the long-haired one began again:—

"It's as good as a warrant for each one, of five hundred balls, and the worst that can happen is five years, six years, ten years at the most!"

The other replied with some hesitation, and shivering beneath his fez:—

"That's a real thing. You can't go against such things."

"I tell you that the affair can't go wrong," resumed the long-haired man. "Father What's-his-name's team will be already harnessed."

Then they began to discuss a melodrama that they had seen on the preceding evening at the Gaîté Theatre.

Marius went his way.

It seemed to him that the mysterious words of these men, so strangely hidden behind that wall, and crouching in the snow, could not but bear some relation to Jondrette's abominable projects. That must be *the affair*.

He directed his course towards the faubourg Saint-Marceau and asked at the first shop he came to where he could find a commissary of police.

He was directed to Rue de Pontoise, No. 14.

Thither Marius betook himself.

As he passed a baker's shop, he bought a two-penny roll, and ate it, foreseeing that he should not dine.

On the way, he rendered justice to Providence. He reflected that had he not given his five francs to the Jondrette girl in the morning, he would have followed M. Leblanc's fiacre, and consequently have remained ignorant of everything, and that there would have been no obstacle to the trap of the Jondrettes and that M. Leblanc would have been lost, and his daughter with him, no doubt.

XIV

In Which a Police Agent Bestows Two Fistfuls on a Lawyer

On arriving at No. 14, Rue de Pontoise, he ascended to the first floor and inquired for the commissary of police.

"The commissary of police is not here," said a clerk; "but there is an inspector who takes his place. Would you like to speak to him? Are you in haste?"

"Yes," said Marius.

The clerk introduced him into the commissary's office. There stood a tall man behind a grating, leaning against a stove, and holding up with both hands the tails of a vast topcoat, with three collars. His face was square, with a thin, firm mouth, thick, gray, and very ferocious whiskers, and a look that was enough to turn your pockets inside out. Of that glance it might have been well said, not that it penetrated, but that it searched.

This man's air was not much less ferocious nor less terrible than Jondrette's; the dog is, at times, no less terrible to meet than the wolf.

"What do you want?" he said to Marius, without adding "monsieur."

"Is this Monsieur le Commissaire de Police?"

"He is absent. I am here in his stead."

"The matter is very private."

"Then speak."

"And great haste is required."

"Then speak quick."

This calm, abrupt man was both terrifying and reassuring at one and the same time. He inspired fear and confidence. Marius related the adventure to him: That a person with whom he was not acquainted otherwise than by sight, was to be inveigled into a trap that very evening; that, as he occupied the room adjoining the den, he, Marius Pontmercy, a lawyer, had heard the whole plot through the partition; that the wretch who had planned the trap was a certain Jondrette; that there would be accomplices, probably some prowlers of the barriers, among others a certain Panchaud, alias Printanier, alias Bigrenaille; that Jondrette's daughters were to lie in wait; that there was no way of warning the threatened man, since he did not even know his name; and that, finally, all this was to be carried out at six o'clock that evening, at the most deserted point of the Boulevard de l'Hôpital, in house No. 50–52.

At the sound of this number, the inspector raised his head, and said coldly:—

"So it is in the room at the end of the corridor?"

"Precisely," answered Marius, and he added: "Are you acquainted with that house?"

The inspector remained silent for a moment, then replied, as he warmed the heel of his boot at the door of the stove:—

"Apparently."

He went on, muttering between his teeth, and not addressing Marius so much as his cravat:—

"Patron-Minette must have had a hand in this."

This word struck Marius.

"Patron-Minette," said he, "I did hear that word pronounced, in fact."

And he repeated to the inspector the dialogue between the long-haired man and the bearded man in the snow behind the wall of the Rue du Petit-Banquier.

The inspector muttered:—

"The long-haired man must be Brujon, and the bearded one Demi-Liard, alias Deux-Milliards."

He had dropped his eyelids again, and became absorbed in thought.

"As for Father What's-his-name, I think I recognize him. Here, I've burned my coat. They always have too much fire in these cursed stoves. Number 50–52. Former property of Gorbeau."

Then he glanced at Marius.

"You saw only that bearded and that long-haired man?"

"And Panchaud."

"You didn't see a little imp of a dandy prowling about the premises?"

"No."

"Nor a big lump of matter, resembling an elephant in the Jardin des Plantes?"

"No."

"Nor a scamp with the air of an old red tail?"

"No."

"As for the fourth, no one sees him, not even his adjutants, clerks, and employees. It is not surprising that you did not see him."

"No. Who are all those persons?" asked Marius.

The inspector answered:—

"Besides, this is not the time for them."

He relapsed into silence, then resumed:—

"50–52. I know that barrack. Impossible to conceal ourselves inside it without the artists seeing us, and then they will get off simply by countermanding the vaudeville. They are so modest! An audience embarrasses them. None of that, none of that. I want to hear them sing and make them dance."

This monologue concluded, he turned to Marius, and demanded, gazing at him intently the while:—

"Are you afraid?"

"Of what?" said Marius.

"Of these men?"

"No more than yourself!" retorted Marius rudely, who had begun to notice that this police agent had not yet said "monsieur" to him.

The inspector stared still more intently at Marius, and continued with sententious solemnity:—

"There, you speak like a brave man, and like an honest man. Courage does not fear crime, and honesty does not fear authority."

Marius interrupted him:—

"That is well, but what do you intend to do?"

The inspector contented himself with the remark:—

"The lodgers have pass-keys with which to get in at night. You must have one."

"Yes," said Marius.

"Have you it about you?"

"Yes."

"Give it to me," said the inspector.

Marius took his key from his waistcoat pocket, handed it to the inspector and added:—

"If you will take my advice, you will come in force."

The inspector cast on Marius such a glance as Voltaire might have bestowed on a provincial academician who had suggested a rhyme to him; with one movement he plunged his hands, which were enormous, into the two immense pockets of his top-coat, and pulled out two small steel pistols, of the sort called "knock-me-downs." Then he presented them to Marius, saying rapidly, in a curt tone:—

"Take these. Go home. Hide in your chamber, so that you may be supposed to have gone out. They are loaded. Each one carries two balls.

You will keep watch; there is a hole in the wall, as you have informed me. These men will come. Leave them to their own devices for a time. When you think matters have reached a crisis, and that it is time to put a stop to them, fire a shot. Not too soon. The rest concerns me. A shot into the ceiling, the air, no matter where. Above all things, not too soon. Wait until they begin to put their project into execution; you are a lawyer; you know the proper point." Marius took the pistols and put them in the side pocket of his coat.

"That makes a lump that can be seen," said the inspector. "Put them in your trousers pocket."

Marius hid the pistols in his trousers pockets.

"Now," pursued the inspector, "there is not a minute more to be lost by any one. What time is it? Half-past two. Seven o'clock is the hour?"

"Six o'clock," answered Marius.

"I have plenty of time," said the inspector, "but no more than enough. Don't forget anything that I have said to you. Bang. A pistol shot."

"Rest easy," said Marius.

And as Marius laid his hand on the handle of the door on his way out, the inspector called to him:—

"By the way, if you have occasion for my services between now and then, come or send here. You will ask for Inspector Javert."

XV

Jondrette Makes his Purchases

A few moments later, about three o'clock, Courfeyrac chanced to be passing along the Rue Mouffetard in company with Bossuet. The snow had redoubled in violence, and filled the air. Bossuet was just saying to Courfeyrac:—

"One would say, to see all these snow-flakes fall, that there was a plague of white butterflies in heaven." All at once, Bossuet caught sight of Marius coming up the street towards the barrier with a peculiar air.

"Hold!" said Bossuet. "There's Marius."

"I saw him," said Courfeyrac. "Don't let's speak to him."

"Why?"

"He is busy."

"With what?"

"Don't you see his air?"

"What air?"

"He has the air of a man who is following some one."

"That's true," said Bossuet.

"Just see the eyes he is making!" said Courfeyrac.

"But who the deuce is he following?"

"Some fine, flowery bonneted wench! He's in love."

"But," observed Bossuet, "I don't see any wench nor any flowery bonnet in the street. There's not a woman round."

Courfeyrac took a survey, and exclaimed:—

"He's following a man!"

A man, in fact, wearing a gray cap, and whose gray beard could be distinguished, although they only saw his back, was walking along about twenty paces in advance of Marius.

This man was dressed in a great-coat which was perfectly new and too large for him, and in a frightful pair of trousers all hanging in rags and black with mud.

Bossuet burst out laughing.

"Who is that man?"

"He?" retorted Courfeyrac, "he's a poet. Poets are very fond of wearing the trousers of dealers in rabbit skins and the overcoats of peers of France."

"Let's see where Marius will go," said Bossuet; "let's see where the man is going, let's follow them, hey?"

"Bossuet!" exclaimed Courfeyrac, "eagle of Meaux! You are a prodigious brute. Follow a man who is following another man, indeed!"

They retraced their steps.

Marius had, in fact, seen Jondrette passing along the Rue Mouffetard, and was spying on his proceedings.

Jondrette walked straight ahead, without a suspicion that he was already held by a glance.

He quitted the Rue Mouffetard, and Marius saw him enter one of the most terrible hovels in the Rue Gracieuse; he remained there about a quarter of an hour, then returned to the Rue Mouffetard. He halted at an ironmonger's shop, which then stood at the corner of the Rue Pierre-Lombard, and a few minutes later Marius saw him emerge from the shop, holding in his hand a huge cold chisel with a white wood handle, which he concealed beneath his great-coat. At the top of the Rue Petit-Gentilly he turned to the left and proceeded rapidly to the Rue du Petit-Banquier. The day was declining; the snow, which had ceased for a moment, had just begun again. Marius posted himself on the watch at the very corner of the Rue du Petit-Banquier, which was deserted, as usual, and did not follow Jondrette into it. It was lucky that he did so, for, on arriving in the vicinity of the wall where Marius had heard the long-haired man and the bearded man conversing, Jondrette turned round, made sure that no one was following him, did not see him, then sprang across the wall and disappeared.

The waste land bordered by this wall communicated with the back yard of an ex-livery stable-keeper of bad repute, who had failed and who still kept a few old single-seated berlins under his sheds.

Marius thought that it would be wise to profit by Jondrette's absence to return home; moreover, it was growing late; every evening, Ma'am Bougon when she set out for her dish-washing in town, had a habit of locking the door, which was always closed at dusk. Marius had given his key to the inspector of police; it was important, therefore, that he should make haste.

Evening had arrived, night had almost closed in; on the horizon and in the immensity of space, there remained but one spot illuminated by the sun, and that was the moon.

It was rising in a ruddy glow behind the low dome of Salpêtrière.

Marius returned to No. 50–52 with great strides. The door was still open when he arrived. He mounted the stairs on tip-toe and glided along the wall of the corridor to his chamber. This corridor, as the reader will remember, was bordered on both sides by attics, all of which were, for the moment, empty and to let. Ma'am Bougon was in the habit of leaving all the doors open. As he passed one of these attics, Marius thought he perceived in the uninhabited cell the motionless heads of four men, vaguely lighted up by a remnant of daylight, falling through a dormer window.

Marius made no attempt to see, not wishing to be seen himself. He succeeded in reaching his chamber without being seen and without making any noise. It was high time. A moment later he heard Ma'am Bougon take her departure, locking the door of the house behind her.

XVI

In Which Will Be Found the Words to an English Air Which was in Fashion in 1832

Marius seated himself on his bed. It might have been half-past five o'clock. Only half an hour separated him from what was about to happen. He heard the beating of his arteries as one hears the ticking of a watch in the dark. He thought of the double march which was going on at that moment in the dark,—crime advancing on one side, justice coming up on the other. He was not afraid, but he could not think without a shudder of what was about to take place. As is the case with all those who are suddenly assailed by an unforeseen adventure, the entire day produced upon him the effect of a dream, and in order to persuade himself that he was not the prey of a nightmare, he had to feel the cold barrels of the steel pistols in his trousers pockets.

It was no longer snowing; the moon disengaged itself more and more clearly from the mist, and its light, mingled with the white reflection of the snow which had fallen, communicated to the chamber a sort of twilight aspect.

There was a light in the Jondrette den. Marius saw the hole in the wall shining with a reddish glow which seemed bloody to him.

It was true that the light could not be produced by a candle. However, there was not a sound in the Jondrette quarters, not a soul was moving there, not a soul speaking, not a breath; the silence was glacial and profound, and had it not been for that light, he might have thought himself next door to a sepulchre.

Marius softly removed his boots and pushed them under his bed.

Several minutes elapsed. Marius heard the lower door turn on its hinges; a heavy step mounted the staircase, and hastened along the corridor; the latch of the hovel was noisily lifted; it was Jondrette returning.

Instantly, several voices arose. The whole family was in the garret. Only, it had been silent in the master's absence, like wolf whelps in the absence of the wolf.

"It's I," said he.

"Good evening, daddy," yelped the girls.

"Well?" said the mother.

"All's going first-rate," responded Jondrette, "but my feet are beastly cold. Good! You have dressed up. You have done well! You must inspire confidence."

"All ready to go out."

"Don't forget what I told you. You will do everything sure?"

"Rest easy."

"Because—" said Jondrette. And he left the phrase unfinished.

Marius heard him lay something heavy on the table, probably the chisel which he had purchased.

"By the way," said Jondrette, "have you been eating here?"

"Yes," said the mother. "I got three large potatoes and some salt. I took advantage of the fire to cook them."

"Good," returned Jondrette. "To-morrow I will take you out to dine with me. We will have a duck and fixings. You shall dine like Charles the Tenth; all is going well!"

Then he added:—

"The mouse-trap is open. The cats are there."

He lowered his voice still further, and said:—

"Put this in the fire."

Marius heard a sound of charcoal being knocked with the tongs or some iron utensil, and Jondrette continued:—

"Have you greased the hinges of the door so that they will not squeak?"

"Yes," replied the mother.

"What time is it?"

"Nearly six. The half-hour struck from Saint-Médard a while ago."

"The devil!" ejaculated Jondrette; "the children must go and watch. Come you, do you listen here."

A whispering ensued.

Jondrette's voice became audible again:—

"Has old Bougon left?"

"Yes," said the mother.

"Are you sure that there is no one in our neighbor's room?"

"He has not been in all day, and you know very well that this is his dinner hour."

"You are sure?"

"Sure."

"All the same," said Jondrette, "there's no harm in going to see whether he is there. Here, my girl, take the candle and go there."

Marius fell on his hands and knees and crawled silently under his bed.

Hardly had he concealed himself, when he perceived a light through the crack of his door.

"P'pa," cried a voice, "he is not in here."

He recognized the voice of the eldest daughter.

"Did you go in?" demanded her father.

"No," replied the girl, "but as his key is in the door, he must be out."

The father exclaimed:—

"Go in, nevertheless."

The door opened, and Marius saw the tall Jondrette come in with a candle in her hand. She was as she had been in the morning, only still more repulsive in this light.

She walked straight up to the bed. Marius endured an indescribable moment of anxiety; but near the bed there was a mirror nailed to the wall, and it was thither that she was directing her steps. She raised herself on tiptoe and looked at herself in it. In the neighboring room, the sound of iron articles being moved was audible.

She smoothed her hair with the palm of her hand, and smiled into the mirror, humming with her cracked and sepulchral voice:—

> *Nos amours ont duré toute une semaine,*
> *Mais que du bonheur les instants sont courts!*
> *S'adorer huit jours, c'était bien la peine!*
> *Le temps des amours devrait durer toujours!*
> *Devrait durer toujours! devrait durer toujours!*

In the meantime, Marius trembled. It seemed impossible to him that she should not hear his breathing.

She stepped to the window and looked out with the half-foolish way she had.

"How ugly Paris is when it has put on a white chemise!" said she.

She returned to the mirror and began again to put on airs before it, scrutinizing herself full-face and three-quarters face in turn.

"Well!" cried her father, "what are you about there?"

"I am looking under the bed and the furniture," she replied, continuing to arrange her hair; "there's no one here."

"Booby!" yelled her father. "Come here this minute! And don't waste any time about it!"

"Coming! Coming!" said she. "One has no time for anything in this hovel!"

She hummed:—

> *Vous me quittez pour aller à la gloire;*
> *Mon triste cœur suivra partout.*

She cast a parting glance in the mirror and went out, shutting the door behind her.

A moment more, and Marius heard the sound of the two young girls' bare feet in the corridor, and Jondrette's voice shouting to them:—

"Pay strict heed! One on the side of the barrier, the other at the corner of the Rue du Petit-Banquier. Don't lose sight for a moment of the door of this house, and the moment you see anything, rush here on the instant! as hard as you can go! You have a key to get in."

The eldest girl grumbled:—

"The idea of standing watch in the snow barefoot!"

"To-morrow you shall have some dainty little green silk boots!" said the father.

They ran downstairs, and a few seconds later the shock of the outer door as it banged to announced that they were outside.

There now remained in the house only Marius, the Jondrettes and probably, also, the mysterious persons of whom Marius had caught a glimpse in the twilight, behind the door of the unused attic.

XVII

THE USE MADE OF MARIUS'
FIVE-FRANC PIECE

Marius decided that the moment had now arrived when he must resume his post at his observatory. In a twinkling, and with the agility of his age, he had reached the hole in the partition.

He looked.

The interior of the Jondrette apartment presented a curious aspect, and Marius found an explanation of the singular light which he had noticed. A candle was burning in a candlestick covered with verdigris, but that was not what really lighted the chamber. The hovel was completely illuminated, as it were, by the reflection from a rather large sheet-iron brazier standing in the fireplace, and filled with burning charcoal, the brazier prepared by the Jondrette woman that morning. The charcoal was glowing hot and the brazier was red; a blue flame flickered over it, and helped him to make out the form of the chisel purchased by Jondrette in the Rue Pierre-Lombard, where it had been thrust into the brazier to heat. In one corner, near the door, and as though prepared for some definite use, two heaps were visible, which appeared to be, the one a heap of old iron, the other a heap of ropes. All this would have caused the mind of a person who knew nothing of what was in preparation, to waver between a very sinister and a very simple idea. The lair thus lighted up more resembled a forge than a mouth of hell, but Jondrette, in this light, had rather the air of a demon than of a smith.

The heat of the brazier was so great, that the candle on the table was melting on the side next the chafing-dish, and was drooping over. An old dark-lantern of copper, worthy of Diogenes turned Cartouche, stood on the chimney-piece.

The brazier, placed in the fireplace itself, beside the nearly extinct brands, sent its vapors up the chimney, and gave out no odor.

The moon, entering through the four panes of the window, cast its whiteness into the crimson and flaming garret; and to the poetic spirit of Marius, who was dreamy even in the moment of action, it was like a thought of heaven mingled with the misshapen reveries of earth.

A breath of air which made its way in through the open pane, helped to dissipate the smell of the charcoal and to conceal the presence of the brazier.

The Jondrette lair was, if the reader recalls what we have said of the Gorbeau building, admirably chosen to serve as the theatre of a violent and sombre deed, and as the envelope for a crime. It was the most retired chamber in the most isolated house on the most deserted boulevard in Paris. If the system of ambush and traps had not already existed, they would have been invented there.

The whole thickness of a house and a multitude of uninhabited rooms separated this den from the boulevard, and the only window that existed opened on waste lands enclosed with walls and palisades.

Jondrette had lighted his pipe, seated himself on the seatless chair, and was engaged in smoking. His wife was talking to him in a low tone.

If Marius had been Courfeyrac, that is to say, one of those men who laugh on every occasion in life, he would have burst with laughter when his gaze fell on the Jondrette woman. She had on a black bonnet with plumes not unlike the hats of the heralds-at-arms at the coronation of Charles X, an immense tartan shawl over her knitted petticoat, and the man's shoes which her daughter had scorned in the morning. It was this toilette which had extracted from Jondrette the exclamation: "Good! You have dressed up. You have done well. You must inspire confidence!"

As for Jondrette, he had not taken off the new surtout, which was too large for him, and which M. Leblanc had given him, and his costume continued to present that contrast of coat and trousers which constituted the ideal of a poet in Courfeyrac's eyes.

All at once, Jondrette lifted up his voice:—

"By the way! Now that I think of it. In this weather, he will come in a carriage. Light the lantern, take it and go downstairs. You will stand behind the lower door. The very moment that you hear the carriage stop, you will open the door, instantly, he will come up, you will light the staircase and the corridor, and when he enters here, you will go downstairs again as speedily as possible, you will pay the coachman, and dismiss the fiacre."

"And the money?" inquired the woman.

Jondrette fumbled in his trousers pocket and handed her five francs.

"What's this?" she exclaimed.

Jondrette replied with dignity:—

"That is the monarch which our neighbor gave us this morning."

And he added:—

"Do you know what? Two chairs will be needed here."

"What for?"

"To sit on."

Marius felt a cold chill pass through his limbs at hearing this mild answer from Jondrette.

"Pardieu! I'll go and get one of our neighbor's."

And with a rapid movement, she opened the door of the den, and went out into the corridor.

Marius absolutely had not the time to descend from the commode, reach his bed, and conceal himself beneath it.

"Take the candle," cried Jondrette.

"No," said she, "it would embarrass me, I have the two chairs to carry. There is moonlight."

Marius heard Mother Jondrette's heavy hand fumbling at his lock in the dark. The door opened. He remained nailed to the spot with the shock and with horror.

The Jondrette entered.

The dormer window permitted the entrance of a ray of moonlight between two blocks of shadow. One of these blocks of shadow entirely covered the wall against which Marius was leaning, so that he disappeared within it.

Mother Jondrette raised her eyes, did not see Marius, took the two chairs, the only ones which Marius possessed, and went away, letting the door fall heavily to behind her.

She re-entered the lair.

"Here are the two chairs."

"And here is the lantern. Go down as quick as you can."

She hastily obeyed, and Jondrette was left alone.

He placed the two chairs on opposite sides of the table, turned the chisel in the brazier, set in front of the fireplace an old screen which masked the chafing-dish, then went to the corner where lay the pile of rope, and bent down as though to examine something. Marius then recognized the fact, that what he had taken for a shapeless mass was a very well-made rope-ladder, with wooden rungs and two hooks with which to attach it.

This ladder, and some large tools, veritable masses of iron, which were mingled with the old iron piled up behind the door, had not been in the Jondrette hovel in the morning, and had evidently been brought thither in the afternoon, during Marius' absence.

"Those are the utensils of an edge-tool maker," thought Marius.

Had Marius been a little more learned in this line, he would have recognized in what he took for the engines of an edge-tool maker, certain instruments which will force a lock or pick a lock, and others which will cut or slice, the two families of tools which burglars call *cadets* and *fauchants*.

The fireplace and the two chairs were exactly opposite Marius. The brazier being concealed, the only light in the room was now furnished by the candle; the smallest bit of crockery on the table or on the chimney-piece cast a large shadow. There was something indescribably calm, threatening, and hideous about this chamber. One felt that there existed in it the anticipation of something terrible.

Jondrette had allowed his pipe to go out, a serious sign of preoccupation, and had again seated himself. The candle brought out the fierce and the fine angles of his countenance. He indulged in scowls and in abrupt unfoldings of the right hand, as though he were responding to the last counsels of a sombre inward monologue. In the course of one of these dark replies which he was making to himself, he pulled the table drawer rapidly towards him, took out a long kitchen knife which was concealed there, and tried the edge of its blade on his nail. That done, he put the knife back in the drawer and shut it.

Marius, on his side, grasped the pistol in his right pocket, drew it out and cocked it.

The pistol emitted a sharp, clear click, as he cocked it.

Jondrette started, half rose, listened a moment, then began to laugh and said:—

"What a fool I am! It's the partition cracking!"

Marius kept the pistol in his hand.

XVIII

Marius' Two Chairs Form a Vis-a-Vis

Suddenly, the distant and melancholy vibration of a clock shook the panes. Six o'clock was striking from Saint-Médard.

Jondrette marked off each stroke with a toss of his head. When the sixth had struck, he snuffed the candle with his fingers.

Then he began to pace up and down the room, listened at the corridor, walked on again, then listened once more.

"Provided only that he comes!" he muttered, then he returned to his chair.

He had hardly reseated himself when the door opened.

Mother Jondrette had opened it, and now remained in the corridor making a horrible, amiable grimace, which one of the holes of the dark-lantern illuminated from below.

"Enter, sir," she said.

"Enter, my benefactor," repeated Jondrette, rising hastily.

M. Leblanc made his appearance.

He wore an air of serenity which rendered him singularly venerable.

He laid four louis on the table.

"Monsieur Fabantou," said he, "this is for your rent and your most pressing necessities. We will attend to the rest hereafter."

"May God requite it to you, my generous benefactor!" said Jondrette.

And rapidly approaching his wife:—

"Dismiss the carriage!"

She slipped out while her husband was lavishing salutes and offering M. Leblanc a chair. An instant later she returned and whispered in his ear:—

"'Tis done."

The snow, which had not ceased falling since the morning, was so deep that the arrival of the fiacre had not been audible, and they did not now hear its departure.

Meanwhile, M. Leblanc had seated himself.

Jondrette had taken possession of the other chair, facing M. Leblanc.

Now, in order to form an idea of the scene which is to follow, let the reader picture to himself in his own mind, a cold night, the solitudes of the Salpêtrière covered with snow and white as winding-sheets in the moonlight, the taper-like lights of the street lanterns which shone redly here and there along those tragic boulevards, and the long rows of black elms, not a passer-by for perhaps a quarter of a league around, the Gorbeau hovel, at its highest pitch of silence, of horror, and of darkness; in that building, in the midst of those solitudes, in the midst of that darkness, the vast Jondrette garret lighted by a single candle, and in that den two men seated at a table, M. Leblanc tranquil, Jondrette smiling and alarming, the Jondrette woman, the female wolf, in one corner, and, behind the partition, Marius, invisible, erect, not losing a word, not missing a single movement, his eye on the watch, and pistol in hand.

However, Marius experienced only an emotion of horror, but no fear. He clasped the stock of the pistol firmly and felt reassured. "I shall be able to stop that wretch whenever I please," he thought.

He felt that the police were there somewhere in ambuscade, waiting for the signal agreed upon and ready to stretch out their arm.

Moreover, he was in hopes, that this violent encounter between Jondrette and M. Leblanc would cast some light on all the things which he was interested in learning.

XIX

Occupying One's Self with Obscure Depths

Hardly was M. Leblanc seated, when he turned his eyes towards the pallets, which were empty.

"How is the poor little wounded girl?" he inquired.

"Bad," replied Jondrette with a heart-broken and grateful smile, "very bad, my worthy sir. Her elder sister has taken her to the Bourbe to have her hurt dressed. You will see them presently; they will be back immediately."

"Madame Fabantou seems to me to be better," went on M. Leblanc, casting his eyes on the eccentric costume of the Jondrette woman, as she stood between him and the door, as though already guarding the exit, and gazed at him in an attitude of menace and almost of combat.

"She is dying," said Jondrette. "But what do you expect, sir! She has so much courage, that woman has! She's not a woman, she's an ox."

The Jondrette, touched by his compliment, deprecated it with the affected airs of a flattered monster.

"You are always too good to me, Monsieur Jondrette!"

"Jondrette!" said M. Leblanc, "I thought your name was Fabantou?"

"Fabantou, alias Jondrette!" replied the husband hurriedly. "An artistic sobriquet!"

And launching at his wife a shrug of the shoulders which M. Leblanc did not catch, he continued with an emphatic and caressing inflection of voice:—

"Ah! we have had a happy life together, this poor darling and I! What would there be left for us if we had not that? We are so wretched, my respectable sir! We have arms, but there is no work! We have the will, no work! I don't know how the government arranges that, but, on my word of honor, sir, I am not Jacobin, sir, I am not a bousingot. I don't wish them any evil, but if I were the ministers, on my most sacred word, things would be different. Here, for instance, I wanted to have my girls taught the trade of paper-box makers. You will say to me: 'What! a trade?' Yes! A trade! A simple trade! A bread-winner! What a fall, my benefactor! What a degradation, when one has been what we have been! Alas! There is nothing left to us of our days of prosperity! One thing only, a picture, of which I think a great deal, but which I am willing to part with, for I must live! Item, one must live!"

While Jondrette thus talked, with an apparent incoherence which detracted nothing from the thoughtful and sagacious expression of his physiognomy, Marius raised his eyes, and perceived at the other end of the room a person whom he had not seen before. A man had just entered, so softly that the door had not been heard to turn on its hinges. This man wore a violet knitted vest, which was old, worn, spotted, cut and gaping at every fold, wide trousers of cotton velvet, wooden shoes on his feet, no shirt, had his neck bare, his bare arms tattooed, and his face smeared with black. He had seated himself in silence on the nearest bed, and, as he was behind Jondrette, he could only be indistinctly seen.

That sort of magnetic instinct which turns aside the gaze, caused M. Leblanc to turn round almost at the same moment as Marius. He could not refrain from a gesture of surprise which did not escape Jondrette.

"Ah! I see!" exclaimed Jondrette, buttoning up his coat with an air of complaisance, "you are looking at your overcoat? It fits me! My faith, but it fits me!"

"Who is that man?" said M. Leblanc.

"Him?" ejaculated Jondrette, "he's a neighbor of mine. Don't pay any attention to him."

The neighbor was a singular-looking individual. However, manufactories of chemical products abound in the Faubourg Saint-Marceau. Many of the workmen might have black faces. Besides this, M. Leblanc's whole person was expressive of candid and intrepid confidence.

He went on:—

"Excuse me; what were you saying, M. Fabantou?"

"I was telling you, sir, and dear protector," replied Jondrette placing his elbows on the table and contemplating M. Leblanc with steady and tender eyes, not unlike the eyes of the boa-constrictor, "I was telling you, that I have a picture to sell."

A slight sound came from the door. A second man had just entered and seated himself on the bed, behind Jondrette.

Like the first, his arms were bare, and he had a mask of ink or lampblack.

Although this man had, literally, glided into the room, he had not been able to prevent M. Leblanc catching sight of him.

"Don't mind them," said Jondrette, "they are people who belong in the house. So I was saying, that there remains in my possession a valuable picture. But stop, sir, take a look at it."

He rose, went to the wall at the foot of which stood the panel which we have already mentioned, and turned it round, still leaving it supported against the wall. It really was something which resembled a picture, and which the candle illuminated, somewhat. Marius could make nothing out of it, as Jondrette stood between the picture and him; he only saw a coarse daub, and a sort of principal personage colored with the harsh crudity of foreign canvasses and screen paintings.

"What is that?" asked M. Leblanc.

Jondrette exclaimed:—

"A painting by a master, a picture of great value, my benefactor! I am as much attached to it as I am to my two daughters; it recalls souvenirs to me! But I have told you, and I will not take it back, that I am so wretched that I will part with it."

Either by chance, or because he had begun to feel a dawning uneasiness, M. Leblanc's glance returned to the bottom of the room as he examined the picture.

There were now four men, three seated on the bed, one standing near the door-post, all four with bare arms and motionless, with faces smeared with black. One of those on the bed was leaning against the wall, with closed eyes, and it might have been supposed that he was asleep. He was old; his white hair contrasting with his blackened face produced a horrible effect. The other two seemed to be young; one wore a beard, the other wore his hair long. None of them had on shoes; those who did not wear socks were barefooted.

Jondrette noticed that M. Leblanc's eye was fixed on these men.

"They are friends. They are neighbors," said he. "Their faces are black because they work in charcoal. They are chimney-builders. Don't trouble yourself about them, my benefactor, but buy my picture. Have pity on my misery. I will not ask you much for it. How much do you think it is worth?"

"Well," said M. Leblanc, looking Jondrette full in the eye, and with the manner of a man who is on his guard, "it is some signboard for a tavern, and is worth about three francs."

Jondrette replied sweetly:—

"Have you your pocket-book with you? I should be satisfied with a thousand crowns."

M. Leblanc sprang up, placed his back against the wall, and cast a rapid glance around the room. He had Jondrette on his left, on the side next the window, and the Jondrette woman and the four men on his right, on the side next the door. The four men did not stir, and did not even seem to be looking on.

Jondrette had again begun to speak in a plaintive tone, with so vague an eye, and so lamentable an intonation, that M. Leblanc might have supposed that what he had before him was a man who had simply gone mad with misery.

"If you do not buy my picture, my dear benefactor," said Jondrette, "I shall be left without resources; there will be nothing left for me but to throw myself into the river. When I think that I wanted to have my two girls taught the middle-class paper-box trade, the making of boxes for New Year's gifts! Well! A table with a board at the end to keep the glasses from falling off is required, then a special stove is needed, a pot with three compartments for the different degrees of strength of the paste, according as it is to be used for wood, paper, or stuff, a paring-knife to cut the cardboard, a mould to adjust it, a hammer to nail the steels, pincers, how the devil do I know what all? And all that in order to earn four sous a day! And you have to work fourteen hours a day! And each box passes through the workwoman's hands thirteen times! And you can't wet the paper! And you mustn't spot anything! And you must keep the paste hot. The devil, I tell you! Four sous a day! How do you suppose a man is to live?"

As he spoke, Jondrette did not look at M. Leblanc, who was observing him. M. Leblanc's eye was fixed on Jondrette, and Jondrette's eye was fixed on the door. Marius' eager attention was transferred from one to the other. M. Leblanc seemed to be asking himself: "Is this man an idiot?" Jondrette repeated two or three distinct times, with all manner of varying inflections of the whining and supplicating order: "There is nothing left for me but to throw myself into the river! I went down three steps at the side of the bridge of Austerlitz the other day for that purpose."

All at once his dull eyes lighted up with a hideous flash; the little man drew himself up and became terrible, took a step toward M. Leblanc and cried in a voice of thunder: "That has nothing to do with the question! Do you know me?"

XX

The Trap

The door of the garret had just opened abruptly, and allowed a view of three men clad in blue linen blouses, and masked with masks of black paper. The first was thin, and had a long, iron-tipped cudgel; the second, who was a sort of colossus, carried, by the middle of the handle, with the blade downward, a butcher's pole-axe for slaughtering cattle. The third, a man with thick-set shoulders, not so slender as the first, held in his hand an enormous key stolen from the door of some prison.

It appeared that the arrival of these men was what Jondrette had been waiting for. A rapid dialogue ensued between him and the man with the cudgel, the thin one.

"Is everything ready?" said Jondrette.

"Yes," replied the thin man.

"Where is Montparnasse?"

"The young principal actor stopped to chat with your girl."

"Which?"

"The eldest."

"Is there a carriage at the door?"

"Yes."

"Is the team harnessed?"

"Yes."

"With two good horses?"

"Excellent."

"Is it waiting where I ordered?"

"Yes."

"Good," said Jondrette.

M. Leblanc was very pale. He was scrutinizing everything around him in the den, like a man who understands what he has fallen into, and his head, directed in turn toward all the heads which surrounded him, moved on his neck with an astonished and attentive slowness, but there was nothing in his air which resembled fear. He had improvised an intrenchment out of the table; and the man, who but an instant previously, had borne merely the appearance of a kindly old man, had suddenly become a sort of athlete, and placed his robust fist on the back of his chair, with a formidable and surprising gesture.

This old man, who was so firm and so brave in the presence of such a danger, seemed to possess one of those natures which are as courageous as they are kind, both easily and simply. The father of a woman whom we love is never a stranger to us. Marius felt proud of that unknown man.

Three of the men, of whom Jondrette had said: "They are chimney-builders," had armed themselves from the pile of old iron, one with a heavy pair of shears, the second with weighing-tongs, the third with a hammer, and had placed themselves across the entrance without uttering a syllable. The old man had remained on the bed, and had merely opened his eyes. The Jondrette woman had seated herself beside him.

Marius decided that in a few seconds more the moment for intervention would arrive, and he raised his right hand towards the ceiling, in the direction of the corridor, in readiness to discharge his pistol.

Jondrette having terminated his colloquy with the man with the cudgel, turned once more to M. Leblanc, and repeated his question, accompanying it with that low, repressed, and terrible laugh which was peculiar to him:—

"So you do not recognize me?"

M. Leblanc looked him full in the face, and replied:—

"No."

Then Jondrette advanced to the table. He leaned across the candle, crossing his arms, putting his angular and ferocious jaw close to M. Leblanc's calm face, and advancing as far as possible without forcing M. Leblanc to retreat, and, in this posture of a wild beast who is about to bite, he exclaimed:—

"My name is not Fabantou, my name is not Jondrette, my name is Thénardier. I am the inn-keeper of Montfermeil! Do you understand? Thénardier! Now do you know me?"

An almost imperceptible flush crossed M. Leblanc's brow, and he replied with a voice which neither trembled nor rose above its ordinary level, with his accustomed placidity:—

"No more than before."

Marius did not hear this reply. Any one who had seen him at that moment through the darkness would have perceived that he was haggard, stupid, thunder-struck. At the moment when Jondrette said: "My name is Thénardier," Marius had trembled in every limb, and had leaned against the wall, as though he felt the cold of a steel blade through his heart. Then his right arm, all ready to discharge the signal shot, dropped slowly, and at the moment when Jondrette repeated, "Thénardier, do you understand?" Marius's faltering fingers had come near letting the pistol fall. Jondrette, by revealing his identity, had not moved M. Leblanc, but he had quite upset Marius. That name of Thénardier, with which M. Leblanc did not seem to be acquainted, Marius knew well. Let the reader recall what that name meant to him! That name he had worn on his heart, inscribed in his father's testament! He bore it at the bottom of his mind, in the depths of his memory, in that sacred injunction: "A certain Thénardier saved my life. If my son encounters him, he will do him all the good that lies in his power." That name, it will be remembered, was one of the pieties of his soul; he mingled it with the name of his father in his worship. What! This man was that Thénardier, that inn-keeper of Montfermeil whom he had so long and so vainly sought! He had found him at last, and how? His father's saviour was a ruffian! That man, to whose service Marius was burning to devote himself, was a monster! That liberator of Colonel Pontmercy was on the point of committing a crime whose scope Marius did not, as yet, clearly comprehend, but which resembled an assassination! And against whom, great God! what a fatality! What a bitter mockery of fate! His father had commanded him from the depths of his coffin to do all the good in his power to this Thénardier, and for four years Marius had cherished no other thought than to acquit this debt of his father's, and at the moment when he was on the eve of having a brigand seized in the very act of crime by justice, destiny cried to him: "This is Thénardier!" He could at last repay this man for his father's life, saved amid a hail-storm of grape-shot on the heroic field of Waterloo, and repay it with the scaffold! He had sworn to himself that if ever he found that Thénardier, he would address him only by throwing himself at his feet; and now he actually had found him, but it was only to deliver him over to the executioner! His father said to him: "Succor Thénardier!" And he replied to that adored and sainted voice by crushing Thénardier! He was about to offer to his father in his grave the spectacle of that man who had torn him from death at the peril of his own life, executed on the Place Saint-Jacques through the means of his son, of that Marius to whom he had entrusted that man by his will!

And what a mockery to have so long worn on his breast his father's last commands, written in his own hand, only to act in so horribly contrary a sense! But, on the other hand, now look on that trap and not prevent it! Condemn the victim and to spare the assassin! Could one be held to any gratitude towards so miserable a wretch? All the ideas which Marius had cherished for the last four years were pierced through and through, as it were, by this unforeseen blow.

He shuddered. Everything depended on him. Unknown to themselves, he held in his hand all those beings who were moving about there before his eyes. If he fired his pistol, M. Leblanc was saved, and Thénardier lost; if he did not fire, M. Leblanc would be sacrificed, and, who knows? Thénardier would escape. Should he dash down the one or allow the other to fall? Remorse awaited him in either case.

What was he to do? What should he choose? Be false to the most imperious souvenirs, to all those solemn vows to himself, to the most sacred duty, to the most venerated text! Should he ignore his father's testament, or allow the perpetration of a crime! On the one hand, it seemed to him that he heard "his Ursule" supplicating for her father and on the other, the colonel commending Thénardier to his care. He felt that he was going mad. His knees gave way beneath him. And he had not even the time for deliberation, so great was the fury with which the scene before his eyes was hastening to its catastrophe. It was like a whirlwind of which he had thought himself the master, and which was now sweeping him away. He was on the verge of swooning.

In the meantime, Thénardier, whom we shall henceforth call by no other name, was pacing up and down in front of the table in a sort of frenzy and wild triumph.

He seized the candle in his fist, and set it on the chimney-piece with so violent a bang that the wick came near being extinguished, and the tallow bespattered the wall.

Then he turned to M. Leblanc with a horrible look, and spit out these words:—

"Done for! Smoked brown! Cooked! Spitchcocked!"

And again he began to march back and forth, in full eruption.

"Ah!" he cried, "so I've found you again at last, Mister philanthropist! Mister threadbare millionnaire! Mister giver of dolls! you old ninny! Ah! so you don't recognize me! No, it wasn't you who came to Montfermeil, to my inn, eight years ago, on Christmas eve, 1823! It wasn't you who carried off that Fantine's child from me! The Lark! It wasn't you who had a yellow great-coat! No! Nor a package of duds in your hand, as you had this morning here! Say, wife, it seems to be his mania to carry packets of woollen stockings into houses! Old charity monger, get out with you! Are you a hosier, Mister millionnaire? You give away your stock in trade to the poor, holy man! What bosh! merry Andrew! Ah! and you don't recognize me? Well, I recognize you, that I do! I recognized you the very moment you poked your snout in here. Ah! you'll find out presently, that it isn't all roses to thrust yourself in that fashion into people's houses, under the pretext that they are taverns, in wretched clothes, with the air of a poor man, to whom one would give a sou, to deceive persons, to play the generous, to take away their means of livelihood, and to make threats in the woods, and you can't call things quits because afterwards, when people are ruined, you bring a coat that is too large, and two miserable hospital blankets, you old blackguard, you child-stealer!"

He paused, and seemed to be talking to himself for a moment. One would have said that his wrath had fallen into some hole, like the Rhone; then, as though he were concluding aloud the things which he had been saying to himself in a whisper, he smote the table with his fist, and shouted:—

"And with his goody-goody air!"

And, apostrophizing M. Leblanc:—

"Parbleu! You made game of me in the past! You are the cause of all my misfortunes! For fifteen hundred francs you got a girl whom I had, and who certainly belonged to rich people, and who had already brought in a great deal of money, and from whom I might have extracted enough to live on all my life! A girl who would have made up to me for everything that I lost in that vile cook-shop, where there was nothing but one continual row, and where, like a fool, I ate up my last farthing! Oh! I wish all the wine folks drank in my house had been poison to those who drank it! Well, never mind! Say, now! You must have thought me ridiculous when you went off with the Lark! You had your cudgel in the forest. You were the stronger. Revenge. I'm the one to hold the trumps to-day! You're in a sorry case, my good fellow! Oh, but I can laugh! Really, I laugh! Didn't he fall into the trap! I told him that I was an actor, that my name was Fabantou, that I had played comedy with Mamselle Mars, with Mamselle Muche, that my landlord insisted on being paid tomorrow, the 4th of February, and he didn't even notice that the 8th of January, and not the 4th of February is the time when the quarter runs out! Absurd idiot! And the four miserable Philippes which he has brought me! Scoundrel! He hadn't the heart even to go as high as a hundred francs! And how he swallowed my platitudes! That did amuse me. I said to myself: 'Blockhead! Come, I've got you! I lick your paws this morning, but I'll gnaw your heart this evening!'"

Thénardier paused. He was out of breath. His little, narrow chest panted like a forge bellows. His eyes were full of the ignoble happiness of a feeble, cruel, and cowardly creature, which finds that it can, at last, harass what it has feared, and insult what it has flattered, the joy of a dwarf who should be able to set his heel on the head of Goliath, the joy of a jackal which is beginning to rend a sick bull, so nearly dead that he can no longer defend himself, but sufficiently alive to suffer still.

M. Leblanc did not interrupt him, but said to him when he paused:—

"I do not know what you mean to say. You are mistaken in me. I am a very poor man, and anything but a millionnaire. I do not know you. You are mistaking me for some other person."

"Ah!" roared Thénardier hoarsely, "a pretty lie! You stick to that pleasantry, do you! You're floundering, my old buck! Ah! You don't remember! You don't see who I am?"

"Excuse me, sir," said M. Leblanc with a politeness of accent, which at that moment seemed peculiarly strange and powerful, "I see that you are a villain!"

Who has not remarked the fact that odious creatures possess a susceptibility of their own, that monsters are ticklish! At this word "villain," the female Thénardier sprang from the bed, Thénardier grasped his chair as though he were about to crush it in his hands. "Don't you stir!" he shouted to his wife; and, turning to M. Leblanc:—

"Villain! Yes, I know that you call us that, you rich gentlemen! Stop! it's true that I became bankrupt, that I am in hiding, that I have no bread, that I have not a single sou, that I am a villain! It's three days since I have had anything to eat, so I'm a villain! Ah! you folks warm your feet, you have Sakoski boots, you have wadded great-coats, like archbishops, you lodge on the first floor in houses that have porters, you eat truffles, you eat asparagus at forty francs the bunch in the month of January, and green peas, you gorge yourselves, and when you want to know whether it is cold, you look in the papers to see what the engineer Chevalier's thermometer says about it. We, it is we who are thermometers. We don't need to go out and look on the quay at the corner of the Tour de l'Horloge, to find out the number of degrees of cold; we feel our blood congealing in our veins, and the ice forming round our hearts, and we say: 'There is no God!' And you come to our caverns, yes our caverns, for the purpose of calling us villains! But we'll devour you! But we'll devour you, poor little things! Just see here, Mister millionnaire: I have been a solid man, I have held a license, I have been an elector, I am a bourgeois, that I am! And it's quite possible that you are not!"

Here Thénardier took a step towards the men who stood near the door, and added with a shudder:—

"When I think that he has dared to come here and talk to me like a cobbler!"

Then addressing M. Leblanc with a fresh outburst of frenzy:—

"And listen to this also, Mister philanthropist! I'm not a suspicious character, not a bit of it! I'm not a man whose name nobody knows, and who comes and abducts children from houses! I'm an old French soldier, I ought to have been decorated! I was at Waterloo, so I was! And in the battle I saved a general called the Comte of I don't know what. He told me his name, but his beastly voice was so weak that I didn't hear. All I caught was Merci (thanks). I'd rather have had his name than his thanks. That would have helped me to find him again. The picture that you see here, and which was painted by David at Bruqueselles,—do you know what it represents? It represents me. David wished to immortalize that feat of prowess. I have that general on my back, and I am carrying him through the grape-shot. There's the history of it! That general never did a single thing for me; he was no better than the rest! But nonetheless, I saved his life at the risk of my own, and I have the certificate of the fact in my pocket! I am a soldier of Waterloo, by all the furies! And now that I have had the goodness to tell you all this, let's have an end of it. I want money, I want a deal of money, I must have an enormous lot of money, or I'll exterminate you, by the thunder of the good God!"

Marius had regained some measure of control over his anguish, and was listening. The last possibility of doubt had just vanished. It certainly was the Thénardier of the will. Marius shuddered at that reproach of ingratitude directed against his father, and which he was on the point of so fatally justifying. His perplexity was redoubled.

Moreover, there was in all these words of Thénardier, in his accent, in his gesture, in his glance which darted flames at every word, there was, in this explosion of an evil nature disclosing everything, in that mixture of braggadocio and abjectness, of pride and pettiness, of rage and folly, in that chaos of real griefs and false sentiments, in that immodesty of a malicious man tasting the voluptuous delights of violence, in that shameless nudity of a repulsive soul, in that conflagration of all sufferings combined with all hatreds, something which was as hideous as evil, and as heart-rending as the truth.

The picture of the master, the painting by David which he had proposed that M. Leblanc should purchase, was nothing else, as the reader has divined, than the sign of his tavern painted, as it will be remembered, by himself, the only relic which he had preserved from his shipwreck at Montfermeil.

As he had ceased to intercept Marius' visual ray, Marius could examine this thing, and in the daub, he actually did recognize a battle, a background of smoke, and a man carrying another man. It was the group composed of Pontmercy and Thénardier; the sergeant the rescuer, the colonel rescued. Marius was like a drunken man; this picture restored his father to life in some sort; it was no longer the signboard of the wine-shop at Montfermeil, it was a resurrection; a tomb had yawned, a phantom had risen there. Marius heard his heart beating in his temples, he had the cannon of Waterloo in his ears, his bleeding father, vaguely depicted on that sinister panel terrified him, and it seemed to him that the misshapen spectre was gazing intently at him.

When Thénardier had recovered his breath, he turned his bloodshot eyes on M. Leblanc, and said to him in a low, curt voice:—

"What have you to say before we put the handcuffs on you?"

M. Leblanc held his peace.

In the midst of this silence, a cracked voice launched this lugubrious sarcasm from the corridor:—

"If there's any wood to be split, I'm there!"

It was the man with the axe, who was growing merry.

At the same moment, an enormous, bristling, and clayey face made its appearance at the door, with a hideous laugh which exhibited not teeth, but fangs.

It was the face of the man with the butcher's axe.

"Why have you taken off your mask?" cried Thénardier in a rage.

"For fun," retorted the man.

For the last few minutes M. Leblanc had appeared to be watching and following all the movements of Thénardier, who, blinded and dazzled by his own rage, was stalking to and fro in the den with full confidence that the door was guarded, and of holding an unarmed man fast, he being armed himself, of being nine against one, supposing that the female Thénardier counted for but one man.

During his address to the man with the pole-axe, he had turned his back to M. Leblanc.

M. Leblanc seized this moment, overturned the chair with his foot and the table with his fist, and with one bound, with prodigious agility, before Thénardier had time to turn round, he had reached the window. To open it, to scale the frame, to bestride it, was the work of a second only. He was half out when six robust fists seized him and dragged him back energetically into the hovel. These were the three "chimney-builders," who had flung themselves upon him. At the same time the Thénardier woman had wound her hands in his hair.

At the trampling which ensued, the other ruffians rushed up from the corridor. The old man on the bed, who seemed under the influence of wine, descended from the pallet and came reeling up, with a stone-breaker's hammer in his hand.

One of the "chimney-builders," whose smirched face was lighted up by the candle, and in whom Marius recognized, in spite of his daubing, Panchaud, alias Printanier, alias Bigrenaille, lifted above M. Leblanc's head a sort of bludgeon made of two balls of lead, at the two ends of a bar of iron.

Marius could not resist this sight. "My father," he thought, "forgive me!"

And his finger sought the trigger of his pistol.

The shot was on the point of being discharged when Thénardier's voice shouted:—

"Don't harm him!"

This desperate attempt of the victim, far from exasperating Thénardier, had calmed him. There existed in him two men, the ferocious man and the adroit man. Up to that moment, in the excess of his triumph in the presence of the prey which had been brought down, and which did not stir, the ferocious man had prevailed; when the victim struggled and tried to resist, the adroit man reappeared and took the upper hand.

"Don't hurt him!" he repeated, and without suspecting it, his first success was to arrest the pistol in the act of being discharged, and to paralyze Marius, in whose opinion the urgency of the case disappeared, and who, in the face of this new phase, saw no inconvenience in waiting a while longer.

Who knows whether some chance would not arise which would deliver him from the horrible alternative of allowing Ursule's father to perish, or of destroying the colonel's saviour?

A herculean struggle had begun. With one blow full in the chest, M. Leblanc had sent the old man tumbling, rolling in the middle of the room, then with two backward sweeps of his hand he had overthrown two more assailants, and he held one under each of his knees; the wretches were rattling in the throat beneath this pressure as under a granite millstone; but the other four had seized the formidable old man by both arms and the back of his neck, and were holding him doubled up over the two "chimney-builders" on the floor.

Thus, the master of some and mastered by the rest, crushing those beneath him and stifling under those on top of him, endeavoring in vain to shake off all the efforts which were heaped upon him, M. Leblanc disappeared under the horrible group of ruffians like the wild boar beneath a howling pile of dogs and hounds.

They succeeded in overthrowing him upon the bed nearest the window, and there they held him in awe. The Thénardier woman had not released her clutch on his hair.

"Don't you mix yourself up in this affair," said Thénardier. "You'll tear your shawl."

The Thénardier obeyed, as the female wolf obeys the male wolf, with a growl.

"Now," said Thénardier, "search him, you other fellows!"

M. Leblanc seemed to have renounced the idea of resistance.

They searched him.

He had nothing on his person except a leather purse containing six francs, and his handkerchief.

Thénardier put the handkerchief into his own pocket.

"What! No pocket-book?" he demanded.

"No, nor watch," replied one of the "chimney-builders."

"Never mind," murmured the masked man who carried the big key, in the voice of a ventriloquist, "he's a tough old fellow."

Thénardier went to the corner near the door, picked up a bundle of ropes and threw them at the men.

"Tie him to the leg of the bed," said he.

And, catching sight of the old man who had been stretched across the room by the blow from M. Leblanc's fist, and who made no movement, he added:—

"Is Boulatruelle dead?"

"No," replied Bigrenaille, "he's drunk."

"Sweep him into a corner," said Thénardier.

Two of the "chimney-builders" pushed the drunken man into the corner near the heap of old iron with their feet.

"Babet," said Thénardier in a low tone to the man with the cudgel, "why did you bring so many; they were not needed."

"What can you do?" replied the man with the cudgel, "they all wanted to be in it. This is a bad season. There's no business going on."

The pallet on which M. Leblanc had been thrown was a sort of hospital bed, elevated on four coarse wooden legs, roughly hewn.

M. Leblanc let them take their own course.

The ruffians bound him securely, in an upright attitude, with his feet on the ground at the head of the bed, the end which was most remote from the window, and nearest to the fireplace.

When the last knot had been tied, Thénardier took a chair and seated himself almost facing M. Leblanc.

Thénardier no longer looked like himself; in the course of a few moments his face had passed from unbridled violence to tranquil and cunning sweetness.

Marius found it difficult to recognize in that polished smile of a man in official life the almost bestial mouth which had been foaming but a moment before; he gazed with amazement on that fantastic and alarming metamorphosis, and he felt as a man might feel who should behold a tiger converted into a lawyer.

"Monsieur—" said Thénardier.

And dismissing with a gesture the ruffians who still kept their hands on M. Leblanc:—

"Stand off a little, and let me have a talk with the gentleman."

All retired towards the door.

He went on:—

"Monsieur, you did wrong to try to jump out of the window. You might have broken your leg. Now, if you will permit me, we will converse quietly. In the first place, I must communicate to you an observation which I have made which is, that you have not uttered the faintest cry."

Thénardier was right, this detail was correct, although it had escaped Marius in his agitation. M. Leblanc had barely pronounced a few words, without raising his voice, and even during his struggle with the six ruffians near the window he had preserved the most profound and singular silence.

Thénardier continued:—

"Mon Dieu! You might have shouted 'stop thief' a bit, and I should not have thought it improper. 'Murder!' That, too, is said occasionally, and, so far as I am concerned, I should not have taken it in bad part. It is very natural that you should make a little row when you find yourself with persons who don't inspire you with sufficient confidence. You might have done that, and no one would have troubled you on that account. You would not even have been gagged. And I will tell you why. This room is very private. That's its only recommendation, but it has that in its favor. You might fire off a mortar and it would produce about as much noise at the nearest police station as the snores of a drunken man. Here a cannon would make a *boum*, and the thunder would make a *pouf*. It's a handy lodging. But, in short, you did not shout, and it is better so. I present you my compliments, and I will tell you the conclusion that I draw from that fact: My dear sir, when a man shouts, who comes? The police. And after the police? Justice. Well! You have not made an outcry; that is because you don't care to have the police and the courts come in any more than we do. It is because,—I have long suspected it,—you have some interest in hiding something. On our side we have the same interest. So we can come to an understanding."

As he spoke thus, it seemed as though Thénardier, who kept his eyes fixed on M. Leblanc, were trying to plunge the sharp points which darted from the pupils into the very conscience of his prisoner. Moreover, his language, which was stamped with a sort of moderated, subdued insolence and crafty insolence, was reserved and almost choice, and in that rascal, who had been nothing but a robber a short time previously, one now felt "the man who had studied for the priesthood."

The silence preserved by the prisoner, that precaution which had been carried to the point of forgetting all anxiety for his own life, that resistance opposed to the first impulse of nature, which is to utter a cry, all this, it must be confessed, now that his attention had been called to it, troubled Marius, and affected him with painful astonishment.

Thénardier's well-grounded observation still further obscured for Marius the dense mystery which enveloped that grave and singular person on whom Courfeyrac had bestowed the sobriquet of Monsieur Leblanc.

But whoever he was, bound with ropes, surrounded with executioners, half plunged, so to speak, in a grave which was closing in upon him to the extent of a degree with every moment that passed, in the presence of Thénardier's wrath, as in the presence of his sweetness, this man remained impassive; and Marius could not refrain from admiring at such a moment the superbly melancholy visage.

Here, evidently, was a soul which was inaccessible to terror, and which did not know the meaning of despair. Here was one of those men who command amazement in desperate circumstances. Extreme as was the crisis, inevitable as was the catastrophe, there was nothing here of the agony of the drowning man, who opens his horror-filled eyes under the water.

Thénardier rose in an unpretending manner, went to the fireplace, shoved aside the screen, which he leaned against the neighboring pallet, and thus unmasked the brazier full of glowing coals, in which the prisoner could plainly see the chisel white-hot and spotted here and there with tiny scarlet stars.

Then Thénardier returned to his seat beside M. Leblanc.

"I continue," said he. "We can come to an understanding. Let us arrange this matter in an amicable way. I was wrong to lose my temper just now, I don't know what I was thinking of, I went a great deal too far, I said extravagant things. For example, because you are a millionnaire, I told you that I exacted money, a lot of money, a deal of money. That would not be reasonable. Mon Dieu, in spite of your riches, you have expenses of your own—who has not? I don't want to ruin you, I am not a greedy fellow, after all. I am not one of those people who, because they have the advantage of the position, profit by the fact to make themselves ridiculous. Why, I'm taking things into consideration and making a sacrifice on my side. I only want two hundred thousand francs."

M. Leblanc uttered not a word.

Thénardier went on:—

"You see that I put not a little water in my wine; I'm very moderate. I don't know the state of your fortune, but I do know that you don't stick at money, and a benevolent man like yourself can certainly give two hundred thousand francs to the father of a family who is out of luck. Certainly, you are reasonable, too; you haven't imagined that I should take all the trouble I have to-day and organized this affair this evening, which has been labor well bestowed, in the opinion of these gentlemen, merely to wind up by asking you for enough to go and drink red wine at fifteen sous and eat veal at Desnoyer's. Two hundred thousand francs—it's surely worth all that. This trifle once out of your pocket, I guarantee you that that's the end of the matter, and that you have no further demands to fear. You will say to me: 'But I haven't two hundred thousand francs about me.' Oh! I'm not extortionate. I don't demand that. I only ask one thing of you. Have the goodness to write what I am about to dictate to you."

Here Thénardier paused; then he added, emphasizing his words, and casting a smile in the direction of the brazier:—

"I warn you that I shall not admit that you don't know how to write."

A grand inquisitor might have envied that smile.

Thénardier pushed the table close to M. Leblanc, and took an inkstand, a pen, and a sheet of paper from the drawer which he left half open, and in which gleamed the long blade of the knife.

He placed the sheet of paper before M. Leblanc.

"Write," said he.

The prisoner spoke at last.

"How do you expect me to write? I am bound."

"That's true, excuse me!" ejaculated Thénardier, "you are quite right."

And turning to Bigrenaille:—

"Untie the gentleman's right arm."

Panchaud, alias Printanier, alias Bigrenaille, executed Thénardier's order.

When the prisoner's right arm was free, Thénardier dipped the pen in the ink and presented it to him.

"Understand thoroughly, sir, that you are in our power, at our discretion, that no human power can get you out of this, and that we shall be really grieved if we are forced to proceed to disagreeable extremities. I know neither your name, nor your address, but I warn you, that you will remain bound until the person charged with carrying the letter which you are about to write shall have returned. Now, be so good as to write."

"What?" demanded the prisoner.

"I will dictate."

M. Leblanc took the pen.

Thénardier began to dictate:—

"My daughter—"

The prisoner shuddered, and raised his eyes to Thénardier.

"Put down 'My dear daughter'—" said Thénardier.

M. Leblanc obeyed.

Thénardier continued:—

"Come instantly—"

He paused:—

"You address her as *thou*, do you not?"

"Who?" asked M. Leblanc.

"Parbleu!" cried Thénardier, "the little one, the Lark."

M. Leblanc replied without the slightest apparent emotion:—

"I do not know what you mean."

"Go on, nevertheless," ejaculated Thénardier, and he continued to dictate:—

"Come immediately, I am in absolute need of thee. The person who will deliver this note to thee is instructed to conduct thee to me. I am waiting for thee. Come with confidence."

M. Leblanc had written the whole of this.

Thénardier resumed:—

"Ah! erase 'come with confidence'; that might lead her to suppose that everything was not as it should be, and that distrust is possible."

M. Leblanc erased the three words.

"Now," pursued Thénardier, "sign it. What's your name?"

The prisoner laid down the pen and demanded:—

"For whom is this letter?"

"You know well," retorted Thénardier, "for the little one I just told you so."

It was evident that Thénardier avoided naming the young girl in question. He said "the Lark," he said "the little one," but he did not pronounce her name—the precaution of a clever man guarding his secret from his accomplices. To mention the name was to deliver the whole "affair" into their hands, and to tell them more about it than there was any need of their knowing.

He went on:—

"Sign. What is your name?"

"Urbain Fabre," said the prisoner.

Thénardier, with the movement of a cat, dashed his hand into his pocket and drew out the handkerchief which had been seized on M. Leblanc. He looked for the mark on it, and held it close to the candle.

"U. F. That's it. Urbain Fabre. Well, sign it U. F."

The prisoner signed.

"As two hands are required to fold the letter, give it to me, I will fold it."

That done, Thénardier resumed:—

"Address it, 'Mademoiselle Fabre,' at your house. I know that you live a long distance from here, near Saint-Jacques-du-Haut-Pas, because you go to mass there every day, but I don't know in what street. I see that you understand your situation. As you have not lied about your name, you will not lie about your address. Write it yourself."

The prisoner paused thoughtfully for a moment, then he took the pen and wrote:—

"Mademoiselle Fabre, at M. Urbain Fabre's, Rue Saint-Dominique-D'Enfer, No. 17."

Thénardier seized the letter with a sort of feverish convulsion.

"Wife!" he cried.

The Thénardier woman hastened to him.

"Here's the letter. You know what you have to do. There is a carriage at the door. Set out at once, and return ditto."

And addressing the man with the meat-axe:—

"Since you have taken off your nose-screen, accompany the mistress. You will get up behind the fiacre. You know where you left the team?"

"Yes," said the man.

And depositing his axe in a corner, he followed Madame Thénardier.

As they set off, Thénardier thrust his head through the half-open door, and shouted into the corridor:—

"Above all things, don't lose the letter! remember that you carry two hundred thousand francs with you!"

The Thénardier's hoarse voice replied:—

"Be easy. I have it in my bosom."

A minute had not elapsed, when the sound of the cracking of a whip was heard, which rapidly retreated and died away.

"Good!" growled Thénardier. "They're going at a fine pace. At such a gallop, the bourgeoise will be back inside three-quarters of an hour."

He drew a chair close to the fireplace, folding his arms, and presenting his muddy boots to the brazier.

"My feet are cold!" said he.

Only five ruffians now remained in the den with Thénardier and the prisoner.

These men, through the black masks or paste which covered their faces, and made of them, at fear's pleasure, charcoal-burners, negroes, or demons, had a stupid and gloomy air, and it could be felt that they perpetrated a crime like a bit of work, tranquilly, without either wrath or mercy, with a sort of ennui. They were crowded together in one corner like brutes, and remained silent.

Thénardier warmed his feet.

The prisoner had relapsed into his taciturnity. A sombre calm had succeeded to the wild uproar which had filled the garret but a few moments before.

The candle, on which a large "stranger" had formed, cast but a dim light in the immense hovel, the brazier had grown dull, and all those monstrous heads cast misshapen shadows on the walls and ceiling.

No sound was audible except the quiet breathing of the old drunken man, who was fast asleep.

Marius waited in a state of anxiety that was augmented by every trifle. The enigma was more impenetrable than ever.

Who was this "little one" whom Thénardier had called the Lark? Was she his "Ursule"? The prisoner had not seemed to be affected by that word, "the Lark," and had replied in the most natural manner in the world: "I do not know what you mean." On the other hand, the two letters U. F. were explained; they meant Urbain Fabre; and Ursule was no longer named Ursule. This was what Marius perceived most clearly of all.

A sort of horrible fascination held him nailed to his post, from which he was observing and commanding this whole scene. There he stood, almost incapable of movement or reflection, as though annihilated by the abominable things viewed at such close quarters. He waited, in the hope of some incident, no matter of what nature, since he could not collect his thoughts and did not know upon what course to decide.

"In any case," he said, "if she is the Lark, I shall see her, for the Thénardier woman is to bring her hither. That will be the end, and then I will give my life and my blood if necessary, but I will deliver her! Nothing shall stop me."

Nearly half an hour passed in this manner. Thénardier seemed to be absorbed in gloomy reflections, the prisoner did not stir. Still, Marius fancied that at intervals, and for the last few moments, he had heard a faint, dull noise in the direction of the prisoner.

All at once, Thénardier addressed the prisoner:

"By the way, Monsieur Fabre, I might as well say it to you at once."

These few words appeared to be the beginning of an explanation. Marius strained his ears.

"My wife will be back shortly, don't get impatient. I think that the Lark really is your daughter, and it seems to me quite natural that you should keep her. Only, listen to me a bit. My wife will go and hunt her up with your letter. I told my wife to dress herself in the way she did, so that your young lady might make no difficulty about following her. They will both enter the carriage with my comrade behind. Somewhere, outside the barrier, there is a trap harnessed to two very good horses. Your young lady will be taken to it. She will alight from the fiacre. My comrade will enter the other vehicle with her, and my wife will come back here to tell us: 'It's done.' As for the young lady, no harm will be done to her; the trap will conduct her to a place where she will be quiet, and just as soon as you have handed over to me those little two hundred thousand francs, she will be returned to you. If you have me arrested, my comrade will give a turn of his thumb to the Lark, that's all."

The prisoner uttered not a syllable. After a pause, Thénardier continued:—

"It's very simple, as you see. There'll be no harm done unless you wish that there should be harm done. I'm telling you how things stand. I warn you so that you may be prepared."

He paused: the prisoner did not break the silence, and Thénardier resumed:—

"As soon as my wife returns and says to me: 'The Lark is on the way,' we will release you, and you will be free to go and sleep at home. You see that our intentions are not evil."

Terrible images passed through Marius' mind. What! That young girl whom they were abducting was not to be brought back? One of those monsters was to bear her off into the darkness? Whither? And what if it were she!

It was clear that it was she. Marius felt his heart stop beating.

What was he to do? Discharge the pistol? Place all those scoundrels in the hands of justice? But the horrible man with the meat-axe would, nonetheless, be out of reach with the young girl, and Marius reflected on Thénardier's words, of which he perceived the bloody significance: "If you have me arrested, my comrade will give a turn of his thumb to the Lark."

Now, it was not alone by the colonel's testament, it was by his own love, it was by the peril of the one he loved, that he felt himself restrained.

This frightful situation, which had already lasted above half an hour, was changing its aspect every moment.

Marius had sufficient strength of mind to review in succession all the most heart-breaking conjectures, seeking hope and finding none.

The tumult of his thoughts contrasted with the funereal silence of the den.

In the midst of this silence, the door at the bottom of the staircase was heard to open and shut again.

The prisoner made a movement in his bonds.

"Here's the bourgeoise," said Thénardier.

He had hardly uttered the words, when the Thénardier woman did in fact rush hastily into the room, red, panting, breathless, with flaming eyes, and cried, as she smote her huge hands on her thighs simultaneously:—

"False address!"

The ruffian who had gone with her made his appearance behind her and picked up his axe again.

She resumed:—

"Nobody there! Rue Saint-Dominique, No. 17, no Monsieur Urbain Fabre! They know not what it means!"

She paused, choking, then went on:—

"Monsieur Thénardier! That old fellow has duped you! You are too good, you see! If it had been me, I'd have chopped the beast in four quarters to begin with! And if he had acted ugly, I'd have boiled him alive! He would have been obliged to speak, and say where the girl is, and where he keeps his shiners! That's the way I should have managed matters! People are perfectly right when they say that men are a deal stupider than women! Nobody at No. 17. It's nothing but a big carriage gate! No Monsieur Fabre in the Rue Saint-Dominique! And after all that racing and fee to the coachman and all! I spoke to both the porter and the portress, a fine, stout woman, and they know nothing about him!"

Marius breathed freely once more.

She, Ursule or the Lark, he no longer knew what to call her, was safe.

While his exasperated wife vociferated, Thénardier had seated himself on the table.

For several minutes he uttered not a word, but swung his right foot, which hung down, and stared at the brazier with an air of savage reverie.

Finally, he said to the prisoner, with a slow and singularly ferocious tone:

"A false address? What did you expect to gain by that?"

"To gain time!" cried the prisoner in a thundering voice, and at the same instant he shook off his bonds; they were cut. The prisoner was only attached to the bed now by one leg.

Before the seven men had time to collect their senses and dash forward, he had bent down into the fireplace, had stretched out his hand to the brazier, and had then straightened himself up again, and now Thénardier, the female Thénardier, and the ruffians, huddled in amazement at the extremity of the hovel, stared at him in stupefaction, as almost free and in a formidable attitude, he brandished above his head the red-hot chisel, which emitted a threatening glow.

The judicial examination to which the ambush in the Gorbeau house eventually gave rise, established the fact that a large sou piece, cut and worked in a peculiar fashion, was found in the garret, when the police made their descent on it. This sou piece was one of those marvels of industry, which are engendered by the patience of the galleys in the shadows and for the shadows, marvels which are nothing else than instruments of escape. These hideous and delicate products of wonderful art are to jewellers' work what the metaphors of slang are to poetry. There are Benvenuto Cellinis in the galleys, just as there are Villons in language. The unhappy wretch who aspires to deliverance finds means sometimes without tools, sometimes with a common wooden-handled knife, to saw a sou into two thin plates, to hollow out these plates without affecting the coinage stamp, and to make a furrow on the edge of the sou in such a manner that the plates will adhere again. This can be screwed together and unscrewed at will; it is a box. In this box he hides a watch-spring, and this watch-spring, properly handled, cuts good-sized chains and bars of iron. The unfortunate convict is supposed to possess merely a sou; not at all, he possesses liberty. It was a large sou of this sort which, during the subsequent search of the police, was found under the bed near the window. They also found a tiny saw of blue steel which would fit the sou.

It is probable that the prisoner had this sou piece on his person at the moment when the ruffians searched him, that he contrived to conceal it in his hand, and that afterward, having his right hand free, he unscrewed it, and used it as a saw to cut the cords which fastened him, which would explain the faint noise and almost imperceptible movements which Marius had observed.

As he had not been able to bend down, for fear of betraying himself, he had not cut the bonds of his left leg.

The ruffians had recovered from their first surprise.

"Be easy," said Bigrenaille to Thénardier. "He still holds by one leg, and he can't get away. I'll answer for that. I tied that paw for him."

In the meanwhile, the prisoner had begun to speak:—

"You are wretches, but my life is not worth the trouble of defending it. When you think that you can make me speak, that you can make me write what I do not choose to write, that you can make me say what I do not choose to say—"

He stripped up his left sleeve, and added:—

"See here."

At the same moment he extended his arm, and laid the glowing chisel which he held in his left hand by its wooden handle on his bare flesh.

The crackling of the burning flesh became audible, and the odor peculiar to chambers of torture filled the hovel.

Marius reeled in utter horror, the very ruffians shuddered, hardly a muscle of the old man's face contracted, and while the red-hot iron sank into the smoking wound, impassive and almost august, he fixed on Thénardier his beautiful glance, in which there was no hatred, and where suffering vanished in serene majesty.

With grand and lofty natures, the revolts of the flesh and the senses when subjected to physical suffering cause the soul to spring forth, and make it appear on the brow, just as rebellions among the soldiery force the captain to show himself.

"Wretches!" said he, "have no more fear of me than I have for you!"

And, tearing the chisel from the wound, he hurled it through the window, which had been left open; the horrible, glowing tool disappeared into the night, whirling as it flew, and fell far away on the snow.

The prisoner resumed:—

"Do what you please with me." He was disarmed.

"Seize him!" said Thénardier.

Two of the ruffians laid their hands on his shoulder, and the masked man with the ventriloquist's voice took up his station in front of him, ready to smash his skull at the slightest movement.

At the same time, Marius heard below him, at the base of the partition, but so near that he could not see who was speaking, this colloquy conducted in a low tone:—

"There is only one thing left to do."

"Cut his throat."

"That's it."

It was the husband and wife taking counsel together.

Thénardier walked slowly towards the table, opened the drawer, and took out the knife. Marius fretted with the handle of his pistol. Unprecedented perplexity! For the last hour he had had two voices in his conscience, the one enjoining him to respect his father's testament, the other crying to him to rescue the prisoner. These two voices continued uninterruptedly that struggle which tormented him to agony. Up to that moment he had cherished a vague hope that he should find some means of reconciling these two duties, but nothing within the limits of possibility had presented itself.

However, the peril was urgent, the last bounds of delay had been reached; Thénardier was standing thoughtfully a few paces distant from the prisoner.

Marius cast a wild glance about him, the last mechanical resource of despair. All at once a shudder ran through him.

At his feet, on the table, a bright ray of light from the full moon illuminated and seemed to point out to him a sheet of paper. On this paper he read the following line written that very morning, in large letters, by the eldest of the Thénardier girls:—

"THE BOBBIES ARE HERE."

An idea, a flash, crossed Marius' mind; this was the expedient of which he was in search, the solution of that frightful problem which was torturing him, of sparing the assassin and saving the victim.

He knelt down on his commode, stretched out his arm, seized the sheet of paper, softly detached a bit of plaster from the wall, wrapped the paper round it, and tossed the whole through the crevice into the middle of the den.

It was high time. Thénardier had conquered his last fears or his last scruples, and was advancing on the prisoner.

"Something is falling!" cried the Thénardier woman.

"What is it?" asked her husband.

The woman darted forward and picked up the bit of plaster. She handed it to her husband.

"Where did this come from?" demanded Thénardier.

"Pardie!" ejaculated his wife, "where do you suppose it came from? Through the window, of course."

"I saw it pass," said Bigrenaille.

Thénardier rapidly unfolded the paper and held it close to the candle.

"It's in Éponine's handwriting. The devil!"

He made a sign to his wife, who hastily drew near, and showed her the line written on the sheet of paper, then he added in a subdued voice:—

"Quick! The ladder! Let's leave the bacon in the mousetrap and decamp!"

"Without cutting that man's throat?" asked, the Thénardier woman.

"We haven't the time."

"Through what?" resumed Bigrenaille.

"Through the window," replied Thénardier. "Since Ponine has thrown the stone through the window, it indicates that the house is not watched on that side."

The mask with the ventriloquist's voice deposited his huge key on the floor, raised both arms in the air, and opened and clenched his fists, three times rapidly without uttering a word.

This was the signal like the signal for clearing the decks for action on board ship.

The ruffians who were holding the prisoner released him; in the twinkling of an eye the rope ladder was unrolled outside the window, and solidly fastened to the sill by the two iron hooks.

The prisoner paid no attention to what was going on around him. He seemed to be dreaming or praying.

As soon as the ladder was arranged, Thénardier cried:

"Come! the bourgeoise first!"

And he rushed headlong to the window.

But just as he was about to throw his leg over, Bigrenaille seized him roughly by the collar.

"Not much, come now, you old dog, after us!"

"After us!" yelled the ruffians.

"You are children," said Thénardier, "we are losing time. The police are on our heels."

"Well," said the ruffians, "let's draw lots to see who shall go down first."

Thénardier exclaimed:—

"Are you mad! Are you crazy! What a pack of boobies! You want to waste time, do you? Draw lots, do you? By a wet finger, by a short straw! With written names! Thrown into a hat!—"

"Would you like my hat?" cried a voice on the threshold.

All wheeled round. It was Javert.

He had his hat in his hand, and was holding it out to them with a smile.

XXI

One Should Always Begin by Arresting the Victims

At nightfall, Javert had posted his men and had gone into ambush himself between the trees of the Rue de la Barrière-des-Gobelins which faced the Gorbeau house, on the other side of the boulevard. He had begun operations by opening "his pockets," and dropping into it the two young girls who were charged with keeping a watch on the approaches to the den. But he had only "caged" Azelma. As for Éponine, she was not at her post, she had disappeared, and he had not been able to seize her. Then Javert had made a point and had bent his ear to waiting for the signal agreed upon. The comings and goings of the fiacres had greatly agitated him. At last, he had grown impatient, and, *sure that there was a nest there*, sure of being in "luck," having recognized many of the ruffians who had entered, he had finally decided to go upstairs without waiting for the pistol-shot.

It will be remembered that he had Marius' pass-key.

He had arrived just in the nick of time.

The terrified ruffians flung themselves on the arms which they had abandoned in all the corners at the moment of flight. In less than a second, these seven men, horrible to behold, had grouped themselves in an attitude of defence, one with his meat-axe, another with his key, another with his bludgeon, the rest with shears, pincers, and hammers. Thénardier had his knife in his fist. The Thénardier woman snatched up an enormous paving-stone which lay in the angle of the window and served her daughters as an ottoman.

Javert put on his hat again, and advanced a couple of paces into the room, with arms folded, his cane under one arm, his sword in its sheath.

"Halt there," said he. "You shall not go out by the window, you shall go through the door. It's less unhealthy. There are seven of you, there are fifteen of us. Don't let's fall to collaring each other like men of Auvergne."

Bigrenaille drew out a pistol which he had kept concealed under his blouse, and put it in Thénardier's hand, whispering in the latter's ear:—

"It's Javert. I don't dare fire at that man. Do you dare?"

"Parbleu!" replied Thénardier.

"Well, then, fire."

Thénardier took the pistol and aimed at Javert.

Javert, who was only three paces from him, stared intently at him and contented himself with saying:—

"Come now, don't fire. You'll miss fire."

Thénardier pulled the trigger. The pistol missed fire.

"Didn't I tell you so!" ejaculated Javert.

Bigrenaille flung his bludgeon at Javert's feet.

"You're the emperor of the fiends! I surrender."

"And you?" Javert asked the rest of the ruffians.

They replied:—

"So do we."

Javert began again calmly:—

"That's right, that's good, I said so, you are nice fellows."

"I only ask one thing," said Bigrenaille, "and that is, that I may not be denied tobacco while I am in confinement."

"Granted," said Javert.

And turning round and calling behind him:—

"Come in now!"

A squad of policemen, sword in hand, and agents armed with bludgeons and cudgels, rushed in at Javert's summons. They pinioned the ruffians.

This throng of men, sparely lighted by the single candle, filled the den with shadows.

"Handcuff them all!" shouted Javert.

"Come on!" cried a voice which was not the voice of a man, but of which no one would ever have said: "It is a woman's voice."

The Thénardier woman had entrenched herself in one of the angles of the window, and it was she who had just given vent to this roar.

The policemen and agents recoiled.

She had thrown off her shawl, but retained her bonnet; her husband, who was crouching behind her, was almost hidden under the discarded shawl, and she was shielding him with her body, as she elevated the paving-stone above her head with the gesture of a giantess on the point of hurling a rock.

"Beware!" she shouted.

All crowded back towards the corridor. A broad open space was cleared in the middle of the garret.

The Thénardier woman cast a glance at the ruffians who had allowed themselves to be pinioned, and muttered in hoarse and guttural accents:—

"The cowards!"

Javert smiled, and advanced across the open space which the Thénardier was devouring with her eyes.

"Don't come near me," she cried, "or I'll crush you."

"What a grenadier!" ejaculated Javert; "you've got a beard like a man, mother, but I have claws like a woman."

And he continued to advance.

The Thénardier, dishevelled and terrible, set her feet far apart, threw herself backwards, and hurled the paving-stone at Javert's head. Javert ducked, the stone passed over him, struck the wall behind, knocked off a huge piece of plastering, and, rebounding from angle to angle across the hovel, now luckily almost empty, rested at Javert's feet.

At the same moment, Javert reached the Thénardier couple. One of his big hands descended on the woman's shoulder; the other on the husband's head.

"The handcuffs!" he shouted.

The policemen trooped in in force, and in a few seconds Javert's order had been executed.

The Thénardier female, overwhelmed, stared at her pinioned hands, and at those of her husband, who had dropped to the floor, and exclaimed, weeping:—

"My daughters!"

"They are in the jug," said Javert.

In the meanwhile, the agents had caught sight of the drunken man asleep behind the door, and were shaking him:—

He awoke, stammering:—

"Is it all over, Jondrette?"

"Yes," replied Javert.

The six pinioned ruffians were standing, and still preserved their spectral mien; all three besmeared with black, all three masked.

"Keep on your masks," said Javert.

And passing them in review with a glance of a Frederick II at a Potsdam parade, he said to the three "chimney-builders":—

"Good day, Bigrenaille! good day, Brujon! good day, Deuxmilliards!"

Then turning to the three masked men, he said to the man with the meat-axe:—

"Good day, Gueulemer!"

And to the man with the cudgel:—

"Good day, Babet!"

And to the ventriloquist:—

"Your health, Claquesous."

At that moment, he caught sight of the ruffians' prisoner, who, ever since the entrance of the police, had not uttered a word, and had held his head down.

"Untie the gentleman!" said Javert, "and let no one go out!"

That said, he seated himself with sovereign dignity before the table, where the candle and the writing-materials still remained, drew a stamped paper from his pocket, and began to prepare his report.

When he had written the first lines, which are formulas that never vary, he raised his eyes:—

"Let the gentleman whom these gentlemen bound step forward."

The policemen glanced round them.

"Well," said Javert, "where is he?"

The prisoner of the ruffians, M. Leblanc, M. Urbain Fabre, the father of Ursule or the Lark, had disappeared.

The door was guarded, but the window was not. As soon as he had found himself released from his bonds, and while Javert was drawing up his report, he had taken advantage of confusion, the crowd, the darkness, and of a moment when the general attention was diverted from him, to dash out of the window.

An agent sprang to the opening and looked out. He saw no one outside.

The rope ladder was still shaking.

"The devil!" ejaculated Javert between his teeth, "he must have been the most valuable of the lot."

XXII

THE LITTLE ONE WHO WAS CRYING
IN VOLUME TWO

On the day following that on which these events took place in the house on the Boulevard de l'Hôpital, a child, who seemed to be coming from the direction of the bridge of Austerlitz, was ascending the side-alley on the right in the direction of the Barrière de Fontainebleau.

Night had fully come.

This lad was pale, thin, clad in rags, with linen trousers in the month of February, and was singing at the top of his voice.

At the corner of the Rue du Petit-Banquier, a bent old woman was rummaging in a heap of refuse by the light of a street lantern; the child jostled her as he passed, then recoiled, exclaiming:—

"Hello! And I took it for an enormous, enormous dog!"

He pronounced the word *enormous* the second time with a jeering swell of the voice which might be tolerably well represented by capitals: "an enormous, ENORMOUS dog."

The old woman straightened herself up in a fury.

"Nasty brat!" she grumbled. "If I hadn't been bending over, I know well where I would have planted my foot on you."

The boy was already far away.

"Kisss! kisss!" he cried. "After that, I don't think I was mistaken!"

The old woman, choking with indignation, now rose completely upright, and the red gleam of the lantern fully lighted up her livid face, all hollowed into angles and wrinkles, with crow's-feet meeting the corners of her mouth.

Her body was lost in the darkness, and only her head was visible. One would have pronounced her a mask of Decrepitude carved out by a light from the night.

The boy surveyed her.

"Madame," said he, "does not possess that style of beauty which pleases me."

He then pursued his road, and resumed his song:—

"Le roi Coupdesabot
S'en allait à la chasse,
À la chasse aux corbeaux—"

At the end of these three lines he paused. He had arrived in front of No. 50–52, and finding the door fastened, he began to assault it with resounding and heroic kicks, which betrayed rather the man's shoes that he was wearing than the child's feet which he owned.

In the meanwhile, the very old woman whom he had encountered at the corner of the Rue du Petit-Banquier hastened up behind him, uttering clamorous cries and indulging in lavish and exaggerated gestures.

"What's this? What's this? Lord God! He's battering the door down! He's knocking the house down."

The kicks continued.

The old woman strained her lungs.

"Is that the way buildings are treated nowadays?"

All at once she paused.

She had recognized the gamin.

"What! so it's that imp!"

"Why, it's the old lady," said the lad. "Good day, Bougonmuche. I have come to see my ancestors."

The old woman retorted with a composite grimace, and a wonderful improvisation of hatred taking advantage of feebleness and ugliness, which was, unfortunately, wasted in the dark:—

"There's no one here."

"Bah!" retorted the boy, "where's my father?"

"At La Force."

"Come, now! And my mother?"

"At Saint-Lazare."

"Well! And my sisters?"

"At the Madelonettes."

The lad scratched his head behind his ear, stared at Ma'am Bougon, and said:—

"Ah!"

Then he executed a pirouette on his heel; a moment later, the old woman, who had remained on the door-step, heard him singing in his clear, young voice, as he plunged under the black elm-trees, in the wintry wind:—

"Le roi Coupdesabot
S'en allait à la chasse,
À la chasse aux corbeaux,
Monté sur deux échasses.
Quand on passait dessous,
On lui payait deux sous."

A Note About the Author

Victor Hugo (1802–1885) was a French writer and prominent figure during Europe's Romantic movement. As a child, he traveled across the continent due to his father's position in the Napoleonic army. As a young man, he studied law although his passion was always literature. In 1819, Hugo created *Conservateur Littéraire*, a periodical that featured works from up-and-coming writers. A few years later he published a collection of poems *Odes et Poésies Diverses* followed by the novel *Han d'Islande* in 1825. Hugo has an extensive catalog, yet he's best known for the classics *The Hunchback of Notre-Dame* (1831) and *Les Misérables* (1862).

A Note from the Publisher

Spanning many genres, from non-fiction essays to literature classics to children's books and lyric poetry, Mint Edition books showcase the master works of our time in a modern new package. The text is freshly typeset, is clean and easy to read, and features a new note about the author in each volume. Many books also include exclusive new introductory material. Every book boasts a striking new cover, which makes it as appropriate for collecting as it is for gift giving. Mint Edition books are only printed when a reader orders them, so natural resources are not wasted. We're proud that our books are never manufactured in excess and exist only in the exact quantity they need to be read and enjoyed.

bookfinity™

Discover more of your favorite classics with Bookfinity™.

- Track your reading with custom book lists.
- Get great book recommendations for your personalized Reader Type.
- Add reviews for your favorite books.
- AND MUCH MORE!

Visit **bookfinity.com** and take the fun Reader Type quiz to get started.

Enjoy our classic and modern companion pairings!

Classic & Modern